Knight of the Demon Queen

By Barbara Hambly
Published by Ballantine Books

The Darwath Trilogy
THE TIME OF THE DARK
THE WALLS OF AIR
THE ARMIES OF DAYLIGHT

MOTHER OF WINTER
ICEFALCON'S QUEST

Sun Wolf and Starhawk
THE LADIES OF MANDRIGYN
THE WITCHES OF WENSHAR
THE DARK HAND OF MAGIC

The Windrose Chronicles
THE SILENT TOWER
THE SILICON MAGE
DOG WIZARD

STRANGER AT THE WEDDING

Sun-Cross
RAINBOW ABYSS
THE MAGICIANS OF NIGHT

THOSE WHO HUNT THE NIGHT
TRAVELING WITH THE DEAD

SEARCH THE SEVEN HILLS

BRIDE OF THE RAT GOD

DRAGONSBANE
DRAGONSHADOW
KNIGHT OF THE DEMON QUEEN

KNIGHT OF THE DEMON QUEEN

BARBARA HAMBLY

THE BALLANTINE PUBLISHING GROUP • NEW YORK

A Del Rey® Book
Published by The Ballantine Publishing Group

www.randomhouse.com/delrey/

LIBRARY OF CONGRESS CATALOGING-IN-PUBLICATION DATA
Hambly, Barbara.
Knight of the demon queen / Barbara Hambly.—1st ed.
p. cm.
"A Del Rey book"—T.p. verso.
ISBN 0-345-42189-2
1. Dragons—Fiction. I. Title.
PS3558.A4215 K57 2000
813'.54—dc21 99-055058

Manufactured in the United States of America

First Edition: February 2000

10 9 8 7 6 5 4 3 2 1

Chapter 1

Jenny Waynest's son Ian took poison on the night of winter's first snowfall. He was thirteen.

She was dreaming about the demon when it happened. The demon was called Amayon, beautiful as the night and the morning, and she had dreamed of him every night since fall, when his possession of her had ended. While her soul was imprisoned in a pale green crystal, he had inhabited her flesh and done such things as still made her wake weeping, or screaming, or speaking his name out of a longing so desperate she thought she would die of it.

In daylight the grief of his loss, and her shame at that grief, occupied her mind against her will, to the exclusion of all other things. Otherwise she would have seen–she hoped she would have seen–the pain and horror growing in her son's eyes.

This night there was a part of her that knew where Ian was. In her dream she saw him in the small stone house on Frost Fell–the house that had been her master Caerdinn's up to the old man's death. Later Jenny had lived there, until she had gone with Lord John Aversin, Thane of the Winterlands and her lover of ten years, to live at Alyn Hold. Asleep in their bed at the Hold now, she saw their son in the old stone house, saw him descend the stair from the loft and with a glance, as wizards could, kindle the wood on the hearth.

He shouldn't be there, she thought. It was past midnight and the snow had been falling since just before dark. *He shouldn't be there.*

Rest, Amayon's voice whispered. *Sleepy dreams are better than plans and schemes.*

Her consciousness drifted away.

Ever since the magics of the Demon Queen Aohila had taken Amayon from her, Jenny had tried to decide whether the pain she felt was a memory that Amayon had left or whether he spoke to her still. Sometimes she thought that she could hear his voice, gentle and trusting as a child's, though he was Aohila's prisoner behind the Mirror of Isychros. At other times she guessed that the coaxing sweetness, the hurtful mocking, were only a poison he'd left to make her suffer. *How like him,* she thought, and she did not know if she thought it fondly or with hatred.

Maybe both.

People who survived possession weren't the same afterward.

Her mind returned to her son. He sat beside the hearth, his head bowed, thin fingers twisting at his dark hair.

She remembered her own pain when the demon who'd possessed her had been driven out.

At least he *still has magic.*

The loss of Jenny's magic, as a result of the final battle with the demons, had been the worst of all.

You saved them, the sweet soft voice whispered in her mind: like Amayon's voice, though sometimes it sounded like her own. *You fought the demons for your son, and for Lord John, and for the Regent of the Realm. You did just as you ought. Yet you lost everything. How fair is that?*

The image came to her of Ian casually brushing aside her spells of ward, running his hands over the terra-cotta pots of her poisons in the brassy dull firelight, but the vision melted with her resentment and her grief. *Sleepy dreams,* the voice coaxed. *Lovely sleepy dreams. Of Amayon. Of magic.*

She saw Ian open a pot that she knew contained monkshood. Saw him dip his fingers into the coarse powder.

Perhaps you'll find the magic again within your beautiful heart.

The sweet voice lured her back to her dream, where she lay in the great bed in the Hold with John breathing soft beside her. His beaky face was turned away; he was clerkish and shortsighted and middle-aged, and nothing like the great thanes who had ruled the Winterlands before him, save for his scars.

Dreaming, she broke open her own ribs and tore her chest apart, as the demon had suggested. She saw her heart, which in her dream was wrought of a thousand crystals, scarlet and crimson and pink. Dreaming, she lifted it out. Blood gummed her fingers together as she fumbled for its catch, as if her heart were a box. The catch was a diamond, like a single poisoned tear.

Fascinated, she watched her heart unfurl in all directions, as if in opening the box she had somehow folded herself inside it. Within it she was, curiously, once again in the curtained bed with John, in a warm frowst of worn quilts and moth-holed furs. Like mirrors within mirrors she saw the scarred husk of her own body, burned in the final battle when she had pinned the demon-ridden renegade mage Caradoc with a harpoon beneath the sea: hair burned away, eyelashes burned away—magic burned away.

John lay beside her, twined in the arms of the Demon Queen.

"Don't wake her," the Queen whispered, and giggled like a schoolgirl. She was beautiful, as Jenny had never been beautiful: tall and slim, with breasts like ripe melons and coal-black jeweled hair. She traced on John's bare flesh the silvery marks it had borne when he'd returned from the Hell behind the mirror, marks that could occasionally be seen in the light of the earthly moon. Then she pressed her lips to the pit of his throat, where a small fresh scar lay like a burn.

She laughed huskily when John cupped her breasts in his hands.

"Let him be!"

Jenny's cry waked her. Like falling through a chain of mirrors, she fell from the imagined tower and imagined bed to the real ones and sat bolt upright, the air icy in her lungs. Beside her, John slept still.

He dreams of her. Rage washed from Jenny all thought of that other dream, the dream of Ian hunting among the ensorceled poison pots at Frost Fell. *Laughs at me with her while I sleep.*

Her cry had not waked him, and that made her angry, too. Hating him, she rolled from the bed and through the heavy curtains. The tower chamber was cramped and fusty: table and chest and large areas of the floor littered with John's books. He had a formidable library, laboriously collected from the ruins of crumbling towns, copied, collated, begged, and borrowed. Since summer's end, when they had returned from the South, John had been reading everything he could get his hands on concerning demons and melancholy and the silent sicknesses of the heart.

As if, Jenny thought angrily, *he can cure Ian by reading!*

But that was always John's answer.

His armor lay among the books: a battered doublet of black leather, spiked and plated with iron and chain; dented pauldrons and a close-fitting helm; longsword and shortsword and a couple of fine Southern cavalry blades; spectacles with bent silver-wire frames; and a pair of muddy boots. Rocklys of Galyon, whose machinations to rule the Realm had set in motion last summer's terrible events, had stripped the Winterlands of its garrisons: John was back riding patrol, as he had done most of his adult life.

He had little time these days to give his son.

And less, Jenny thought, to give to her.

Fingers stiff with scars, she shoved up the latch of the heavy shutters and stood gazing into darkness only a degree less heavy than that in the room. Snow covered the bare fields, the bare moor beyond. The smell of the sky calmed her, dispelled the envenomed miasma of her dreams.

Ian. The dream of him stirred at the edge of her thoughts.

Sleepy dreams. The sweet voice whispered and pulled at her heart. *Sleepy dreams, not plans and schemes.* Somehow it sounded rational, true in its simplicity, like a nursery song.

When she'd left the bed, the burning heat of the change of life had been warming her flesh, but that fled away now and her limbs were cold. Better to return to bed and the comfort of her dreams.

"Jen?"

The cold from the window must have waked John. Anger and resentment burned her. She wanted to be alone with her wretchedness and her grief.

"You were dreaming of her, weren't you?" Her voice snapped in her own ears, black ice breaking underfoot and miles of freezing water beneath. She spat the words back at him over her shoulder. She knew that he stood next to the bed, wrapped in one of its shabby furs, long hair hanging to his shoulders as he blinked in her direction, seeing nothing.

And just as well, she thought bitterly. Face and scalp and body scarred by demon fire and poisoned steam, and scarred within by the heats and migraines and malaises of the change of a woman's life. *Better he be half blind and in darkness than see me as I am.*

"I can't help me dreams, Jen." He sounded tired. They'd fought before going to bed. And yesterday, and the day before.

"Then don't deny me mine."

"I wouldn't," John retorted, "if dreams was all they were. But you had a demon within you . . ."

"And you believe them, don't you?" Jenny swung around, trembling. "Believe those people who say that anyone who has been taken by a demon should be killed? That's what all those books of yours say, isn't it?"

"Not all." There was a warrant out in the South for his life for trafficking with the Demon Queen. Had Rocklys of Galyon not taken the King's troops from the North to fuel her demon-inspired rebellion, he might already have been executed.

"Is that what you want?" She struck at him with her words as if it were he, and not the archdemon Folcalor's final outpouring of magic, that had robbed her of her power. "To kill me, as the books say? To kill Ian, for something neither of us wanted, for something that happened against our wills?"

He was a man who had grown up keeping his thoughts to himself, and he said nothing now.

"I was taken trying to save him!" she cried into his silence. She had a sweet small voice: gravel veined with silver. It sounded brittle to her now, and shrill. "For trying to save him, for trying to save you, and all these precious people of yours around here! This is what came of it! I hated the demon!"

"Yet you did every damn thing you could to keep me from sending it away behind the mirror." There was an edge of anger to his quiet words. "And you've been mourning it since."

"You don't understand." Jenny had learned that it was possible to hate and love the same thing at the same time.

"I understand that neither you nor my son has eaten nor slept well for months, and that as far as I've been able to see you haven't done a hand's turn to help him."

You don't understand, she wanted to say again. To scream the words at him until he knew what she felt. But instead she lashed at him, "*Your* son?" How *dare* he?

And at the same time she thought, *Ian,* and her mind snatched at shredded images of a boy sitting in despair beside a hearth. She remembered stick-thin white hands tracing away wards from jars on a shelf.

"Well, you never did want him, did you?" The resentment, the buried rage, of all those years of her uncertainty spurted up in his voice. "And if you'd been here in the first place when Caradoc showed up—"

"If you wanted a woman here during the years I was seeking my own magic, John," Jenny said with harsh and deadly sarcasm, "I can only say you should have convinced one of your regiment of village lightskirts to bear you a child. Any one of them would have."

"Papa?" The door hinge creaked. A yellow thread of candlelight fluttered, illumined the sturdy eight-year-old in the doorway: face, hands, rufous hair, and bright sharp brown eyes all the mimic of John's burly father. He'd girded his small sword over his nightshirt: *A man must go armed,* he liked to say. "Ian's gone."

Jenny led them to Frost Fell. The moment her second son, her little ruffian Adric, had spoken, her dream rushed back to her and she knew where Ian was and what he sought. Snow fell steadily as they saddled the horses, Jenny's scarred fingers fumbling half frozen with buckles and reins until she wanted to scream and strike everyone around her for being so slow. The air was filled with drifting white as they crossed over Toadback Hill, and the horses skidded on the ice of the cranberry bog.

They found Ian outside the little house, unconscious. By the tracks, he'd crawled there in delirium, but the snow already lay over him like a shroud. John and Sergeant Muffle, John's bailiff and blacksmith and bastard older brother, fed the dying fire in the hearth and dragged the bed over beside it while Jenny worked desperately to mix an antidote, to force saline water down her son's throat, to induce vomiting and keep him warm. All the while she cursed, for the one thing that would surely drag him back from the shadowlands where he now walked—the magic of her healing—was gone.

Looking up, she saw this, too, in John's eyes.

"You knew he was here." He sounded numb, like he couldn't believe any of this was taking place.

"I saw him in a dream." Between them the boy's white face was slack, shut eyes sunk in bistered hollows of pain.

And you didn't think to mention it to me. She could all but hear his thought. But he only looked away and brought more water to bathe his son's face. Frantic, Jenny traced the marks of healing, the runes of life, on her son's forehead and chest and hands. In her mind she drew first the limitations and the power lines, then the summoning of power, the calling of the magic from her bones and her heart, from the stars above the sullen cloud and the water beneath the earth, as she had done all her life.

But it was only words. The sparkly slips of fire that she'd felt in her days of small power and small learning, the great golden river of fire that had been hers when the dragon whose life she had saved had given her the gift of dragon magic, the gorgeous envenomed rainbow of demon power—all these were gone. She was just a middle-aged woman repeating nonsense words in her mind, hoping that her son would not die.

And thinking, in spite of all she could do, of the demon she had lost.

In the black cold before dawn, when John went out to fetch more wood and Sergeant Muffle dozed by the blood-colored pulse of the hearth, Jenny stretched across the furs and wept, whispering a prayer to the God of Women: *Do not let him die. Do not let him die.*

The hollow within her yawned to a chasm that would swallow the world, her soul, and John, Ian, and Jenny together, leaving nothing. *Do not let him die.*

Like the touch of an insect's feelers on her scarred scalp, she felt the brush of her son's finger. Ian whispered—or perhaps only thought—"Folcalor." And then, "I will not go."

Even in her extremity, before she passed over into sleep, Jenny thought it curious. Folcalor was not the demon who had possessed Ian's body and imprisoned Ian's soul.

Folcalor was the archdemon who had whispered to the mage Caradoc in dreams. Once in possession of Caradoc's flesh, he'd had the magic to open the doors to Hell, to bring through the other Sea-wights—wights who in turn had enslaved dragons and wizards alike.

When Jenny dreamed of that time, she dreamed of Amayon. She assumed Ian dreamed of his own jailer, lover, rapist, master: a minor gyre called Gothpys.

But it was Folcalor she saw now in dreams.

The wizard Caradoc's body was gone. She had slain him beneath the sea, and fish had devoured his flesh. Dreaming, she saw Folcalor as she'd always known he looked: a bloated soft thing of quicksilver and green fire in which the half-digested glowing remains of other Hellspawn fitfully moved. His eyes were like fire seen through colored glass: cold and intelligent, as a pig's are intelligent, or a rat's: uncaring. Her flesh crept, as it had during the days of her imprisonment, seeing him for what he was.

Intelligence and patience and power. Power beyond any demon she'd encountered or heard of, even in John's ancient lore; power not only to shove aside the spells and exorcisms of a trained mage, but to devour that mage through the magic itself. Not in a thousand years, according to the lore, had demons of such power existed.

A thousand years ago they had been vanquished, but no one knew how.

Now they had returned. No one knew why.

In his hands—hands of human flesh, she saw, small and stubby and crusted thick with rings—he held the sapphire in which Ian's soul had been imprisoned, the sapphire Jenny had herself cast into the River Wildspae when she'd returned her son's soul to his flesh.

The demon looked at her and smiled.

In the morning John's aunts arrived. His father's bossy brood of sisters—Jane and Rowan and Umetty—and Rowan's daughters Dilly and Rowanberry, and Muffle's mother Holly, who had been old Lord Aver's mistress for years, lived at the Hold in their assorted states of spinsterhood and widowhood, running the Winterlands as they had run it in John's father's time. Aunt Jane brought eggs and a milk pudding, and brandy to bathe her great-nephew's hands and feet; Rowan and Dilly brought clean sheets and pillows. They wrapped the boy and put hot bricks about him to warm him, pushing Jenny aside as if she were a scullery maid. Though it was quite clear that he heard nothing, Aunt Umetty told the boy endless stories that she generally told to her dogs, and she sang him the little songs she sang to them.

Jenny retreated to a corner of the hearth, willing herself not to be seen. She understood why Ian had taken the poison, and she thought about taking it herself. They all seemed very distant from her. Certainly they seemed less real than her memories of what it had been like to be beautiful and powerful and able to do exactly as she pleased. She knew that this was not right, yet she could not do anything about this part of her thoughts.

Snow fell again in the afternoon and drifted high against the stone walls. The grooms who'd come with the aunts brought shovels from the stable and labored to keep the yard clear. Jenny wondered once or twice, *Why Folcalor?* Then the darkness that pressed her heart overcame her again, and she retreated to sleepy dreams.

The following day Ian opened his eyes. He said, "Yes," and, "No," in a blistered whisper when John spoke to him, no more inflection in his voice than it had had since the demon had been driven out of him. Then the wind came up in the afternoon, flaying the land and driving the snow into drifts. It was best, John said, propping his spectacles more firmly on his long nose, that they go soon, for he knew bandits were abroad even in the bitter world of winter.

While the grooms brought out the other horses, with the wind tearing manes and plaids and blankets, Jenny took her mare Moon Horse from the stable and saddled her. There was a great boiling of people in the yard just then, and John was entirely occupied with making sure Ian was wrapped warm. Jenny had no magic anymore, but long years of living in the Winterlands with only slight powers had taught her to see when people turned their heads. As aunts and grooms and John and Muffle rode out of the yard, she led Moon Horse back into the stable and unsaddled her, and from the little attic window she watched them ride away across the moor. Snow filled their tracks before they were even out of sight.

In the ballads of the great heroes, she thought, watching them go—Alkmar the Godborn or Selkythar Dragonsbane or Öontes of the Golden Harp—the heroes frequently sustained injuries in slaying the dragon or overcoming the cave monsters or outwitting the evil mage. So they must, for there is no sacrifice unless blood is shed. But they survived and came home, and everything was as it was before, only happier.

No desolation. No regret. No wounds that cannot heal.

Part of her thought, *Oh, John.*

And another whispered Amayon's name.

She went down the ladder and built up the fire in the hearth again and found food the aunts had left. She made herself a little soup but didn't eat it. She only sat, wrapped in a quilt, watching the fire and seeing nothing in it but flame and memory.

Sleepy dreams, not plans and schemes.

She slept and dreamed of the demon still.

Chapter 2

"Lord Aversin."

John woke with a start. His son's hand was cold in his. The fire in the tower bedroom had almost died. The Hold was silent below.

The Demon Queen was in the room.

She looked the way she'd looked when he'd gone into the Hell that lay behind the burning mirror, away in the South in what had been the city of Ernine: a slim long-legged woman with a face that combined a girl's fresh beauty with the wise sardonic wit of thirty. Her black hair was an asymmetrical coiled universe of braids and ringlets and rolls strung with pearls and jewel-headed pins. Things lived in it. He sometimes saw them move.

Her eyes were gold and had squarish, horizontal pupils like a goat's. She had a magic that she used to keep him from noticing this—magic and the fact that her peach-perfect breasts were defended by a silk drape no thicker than a breath of smoke. He was further aware that her whole appearance was a sham, a spell, a garment that she wore. Without knowing quite how he knew, he knew what she really looked like, and this turned him sick with terror.

Her name was Aohila.

She smiled with her red lips and said, "John."

"Better stand on the rug." With one foot he scooted it toward her, a much-mangled sheepskin that the cats hid twigs and bird feet under when they weren't concealing them among the quilts on the bed. "Me Aunt Jane'll be up in a minute and make you wear slippers. She don't hold with bare feet even in summer." He fumbled on his spectacles, feeling better for being able to see her clearly. "Sorry about the star you sent me for, and the dragon's tears, and all that."

He saw her face change, anger like a holocaust of summer lightning in those yellow eyes at the reminder of how he'd tricked her when he paid the tithe he owed her for the spells she'd given to save

Ian and Jenny. The snakes—or whatever they were—stirred eyelessly in her hair and opened their small toothed mouths.

"You're a clever man, Lord John." The seductive note vanished from her voice. She ignored the sheepskin; instead she came to stand by the bed before him, close enough that she could put her hands on either side of his face. His grip tightened on Ian's fingers. Not, he thought, that he could do a single thing to stop her from hurting his son, but he felt better with his body between her and Ian. "I appreciate cleverness."

"You're one of damn few, then." He kept his voice steady and his eyes looking up into hers. "Me dad didn't. 'Don't you be clever with me,' he'd say, and I'd get the buckle end of his belt; he'd only get wilder if I asked, 'Do you want me to be stupid?' But of course I did ask, so maybe I wasn't so gie clever after all." As with her appearance, her smell was sometimes human and seductive, and sometimes something else.

She got out from behind the mirror somehow, he thought, blind with panic. And then, *No. This is a dream.*

Like all those other dreams.

He couldn't breathe.

"I can heal your son," she said.

She spoke offhandedly, not even looking at Ian, as if she offered to use her influence with a friend to secure the pick of a skilled herd dog's litter.

"Me Aunt Jane says he'll live." Demons always wanted something from you. That was what the ancient lore said, and he had found it to be so. Wanted something from you and would promise something in return.

"I can cure his heart," she said. "Close up the wound the demon Gothpys left in him. It isn't much. Gothpys is my prisoner—" And she smiled with evil reminiscence. "—but I know his voice still whispers in your son's dreams."

He took her wrists and pushed her from him. Still, he did not rise from the stool on which he sat, or dreamed that he sat, beside the bed. Fat Kitty and Skinny Kitty, who had been sleeping on the coverlet when the Demon Queen entered, peered now from the bedchamber's darkest corner, mashed together into a single silent terrified ball.

"That makes about as much sense as tryin' to drink yourself sober," he said quietly. "He'll heal when he learns how to heal from the hurt the demon laid on him. Not before." It was hard to speak the words, for he knew that Gothpys and Amayon and all the other demons who'd possessed Folcalor's slave mages were this creature's prisoners now. He didn't clearly understand the machinations within and between Hell and Hell, Demon Lord and Demon Lord, but he'd heard how the Sea-wights had screamed when they'd been taken into the Hell behind the mirror.

"Your touch will only put him in greater danger. I may be no more than a soldier and not such a very clever one at that, but I know there's things that bring naught but grief, and makin' bargains with demons, even in me dreams, is one of 'em. Now get out."

Her voice was broken glass. "You owe me."

"I paid you."

"With gifts that melted into smoke or were only tricks of words."

"You asked for a piece of a star, and I gave you some of what a star is truly made of: light. You asked for a dragon's tears, and you didn't say I shouldn't put 'em in a bottle that would evaporate and consume them before you could use 'em to make a gate into this world for your wights to come through. You asked for a gift from one who hated me, thinkin' I'd fail to get one and become your servant here, so you could feed on the souls of men and women like Southern gourmets feedin' on baby ducks."

He tried to shut from his mind the demon light he'd seen in Jenny's eyes and the obscene evil he'd watched her do. But he knew the demon saw it in his face. "And with what I've seen of the way you get into the heart and the skin and the brains of those you deal with, I don't blame those who've a warrant for me for traffickin' with your lot. I'd turn meself in if it wasn't me."

She stepped back from him while he spoke, but still she could have put out her hand and touched him, or he her; she stood with her garments–if they were garments–lifting and floating about her as if on the breath of some hot exhalation that he himself could not feel. Her spells of lust, of wanting, stroked him, clouding his mind like a perfume.

"Well, I won't be your lover, and I won't be your slave. Not in the world, not in me dreams—nothing. So you might as well go home and torture the other little demons in Hell, and let me take care of my son."

"I can bring Jenny back to you."

It was like an incautious step on a broken foot—he didn't think her words concerning Jenny would hurt that much. He saw Jenny's eyes again, across Ian's waxy face; saw the set of her shoulders, braced against whatever he should say or think. Saw himself, blind with grief and rage and anxiety, not thinking that she would feel all those things, too.

"If she didn't come back on her own, it wouldn't be Jenny."

The Demon Queen said nothing. On the hearth John saw how the flames had turned low and blue, as if the very nature of air were changed. The shadows of the chest, the table, and the heaped books and tumbled scrolls and note tablets dimmed and loomed and ran together, and he could hear his own breath, and Ian's: a slow desperate drag as if the boy struggled with horrors in his sleep. He wondered—as he always wondered—if the Demon Queen wore her own form when he wasn't looking at her.

"John," she said, and he looked back at her quickly. Almost it seemed he caught her shape changing, just enough to know that she had.

"Look at your son."

Ian's hand burned in his. As the fire licked up brighter again, unnaturally brighter, he saw the boy's swollen tongue protruding from lips gone purple with blood. Even as he looked, brown spots formed under the clear thin skin, as if the blood vessels were dissolving in the flesh. Blisters bulged taut and yellow around the mouth and on the neck. Ian cried out in his sleep, weeping in pain, and kicked and clawed at the blankets.

"Stop it," John said softly. "This is only a dream, but stop it."

"You think I'm powerless in this world, Aversin," the Demon Queen said, "because I and my kind cannot cross through the gate without being summoned from this side. But there are little gates everywhere that open now and now, and the season of demons is on the world. My hand is long, and it is stronger than you think."

He stood and, catching her by the arms, thrust her back from the bed. Her body was light, as Jenny's was, but there was something about the weight of it, and its relationship to the softness of her flesh, that was wrong. He felt it as he shook her, and the things in her hair put forth their heads and hissed at him from among the darkness and the jewels.

"Get out of here."

She only looked at him full with those terrible eyes.

"Get out of here!"

He hurled her from him, then turned and pressed his forehead to the carved bedpost until the graven leaves and flowers dug into his flesh. He could hear Ian crying, moaning as the fever consumed him, but he kept his eyes shut tight, willing himself not to see either his son or the Demon Queen. *This is a dream. A dream. A dream.*

He woke trembling, on his feet, holding the bedpost, weak with shock and bathed in sweat. The flames had sunk low in the hearth, but only because the log was nearly consumed. The warm amber light was normal after the glare and blackness of his dream. Ian slept, and the hand that lay outside the shadows of the bed-curtain relaxed, its skin unmarred. Skinny Kitty raised her little triangular head to regard John in sleepy inquiry; Fat Kitty dozed, a mammoth lump of ruffled gray somnolence.

John looked back at the hearth. The sheepskin rug had been moved, and lay where he'd kicked it toward the Demon Queen's bare alabaster feet.

The next day John sent out a five-man troop of militia under the command of Ams Puggle, whose turn it was to ride patrol with him, without too much misgiving: Puggle was a stolid young man who didn't think quickly in emergencies, but this was ordinarily a quiet time of year.

Still, this was not an ordinary year, and guilt tormented him—guilt at sending his men out while he stayed behind, and guilt at not doing more for his son.

He brought an armload of books down and sat by Ian while the boy slept, waking him twice from dreams that left him shaking with terror but about which he could not be brought to speak. After a time Ian lay quiet, smiling if required to do so and thanking him, but terrifyingly distant, as if the words were spoken through a small window by someone prisoned in an unimaginable room.

Throughout that day John combed his books for mention of demons and how he might keep his son safe.

What he found was not encouraging. According to Gantering Pellus' *Encyclopedia of Everything in the Material World*, demons could take the form of mice and rats and slip into the beds of their victims while they slept, although it was not clear how the ancient scholar knew this. Polyborus' *Jurisprudence* said that demons could take on the seeming of household members and kill children or betray husbands with nobody the wiser, at least not at the time. An old ballad the Regent Gareth had played for him detailed how demons disguised themselves as candies, cakes, and tarts, so the king of an ancient land ate them and became possessed, and perversely this tune jingled in his head for the rest of the afternoon.

Peaches and prunes,
Sugarplum moons,
And mountains of glorious cheese.

Polyborus listed eight ways of killing those who had dealings with the Hellspawn, depending on whether they were still possessed, had been possessed, or had merely made bargains with wights. Demons could enter a corpse and do terrible mischief between the time life was extinct and the body destroyed, he said, so it was important that the culprit be burned or dismembered alive.

John recalled clearly the smell of the oil on the pyre they'd prepared for him, and the way Ector of Sindestray, treasurer of the Southern Council, had smiled when the old King had ordered John put to death.

Demons destroyed trust. You never knew, afterward, where you were with one who had dealings with them. You never knew to whom you were speaking.

Jenny. The ache in his heart overwhelmed him as he looked out across the moor from the tower window and saw the thin gray smudge of smoke rising above Frost Fell. *Jenny.*

Despite the snow, and the day's growing cold and darkness, he thought of going there. But though Ian seemed a little better, still he felt uneasy at leaving him. Nor could he put from his mind Jenny's desperate and dreadful silence, silence from which, apparently, she could not even reach to help her son. Nor could he forget his love. There was a time when he would have gone on harrowing himself, forcing meetings with her, trying stubbornly to cut through the wall around her, but he saw with strange clarity that there was nothing he could do.

He could only trust that wherever she had gone, she would come back.

Puggle and his men returned the following forenoon, frosted to the eyebrows and grumbling. No sign of bandits or wolves, nor of the Iceriders who raided two winters out of three from the lands beyond the mountains. They'd checked with the depleted garrison at Skep Dhû, and the commander—a corporal promoted when all the troops had been drawn off to join Rocklys of Galyon's attempt to conquer the South—said the same. Corporal Avalloch also reported that yet another message had come from the King's councilor Ector of Sindestray, ordering him to arrest John Aversin on charges of trafficking with demons and put him to death.

"You think Avalloch'd agree to send a message to this Ector bloke telling him that's what he'd done?" Muffle inquired from his seat on the big table in the kitchen where the patrol had come to drink hot ale and report.

"I asked him already," John said, breathing on his spectacles and rubbing them on a towel, for the kitchen was far warmer than any other room in the Hold. "I even pointed out as how it'd be a savin' of money for the council, in that they wouldn't always be sendin' messengers. Avalloch just gave me those fishy eyes and said, 'I could not do that, Lord Aversin.'

"Anythin' else?" he added, turning back to Puggle.

"Only sickness," the corporal said, "over at Werehove Farm."

Warm as the kitchen was, John felt suddenly cold.

I can heal your son. And, *My hand is long.*

"Ema Werehove was near frantic when she spoke to us. She said it was nothin' she'd ever seen nor heard of: fever, and sores on his lips—Druff it is who's sick—and brown spots that spread if you touch them. Should we ride out to the Fell and fetch Mistress Jenny, d'you think? Your Aunt Jane was tellin' me all's not right with her either . . ."

Puggle's words washed over him, barely heard.

"Did she say when Druff had been took sick?" John's voice sounded odd in his own ears, as if it belonged to someone else.

"Night before last, she said. Close to dawn."

Within hours of his dream of the Demon Queen.

"Where you goin'?" Puggle asked as his thane paused in the doorway only long enough to gather up his winter plaids and his heaviest sheepskin jacket.

"Get Bill to saddle Battlehammer."

"You're mad, Johnny," Muffle protested. "It's comin' on to storm before midnight!"

"I'll ride fast."

Werehove Farm lay in a tiny pocket of arable land, under the backbone of the Wolf Hills, close by the spreading desolation of Wraithmire Marsh. Aversin shivered as he rode past the marsh, for even in the cloud-thinned sunlight it had a dreary look. No sign now of the fey lights that jigged across the brown pools and root-clotted black streamlets once the sun was down. Nothing but silence, though on five or six occasions John had heard the whisperers calling to him from the marshes at evening, in Jenny's voice, or Ian's—once in his father's.

They live on pain, Gantering Pellus said in his *Encyclopedia*, and John knew how true this was. Pain and terror and rage, lust and guilt and shame. They drank those emotions like dark nutty Winterlands beer. Cut your wrist in the Wraithmire, and the glowing little whisperers—the stoats and foxes of the Hellspawn, compared to the tigers like the Queen—would come round to drink the blood. Weep there, and you would see them seeping out of the ground to lap your tears.

And they'd tease and twist and lure to increase those intoxicating delights. If humans were not available, they would torment cats or pigs or anything whose blood and fear would warm their coldness, feed their hunger for life.

Maybe the Demon Queen had offered to heal Ian only to sup on the surge of hope and grief and pain her words had brought.

"Cannot Mistress Jenny come?" Ema, matriarch of the Werehove clan, asked, meeting him in the stable yard wrapped in sheepskins and scarves. The light had sickened, and harsh wind yanked at John's hair and plaids, tore at the woman's gray braids as she led him toward the thick-walled stone house. "I'd heard she was hurt and not able to do magic as she used. But she've still the knowledge of herbs, and sickness, and worse things belike. This is an ill such as we've never seen, and it's eating Druff up alive."

Druff Werehove, Ema's oldest son, lay in the loft, his bed set against the chimney. A few candles burned around him, and Winna, his wife, knelt by him bathing his face. As he climbed the loft stairs, John smelled stale blood and sickness. He stopped, looking down at the man—one of his militia, and with his brothers the core of the little farmstead—and felt sickness clutch his own breast. For he was as Puggle had described him: His face was blistered around the mouth and across the nose and forehead, and his arms and breast were spotted with brown. His swollen tongue filled his mouth so that he could barely breathe, and his thick gasping was dreadful to hear.

"He's burnin' up." Winna raised frantic eyes to her mother-in-law. Her hand trembled as she sponged her husband's face again. "Burnin' up. And Metty from over Fell Farm, she tells me her girl's down with this here, too. Cannot Mistress Jenny come?"

"I'll tell her." John's heart shrank up to a coal inside him, a black nubbin of dread. "As soon as I return to the Hold."

But it was night, and storm was coming on hard when he crossed the drawbridge again. And in any case he knew whence the sickness came, and how it could be ended.

Muffle met him in the courtyard, wrapped to the eyes in plaids and leaning against the beating wind. "There's fever in the village," he said, "two cases of it. Blisters on the face, and brown spots. We sent for Mistress Jenny, but by that time the snow was too bad to get near the Fell."

"Anyone here down with it?" In John's mind he saw Ian, writhing and sobbing. Everything seemed to have gone blank within him, beyond thought or reasoning. Only, he thought, *I'll kill her if she's harmed him. Demon or not I'll destroy her somehow, though it cost my life.*

"Not yet." The smith led the horse back to the stable, John stumbling behind. They stripped Battlehammer of his saddle by the light of a wavering flare, then John went up the tower stairs two at a time, shedding his wet plaids and sheepskin coat as he went. There was a part of him that did not want to reach the door of his room.

But Ian lay propped in the shadows of the bed, and something altered in the blank blue gaze as John came through the door. "Papa?"

"You all right, Son?" And he cursed himself for the offhand tone in his voice—offhand, as he'd had to be about everything when he was a child Ian's age and younger, fighting not to let his own father crush him inside.

Ian nodded and let himself be embraced. He started to speak, as if to remark on the cold that still clung to the metal plates of John's rough leather doublet and to his snow-flecked hair, but then did not. John didn't know whether this was something the demon had done to him—this trick of reconsideration, of backing down from any speech, as if fearing it would reveal or disarm or obligate him—or whether it was a thing of his years, or perhaps only of his self. Still Ian held onto his arm for a moment, the first reassurance he had sought, his face pressed to the grubby sleeve.

And John fought not to say, *Why did you take the poison? Why didn't you speak to me?*

Uncharacteristically it was Ian who broke the silence. He coughed, his voice still barely a thread. "I heard Muffle talking about fever . . ."

Of course he would. He had a mage's senses, which could pick up the murmur of voices in the kitchen three floors below.

"Should I get up and go down to the village?"

"In a while." John sat on the edge of the bed. A protesting *meep* sounded beneath the quilts, and one of the humped covers moved. John wanted to say, *Your mother can handle it,* but he let the words go. He suspected Jenny would be helpless against this illness, and Ian also.

In any event this was the first interest Ian had shown in anything since his return to the North.

"It doesn't sound like any of the fevers I've read about in Mother's books." Ian sank against the pillows, exhausted by the effort of sitting up, and Skinny Kitty emerged from beneath the comforters to sit on his chest. "Tonight could you bring down from the library what you have about diseases? There has to be some cause."

"Aye," John said softly, knowing the cause. "Aye, son. I'll do that."

He remained until Ian slept again. It wasn't long. Even after the boy's eyes slipped closed John stayed seated beside the bed, holding his hand. Watching the too-thin face in its tangled frame of black hair, the wasted fingers twined with his own. Remembering the child Jenny had borne but had not wanted to raise—the child she had left at the Hold for him when she returned to Frost Fell to meditate, to concentrate, to patiently strive at increasing her small abilities in magic to the level of true power. He saw again the demon fire in the boy's eyes as Ian was drawn toward the dragon Centhwevir, already under the wizard Caradoc's control.

Where had these demons been for a thousand years? he wondered, riffling Skinny Kitty's gray fur. It had been that long since spawn from the Hell behind the burning mirror had destroyed Ernine, that long since the mages of the forgotten city of Prokeps had summoned Sea-wights to aid them in what human magic couldn't do alone. Fighting wars among themselves and leaving humankind at the mercy of the smaller pooks and gyres, which could be cast out or guarded against with a spell?

Why a thousand years ago?

Why now?

Gently he disengaged his hand from Ian's and peered into the boy's face. His son slept calmly, something he had seldom done since he was a child. Skinny Kitty purred drowsily and kneaded with her paws.

I can cure your son.

John blew out the candles by the bed and by the fire's dim glow crossed the room to seek the steps that led to his library.

Asleep before the hearth, Jenny dreamed of Amayon. Dreams of him—of his love and of the power he'd given her—were so much easier than waking now.

She dreamed of the mirror chamber in the ruins of Ernine in the South, of John standing before the blacked-over doorway of the glass with the seven spikes of crystal and quicksilver that Caradoc had used to dominate and control the dragons. With the spikes lay seven vessels—seashells, snuff bottles, hollowed-out stones—containing the Hellspawned spirits that had possessed the mages: old Bliaud, Ian, the two Icerider children Summer and Werecat, the witch girl Yseult, little Miss Enk the gnomewife . . . And herself.

She could have sketched from memory every bump and spike and curve of the seashell that prisoned Amayon. It was the only one that she had truly seen. The only thing that she truly thought about.

It, and Amayon's screams when Aohila had taken those fourteen spirits behind the mirror, to torture them for eternity.

In her mind she heard again Amayon's desperate pleading, telling her how the mirror demons hated the Sea-wights, how they could never die, could never be free of pain. She had hated John then for giving them over, and the hatred stirred anew, drawing her mind back to its old circular paths.

Drawing it aside from the fact that there should have been eight vessels there, not seven.

Folcalor, Ian had said.

And, *I will not go.*

In the first second of waking, Jenny thought, *Folcalor wasn't taken. Folcalor wasn't sent behind the mirror. He was the demon who possessed Caradoc, the rebel demon who started this whole affair...*

And then a voice whispered in her mind, *Sleepy dreams, Jenny. Sleepy dreams, not plans and schemes. It's all over now.*

She saw John's eyes looking at her across Ian's body and wanted only to sleep again.

Snow had piled thick before the house door. She made herself get up and slipped through a tiny passway from the kitchen that let her into the stable. There she fed Moon Horse and mucked out her stall, her numb hands crooked as bird claws around rake and hay fork. The effort exhausted her, and without eating or washing—it seemed too much effort even to boil water for gruel—she returned to her quilts and the comfort of her dreams.

All care for her life seemed to have dried with her menses. The symptoms she had once kept at bay with her spells returned to tear at her, so she could not rest. Blind with migraine, she crept about her few tasks like an old woman, feeding the fire and boiling a little snow water to drink.

In her memories Amayon was still with her. Magic flowed in her veins.

Let your magic go, Morkeleb had said to her, Morkeleb the Black, the dragon of Nast Wall.

Let your magic go.

She hadn't known then that it would not come back.

In her dreams she saw him, beautiful beyond beauty: the black glittering specter in the darkness of the gnomes' Deep at Ylferdun, the cold voice like the echo of far-off singing that spoke in the hollows of her mind. *Know you not your own power, Wizard-woman?* he had asked her once. *Know you not what you could be?*

And later, when he had begun to change, to become a dragon-shadow of smoke and starlight: *I would that I could heal you, my friend, but this is not possible: I, who destroyed the Elder Droon and brought down the gnomes of Ylferdun to ruin, I cannot make so much as a single flower prosper when frost has set its touch upon it.*

She saw him again, as she had seen him last: near invisible, beautiful, a ghost of peace and stillness, flying away to the North. Not sleepy dreams, she thought, but clarity, an acceptance of time and change.

Waking, she felt still the deep peace of his presence. Wind screamed around the walls and in the thatch, and the cold draft streaming from the attic reminded her that in summer she'd gathered herbs and dried them on the rafters, herbs to ease the ill of other women's change: primrose and pennyroyal and slippery elm.

She worked the door open enough to scrape some snow into a pan, which she put on the hearth to boil. She wedged herself through the cranny to the stable and pitched fodder for Moon Horse again and cleaned her stall, shivering in the colder atmosphere of the stable but glad to have the care of another creature to occupy her thoughts. Returning to the kitchen, she checked the water, touched a candle to the flame, and dragged herself up the attic stair.

It was cold up there. The window through which she'd watched John depart three days ago was unshuttered, cold seeping through the glass as if there were nothing in the space at all. No light trickled in with the cold–Jenny had no idea what time it was. With the wind rising and dense cloud covering the stormy sky, it could have been dawn or twilight or midnight. Her candle glow touched the herbs, homey comforting bundles, like an upended forest over her head.

Yet there was something wrong. Jenny stood, candle in hand, listening, trying to sense what exactly it was.

Her dream? she thought. *Folcalor?*

She had the sense of having had another dream, or some other awareness while she dreamed—eternally and repetitively—of Aohila, of Amayon, of John's betrayal. Closing her eyes, she walked back in her mind to the mirror chamber, as she'd seen it in her dream, and it seemed to her for a little time that she could hear something else, some voice whispering . . .

It seemed that as she stood in the mirror chamber, looking at John in his flame-scarred and grubby doublet with the fourteen prisoned Sea-wights around his feet, someone or something was standing behind her. Someone that she knew with a hideous intimacy.

Someone who had hurt her and had laughed at her while she wept.

She knew if she turned around she would see him—it. And the sight would destroy her, because the horrible thing she would see would be herself: a woman capable of causing her own child's suicide, a woman who had betrayed the man she loved a thousand times.

Go downstairs and dream again by the fire.

You do need to rest.

In that mirror chamber in her heart she turned around. And of course there was nothing there but shadows.

She opened her eyes. Her single candle flame bent and flickered in the draft, the heavy rafters she had known since girlhood taking on sinister weight and darkness overhead. There was a bundle of candles under the spare bed, candles she'd made five summers ago, and she took half a dozen and lit them, looking carefully around her for any sign of the wrongness she felt.

But the light seemed to dispel whatever it was that had troubled her. The room was as it had always been: a big open space beneath the tall slant of the thatch. Spare bed, bundles of candles, bags of dried corn and barley spelled a year ago against mice. Blankets and quilts and old coats, snowshoes and boots. The sense she had had, of wrongness and evil, seemed to have folded itself away into a shadow.

And maybe a shadow was all it had been.

Storm winds smote the house, and all the candle flames bent and jittered with it. *More snow,* Jenny thought.

But the thought didn't bring with it the urge to sleep again, merely a reflection that with her hands twisted as they were, it would take longer to wield the shovel to dig herself clear. She opened the window long enough to pull the shutters closed and bar them, then made her choices among the dried herbs, gathering the little bundles and holding them in her skirt. As an afterthought she looked for a clean skirt, a clean shift, a clean bodice from the chest of spare clothes, then went downstairs to tidy the kitchen.

Behind her she thought the shadows whispered, but she did not look back.

Chapter 3

John's study was a round chamber at the top of the tower that in his father's time had doubled as a depot for emergency food stores and a lookout post in bad weather. Wide windows faced the cardinal points and made the place almost impossible to heat. As a child, John had fallen into the habit of studying there, away from his father's eye, and hiding his books among the grain sacks.

Now a lifetime's plunder of learning stacked desk, worktable, and the plank shelves that filled every available inch of wall space. Candles—or the slumped, exhausted remains of them—sprouted like fungi among the dilapidated volumes, stalagmites of tallow bearding every shelf, corner, and lamp stand. Scrolls, parchment, piles of papyrus drifted every horizontal surface like dried leaves. The rafters were a spiderweb of experimental hoists and pulleys, the shelves a ramshackle graveyard of disemboweled clocks. A telescope, built by John according to accounts he'd found in a volume of Heronax, stood before the eastern window, the gnome-wrought crystal lenses pointed at the quadrant of the sky where six hundred years ago Dotys had predicted the rising of a comet at last summer's end.

Unerringly John picked from the disarray an onyx bottle that had once contained silver ink. Terens had described such a thing in *Deeds of Ancient Heroes* in writing of the villainous Greeth Demoncaller, who had been dismembered alive on orders of Agravaine III. John tied a red ribbon around it—*why red?* he wondered—and put it in his pocket. From a cupboard he took five new candles—marveling a little that he could find five unburned—and Volume VII of Gantering Pellus' *Encyclopedia* and finally, from the litter of the desk, a piece of black chalk.

Gantering Pellus strongly recommended that experiments concerning demons not be conducted under roofs that would ever again shelter humans. In fact, he'd strongly recommended that such experiments not be conducted at all. *For whoso speaketh with the Spawn of*

Hell, even in their dreams, the encyclopediast wrote, *is never after to be trusted in any congress with men. It is the whole art and pleasure of such wights to cause suffering. They are cunning beyond human imagining and, being deathless, will stay at nothing to avail themselves of access to the affairs of men.*

All of this, John reflected as he climbed from the tower, was true.

As true as fever, and love, and duty, and death.

He fought his way through the snow to his work shed. His hands would barely work the catch on the door. Drafts tore at the flame as he hung his lantern on a low rafter, shadows jittering among the bones and sinews of his larger experiments: the clockwork engine of his flying machine, the webby drape of the parachute that had cost him a week in bed with a broken collarbone the summer before last. Trying not to think of anything beyond the moment, he cleared the wheels and gears of the dragon-slaying machine away from the center of the room and with the black chalk drew a pentagram on the dirt floor.

Let the flame be virgin as the waxe, the encyclopediast said of the candles. Their wobbly light threw his shape huge on the rough-cast walls. He placed the ink bottle beside him and settled himself cross-legged in the pentagram's center, breathing deep.

He had none of his son's magic, none of the power Jenny had lost. *By all rights,* he thought, as the fivefold candleflame bent and shivered, *the world should have no more to fear from what I am doing than from a child's game.*

But his heart felt as if it would break in his ribs with pounding, and his whole body was cold.

"All right," he said into the silence. "You win. What do you want?"

Once on a time, staring into the fire, Jenny could have seen them.

Seen Ian sleeping–in the room he shared with Adric? In the great bed she'd shared with John? Did Aversin sit beside his son, awake or asleep?

Jenny closed her eyes, the ardent changefulness of the flame a color visible yet. But the images she saw in the dark of her mind were only those created by her thoughts.

Ian sleeping, as she'd seen him sleep a thousand times.

Low red firelight playing over the strings of her harp in its corner. Her hands were too stiff with scars now to coax music from its strings.

John . . .

Where would he be? And what would he be doing, in the wake of his son's attempt to take his own life?

She shivered, remembering him clinging to the spikes and horns and hammering wings of two dragons as they fought hundreds of feet above the ground, trying to reach his son with the talismans he'd bartered his soul to get. She remembered herself riding the black dragon Morkeleb down into the sea in pursuit of Caradoc as he fled, and she saw again the distorted demon fish circling and attacking in the blue-black water as she and the dragon drove Caradoc back among the coral and rock. She saw the devil light streaming from the old mage's open mouth, his open eyes, the smooth white moonstone in his staff's head.

The water had burned her as she pinned the renegade wizard's body to the rocks with a harpoon. She had pulled the crystal spike from the dragon Centhwevir's skull, freeing Centhwevir of the demon. She'd torn away from Caradoc's neck the silver bottle containing the jewels that imprisoned the captive wizards' souls. But Folcalor had rushed forth out of Caradoc's body, leaving the wizard's emptied corpse to be devoured by fish.

Later, when they'd returned the souls of the wizards to their bodies again, they'd found among the jewels in the bottle a topaz that they'd assumed contained Caradoc's soul. This they had smashed—as they'd smashed that of the Icerider boy Summer, whose body had been killed in the fighting—to release the soul into the next world.

Now, as she tried vainly to call John's image in the fire, all she saw was that underwater darkness, that blue-black world near the Sea-wights' abyss. The whalemages had closed the demon gate by piling rocks before it. Closing her eyes and letting her mind drift, Jenny did not know whether what she saw was in truth a scrying or only the pictures in her imagination.

But she smelled the cold salt strangeness of the deep sea and heard the movements of the water around the black columns of rock where Caradoc had been pinned. Like vast moving shadows she saw the whalemages above her, and far below, silver stealthy shapes whose eyes flared with green light.

* * *

"A knight went out on errantry,
Sing the wind and the rain . . ."

The song seemed to come from a great way off. Children singing, he thought, as Ian had sung to Adric when they were small. Thin frail voices down a long corridor of darkness.

"A knight went out on errantry
In shining silver panoply,
And none could match his gallantry,
Sing the wind and the rain . . ."

The air in the room changed. He smelled sulfur and scalded blood.

"Sing the wind and the rain."

She was there, in the shadows near the western wall.

John drew breath, queasy with fear.

He knew he was asleep. The quality of the candlelight and the way the darkness in the work shed vibrated with colors unknown to waking sight told him this, along with the fact that he felt only vaguely cold although he could see his breath. Looking hard at the shadows he couldn't see her. Things that appeared one moment to be her turned out the next to be only pale shapes in the plaster, or shadows thrown by an engine's pulleyed wheel. It was worse than seeing her, because he couldn't imagine what form she wore.

"You said you wanted aught done, an' all." It took him everything he could muster to speak. "What is it you want, that you'll kill half me people to get?"

Her chuckle was like a torturer's little silver hook slipped down a victim's throat. "My darling, I'd kill half your people for the amusement of hearing you weep for them. You know that."

He made no answer. Droplets of blood began to ooze from the

coarse plaster wall, glistening in the five candles' light. The smell of it went through his head like a copper knife.

"It isn't much that I want," she purred in time. "I'm not an ogre." She spoke, he saw now, out of a running wound that opened in the wall. The voice came out with a clotted trickle of blood, nearly black in the flickering shadows. He wanted to look away but couldn't.

"But there are things a man can do, and places a man can ride, that the Hellspawned cannot. The world is differently constituted than you think, Aversin."

Still he said nothing. Storm wind had been howling around the Hold walls, and he could not imagine that it had ceased to do so, but the work shed was silent as if it had been plunged to the center of the earth.

"When you passed through the burning mirror this summer past, you entered Hell." Like a dragon she spoke into his mind, placing images there. He saw himself pasting the gnomewitch Mab's sigil on the enamel that covered the mirror's unholy glass, felt the cold, burning touch of the Demon Queen's mouth on his. The horrors of illusory death, illusory pain, as if he were dreaming within a dream about being tortured and killed, without the ability to wake up.

"But there are other Hells," she went on. "The Hell of the Seawights, whence the Archwight Adromelech sent Folcalor to trap the mages and the star-drakes, is not the Hell of my Realm. All Hells are not alike. Nor are all demons, and in some Hells it is deadly for the demonkind to tread." These images passed beyond his ability to picture them: only suffocation, dread, and the promise of horrible pain.

"You're goin' to give me a couple of coins, then, and a little basket and send me to market?" His mouth was dry. He couldn't imagine a place where the thing he spoke to would fear to enter. "For what?"

"Only water." Her voice was as casual as a child pretending disinterest in a coveted toy. He saw it in his mind even as she spoke of it, if she did speak. "There's a spring in the mountains there, where the rocks are silver and red." It felt as if he were recalling something once visited, or known long ago and forgotten. "Its water has a virtue against the demons who dwell behind the mirror. It is a grievous life, to be Queen of Hell." Her lovely voice grew sad.

"Demonkind are fractious and divisive, ignorant of their own best good. There have been attempts to unseat me, to devour me, by those who should thank me for the steady strength and kindness of my rule." He remembered her tearing the head off a small wight and throwing it aside, then continue speaking to him with gore dripping from her chin.

"The Hell to which I will send you is inimical in many ways to us and our kind. Some of our spells continue to work there, but many do not. This water is a weapon I need to maintain my power. But you understand that I cannot fetch it myself. Nor can any of those loyal to me go there."

"Yet you trust me."

She smiled. He could not see her—could see nothing but the stream of black-red running down the wall—yet he could feel her smile. "John." Almost he could feel the touch of her cold hand on his hair. "You know what I can do."

She had tried to trick him once into paying for the spells against Folcalor's Sea-wights with a thunderstone, meteor iron whose origin—being extraterrestrial—was not affected by the magics of the world because those magics knew nothing of its origins. At least that was what Jenny and Morkeleb had said. Rightly, the gnomes had refused to part with one. With the thunderstone she could have wrought a gate into the world of humankind that could not be closed by human magics and probably, like the burning mirror that was framed in meteor iron, couldn't be destroyed.

Was the water the same? If she'd ruled the spawn of the Hell behind the mirror for countless thousands of years, it was likely she was perfectly capable of carrying on for another few millennia, water or no water. Or were these new and stronger demons a threat to her as well?

His hands felt cold, and he stared at the flowing wound in the shadows, wondering how to get himself out of this alive. He was far beyond anything he had ever read in Dotys or Gantering Pellus or Polyborus, far beyond the craziest hints of dreams or magic or madness.

And if he guessed wrong, he knew, people would die. Muffle or Aunt Rowe or any of a hundred others whose lives had all his days been his charge. Ian or little Maggie, his and Jenny's youngest child. Adric or Jen herself.

"And I can just sashay on into this Hell with me little bottle and fetch you this water, then?" He pushed up his spectacles again and scratched the side of his nose. "Nobody's goin' to ask me what I'm doin' there?"

"Naturally," she crooned, "I will not send you on your errantry naked. You will know the way from the place where the gate is to the spring in the mountains. And you will have a helper to advise you."

"I can hardly wait," he said.

And a wind blew the candles out.

Dreams opened, windows into windows in his mind. In his dream he had been walking for hours and days, weeks maybe, in a bleak stony country where nothing grew but tufts of herbage in crevices. The rock was carved and twisted into waves, caverns, combers, dragons, and razor-edged ridges as if by violent winds, but he felt no wind. Sun hammered on its silver-threaded rusty glassiness. In pools he saw asphalt bubble and drip, but he felt no heat, nor did the steam that rose from the deep clefts have any smell. He came down out of the rock mountains to a maze of dry gullies, sandy flats, and knots of black, wasted trees among gouged walls of rock and earth. He saw the dust scamper, the black trees bend and shake.

He was a naturalist and a tracker. He could call to mind every foot of the Winterlands, every root and rock and trail. That was what it took to stay alive in his land. Looking around him now he made note of the shape of the land—the notches and ridges that would let him climb to the higher red-and-silver peaks where, he knew, the spring would lie.

Later still he was beside water and made note there, too, of the windings and changes of the riverbed. Lake flats lay near, speckled with humped gray silent plants barely poking their heads above the surface.

In this place he saw no life, but something told him that life was there.

In one hand he held the onyx ink bottle on its long red ribbon. In the other, three flax seeds, like little black beads in his ink-stained palm. The ink bottle was unstoppered and empty, though he had the stopper with him, too. Holding both was awkward, so he put the flax seeds in the bottle.

At once smoke began to coalesce from the dry air around him. He heard a voice cursing him, foul and furious. The smoke poured into the bottle, and he felt the onyx turn hot in his hand. He stoppered the bottle. The cursing stopped—or, in the ensuing silence, could still be heard muffled and tiny from within the bottle—but the bottle itself was warm, like bread new-taken from the oven.

You will have a helper to advise you, he heard the Demon Queen's voice say again. Looking down, he saw a little puddle of blood on the dark rock at his feet. The words came out of that. He shivered, knowing what kind of a helper it would be.

Let him who has trafficked with demons, and bought and sold whatever of money or goods to them, for any reason whatever, be burned alive on a pyre of dry wood soaked with oil, and all those goods with them, Polyborus had said.

Let him who has summoned demons through a gate into this world be cut into pieces alive, and those pieces afterward burnt, not leaving so much as a finger unconsumed by the fire.

Let him who has willingly taken a demon into his body be cut to pieces and burnt, and the ashes mixed with salt and silver and cast into the sea, that nothing of his substance may afterward be used by the Hellspawnedkind.

Let him who has gone through the gates into Hell be burned, upon dry wood and a hot fire, and bound with chains rune-warded to hold demonkind, for it must be assumed that any man who goes into Hell comes back changed in his body and his soul, if indeed it is the same man, and not merely a semblance of him, who emerges.

For there is no lawful reason for humankind to touch, or speak to, or have traffic with the Hellspawnedkind. Rather should that man perish, and suffer his wife, or his son, or his goods all to perish utterly, than that demons be given a gate into this world.

John knew the words. He'd read them a dozen times over fifteen howling winters, back when he'd only sought knowledge for knowledge's own sake. He'd read them a hundred times since his return with Jenny from the South, seeking desperately for an answer to Jenny's terrible silences, to Ian's debilitating grief.

He woke suddenly, lying on the dirt floor with the late winter dawn oozing leaden through the cracks in the shutters, the stink of burned tallow heavy on the air. Of the five candles only long winding sheets of brown wax remained. The pentagram could still be seen, scratched into the floor. The air smelled faintly of blood, though no trace of it showed on the walls or the floor. John found he could not look at the place on the plaster where the wound had been.

He sat up shivering, aching in his bones and in his heart. Outside he could hear Bill the stablehand talking to Aunt Umetty, with the scrape of a shovel on the ground.

"...broke around midnight," Bill was saying, "and she's been sleepin' natural ever since." Snow scrunched, fell. The air was iron cold. "They tell me Genny Hopper's boy's better, too, though they sure thought he was a goner; even them spots are fadin' off him. I thought sure, it has to be either Master Ian or Mistress Jenny, and not meanin' to slight the boy I hoped it was Miss Jenny, since I hear she's been unable to do spells as she used ..."

John put his fingers to the pit of his throat. A small oval scar marked the place where the Demon Queen had pressed an ensorceled jewel when he had first gone to beg her help in Hell.

And there was no getting past the fact that she had helped. She had given them spells to protect the dragon-slaying machines so they could defeat Caradoc's—Folcalor's—enslaved star-drakes and free them of their demon possessors. She had given them spells to free the wizards in Folcalor's thrall. And she had given them a spell of healing, without which Ian might now be in even worse shape.

Now she asked his help.

She was lying, he was almost certain—he wondered what that water actually did. But she was asking his help.

As he climbed stiffly to his feet something dropped from his plaids, rolled to the earthen floor. He picked it up. It was the onyx ink bottle, stopper still tightly in place. When he touched it it was warm, like bread new-brought from the oven. Putting his ear to it, it seemed to him that he could hear a whispering inside.

Chapter 4

"Don't do it, Johnny." Once Muffle would have growled the words in exasperation, or shouted them in rage. But his voice was now very quiet, and the light from the burning work shed showed the profoundest fear on his face.

"You don't even know what I'm at." Aversin didn't look at him, only stood gazing into the flames where half a lifetime's work slowly crumbled in red heat and smoke. The wicker gondola and silken air bags of the *Milkweed,* which had borne him north to the isles of the dragons, the Skerries of Light. The jointed frame and waxed canopy of his infamous parachute. Pieces of five or six early versions of his dragon-slaying contrivances.

Gone.

Against his overwhelming regret he had only to place the mental image of Mag or Adric entering the building or touching any single thing that had been in it during last night's manifestations.

He drew a deep breath and turned to regard his brother. "It's only demons can undo the magic of demons," he said.

The heat of the fire made the snow on Muffle's plaids steam and glitter in the red-gray stubble on his cheeks. The older man's small bright brown eyes searched John's but met only the reflection of flame, mirrored in the rounds of spectacle glass.

"And Ian's like a visitor that's got his coat on to leave," John added. "What would you have me do?"

"Take Jen with you."

"No." John pitched his torch into the flaring ruin, trying not to remember the demon in Jenny's eyes, or Amayon's name whispered in her sleep. When the shed roof fell in, he picked up his loaded saddle-bags, made sure the little bag of flax seeds was in his pocket, and ascended to the stable court. Gantering Pellus alleged that demons were obliged to count seeds, though he'd claimed it was millet seeds, not flax. Muffle climbed behind John, water skins slung over his shoulder, slipping a little in the snow that heaped the steps. The lower court was sheltered. Once they came up the wind hit them, cold as a flint knife and stinging with sleet.

"Ian, then. He'll be on his feet in a day or two . . ."

"No." John ducked through the low stable door, where Battlehammer stood saddled and waiting. He pulled off the rug Bill had laid over the big liver-bay warhorse and fastened on saddlebags and water skins. It wasn't a day on which he would turn a stable rat out-of-doors, and by the smell of the wind he'd be lucky if he reached the Wraithmire before more snow hit. But the fever wouldn't wait.

Snow lay drifted in the gateway. Peg the gatekeeper and Bill the yardman straightened from their shoveling. "If I was you, I'd think again—" Peg began.

"If I was you, I would, too," John reassured her. He wrapped his brown-and-white winter plaid tighter around his lower face. His very teeth hurt with the cold.

"Jen's taught Ian how to use the ward wyrds that'll tell if Iceriders are on their way," he said, swinging up into the saddle. He felt bad about taking Battlehammer into peril that would almost certainly get him killed—poor payment for a beast of whom he was dearly fond—but he knew he would need a trained mount, and a fast one. "But if that happens, for God's sake, don't forget to send someone out to the Fell to fetch Jen in, whether she wants to come or not. Tell her I'm on patrol."

"Since when have you taken water on patrol?" Muffle demanded. "Or your harpoons?" He slapped the backs of his fingers to the heavy iron weapons slung behind Battlehammer's saddle, three of the eight that John had made to use against dragons. Even without the poisons and death spells Jenny—and later Ian—had put on them, they were formidable, and something about the empty lands he'd seen in his dream last night had warned him that there were things about which the Demon Queen had lied.

"Keep watch." John bent from the saddle to lay a hand on his brother's shoulder. "There's aught afoot, Muffle, and I don't know what it is or how it's to be fought." *I'm not a mage!* he wanted to shout, *I shouldn't even be doing this!* But he'd never considered himself a warrior, either. "Keep watch for anythin'. Not only outside the bounds, outside the walls, but inside as well. Stay here at the Hold tonight, if you would, and until I return. Bring Blossom and the children—tell 'em it's because I don't know how long I'll be away. Tell 'em anythin'. But every night, walk about the place. Down the cellars, along the walls, go in the crypt underneath the main hall. Just look."

"For what?"

Peg was lowering the drawbridge, working the crank to raise the portcullis. Wind slammed through the gate with renewed viciousness, slicing John's sheepskin coat and winter plaids, the mailed leather beneath.

John shook his head. "I don't know."

"And who do I tell," the blacksmith asked, "if I find what I shouldn't?"

Ian. John felt a pang, less of fear than of grief, thinking of what his son might have to face.

He's too young, he's been hurt too bad . . .

But he had grown up in a land that did not make allowances, not for youth, not for innocence, not for the wounded.

"Jen," he said. "Ian, if Jen's not to be reached."

Sergeant Muffle nodded, silenced by whatever it was that he saw in John's eyes. "How long will you be gone?"

"That I don't know." He gathered the reins, Battlehammer's breath a white mist like a monster of legend. Beyond the gate the world was marble and ash, treeless to the horizon.

He turned back. "Pray for me."

"Every day, Johnny," Muffle said quietly. "Every day."

Aversin turned his back on the Hold and rode for the Wraithmire. The smoke of the burning work shed made a hard white column in the gray air, and the hot onyx of the ink bottle burned against his flesh like a second heart.

In summer or fall he could reach those dreary marshes in a matter of hours. Riding against the wind, with Battlehammer foundering in the drifts, the day was dying when he came to the edge of the slick flats of brown ice, the snow-covered humps of bramble and hackweed that filled the sheltered ground. No one could tell him now whether the flooding had come first and the infestations of whisperers later, or whether the lands had been abandoned to the water when those glowing, giggling things had begun to haunt the nights.

In either case it hadn't surprised him to learn that a gate of Hell was located there.

A man named Morne had had a house hereabouts—before the marshes had spread this far—and had farmed a little. One afternoon Nuncle Darrow came to the Hold saying that Morne's wife had cut her husband and then their four children to pieces with a carving knife. Old Caerdinn and Jenny had exorcised the woman, but they didn't know whether they'd succeeded, for after they were done with their spells the woman turned the knife on herself.

The house still stood. John could distinguish its pale shape among the half-dead trees in the gloom. None of the neighbors had torn it down, not even for the bricks and the dressed stone.

He dismounted cautiously and led Battlehammer into the labyrinth of hummocks and ice. In the graying twilight he found where animal tracks turned aside in fear of the whisperers but saw no mark, no sign of the Hellspawn themselves.

He made sure Battlehammer was stoutly tied to a sapling before reaching into his coat for the ink bottle. It felt heavy in his hand, and for a time he stood, wondering if there were any way whatsoever he could accomplish the bidding of the Demon Queen without the help of the thing inside.

But he couldn't. He simply didn't know enough. So he pulled off his glove, took three flax seeds from the pouch at his waist, and held them ready between thumb and forefinger. Only then did he pull the stopper from the bottle.

A momentary silvery glitter played above the hole, like a very tiny flame.

And Jenny stood before him.

Jenny beautiful, as she had been when first he'd seen her at Frost Fell: black hair like night on the ocean, blue eyes like summer noon. Smiling and relaxed and filled with the joy of living, with daffodils in her hands.

John held the flax seeds above the bottle's mouth and said, "You take that form ever again, and I swear to you I'll seal this thing with you in it and bury it in the deepest part of the sea."

"Darling, how serious you're being!" It wasn't Jenny anymore; it never had been, in the way faces and identities shift and merge in dreams. A slim boy stood before John, fourteen or fifteen years old. Like Jenny he was black haired and blue eyed, with long lashes and red pouty lips in an alabaster face. He wore plain black hose and a coat of quilted black velvet, just as if the world were not frozen all around them; his little round cap was sewn with garnets. "Could it be you're jealous? Do you suspect those legions of men she had weren't entirely because she was allegedly possessed? We can't force anyone to do anything that's truly against their secret natures in the first place, you know."

"No," John returned mildly. "I don't know that. In fact, what I do know is that the lot of you are liars who couldn't ask straight-out for water if you were dyin'."

The boy shrugged. "Well, I'm sure you'll go on believing whatever makes you comfortable." He held out his exquisitely kid-gloved hand. "I'm Amayon." And, when John did not react, he added, "*Jenny's* Amayon."

"And *my* servant," John pointed out maliciously and for a fleeting instant saw the flare of rage and piqued pride in those cobalt eyes. "I trust Her Majesty told you your duties an' all."

"Tedious bitch." Amayon yawned elaborately, though John had already seen that the demon did not breathe. "I suppose you know she uses the mucus of donkeys as a complexion cream? You haven't, I hope, been taken in by that antiquated lust spell she throws over everyone she encounters."

"Like the one you used on Rocklys' cavalry corps?" John returned, refusing to be goaded.

"Oh, darling, did Jenny tell you that was me?" The demon simpered, but he was watching John's eyes. "How very simple of her."

Not for nothing, however, had John grown up his father's son, his heart and his face a fist closed in defense. He merely regarded Amayon without expression, and the demon shrugged and smiled.

"Well, I'm sure if it makes you feel better to believe that ... The gate's this way, Lordship." He threw a mocking flex into the title. "Generally only the small fry can leak through, but Her Reechiness has given me a word."

"Do you hate that animal?" he added, raising delicate brows at Battlehammer, who stood, ears flat to his neck and muscles bunched, regarding him as he would have a snake.

"Should I?"

"It's up to you, of course, Lordship. But unless there's some reason you'd like to see him die, I suggest you don't bring him with us. Your mistress has made arrangements."

"Ah," John said. "Thinks of everythin', she does." And he dropped the seeds into the bottle.

It was Aversin's intention simply to keep the demon where he couldn't do mischief while he took Battlehammer to the nearest farm, which was old Dan Darrow's walled enclave in the bottomlands adjacent to the Mire. But with the snow and the wind, and his exhaustion from a sleepless night, it took him nearly two hours to reach the place.

" 'Twill be black as pitch by the time you get back to the Mire," the farmer protested when John explained that he wanted the loan of a donkey and a boy to lead it back to the farm again.

A little uneasily, he acceded to the patriarch's invitation to spend the night. He was conscious of the demon bottle around his neck as he sat at supper with the Darrow clan and their hired men and women, watching the old man's fair-haired grandchildren tumble and play before the hearth. He guessed that Amayon was perfectly aware of his surroundings; he had no business, he thought, bringing even a bottled demon into a house where there were children.

When he slept, he dreamed again and again of a rat, or some huge insect, creeping up the frame of each child's bed, demon light glittering in its berry-blue eyes. Reaching toward them . . .

He woke at the touch of a hand on his neck.

The Darrow farm was a big place, but simple and rustic. John had bedded down among the men of the household in the loft, on blankets and straw tickings spread around where the chimney came through from the floor below. They'd have put the King himself there, had he come calling. Remembering that demons had spoken to Caradoc in his dreams, offering him greater power and wider wisdom if he would but open a gate for them, he'd tied the red ribbon that held the ink bottle in a knot up close to his throat so it couldn't be slipped off over his head while he slept.

Sure enough, as he opened his eyes he felt a man's hands fumbling with the ribbon and heard the slow thick breathing of a sleeper near his face, not the short breaths of a man nervous about robbing a guest. John caught the sleepwalker by wrist and shoulder and flung him bodily onto as many men as he could; there were shouts and curses, and by the thread of dim hearthlight that leaked up through the ladder hole at the far end of the loft he saw his attacker bound to his feet, eyes blank, knife in hand.

The attacker—a huge stablehand named Browson who'd helped unsaddle Battlehammer—lunged at him, but men were scrambling up, grabbing, clutching. Shouts of "Murder!" and "Bandits!" barked through the dark. Another of the hired men grabbed Browson and threw him down, and then Dan Darrow and his two sons-in-law swarmed up the ladder in their nightshirts. "Browson, what in Cragget's name are you at?"

Browson was blinking, stupid with sleep and scared. He saw the knife in his own hand and dropped it in terror.

John fumbled his spectacles on as one of the men said, "He pulled steel on His Lordship here, sir!"

"I didn't! I didn't do nuthin', sir!" Browson gasped. Darrow's eyes grew flinty, for it wasn't an unheard-of thing for bandit gangs to buy the loyalty of hired men to slit the throats of as many potential defenders as they could in the vanguard of an attack. "I swear it, sir! I didn't mean no harm! I had this dream . . ."

"I thought so," John said briskly and gestured stillness to those who'd pulled their weapons from beneath their blankets. "*Somnambulistis truncularis,* that's what it is."

"Somna-what?" They regarded him with respect, for he had a wide reputation as a scholar. Only old Dan glanced sidelong, suspicion in his dark eyes as he stroked the huge white fangs of his mustache back into something that resembled their daytime order.

"*Somnambulistis truncularis.* Polyborus describes it in his *Materia Medica,*" John went on, inventing freely, "and Heronax says it's caused by conjunctions of Saturn and Mars at the midwinter solstice, though meself, I agree with Juronal that it's caused by the bite of the brown hay toad, which is near extinct here in the North."

He shoved the ink bottle back under his shirt and checked that the sack of flax seeds was still safe in his pocket. "In places in the

South, though, people regularly put pots and pans round their beds in case the servants come sneakin' in like this, for it gives 'em dreams about killin'. What'd you dream, son?"

"A voice." The farmhand looked tremblingly from John to his master. "It was a King, like, all in a golden crown, tellin' me to get this bottle away from . . . from His Lordship here. He said as how His Lordship had stole the bottle, and I was to take and open it. Take and open it, he said, and there'd be treasure for me inside as well."

John nodded wisely. "Way common in these cases," he said. "In Greenhythe only last year there was a quadruple case of it, when four village women all dreamt they had to bathe the mayor and converged on his house in the middle of the night with soap and towels, and not one of 'em remembered in the mornin' why it was so twilkin' important that he be clean. So I'm just grateful the case is no worse."

That got a laugh, as he'd hoped it would, and those men who'd had their swords in hands stashed them beneath their blankets again. Even Darrow, who wasn't one to endanger his family by leaving a suspected traitor unhanged, relaxed.

But John spent the remainder of the long night awake, pinching himself when he felt in danger of falling asleep. Twice or thrice, when he did drift off, he dreamed again about the blue-eyed rat that sniffed and scrabbled about the beds where Dan Darrow's little grandchildren slept.

"And that was your idea of a joke?" he asked when Darrow—who had himself accompanied him to the edge of the Wraithmire with a donkey laden with supplies—disappeared between the snowy deadfall hummocks, leaving Aversin alone.

Amayon flickered into view out of the smoke from the newly opened ink bottle. "Oh, don't be squeamish." He pouted. "I wouldn't have harmed the little bastards. You've said yourself a thousand times that that youngest boy needs to be thrashed more often."

John studied the elfin face, the innocent eyes in their dark fringes of lash. Just enough like Ian, he realized, to twist at the grief he felt about his son. The voice melodious, sweet and childlike. But he knew that Amayon no more looked like this than the Demon Queen looked like the woman he saw in his dreams.

He slipped the straps of food sacks and water satchels over his shoulders, flexing his knees to test the balance of the load. One sack contained other things: bits of silver and dragonbone, whatever he could find in Jenny's workbox that wouldn't add too much weight. "And I suppose Browson needs to be hanged, for attackin' a guest?"

"They wouldn't have hanged him." Amayon gestured airily. "Now come along. Her Poxship went to a great deal of trouble to get you a beast worthy of you, so we'd better get through the gate before it wanders away."

He set off through the snow-choked thickets, John at his heels. Every tree they passed, every frozen pond they skirted, John noted, remembering the way so he could come back and do something—he wasn't sure what—about the demon gate. He had packed also as much clean parchment and paper as he could, had drawn from memory what he remembered of the route Aohila had shown him in dreaming, and had made note of Amayon's remark last night about gates that would admit only tiny spawn, not great ones.

He didn't know what any of it meant or might mean, but someone, sometime, would.

The mists that always hung over the Wraithmire thickened, making it hard for him to get his bearings; Amayon stopped twice and waited for him, knee-deep in swirling white vapor. John followed carefully, reflecting that it would be exactly like the demon to lead him thus onto thin ice, for the amusement of watching him lose toes to frostbite when his boots got soaked. Then through the fog a warm wind breathed, alien and frightening, and on it drifted a smell John knew he'd scented before hereabouts: sand and sourness, and something like burning metal.

The light altered.

The squeak of the snow turned to the crunch of pebbles underfoot.

And a thing rose up before them in the mists, with a blunt stupid head on a long neck balanced by a blunt heavy tail. Between tail and head were tall haunches and two long legs, like a sort of flabby featherless hairless bird, saddled and bridled like a horse.

A creature of Hell, regarding him with a black dead porcelain-shiny eye.

The hot wind breathed the mists away. Dust stung Aversin's nostrils, burned his eyes.

Black harsh mountains stained with rust scraped a colorless sky. Something like a cloud moved across it, curling and uncurling with a floppy, obscene motion, running against the wind.

Amayon smiled, and John knew it was because the demon tasted his fear.

"Welcome to Hell," the demon said.

Chapter 5

It took Jenny most of the day following the storm to dig out. In this she was helped by her sister Sparrow and Sparrow's husband and Bill, the yardman from the Hold, who came up with milk, cheese, and dried apples and to make sure she was well. "Aunt Umetty seems to think as you'd laid in the corner all this time and would need feedin' with a spoon," the sallow, lanky little servant said with a grin.

Jenny, who had convinced herself that everyone in the Hold and the villages round about would stone her on sight, returned the smile shakily and said, "I hope you brought a spoon."

After days of sleep, of migraines and troubled dreams, the company made her feel better, more alive. Ian was better, Bill reported, though he slept a good deal, which wasn't to be marveled at, poor lad. Bill hoped as Mistress Jenny wouldn't be moved to do herself a harm, having had traffic with demons same as her boy. He said that John had ridden out by himself this very morning, as his father had used to do sometimes, then asked what Jenny thought of prospects for spring.

Though Jenny quivered a little at the thought, she walked over to the Hold the following morning, a tiny brown-and-white figure in the bleak vastness of the snow-choked cranberry bog. As Bill had predicted, she found Ian asleep.

"And I'll not have you wake him," Aunt Jane, who had insisted on walking up to the boy's room with her, said. A big woman with thick dark hair slashed now with gray, Aunt Jane had never liked Jenny, though for years the two women had existed in a state of truce. Jane had said many times—as reported to Jenny over the years by various people whose business it wasn't—that no good ever came of mixing with witchery, meaning that she had passionately loved her brother Lord Aver and had hated Kahiera Nightraven.

It was Kahiera that Jenny saw now in Jane's eyes, as they stood together in the doorway of Ian's room.

Icewitch and sorceress, an outcast of her own people and a battle captive of Lord Aver, Nightraven had been Jenny's first teacher in the arts of magic when Jenny was a child; she had been the only one in the world who understood. Jenny had been five when that tall cold beautiful woman had been brought to the Hold, and for six years she had tagged at her sable skirts. Every word and spell and fragment of lore that came from those pale lips she had memorized, and she had seen how the witch used her magic, and her wits, to ensnare her captor. Leaving him at last—leaving their son—she had laid on Lord Aver spells such that he had never loved another woman.

And all this was still in Jane's resentful eyes.

Ian looked peaceful, curled on his side in the bed that the boys shared, its curtains drawn against the chilly forenoon light. He was terribly thin, Jenny saw, guilt prodding and twisting at her heart, but he did not seem to be tormented by the dreams that had tortured her.

Was that why he had tried to take his own life?

She shrank from the thought, guessing it to be true. Her own pain had blinded her. Her self-absorption in the loss of Amayon had kept her from even asking whether he suffered as badly . . .

What made her think her own agony was the worst possible?

Did Gothpys croon little rhymes to Ian still, in dreams? Did Ian hate his father for having taken the demon from him?

But even had Jane not been there, she would not have broken his healing sleep to inquire.

"Where's Adric?" she asked as she turned from the door and descended the stairs to the kitchen again.

"He and Sergeant Muffle went hunting." Jane's voice was frosty. "You're welcome to wait."

Since this was patently untrue, Jenny thanked her and took her leave, staying only long enough to play a little with Mag by the warmth of the kitchen hearth. Pursuant to her decision to be a spider when she grew up, Mag was currently practicing weaving webs with Aunt Rowe's yarns; she accepted her mother's presence as peacefully as she had accepted her various absences, evidently considering this merely another journey. From Sparrow and Bill,

Jenny had already heard of the mysterious fever, though there were no further cases of it and those who had been like to die were already on their feet. *Curious*, she thought, disquieted. On her way back to Frost Fell she resolved to return on the morrow, later in the day when Ian would be awake, though it meant walking home in the dark.

But as she trudged homeward, the flinty dazzle of the snow resolved itself into the wavering firefalls of migraine, and through the following day Jenny was barely able to do more than make sure Moon Horse was watered and fed and stagger back to bed. She dreamed again of the sea bottom and the great weightless graceful shadows of the whalemages passing like dancers overhead. The migraine seemed to have gotten into her dreams as well: fire shimmering in the water among the great columns of rock where Caradoc had died and things appearing and disappearing on the current-sculpted sand of the seafloor below.

The next day she felt better, though lightheaded. She trekked the woods in early morning, digging herbs patiently out from beneath the drifted snow. She could put no magic into them as she'd used to do, but they would have virtue nonetheless. There was peace, too, to be found in the secret tales told her by fox track and rabbit scat in the snow. She returned home and made herself a tisane against the migraine's return. Lying in bed she heard the shutters rattle with new-risen wind. She stepped to the door and smelled the wind: It would be worse long before nightfall.

So she performed her chores and baked bread and carried in wood to last the afternoon and the night. The small tasks brought peace to her, and she tried to put from her mind what Jane would be saying of her—probably had been saying about her for years—behind her back. In the afternoon she climbed the attic steps with a broom and dust rags, to sweep and cleanse it and make it sweet for the drying of herbs. She relit the candles she'd set up four nights ago and, finding that light insufficient, untied the bundle and set another dozen in place: The darkness in the attic had disquieted her.

She no longer had a wizard's skills, but, she found, something of a wizard's awareness remained. And there was something about the attic that made her scalp prickle.

She opened another bundle of candles and saw that five were missing from it. The number skittered in the back of her mind with a sensation like the scratching of rats, catching at her breath. She lit all that remained of the candles and moved the spare bed out of the way; shifting boxes and sacks, her tiredness dissolved and even the ache in her crooked hands retreated before the dread in her heart. The dust on the trunks and bundles had been disturbed already. Thrusting aside two sacks of barley, she found the ghost of a mark on the floor, rubbed out with rags but not rubbed out enough.

It was a single curving line, ending in a sigil she recognized—a sigil she had never before seen in any of John's books or the books left her by old Caerdinn. But she recognized it still.

She stood, candle in hand, looking down at it, wondering why she knew it, why the sight of it turned her sick.

Then she understood.

The memory of it was not her own. It had been left in her mind by Amayon when he had inhabited her body and her brain. It was one of dozens—ugly and dirty and disquieting, like fruit parings cached in corners by an unwelcome and uncouth guest.

The line was part of a complex power circle designed for the calling of a demon.

Ian.

The thought smote her like the toll of an iron bell.

Folcalor.

I will not go.

Nausea twisted her—nausea and pity and horror—and she scraped and hurled and tore at the boxes, the firkins, the bundles that had been stacked over the place.

Ian, no! Oh, my son ...

She found the fragments of a china bowl, not merely broken but stamped and smashed until the clay was powder, ground into the scratched planking of the floor. Powdered, too, were bits of black chalk, as if they'd been crushed and ground under a young boy's boots ... *I will not. I will not. I will not.* In the darkest corner she found the five candles.

They were unlit.

He had not completed the rite.

Jenny knelt, holding her hands over her mouth, her breath glittering in the soft amber light that filled the attic.

He had not completed the summons of the demon.

Instead, he had gone downstairs and drunk poison in an effort to silence those demands.

Oh, Ian.

She closed her eyes.

Oh, my son.

The Winterlands' wind screamed across the thatch.

When morning came, Jenny patiently dug the snow from the doors of the kitchen and the stable, wrapped herself in a sheepskin coat and her thick winter plaids, tied her sheepskin cap over her bald scalp, and set out for Alyn Hold. *It has to be Folcalor,* she thought, as she waded through the drifts on the downhill road through the bog. Gothpys—the demon who had inhabited Ian's body and heart as Amayon had inhabited hers—was a prisoner behind the Mirror of Isychros. He would not be able to benefit from being summoned even had he had the power to invade Ian's dreams with the demand.

Folcalor had seduced Caradoc, imprisoned his soul in a jewel, and inhabited his body. He had used the enslaved mage's powers to capture and imprison other wizards.

Why?

And he was seeking to do it again.

Why?

At the Hold, Peg told her Ian and Muffle had ridden out that morning to deal with sickness in the village of Great Toby. "They hadn't heard over there yet that you wasn't at the Hold," the gatekeeper explained apologetically. "The sickness isn't much—Granny Brown's rheumatism—so Master Ian said not to trouble you with it."

"Thank you," Jenny said, tucking her halberd against her shoulder and blowing on her hands. Even if Ian and Muffle were a few hours ahead of her, she'd encounter them in Great Toby. It would be near dark by the time she reached the village, and almost certainly snowing again.

"Would you do me a favor and ask Sparrow to send one of her

girls up to the Fell to look after Moon Horse, if I'm not back tonight?" Jenny asked. Diffidently, she added, "John hasn't returned yet, has he?" For through the gate arch she saw Bill lead Battlehammer across the yard.

Peg shook her head. "Dan Darrow brought the old boy back yesterday," she said, turning to follow Jenny's eyes. "He says His Lordship was there at the half moon; left the horse and went on into the Wraithmire alone. Old Dan said he thought as how John might be tracking something, by the weapons he bore."

"The half moon?" Jenny said, and glanced at the sickle of the day moon just visible among the slow-gathering clouds.

"I don't like it." Peg hunched her shoulders in her mountain of wolf hides, plaids, and bright-colored knitwork scarves. "Muffle don't like it, neither. He's been pacing over the place at night as if he'd left something somewhere, looking in all the same places."

The half moon, Jenny thought, quickening her stride as she passed through the village and over the barren fields. The road to Great Toby was laid out to avoid a slough, and Jenny knew she could cut nearly an hour off her walk by going through the woods. She moved with instinctive caution, seeking out deadfalls and places where the snow had been rucked and trampled by wild pigs or scoured by last night's winds. It wasn't unheard-of for bandits to come this close to the Hold walls, or even for them to raid one of the few isolated farms hereabouts, and she was acutely aware that she no longer had spells of "look over there" to keep her from their sight.

Even in the days of the kings, gangs of bullies and outlaws had preyed on the farms, hiding in the woods to steal cattle or pigs or to capture the occasional villager to sell as a slave to the gnomes of the mountains. With the return of the King's troops and the King's law three years ago, John had for the first time in anyone's memory been able to make headway against them.

But with law, the King's troops had brought more men, insubordinates and hard cases both in the legions and among the serfs of the manors established to feed the garrisons. In the past year, John had been certain that the bandits had entered the slave business in earnest, systematically kidnapping serfs who for the most part had been forcibly relocated to the North anyway.

Thus when Jenny saw the quick darting of half a dozen foxes away to her left in the white woods and found they'd been feeding on a dead sheep at the end of a long blood trail, the first thing she thought was, *Bandits.* When she followed the trail back to Rushmeath Farm, she knew it.

House and barn stood open and empty. By the trampled tracks and the blood on the snow Jenny read the tale of the attack: read, too, that it had taken place just after dawn. Heartsick with dread she searched for Dal and Lyra's children, knowing that the gnomes had no use for anything but healthy adults in the deep tunnels of their endless mines.

But she found no trace of the youngsters, queer—no blood, no torn clothing, no sign of wolf tracks hauling a tiny corpse back to a lair. And in the mucked stew of tracks she picked out those of Gerty and Young Dal, as well as those of their parents, heading south and east, deeper into the Wyrwoods.

Jenny glanced around her as if taking counsel from the zebra-striped silence of the winter woods. It was two hours' walk back to the Hold, nearly three to Great Toby. According to Peg, the Alyn militia was out on patrol and might not return until dark. It would be snowing by then, and these tracks would be covered. And the half dozen bandits who'd raided the farm would have rendezvoused with either the gnomes or with the main body of their own gang. In either case someone would have pointed out that the gnomes wouldn't buy the children.

As she set out after the tracks, she identified in her mind the three possible camping places they'd make for. Almost due south was a hollow with a spring, thickly covered by trees, that would provide protection against the snow. More easterly lay a cave in the bank where the Queen's Beck cut under the hills on the edge of the bleak fell country, and north and east of that was a deeper cut protected on three sides by the fells.

It quickly became clear they weren't moving south. As she followed the tracks through the quick-falling darkness, Jenny counted footprints and estimated the strength of the party: seven men, two of whom scouted ahead and to the sides in a businesslike fashion. They'd taken Dal's two cows, his horse, and to judge by the depth of the tracks, a good deal of food. They were pitifully easy to follow. If they were heading east, Jenny thought, they'd be making for the old Brighthelm Tower in the hills. If northeast, they'd be meeting in either Shern Hollow or the big caves under Wild Man Fell, all customary haunts of bandits. She could overtake them there . . .

And what?

Even as a witch-wife of small powers, before dragon magic had entered her flesh, Jenny had never truly thought she could be enslaved. Killed, possibly. But never carried off like a common woman: raped, sold to the gnomes. She was a solitary woman, alone in the woods with her knife, her halberd . . .

. . . and forty-three years' knowledge and experience of tracking, of watching, of silence.

When it became obvious that the bandits were headed due east, Jenny veered away and sought the low ground of a frozen pond deeper in the woods, where nightshade grew in the summer. She found thickets of it buried under the snow, and as darkness gathered and snow began to fall, she harvested handfuls of the dried leaves. In the shelter of an oak tree she made a small fire, and in her drinking cup, the only open vessel she had with her, boiled snow water and the crushed leaves, over and over, until she'd made up a tincture. This she stored in her water bottle, wrapped herself in plaids and coat and cloak beside the fire, and fell to sleep hungry.

Mother Mag, she prayed to the One who watched over children, *don't let them kill them before I get there . . .*

Look after Ian. Look after John.

Next morning she found where they'd camped, in the cave by the Queen's Beck, where she couldn't have got to them anyway. By now they'd be on their way to Brighthelm Tower. With five prisoners and livestock, the bandits wouldn't be moving fast. Jenny swung wide to avoid their scouts and eventually reached the tower: a couple of stories of the keep, a broad ring of crumbled stone that had been a court, and a clutch of pine trees that John would never have suffered to grow anywhere close to any defensive position of his.

Jenny climbed a pine tree and stayed there. The tower would be the first place the scouts would search, and there was no other place close where her tracks would not show in the new-fallen snow. Though she swept behind her with a pine bough and leaped from occasional bare rock to bare rock beneath the trees, she wasn't sure the deception would pass by daylight.

But the bandits didn't arrive until dusk, as the last thin nail paring of the old moon set. Cramped, frozen, and aching with hunger, Jenny heard their voices and the squeak of booted feet in the snow, far off. She found herself holding her breath until they came into sight among the twisted trees of the dale below: The boy and girl were still alive, and little Sunny was a tiny bundle clinging to her father's bent back.

Even as she breathed a prayer of thanks Jenny wondered, *Why keep children alive?* They couldn't have been easy to travel with. Young Dal was eight and barely keeping up; the rope that circled his wrists was being dragged on by a thickset oaf with a beard like a dead dog. Lyra, too, was staggering, her bloodied skirts and her husband's averted eyes speaking clearly of how the bandits had used her. Jenny shivered with anger, and her hunger and fatigue dissolved.

"They festerin' better be here soon," the bandit leader grumbled, making a careful check of the encircling wall while Dead Dog Beard scouted inside the tower. "You, Hero—" He motioned to Dal. "You clear the snow off there." He pointed to the half-covered remains of the hall at the tower's foot. "We're too festerin' close to Alyn for me."

"We can see the track from the top of the tower," a blond-bearded man pointed out soothingly. "We'll have plenty of time to see a patrol."

"Well, I didn't know you could witchfesterin' motherless see in the dark, Crake. But since you can, you can be the one who keeps witchfesterin' watch tonight if they don't show up."

"Just send me up a bottle of that wine and I'll watch all you can ask for," Crake responded.

"Mother Hare's tits, I'm thirsty."

"You leave that wine alone," the leader snarled.

"What, the gnomes ain't gonna bring their own wine?"

From her post in the pine Jenny listened, coldly calculating what had to be done. She recognized two of the bandits from Balgodorus Black-Knife's band, whom she'd helped Baron Pellanor of Palmorgin fight last summer. When they finished checking the tower, they sent up a watchman to its top, then proceeded to make themselves comfortable around a fire in the semiopen hall ruins; it was a fairly easy matter for Jenny to creep along a branch to one of the broken-out windows of the tower and down to where the packs—and the wine bottles—were stowed in the jumble of broken rafters and fallen tiles that was the tower's lowest room. As she poured the nightshade into the bottles, she could hear the bandits outside.

"Can we have the skirt again 'fore the gnomes take her away?"

"You keep your mind on your business and your cod in your britches."

"You, junior—you're ten, remember? You think they'll take that little 'un anyway? They said from ten up."

"Let's see. They may want 'em younger. If not, no problem."

Just after dark the man on watch called out, "Company coming!" and Jenny heard a man's voice speak out of the darkness, "In whose name are you here?"

"In the name of the King beneath the Sea," the bandit leader called out. The King beneath the Sea was Giton, boy-husband of the Yellow-Haired Goddess Balyna in Southern legend, but the name could as easily be applied to Adromelech, the Archdemon Lord of the Sea-wights, or his servant Folcalor.

Jenny, crouched in the darkness, held her breath. Having inspected the tower ruin once, the bandits were not disposed to do it again, and any chance sound she might have made was amply covered by the cows and horse they'd penned there. Still her heart pounded as the bandit leader came in and took the wine bottles.

They drank to one another, and to their bargain, the deep, oddly timbred voices of the gnomes bickering over prices and deferring to their human leader about the little girl Sunny. "Well, we can certainly try—" that voice said, and Jenny felt a queer cold stirring of recognition. She knew it, or one like it "—so long as she gives no trouble."

"You hear that, Sweetlips? You keep your brat quiet and don't lag behind . . ."

The wine bottle clinked on a cup.

"Cragget's balls!" A man staggered through the black doorway and tried to fumble his britches down, then fell to his knees and vomited. Jenny slid her knife from its sheath, took a better grip on her halberd, and settled herself deeper into the dark corner to wait. The man Crake came down the dark stair from his watchpost above when he heard the other men cursing and puking; Jenny took him from behind, half severing his head before he could reach the door. She listened for a little time more, until all was silence outside, then crept to the door to look.

Dal, Lyra, and their children were clustered in a corner of the firelit shelter, their hands bound behind them to the wrecked beams, staring at the dead men and gnomes strewed between the shelter and the far wall of the open court. Lyra's face wore a strange, hard, bitter smile. They turned sharply as Jenny appeared in the doorway. "Mistress Waynest!" Dal cried. "Thank God!"

"Did you use magic?" Gerty whispered as Jenny cut their bonds. Her eyes were huge with shock and wonder. "Cousin Ryllis told me you couldn't use magic anymore."

"Just because you can't use magic, you aren't helpless," Jenny said softly. "Could I have used magic I would have spared these men. Now quickly, gather up what provision we can and let's be away from here. They may have been part of a greater band. We must tell Lord John to bring out the militia . . ."

Lyra, who had gone over to gather up the little sack of money from the hand of a dead gnome, screamed.

The human leader of the gnomes, a man in a long green cloak, sprang from the ground and snatched at her wrist.

Jenny leaped toward her, halberd raised to strike, then halted in her tracks in shock. Lyra had darted clear of the man's lunge and stood back, gasping and trembling, as he fell, clutching his belly, his whole body convulsing again with the effects of the nightshade. *He should be dead,* Jenny thought blindly, blankly. *He should be dead . . .*

Her mouth was dry and her breathing fast as she stared at that cropped gray head, the beaky nose, the patch over the eye.

Foolish, she thought. *He* is *dead.*

The man was crawling toward them, muttering curses and vomiting again though there was nothing in him to bring up. Clinging together, Jenny and Lyra backed away before him, while Dal and the children brought the stock out of the tower, making a wide circuit around the crawling body.

I saw him die in the infirmary tent after the battle at Cor's Bridge, at summer's end. The eye now covered with a patch had been pierced by an arrow . . .

And in the other eye, as Pellanor of Palmorgin raised his head, glared the greenish light of a demon.

Jenny stepped forward with her halberd and struck off his head.

The body continued to crawl toward them.

Jenny and the little family fled into the snow-blanketed night.

Chapter 6

There was Hell, reflected John, and there was Hell.

This was something no one—not Gantering Pellus, not Juronal, not the author of the mysterious *Elucidus Lapidarus*—had known: that not all Hells were the same.

He had passed beyond any information or assistance from the writings of anyone he had ever read, and he supposed this was why the Demon Queen had wanted him as her agent. Having survived the Hell behind the mirror—as he had survived one dragon slaying, with the assistance of a certain amount of magic—he had learned just enough to survive the next.

He supposed, too, that the Demon Queen had given him Amayon as a servant because he was the one demon she knew John would hate the most: the demon who had hurt Jenny. The one demon to whose charm John would be almost guaranteed not to yield.

Not that Amayon didn't try.

"That's very good," the demon said softly, looking over his shoulder during one of their rests, in the dense shelter of a thorny watercourse between two walls of striated black rock. John sketched the thorns and the shape of the barren upland that stretched beyond; sketched the carry beast, whom he'd named Dobbin, bending its long neck down to the pool to drink, and the shape of the herds of such creatures that could be distantly seen on the top of the opposite cliff. "You've captured the look of it well."

Amayon now wore the form of a girl, dark curls framing a nymph's triangular face, fragile hands resting on John's shoulder as she stood behind him to look at the sketch. She glanced around her nervously at a quick soft scraping sound from the rocks and pressed a little closer to him. Genuine fear? John wondered. Or the imitation of it, to coax him into protectiveness?

He didn't know. The landscape in his dream had been without life, but he sensed there was life here.

Waiting in the shadows. Watching.

"It'd help if I knew if it was real," he remarked, sketching the long necks of the herd beasts with a charcoal stub. "I mean, the Queen's palace behind the mirror was whatever she fancied it to be: We'd pass one window where it was rainin' outside, and the next there'd be a sandstorm, and the next it'd be a sweet summer night. So maybe the next chap who rides through here isn't goin' to see these things at all."

"Is that why you're doing this?" Amayon regarded him through lowered lashes. "To help another who may ride after you?"

"I'd like to say yes." John grinned and shoved the parchments into his satchel. "That'd sound a bit noble, wouldn't it? But it's just I can't pass up the chance to make notes of all this, to remember it by."

He stepped over the watercourse, holding out his hand in automatic assistance to the delicate girl who followed, though he knew Amayon needed no such assistance. She stumbled a little on the rocks and clung to his arm. *There's a small favor to be thankful for,* he thought: The Queen had said that the spells of one Hell's demons might work in another Hell, and might not. Evidently Amayon's spells of lust didn't work, which was a relief.

"There's no need for us to be enemies, you know." Amayon stroked his arm as they came up on Dobbin, who made a noise at them like an angry goose and lashed his heavy tail. "We're going to be traveling together for quite some time. We need one another, you know."

"And you need me for exactly what?" John half turned in the saddle as Amayon arranged her gauzy skirts. Her eyes met his, haunted and beautiful and filled with tears.

"To help me," she whispered. "I know I was wrong, to hurt your lady Jenny. You were justified in sending me behind the mirror, to be slave and captive of the Demon Queen. I know that now. But oh, John, she is monstrous, terrible! Nothing, *nothing* that I ever did merits the things . . ." She dropped her voice, her eyes, turned her head slightly aside and caught her red underlip between delicate white teeth with the memory of pain. "The things she has done to me."

"And you hope I'll forgive you?" John asked, keeping his voice uninflected. "And help you escape her?"

Her hand slid over his thigh. "I would do anything to escape her, my lord. I would be your servant for life, your slave. Demons are very loyal to those who treat them kindly. If you knew what she is . . ."

John knew what she was. But before he could reply a thin shriek rent the sullen air, and a hairy insectile thing the size of a dog bounded down the watercourse, fleeing in desperate terror from seven or eight greater creatures, now running, now flying—demons or animals, John didn't know, until the larger beasts caught the small. Instead of eating it they played with it: torturing it, tearing it to pieces while the victim shrieked on and on in undying agony as nerves and flesh and entrails were shredded.

And Amayon watched, rapt. Drinking in what she saw with trembling nostrils and ecstatic eyes, as if savoring the most exquisite of meals.

Disgusted, John pushed her hand aside and yanked Dobbin's reins.

There was neither night nor day in Hell. The light came from nowhere, without shadow—or maybe the Demon Queen had put on him a magic that enabled him to see in the dark. Dry heat seemed to radiate from the ground and varied from place to place: It was colder, John had noticed, when they'd crossed a limb of the black stone uplands, where bands of Dobbin's brethren strode with their gangling, purposeful strides. Observing them, he saw they avoided the watercourses for as long as they could: They'd descend, drink quickly, and depart.

No wonder, he thought, considering the slumped squeaking wights that rustled and darted in the black leathery vegetation that grew along the water. Twice, also, during that first long ride he glimpsed signs of human hunters, or humaniform creatures anyway: things that walked upright and bore crude weapons. When, in exhaustion, John had just begun to argue with Amayon that they stop and rest—Dobbin was stumbling, too—he heard a stealthy rustling in the thorn along the bank tops that had not the sound of demons and looked up to see a dozen men and women, dirty and clothed in skins.

"Skin and ream the lot of them," Amayon muttered, sliding down from Dobbin's cantle. "Wait here." She climbed the bank toward them, holding out her hands and speaking in a sweet musical language that John heard as his own in his mind: "Please let us pass, dear friends. My brother and I mean no harm to you or to any in this place."

"You have food," the leader said, the tallest and strongest of the men. Looking up, John saw a face bearded and brutish, and eyes that were filled with suspicion, fear, and rage, but without the curious glitter of a demon's. These were indeed men and women. Native to Hell? he wondered. Had they been born here? Trapped here while passing through by eating food and drinking water of this place? Had some demon who ruled the place enslaved them, as Aohila had sought to enslave him and trap him forever behind the Mirror of Isychros?

"We can spare neither food nor drink," Amayon said, "for our road is long and we cannot tarry to hunt. But another gift I will give you, to show our love for you." From the tight-laced gauzy bodice of her dress she drew two coins, one gold and one silver. Cupping the silver in her palm, she struck it gently with the gold three times. On the third strike sparks leaped forth. Bending down, she showed how by holding a little of the dry vegetation of the uplands near to the coins, fire could be produced.

"Only don't do it too often," she cautioned as the leader performed the same feat and kindled a little scrap of brush held close. "The fire takes the virtue of the coins away for a little time, and they need to rest. But they will always return to their power."

"I take it spells of fire are easier to work than spells of lust?" John remarked as Dobbin bore them away down the gully with his jogging, bone-jarring stride. Glancing back over his shoulder he saw the snaggle-haired warriors crowding around, saw the leader gesture them away from the precious coins in his hand. "Or will fire spells work just about anywhere?"

"They're very simple." Amayon shrugged.

"Are you speakin' of the fire spells or those folks you just cheated?"

The demon regarded him from beneath long black lashes. "The way you cheated Aohila, with the phial of dragon tears that evaporated from her hand, and the gnomish hothwais crystal charged with starlight in place of the metal of a falling star? She was furious, by the way, just livid. I don't think I've ever heard such cursing." The pale rosebud mouth curved in a spiteful grin. "Aren't you going to ask me who those people are?" she went on after a moment, when John relapsed into silence, thinking of what she had said.

"I'm a bit interested in the kind of tale you'd tell me," John replied evenly. "But I'd be a fool if I thought it the truth."

She put her arms around his waist and leaned her cheek on his shoulder. "It might be."

Dobbin was stumbling, and Aversin drew rein. "Don't," Amayon protested, glancing over her shoulder at the cliff tops that hemmed in the gorge. Hot winds lifted the fragile layers of her dress, her dark hair; she looked wild and young and scared.

"It won't do us a bit of good to ride the poor thing to death." John swung down and neatly avoided the beast's kick.

"You worry too much. They're very tough."

"Well, I'm not." He unhooked the water skin from the saddlebow, took a cautious drink. He'd rolled his doublet and his plaids into one of the saddlebags, but the heat in the gorge was dry and suffocating. Sweat soaked his shirt and made long wet strings of his hair. "And I'm not ettlin' to get meself killed because I'm too tired to react to danger."

"Oh, surely not," she protested. "I think you're very tough, too." He took her by the waist and lifted her down, and she slid into his arms, holding him tight as if she feared she would fall, her face raised expectantly to his. "Well," she agreed softly, "maybe we can rest here a little."

"Aye." John fished in his satchel and found the bag of flax seed and, disengaging his other arm from Amayon's pressing hands, opened the ink bottle. "But tough or not I think I'd rest a bit quieter without you wrapped round me neck."

"Don't!" The demon started back, genuine panic in her eyes. "Don't–"

John dropped in three seeds and stoppered the ink bottle, then went over and kicked Dobbin several times to wake him–it was like kicking a stack of cowhides–and led the beast up out of the smothering bottomlands and a few hundred yards out onto the rocky plateau. In his dream–and in the endless, aching ride–he'd seen how the upland rock flawed and faulted into smaller gorges and overhangs. Had seen, too, that the pooks and wights that infested the streambeds were far fewer on the higher ground. In a dip in the stone like the trough beneath a wave the carry beast hunkered down, tucked its head under one thigh, and wrapped its tail around tight until it was an impenetrable bulb of dappled pinkish leather. John leaned his back against it as if it had been a bedstead, forced himself to remain awake long enough to jot a few notes about the hunter folk who'd barred their way, then slept.

He discovered why it is not recommended to put oneself in the position of dreaming dreams in Hell.

Foulness, pain, blackness leading down into blackness—

Ylferdun Deep, he thought. He had battled the dragon Morkeleb and was wounded unto death. He and Jenny and Prince Gareth had taken refuge in the darkness of the gnomes' deserted Deep while the witch Zyerne's followers besieged the gates. And in the heart of the Deep he'd heard whispering, the whispering of the thing that the gnomes worshiped: Crypt below crypt, vaults beneath subvaults, and in the dark at the bottom of the mountain it dwelled—the Stone within the Deep.

The Stone that drank souls.

It was before him now. Emerging from the coarse black basalt of the ground as a whale slowly rises from the sea, smooth and bluish and without mark. A Drinking Stone, the gnomes called such a thing. Drinking life. Drinking souls.

Dobbin was dead. John could see the consciousness of the animal trapped already in the Stone, alive and completely present, along with the half-deteriorated spirits of dozens of his kind and broken fragments of demons, beasts, men, and women . . .

He could see them clearly, even as he felt his own spirit, his own life, being drawn by the thing.

Damn it, no! he thought, and tried to drag his mind away.

And could not.

Damn it, he screamed against that slow-growing warmth, *I will not!*

But it was like sleep too long denied, or a slow-tilting floor when it has gone too far to be climbed. His hand jerking as if with palsy he fumbled the ink bottle from his shirt, dragged loose the stopper, wondered if the Stone would trap Amayon as well.

Evidently it didn't, for he could hear the demon shrieking curses at him, as if from some great distance away. Then the curses stopped, and there was only a slow-growing weariness, like weight too heavy to be borne or fought. A sinew-cracking drag that could not be resisted . . .

He felt the Stone's hold break and shift, diverted to something else, and in that momentary relaxation of its power he rolled, scrambled, dragged himself across the rock and away from the thing. Small hands grabbed his wrists and pulled him farther away, and he heard Amayon call his name. "Wake up! Wake up, damn you!"

"I'm all right." Gasping, John looked back past the fragile, half-bared shoulder. Dobbin lay uncurled in death. A young hunter of the savages sprawled just where the Drinking Stone had been. John couldn't make out his face—even at two feet it would have been a blur to him—but his body lay disposed calmly, without sign of struggle, his spear still grasped in his hand. Of the Stone itself there was no sign.

"You blundering, imbecelic fool . . ." Amayon's hands were as cold as marble. *Odd,* thought John, *after the warmth of the ink bottle. Must make a note of that.*

"Would it have got you, too, then?" He scratched his hair and squinted hard at Dobbin's carcass, beside which, if he recalled, he'd left his spectacles. He couldn't see them—he was lucky, he reflected, that he could see the carcass—and got up to make a move in that direction, then stopped and glanced inquiringly at the demon.

"It's gone." Amayon still sounded shaken to pieces. "And no, it wouldn't have 'got' me, too. I just don't fancy remaining trapped in an onyx bottle for eternity because of some bumpkin's prudishness."

John edged cautiously nearer and found the light frame of wire and glass where he'd left it, unbroken in all the ruckus—the spell Jenny had long ago put on them seemed to be still in force. He put them on, then knelt beside the young hunter. At his touch the man opened his eyes, but they were blank, empty. A trickle of drool ran down through the fair beard.

"The Stone has drunk him."

John looked up quickly at the voice. The tall hunter leader stood nearby, spear in hand. A woman whom John had not seen before was with him, gray haired and tough, with bitter eyes.

"He left us with a cry and ran toward this place," the hunter woman said, her words speaking in John's mind, though he understood that they used another language than his own. "That girl of yours called to him." From around her neck she took a fragment of smoky glass tied on a piece of braided sinew. This she held up, and like a mirror John saw reflected in it his own face. The woman regarded the reflection, then walked to Amayon and did the same.

Whatever she saw in the glass caused her to say "Faugh!" and step back in loathing.

"Take her," she said. "Take your demon whore and go from here. She has saved your life by bringing Lug here to the Stone. Now Lug must die, that the spirits by the river will not enter into his body, for the Stone has drunk away his mind."

John stood back while the woman and the hunter got Lug to his feet. The young hunter seemed dazed, his eyes empty and dead. From the corner of his eye John could see the flickering movement of the small glowing wights of the riverbed, moving cautiously out over the rock toward them. When Amayon came near to him, he said, "You brought him here for the Stone to take, instead of me." He felt shocked and empty, glad to be living still but hating the demon.

"Well, I couldn't very well get *him* to continue the Queen's stinking quest." Amayon swished her skirts and stepped across to Dobbin's side. "Drat," she added. "I was afraid it would come to this in the end. I will truly see to it that that bitch Aohila gets trussed and left for a satyr of iron."

She pressed her hands to the dead beast's outstretched head. Her body melted to smoke, and the smoke then flowed into Dobbin's nostrils and slack mouth. A moment later the beast rolled lightly to its feet, shook itself, and strode to John with the same swagger that characterized Amayon's walk.

The hunter and the woman watched all of this, stone faced, and made no move while John saddled and bridled the demon beast. Looking back as he rode away, John saw the young hunter stretched on the ground again, the two elders walking off in the other direction. Demons were already chittering around the new corpse, fighting one another over its blood.

Amayon carried him swiftly toward the mountains, more swiftly than Dobbin would have, for Amayon did not pause to rest. John clung doggedly to the saddle while the demon drove the borrowed muscles along ground that grew ever steeper and more harsh. Ravines gaped below them, and cliffs climbed ever higher above: dark clefts of shadow where pallid lights darted, shed by creatures he could not see.

The callused pads of the beast's feet tore open, and eventually ripped entirely away, leaving blood on the rock that drew small scavengers in their wake. In time the beast began to stink, rotting deep within, and to swell, the girths cutting its belly. Twice Aversin fell asleep, jerking to wakefulness as he began to slip from the saddle. The third time he dismounted, insisting they stop.

"What, had too much already?" Amayon swirled from the blood-slimed nostrils of the dead beast. "If you're like this with a woman, it's no wonder Jenny craved real men, poor thing. Get up. It isn't far."

John knew from his dream that there were at least two days' travel yet to the spring. "Whatever it is you're afraid of," he said wearily, "I'll be in gie better shape to deal with it if I've slept."

"Who said anything about afraid?" Amayon glanced over her shoulder. "There isn't anything . . ."

She broke off, staring, eyes showing white all around their rims for one second before she turned and fled, and John, turning, saw it, too.

He smelled it and felt it before he saw it, a kind of cold radiance and a scent like storm sky and lightning. It came whipping and rolling through the rocks of the rising land, concentric turning rings of light, a half-seen coruscation of wings and eyes. Amayon had wedged himself into a sort of rock chimney among the great boulders, casting rocks at the thing in desperation and sending forth small spats of fire spells that fizzled in the air around the creature.

"Kill it!" she screamed—it screamed, for so great was Amayon's terror that all semblance of human form, male or female, melted away, leaving the demon as it truly was.

John caught up a harpoon from Dobbin's saddle and flung it at the attacking creature as it passed him—passed him without pausing, heading straight for Amayon in the rocks. John's second harpoon took the Shining Thing through one of its many eyes, and it wheeled like a gyroscope and shot at him in a storm of jabbing stingers and wings like slices of primal light. John struck at it with his sword, the cold of it enveloping him and the sound it made piercing his brain. *If Amayon's killed, I'm stuck here forever,* he thought. And then, *What if I'm killed here?*

Were those things souls, that the gibbering pooks chased down among the black reed beds? Is that what he would become, if he were to die here: a soul for the pooks to chase?

The Shining Thing veered from him and went back toward Amayon, dripping ichor that smoked on the rocks. *It can be cut, then.* John followed it, slashing, drawing it back from the huddled, shaking demon. He sliced off one of the stingers, then one of the wings. That seemed to decide the thing, for it whipped away from him and raced up the mountainside faster than a horse could run. Reaching a cliff, it scooted up the sheer rock like a roach on a wall and was gone.

The smell of it lingered, less an odor than a wildness that lifted the hair on John's scalp.

The harpoon he'd flung lay smoking on the ground in a puddle of glowing acid. He cleaned his sword as well as he could on one of his plaids and cut the fabric off when it began to burn. Amayon still crouched in the rocks, weeping with shock and fright. John didn't want to touch it, but he did; and for one instant the demon looked up at him, not with gratitude but with such a fury of resentment and hate that he stepped back.

Amayon quickly resumed the shape of a girl and held out her hands to him, her face running with tears, but the illusion was too late. "Fair try." John took her arm and held her firmly away from embracing him. "There's more of 'em about—can you smell 'em? Let's see if we'll be a little safer farther on."

They journeyed a little farther, and Aversin wrote up an account of the fight with as accurate a drawing as he could make of the shining thing that had attacked them and another sketch of Amayon, a slumped silvery-green homunculus like a skeletal salamander. When he wakened again from nightmare-riddled sleep it was to find—revoltingly—that the carcass of the carry beast had deteriorated to the point where it could no longer be made to bear weight, and they continued their quest on foot. The squeaking, gibbering demons of the bottomlands seemed to have been left behind, and the high peaks were the province of the shining things, small and large. Twice more they were attacked, once by wolf-size creatures of rings and wings and eyes, and again by a thing like a glowing slug that oozed from the gravel and seized Amayon by the foot.

Only when John had chopped the thing away from the shrieking demon and the pieces receded sullenly into the ground again did he guess the truth.

"They can kill you, can't they?" He lowered his sword and wiped the sweat from his face. It burned in the cuts left by the earlier attackers' stings and made tracks in the fine dust on his cheekbones and throat. "Not devour you, the way demons do in the Hell behind the mirror. Not imprison you and torture you forever. Not cut you into little bits, each bit livin' on in pain. Kill you."

"You know nothing of it." Amayon staggered to its feet, slowly, shakily resuming the shape of the girl, dress in rags over the tender breasts and the illusion of blood running down from a dainty cut on her leg where a swollen, ichorous sore had been.

"I do, though." John felt something that was almost pity as he helped her up. "I grew up knowin' I was to die, see. I was raised by those who knew they would die—would cease to be. Would have it all go away, and be nothin'. You never were."

Amayon wrenched her arm from his grip and spat at him, poison that burned his face. "Whore's son! Coward!" She would have run from him, but she staggered on her hurt leg. In any case he still had the ink bottle and the flax seeds. "You're so puffed with pride about what you think you know, and you're the most ignorant and stupid son of the children of earth, sitting on your dungheap of fragments and crowing at your learning, like an ape with half a book in its paws! And all the while you neglect those who're stupid enough to depend on you! You can't even keep a woman as old and homely as the bitch you got to bear your bastards, much less protect your feeble-witted son! So don't go preaching to me about what I feel or what I think!"

But John saw the demon-girl tremble in her cloudy rags of lawn and velvet and heard the crack of terror behind the rage in her voice. He knew that he had guessed right. And Amayon would never forgive him that.

Darkness covered the mountain, as it had covered it in his dream. It might have been night at last—Morkeleb had spoken to him once of places where night lasted years, so that all things perished for want of light—or it might have been a quality peculiar to that place, as heat seemed peculiar to the lowlands. No star could be glimpsed, and the only light was a sort of glow that pulsed along the silver lines in the rocks. The silence was dreadful.

But the place was known to John through the dreams the Demon Queen had sent. A dreadful déjà vu tangled with other memories that he could not clearly identify as either true or illusory. In sleeping, other dreams had come to him, terrible dreams from which he would wake crying out or weeping and see lines of filthy little pooks perched on the rock rims above his camp, puffing and crooning with content at the pain and terror they drank.

The rivulet was exactly as he had seen it in his dream. It dribbled from a crack high in the rock face and ended in a pool perhaps the size of the communal wash fountain of Alyn village, and the air above it shone with the sickly luminosity of the shining creatures that had attacked them. In her delicate flutter of revealing rags, Amayon stared transfixed.

There have been attempts to unseat me, Aohila had said. She might even have been telling the truth. Aversin wondered what Folcalor's summer gambit with demon-ridden wizards had to do with such matters, if anything, and what Folcalor's lord—Amayon's lord—the archdemon Adromelech would give for this water.

And what would Aohila give Amayon for it, if the demon returned with it instead of John and bargained for freedom?

Deliberately Aversin unslung the satchel from his shoulder—much lighter now, for food and water were scant—produced the ink bottle, and dropped half a score of flax seeds inside.

Amayon cursed him and tried to snatch the bottle from his hand. But even as she reached, her white fingers thinned to smoke and whirled into the tiny aperture. John stoppered the bottle, stuffed it into the front of his tattered and sorry doublet, and stood for a time listening.

But the only sound was the lick and twitter of the water over the rock.

The Queen had given him nothing in which to carry the water, nor had there been any vessel save for the onyx ink bottle in his dream. Among the things he'd brought from the Hold were two small silver flasks: If spells changed from Hell to Hell, he hoped anything watertight would do. And he hoped, too, that whatever this water really did would not work to the peril of his own world. He filled both bottles, placing one in his satchel, the other in the bottom of a food bag.

"Now let's hope she can't see from one Hell to the next," he muttered and slung both satchel and bag over his shoulder.

He made a careful examination—and a sketch—of the desolate fountain but saw no rune, no wyrd, no sigil; there was no indication at all that the place was anything other than what he had been told.

Aching in every limb and joint, he began his slow descent of the mountain.

Chapter 7

"He said there was aught he had to do." Sergeant Muffle turned back from the milky brightness of the doorway into the gloom of the smithy where Jenny had sought him out. "He wouldn't say where he was bound. But he burned his work shed before he left."

"*John* burned the work shed?" Jenny had heard from Bill, when he'd helped dig the snow from her doorway, that the shed had burned. She had grieved for John, knowing how he loved all those half-made projects, how he'd sought the length and breadth of the Winterlands for metal and springs and silken cord.

She put out her hand half blindly to touch one of the roof posts that surrounded the low brick forge, the warmth and amber light beating gently up against her face. And she saw her own shock, her own fear at the implications of such a deed, reflected in the smith's small bright brown eyes.

"And none have seen him." John's brother picked up again the pot he'd been repairing when Jenny came into the forge and set it over the horn of the anvil to tap and file the patch smooth. "Not since Dan Darrow took him to the borders of the Wraithmire."

"Wait a minute. *That's* the last anyone saw of him? That was eight days ago."

The new moon, chill and thin, stood high in the afternoon sky above the Hold.

Across the court, Bill and Ams Puggle were deep in conference with Dal. One or two others of the little Alyn garrison clustered around, gesturing and muttering. Jenny could catch an occasional oath or a question about the number of gnomes in the slave-buying band and if they'd said anything about who their master was. Dal held out something that was passed around among the men—probably one of the gold pieces with which the bandits had been paid.

Pellanor, Jenny thought. *Pellanor of Palmorgin. Dead these three months . . .*

"I put the word to old Dan to keep mum about it, and he has, pretty much. But there's been talk nonetheless. Nobody knows what to make of it." Muffle turned the pot to the light to see how even the join was, then went back to work with his rasp. He'd been the town bully as a child, Jenny recalled, and always Lord Aver's favorite. "Come indoors, Jen, you look froze through. The children will delight to see you."

Aunt Jane, too? But her heart ached at the thought of little Mag and Adric . . .

"And do *you* know what to make of it?"

Muffle's eyes slid sideways to her, and his heavy mouth set. Then a slight shadow darkened the smithy door, and Ian said, "Mother?"

While everyone in the Hold had crowded around Lyra and Dal and the children, cold and exhausted after two nights of hiding in the woods, Jenny had hung back. She still felt stung by the chilled animosity in Aunt Jane's eyes—and no wonder, she thought. John's eldest aunt was ferociously protective of all three of her nephew's children. Of course she would blame Jenny for Ian's attempted suicide and try to keep her from him if she could.

Jenny had felt apprehensive at the idea of meeting John, and more so at the thought of speaking again to Ian.

Now all her apprehension melted as her son stepped forward and caught her in his arms.

"Don't be angry," he said, hugging her tight. His voice was desperate in her ear. She saw he stood an inch taller than she, and the arms that crushed her to him had the beginnings of a man's strength. "I'm sorry. I'm so sorry . . ."

"If you say that again, I'll put you over my knee!"

He laughed, the release of it shaking his whole body. It was the first time she'd heard him laugh since the summer, and it turned his face from a ghost's to that of a living boy again, and that boy only thirteen. She laughed, too, looking into the sea-blue eyes.

Then her laughter faded. "It was Folcalor, wasn't it?" she asked.

His face grew still.

"In your dreams?"

His mouth flinched, and he looked away. Beside the door Muffle stood silent, watching them with wary eyes as if he had seen them suddenly transform from people he knew—his brother's wife and son—to something uncanny, speaking a language only they fully understood.

"Yes," Ian said. "I think so. Yes." And he met her gaze again. *"Love can't wait, so open the gate,"* he rhymed, with a faint flush of shame tinging his dead-white cheeks. "It sounds so stupid when I say it, but it comes to me just as I'm drifting off to sleep. And it sticks in my mind. *Love can't wait, so open the gate.* As if by opening the demon gate, I'll have all the love I'll ever want. I'll never be lonely again."

The love I never gave him. She looked, mute, into her son's face. But there was no blame there, or even thought about why he felt unloved. It was just a part of him that he accepted and dealt with as best he could.

"It makes a whole lot more sense when you're asleep," he added apologetically. "And it . . . it got so strong. Sometimes it's just a whispering, and other times it seems like it's the only thing real in the world. And it won't leave me alone." His voice sank to a whisper. "I was so afraid. And I felt . . . I felt so empty . . ."

"After the demon left?"

Ian nodded, his face crimson now.

Jenny touched his cheek. "Ian, I did, too. I do still, sometimes. In spite of everything."

His eyes flicked to hers, then away—understanding and thanking her for her understanding.

"Do you know where he is?" she asked gently. "What he looks like now?"

Her son shook his head. "I see him but I can't really see him." He glanced at her and she nodded. "Just the whispering. It was worse before. I could see how the gate was to be made, where the power would source from. That's when . . . That's what . . . I woke up from a dream and found myself in the house on the Fell, up in the attic, writing things on the floor." The words blurted from him in terror and in shame, an admission he had kept and hidden. "I swear I didn't . . . I'd been dreaming about having power. About being able to do anything. And then I woke up, and I was there, with the chalk in my hand . . ."

He shuddered and averted his face again, and Jenny caught his hands. The fingers were chill as frozen sticks.

"I didn't want to go back. I knew what he'd do to me if he came through the gate, and I didn't want to go back to being what I was."

"No." Jenny put up her hand, stroked his hair, as black and coarse as hers had been. "Ian, I think I would have done the same thing."

"No, you wouldn't," Ian said. "Because you'd have been stronger. You could have gotten rid of him."

And she laughed, bitterly, remembering her own desolation of sleep and despair. "Thank you for the compliment, but believe me, I don't deserve it. I don't."

Their eyes met again and held.

At length she said, "So you rubbed out all the marks?"

He nodded. "I couldn't . . . I was just afraid the next time he'd get me all the way through the rite. I hadn't been sleeping . . . I was so tired." His mouth tightened. "You don't think it was–was Folcalor that Father tried to contact? Because I'd hear him whispering to others sometimes–Folcalor, I mean. Reaching out to others. And Father . . ."

He held his thin hands out toward the heat of the forge. Outside in the yard Aunt Jane had joined the group around Dal and was giving them the benefit of her advice. Adric, sword at belt, was there, too, clearly trying to talk the men into letting him ride patrol with them.

"I went into his study, on the night of the storm, and found his books all spread out over the study table. Everything he had about the Hellspawn: how to summon them, how to speak to them, how to protect himself from them when they'd been summoned. I went to the window and looked out, and I could see candlelight through the cracks around the work shed door."

"Folcalor wouldn't have any use for your father," Jenny said. "I'm fairly sure the demon he called was Aohila, the Queen behind the Mirror." And she kept her voice level with an effort, against the hot spurt of jealousy that flared through her. And hard on the heels of her jealous anger, she thought, *He has no magic. The ward lines he drew wouldn't protect him.*

"Who else was Folcalor summoning, do you know?" Jenny asked after a time. "Who else was he trying to speak to?"

Ian shook his head. "If he's tried to reach me, he must be trying to reach Master Bliaud as well."

She recalled the little gray-haired wizard from the South fussing ineffectually around the mule train in the courtyard at Corflyn Hold.

Already the demon had been in him, imitating the old man's mannerisms so his sons would not suspect. Later, after the demons had been driven out, Jenny had worked with the old man to restore and heal the other mages. He'd drawn sigils of healing on her forehead, lips, and eyelids in the thin blue-white powder John had obtained from the Demon Queen.

But there had been no healing.

"And I heard him . . ." Ian said slowly. "I heard him calling Master Caradoc's name. I thought I had to be mistaken, because Master Caradoc is dead. But . . ."

"Calling him?" An icicle seemed to have formed somewhere behind her heart. "Calling him how?"

"Differently," Ian said. "Singing to him. *Loved you so long, raise your voice in a song . . .* Something like that. It was a love song, like—" He stammered and left the words unsaid, so Jenny finished for him.

"Like Amayon used to sing to me."

Ian nodded, the sudden woodenness of his face telling her that Gothpys had sung such songs to him. They were beautiful beyond mortal music and erotic past the ability of mortal flesh to withstand.

"*'Sing to me, love,'* he keeps saying. *'Sing to me.'* But I know Master Caradoc is dead. You killed him beneath the sea, and the crystal that—that held his soul."

"We smashed *a* crystal," Jenny said quietly, all her dreams of the dark seafloor returning: the weightless beauty of the whalemages drifting among the columns of rock, the silver flicker of demons down below . . .

Searching for something.

Closing her eyes, she could see Caradoc's face again, framed in the floating curtain of his silver hair, green demon light streaming from his eyes, fire pouring from his mouth. He raised his hand, and in his hand was the staff of his power, with its carven goblin head that held a moonstone in its mouth.

Then from the court a voice cried "Mama!" And Adric and Mag pelted over the snow-grimed cobbles and threw themselves into Jenny's welcoming arms.

Standing just clear of the trees, the moon was a segment of a silver orange, so bright that a frail wedding ring of light limned the whole of its velvet disc. John drew his decayed plaid close around him and shivered, but only thin snow dusted the ground, and there was no wind.

The stars were yet the stars before midwinter, even to the Wanderers where they camped among the Watcher's jeweled belt loops, and the White Dog's rough wet fur.

"Don't you yet know how it is with the Hellspawn and time?" Amayon's jeer held its usual edge of impatient contempt. He had resumed the shape of a pretty youth, though the blue eyes were the same, and the black grapevine curls. "We'll still be beautiful–not to mention continent and in possession of all our wits–when you're lying crippled with arthritis in bed wondering if anyone will come in time to get you to the chamber pot. The God of Time has no authority over us."

"Well, you don't know that yet, now do you?" Hands stuck behind the buckle of his sword belt, John gazed at the marshes around him. Not the Wraithmire–he'd never seen willows like these growing anywhere north of the Black River. "That's the tricky thing about the God of Time." Though the mountain wall to west and south was cloaked to its toes in snow, the ice that scummed the edges of the pools thinned over the centers, where a little open water gleamed black, like the pupil of a cataract-dimmed eye.

What had been a chapel surrounded them. The roofless, isolated pillars and the bone-white glimmer of shattered statuary in elongated arches told John clearly enough that they were no longer in the Winterlands, even had it not been obvious from the stars. "You want to think about goin' into the fancy fish business, bringin' things down from the Winterlands to Ernine like this–I take it we are in Ernine?–without the moon a day older on the way? I have it that you pay as much for a salmon in Greenhythe–half spoiled and poor to begin with–as you'd pay for a trained huntin' dog up north, where we get so sick of salmon we use 'em for pig food . . ." He forced his voice to show nothing but a Northman's bland practicality, unwilling to give Amayon the satisfaction of knowing his shock and wonderment, the shaken disorientation that came in the aftermath of stepping from the demon mist to find himself in his own world again and not a day later than he'd walked out of it.

He certainly felt as if he'd tramped and done battle for the best part of ten days, the last two virtually without water or food. The shining things, the rock slugs and once, terrifyingly, a many-legged creature of wings and mouths and spines ... Had those fights been like the tortures he'd undergone in the Hell behind the mirror, illusion only, for the amusement of the Demon Queen? Gingerly he parted the ripped and blood-crusted linen of his sleeve to see the rough bandage still on his arm, a souvenir of that final attack. The flesh was sore underneath, but not until he nudged the dressing aside and looked at the scabbing wound did he understand that the things that had happened to him in Hell had actually taken place.

Amayon snickered and mimicked the movement with an exaggerated mime of fear, concentration, bumpkin astonishment. "I wish you could see your face," he jeered.

John scratched the graying auburn stubble on his jaw. "Just as well I can't," he agreed mildly and, kneeling, scrubbed the filth from his hands in one patch of snow and scooped up the cold white crystals from another to eat. "And to spare you further sight of it, I think it's the inkwell for you, me bonny boy, and I'll find me own way into town."

"No!" the demon cried. "Stop it!" But John dropped the flax seeds into the bottle.

Better to be safe than sorry, he thought, unshipping from his shoulder the goatskin bag that contained his own silver vessel of the enchanted water and hanging it from the high limb of an oak. Despite whatever spells Aohila had placed on Amayon to make him serve John, he wouldn't put it past the demon to betray him and take the vessel of water for himself, to trade to the Queen for his freedom.

Not that John blamed him. He'd seen what the Demon Queen did to those in her power. Aohila didn't look like the kind who would forgive even the smallest of the demons who had aided in sealing her and her minions behind the mirror, and he knew from experience a little—the smallest part—of the torments meted out in Hell.

He wondered, as he made his way out of the marshes through vapor and shifting moonshine, what teind the mages of Prokeps had had to pay for the Lord of the Sea-wights' help. He came around the shoulder of the hill and recognized the maze of gashes and gullies, of fallen pillars and half-buried statues through which he and the gnomewitch

Miss Mab had ridden in the last moon of summer, seeking some way to save Jenny from enslavement to Caradoc and his demon master.

No magic of humans or gnomes, Miss Mab had said, could guard him from the spells of the Hellspawn. They were supreme in their own worlds. Such spells as could be wrought in this world could only strengthen him in the ways he was already strong.

And it was that strength, those spells, he understood now, that had saved him behind the Mirror of Isychros. That strength was why the Demon Queen had sought him out when she needed a human to do her work. The strength of his love for Jenny, and his stubborn refusal to be fooled.

But it had to be done, he thought. A fool's errand, yes, and a madman's, but there had been no other way to free them. The image of Jenny rum soaked, naked, and flashing with cheap finery had tormented him for months, until he'd made Amayon's acquaintance and heard in the demon's voice the disdainful mockery that had come, in those days, from Jenny's mouth. With Ian and his possessing demon it must, he knew, be the same.

Just take from them that memory, he thought, his legs aching as he waded through flowing ground fog and ivy up the curving sandstone stair. *Just free them of that pain.*

I can heal your son.

John had feared and mistrusted demons before riding with one to Hell. He hated them now, and the Queen among the rest.

The passageway into the rock, and the crypt where the mirror stood, were knee-deep in opal mist. Tendrils of it curled to the ceiling, where the light of John's lantern flashed on the stars writ there in gold, the comet with its trailing plumes. Then the flame burned low, chill and blue within the glass chimney, and dwindled to its death while a sort of greenish light formed up within the mist itself. The mirror chamber shifted, uncomfortably like chambers in the queen's palace, filled with vapors through which demon courtiers passed in semblance of handsome lords and ladies: heartstoppingly beautiful until you turned your head and caught a glimpse of them from the corner of your eye. John took the remaining silver bottle from his satchel and put it on the stone floor before the mirror, among the scuffed lines of summoning that remained from the last time he had stood here to pay the Demon Queen's teind. Beside it he laid the ink bottle, and as if there were a thorn caught in his clothing somewhere the memory stabbed him of Jenny leaving him here because she could not bear to see him deliver Amayon to the punishment he deserved.

He drew a shaky breath. "Here I am, love," he said to the covered mirror. "And here's your present, all exactly as you asked this time and no jiggery-pokery to it. And I hope you don't mean that I should walk home from here, for it'd be a gie shabby trick if you do."

"As shabby as those you played me?" Hands closed over his shoulders, death-cold hands strong as steel. He could feel the claws prick through his doublet and his shirt and dared not turn his head. Her slow evil smile was in her voice. "Something can doubtless be arranged. Pour out the water onto the floor."

Bottle and floor were invisible under the mists. When John picked up the flask and obeyed, the vapors cleared from the spot as if blown upon, rising up and ringing them in a wall that hid even the door from sight. "Look into the water," she said. John stepped forward, barely breathing, remembering the smoky mirror the gray-haired woman hunter had held that would reflect the true semblance of the Hellspawn.

But when he looked down he saw nothing behind him at all. His own reflection lay in the water as if in a pool miles deep, with the stars of the ceiling twinkling above his head. Though he felt the weight of the taloned hand and sensed the iciness radiating from her against his flesh, in the water it was as if he stood alone. Beneath and beyond his reflection he could see down into the stone floor and past it—past subcrypts and potsherds, past grass roots tangled in men's bones, down and down to the heart of the earth, to a darkness where ill things lived.

The Queen's hand moved on his shoulder, and blue lightning ran over the surface of the water then sank away, still flickering, into its depths.

John's reflection dimmed into a wilderness of winds and howling sands. Lightning scorched across rocks more barren than a miser's heart. Then the vision shifted to a sweet promise of birch trees in summer twilight, of butterflies, lilacs, and vines. Finally he saw black walls rise hideously tall and glaring with light, smoke-wreathed and sluiced by rain that fell endlessly from a filthy sky.

A woman. She staggered as she ran through the maze of walls, clothing torn and blood on her face, gummed in disheveled hair that was streaked lavender, after the fashion of the courtiers in the South. She ran with her arms folded before her breasts as if to protect herself. Her foot caught and she stumbled, the heel breaking off one garish pink shoe, but she picked herself up and fled on, panting with terror, feet splashing through shallow standing water, leaving trails of blood. She threw herself between two shapes—metal? rock?—where darkness pocketed. She leaned on the wall, gasping, one hand pressed to her mouth, the other wrapped around her belly, half doubled over, shaking with shock. Light fell down from somewhere near, and it showed not only cuts on her arms and face but the burned edges of those gashes, the rings and dots of branding on jaw and throat and chest. Bracelets glinted gold. Gold chains crossed the burns and scratches on her neck. Tears of pain rivered her face, but she bit her bleeding lips. John knew that she knew it would be death and worse than death for her to make a single sound.

She was listening. Listening for her life. Black streaks from tears marred her eye paint, and the distant colored lights showed her flesh glabrous with sweat.

Damn it, stay where you are, John thought. *Whatever's pursuin', d'you think it doesn't know you're there?* In his mind he saw the line of tiny demons on the rock, drinking greedily of the horror of his dreams.

Stay where you are!

But she didn't. She didn't know. Like a new-foaled calf on shaky legs, she crept out of her hidey-hole—*no!*—and looked up and down the alley.

It *was* an alley. What was the matter with those who must have been in the lighted rooms so far above her, that they didn't come? Blackness, brightness, mold and filth growing on the walls, the gleam of water everywhere, rain beginning to fall once more. Lights visible perhaps fifty feet away, reflected on the water that stood in the alley ... The illusion of safety.

She ran for them. And running, turned back at a sound John could not hear.

Mouth stretching, eyes stretching, wider and wider. The lights from above flickered on the gold of her bracelets as she raised her arms over her face.

Darkness bore her back against the wall.

If she screamed, John couldn't hear it. But he saw the blood. It splashed the brick of the walls for yards and made lazy black spirals in the water underfoot, after her pursuer was done. He tried to turn his head away, but the Demon Queen's hand closed over the side of his face and forced him to look again.

This time a man sat in a great chair entirely padded in green leather. John saw him in the pool: the room behind him less clearly, though he had an impression of opulence, of heavy hangings stamped with gold and statues and candlesticks wrought of the same gleaming metal. A small man, trimly handsome. A hooked thin profile and a mass of white-streaked dark hair. Like John he wore spectacles, oddly shaped, and with glass smoked dark so that his eyes were protected from even such small lights as burned in the room. He turned the woman's gold bracelets over and over in white-gloved hands.

"Ah," Aohila said, and there was deep satisfaction in her voice.

"Who is he?"

The clawed bone moved on his cheek. The tiny gashes its talons left bled, hot on his chilled skin. "He was my lover." Though he knew there was no human mouth behind him, he heard the little click of her tongue. "Faithless."

"Now how could any man be so to you?"

The claws contracted warningly on the back of his neck. "Not like you."

"I take it you want him."

"Men don't leave me, Aversin." The grip tightened. Whatever was behind him, it was huge. The voice spoke above as well as behind his head. "Mostly they come back of their own accord. You will."

"In time I might." He grabbed her wrist and whirled to face her, to see her . . .

And behind him she was as she had always been. Tall but not quite his own height, snake-slim and beautiful as nightshade blossoms. A glitter of jewels, a suggestion of uneasy movement in her hair. The hand he held was a woman's hand. It had always been.

"Bein' that I don't die of old age first, which I think is more likely.

Do I get to take our boy Amayon with me for company again? Or have you got a trained scorpion you'd like to send along instead?"

Her mouth flexed with anger at this sarcasm, and something appeared on his hand: a scorpion the length of his finger, coal black with human eyes. His hand flinched to strike it, and her fingers turned in his grip and closed around his, holding them immobile. Angered, the vermin raised its tail. John stood paralyzed, not breathing, while the thing walked up his arm. It disappeared just short of his shoulder.

"Don't jest with me," the Demon Queen said softly.

Sweating, trembling, he only looked at her. It was probably, he realized belatedly, only an illusion. That wasn't a theory he felt like putting to the test.

"Amayon is there to help you," she added after a moment. "You'll need it. Heed his advice." When he drew breath to speak, she added, "Did you think your errantry was done?"

From her robes she drew out a box wrought of pale brown dragon-bone, mounted and clasped in silver, lidded with a baroque opal perhaps the diameter of a cut lime.

"You've got to show me how you do that one day," John remarked, cocking his head and considering the naked, sinuous body so clearly visible beneath its single layer of blowing, smoke-hued gauze. "Girls'd pay a fortune to be able to carry combs and shawls and eye paint in their pockets and not have 'em make lumps. You invent that and peddle it in Belmarie, and you wouldn't need to be Queen of Hell anymore, nor tell lies about what you want a cup of water for that has to be fetched from the ends of creation. You could marry a nice man—a tailor, he'd have to be, to get the first couple stitched up for sale—and have a house on the Street of the Sun with servants and tea parties for your friends, and be done with all this worryin' about other demons tryin' to push you off your throne and eat you and have you talkin' to 'em out of their stomachs and all that."

"You are frivolous," the Queen said softly. When she lifted back her lip from her teeth, he saw there was blood on them. "It will be your death."

John looked up from examining the inside of the box, an expression of surprise on his face. "Oh, it gie near was," he said and rubbed the back of his neck. "Me dad didn't have any more sense of humor about it than you do. Meself, I never thought he was the happier for takin' everything in life so serious as he did. He came close to throwin' me off the walls more than once."

"I sympathize," she said, her voice grim. She held out to him a flask of bronze, scarcely bigger than a Southern double-royal coin. It tinkled softly as he shook it. "Open the box in his presence, and pour these inside. He will be drawn into it, as Amayon is drawn into the ink bottle. After that the box will not open again." Something glinted, cold and more frightening than anything John had seen, in the alien yellow eyes. "Bring it to me. And then we are quits."

The mist flowed down from the walls again. It covered the floor, then swirled up around her, a column of vapor through which the mirror glowed like the lightless door of an oven. She moved toward the incandescent Hell mouth, all the writhing life lifting and hissing in her hair.

"And me son?"

She stopped and faced him. "Your son will heal." Casually, like a penny thrown to a beggar.

"And Jen?" She was already melting into darkness and fog, but her eyes remained, copper gold and narrow: jealous. Her voice came to him, it seemed, from the mists all around: an echo in the dark of his mind.

Mortals heal, John Aversin. And mortals die. Man can only do as he must.

He woke on the stone floor of the mirror chamber with his lantern burning and his bones aching with cold, the round bone box in his hand.

Chapter 8

Ian and Jenny set forth next morning, under a thin, new-risen day moon. They rode alone, burdened as lightly as possible for travel in the bleak Winterlands. It was hard going, though they followed the old road to Eldsbouch and Ian could turn the worst of the weather aside. He cloaked them both with spells to send bandits elsewhere, too, but Jenny doubted that even such hardies as Balgodorus Black-Knife would be abroad in cold and rising wind like this.

In the days of the kings, Eldsbouch had been a walled city of many towers, spread over its four abrupt hills and along the shores of the great Migginit Bay. So rough were the riptides and currents of the bay that the ancients had built a mole to protect the deep-water harbor, which could still be seen at low tide. Rotted pillars clung to it where a colonnade had run, and when the tide was up they tusked the black foaming water like a broken comb. During the summer ships still put in at Eldsbouch, for the gnomes of Tralchet brought their trade down to the little town: silver from the mines, amber, and tin. The city wall had been rebuilt three times, each time nearer the harbor itself as the population shrank and the surrounding farmlands grew less and less able to give forth crops.

Still there was an inn there, called the King's Great House, and everyone in the Winterlands called its landlord His Majesty King Mick the Fourth, his father and great-grandfather having been, respectively, Kings Mick the Third and Second. He was a small dark cheerful man who made the travelers welcome when they reached the place in the sleety darkness of the forenoon, and he asked after John and Muffle and the folk of the Hold. Asked, too, if they'd heard whether the King would be sending garrisons back any time soon.

"I hear the gnomes have put word out they're buying slaves," he said to Jenny as he guided her and Ian to rooms above the kitchen, the best in the house in weather like this. "And not just among the bandits as they used to. Word is they've let it be known here in the town that any who wish to rid themselves of old folks, or cripples, or the simpleminded can earn good silver by giving them over to the brother kings. Have you heard this?"

"Old folks?" Ian unslung his pack and dropped it on the bed. "Cripples? Why would Lord Ringchin and Lord Ragskar buy those?"

His Majesty shook his head. "That I don't know." Outside, the winds that had whipped the travelers for two days had risen to a scream, and even through the thick rock walls they could hear the pounding of the waves against the seawall. "But Prowser Gorge, that fishes out beyond the mole, was putting it about last week that the lung fever carried off his crippled sister and that poor daughter of his, her that was so fragile and not able to do any work or find a husband. His sons have been more than usually shut-mouthed, and all of them spending gnomes' silver that they didn't get for their fish."

He turned his head as a particularly violent gust shook the building, and he made the trident sign of propitiation against that most capricious of Goddesses, Yellow-Haired Balyna of the Sea. "I think you should let Lord John know of this." He made as if to go, then turned back.

"Not meaning to trouble you, my lady, nor your son, but if you could see your way clear to putting a bit of a word on the storm . . . There's three or four of the boats that were out beyond the breakwater when the wind grew bad. A trading vessel was wrecked there a week ago, and I've heard as how in times past you've witched the weather."

"There isn't much that can be done," Jenny said gently, "with a storm like this, nor once the storm is upon us. But we'll do what we can."

After the man had left, Jenny said, "I haven't the smallest trouble believing old Gorge would sell his sister to the gnomes, or his daughter Ana either." She'd met the disagreeable fisherman on a number of occasions and had heard stories about him all her life. "But who in their right head would buy a cripple for a slave? Or a girl who's always ailing and in bed?"

As she helped Ian lay out a circle of power to slack the winds and try to make a break in the storm, she saw Pellanor again in her mind, crawling toward her in the firelight, with his dead demon eye.

She had lived cheek-by-jowl with the gray-haired baron under siege conditions for nearly a month, had fought beside him in battle. She knew absolutely that the man had had no flicker of magic in his blood.

So why had the demons taken over his body once life was gone?

Because the men in the Northern garrisons wouldn't have heard he was dead? Was it only her experience that had let her see the demon light in his eye?

After Ian had finished his spells to work the wind—which did slacken a little for an hour or so—Jenny opened the satchels that contained substances she'd thought to put away forever: silver dust and powders compounded of herbs and ash, tiny crystals ensorceled long ago to hold certain powers, candles of virgin wax. Under her instruction, as he had done nightly since setting forth from Alyn, Ian ceremonially cleansed the bigger of their two rooms, set limitations at the cardinal points, and traced out circles of power on the foot-smoothed plank floor. From her long studies and meditations in her days of small power, before the dragon's magic and the dragon's touch, Jenny knew the disciplines of sourcing power and took her son through them, calling on the name that the moon bore when it was five days old and on the tide as it came in over the breakwater. Assembling, too, the fragmentary magics to be gleaned from trines and quarts of position: a wyrd that had strength when drawn between running water and oaks on a hill, a sigil that drew power when made equidistant from silver, which could be found in the Tralchet Hills, and coal, which her dragon senses had detected years ago under the Snakewater Marshes.

Small magics, yes, but collected together, like a slave's two-penny tips and peddled handcrafts, they could build up and buy freedom.

Thus Ian called power, enough to source the summoning Jenny had described to him as well as she could. Through the howling of the storm Ian cast that summoning once more out into the ocean, and sleeping that night Jenny dreamed of those vast dark gliding shapes swimming northward, deep in the still safety beneath the waves.

In the morning the storm had abated, though the wind still

shrieked and small flotillas of cloud raced before it. The cold was bone breaking. As she and Ian walked down to the harbor together they could see where two fishing boats lay tied up at the old wharves with broken masts and torn sails, exhausted men telling their families how only the unexpected slacking of the wind for an hour in the night had let them make land. A third boat lay wrecked on the breakwater, its splintered masts and shattered timbers floating and crashing with the surge of the waves.

The gray heaving waters of the gulf stretched away to the west, bordered on the south by low shores dense with pine and spruce, uncut and unbroken since time's roots. North, the glacier-shawled rock of the Tralchet Hills gouged the blue air.

And beyond the gulf to the west, nothing. Only, far off, invisible and beyond the flight of all but the strongest birds, the Skerries of Light, where the dragons dwelled.

Ian found a plank from the wrecked fishing boat to lay from the shore to the first of the mole's great founding stones, for the massive piers had been plundered by villagers over generations for cut stone for houses and defensive walls. Water slopped constantly over their boots as Jenny led the way along the line of the old masonry; spray soaked their plaids and their sheepskin coats and now and then a great wave would douse them, like a child playing a prank. If any dead had remained in the wrecked boat when it had been driven on the mole, their families had come for them already. But as they edged past the broken body of the vessel, Jenny found herself thinking of the lightless deeps below the wall, of the cold violence of the storm that could drown men as casually as if they had been newborn kittens.

At the far end of the mole, wet and shivering, Ian raised his arms. Jenny heard nothing of the call he sent forth again, but she remembered how the dragon Morkeleb had called, extending his thought through the green deeps and the blue deeps, down to the lightless abysses below the sunken isle of Urrate in the South.

She remembered the dark forms rising from blackness, weightless and beautiful as they crossed into the violet zones where the sunlight touched. Remembered the deep slow hooning of their songs.

Those songs reached now into her mind and touched her as the singers of the deep, the Calves of the Abyss, rose up to answer Ian's summons. In the notes were endless tales of the deeds of ancestors. Songs of lost ships and lost treasure, love and gems alike drowned in the sea. Mudflat and trenches, warm currents and cold: the curious worlds and creatures hidden and unimagined beyond where the sunlight failed.

Hesitant, fumbling, she formed the thought, *Squidslayer!* as if she were trying to pronounce his name through mutilated lips and tongue. *He will not even hear, now that magic is gone.*

But his reply came to her, music from the gulfs of the sea. *Dragonfriend.*

They breached, curved slate-dark backs breaking the water in great smooth shining islands, and the steam of their spouts whipped away white on the wind. Tails waved, massive as trees, then slid soundless back into the waves. Ian's eyes widened with awed delight. The water thinned and rolled glossy over the rising backs once more, and they breathed again, little puffs this time, not long held. Then they were lying on the surface, a hundred feet from the breakwater, minds and thoughts surrounding the two humans like a slow deep echoing song.

Dragonfriend, slayer of demons, long-long tales of sorrow hurting the soul, and this thy calf?

Calf, Jenny agreed, groping and fumbling to reach to them with her crippled mind.

Motherfriend battleinjured. She heard Ian's voice shaping words clumsily, in imitation of what she'd taught him. *Lying in the deep trench resting, healing with time.*

Time, time. The whales passed assent and agreement among them, the music of their thoughts blending with those soft leathery hoons and drones. *Healing time. Good good good good good.*

Their word for time—their concept of it—differed utterly from the cluster of meanings humans used; though it was not, she realized, as alien as the way dragons thought of time. She was surprised, too, at Ian's perception of her winter's progress and pain.

Caradoc.

The image shaped in Ian's mind of the gray-haired, square-jawed face of the man who had done this thing to them, strong fingers holding up the jewels into which Ian's and Jenny's souls had been sent while demons inhabited their bodies. The big man was sitting by the hearth of

Jenny's cottage on Frost Fell, waiting for Ian to arrive, his goblin-headed staff upon his knees. There was a glass shell on the doorstep, and a little slip of quicksilver. Caradoc said, *Bring it to me ...* And Ian reached out with his hand. There was a memory of unbearable pain.

It was hard to remember, through all that had happened after, that it was not Caradoc who had done those things, but Folcalor. Folcalor had seduced Caradoc years ago in dreams, coaxing him to open a demon gate. And after that he had been a prisoner, as Jenny and Ian and the other mages had been, while the demons used their bodies and their magic to enslave the dragons and attempt to conquer the Realm of Belmarie.

Nevertheless she felt hatred in her heart as she thought of him. Were it not for Caradoc's stupidity and greed, she would have the dragon power that she had attained from Morkeleb; she would have even the original small powers with which she was born. She would not now be standing—a skinny, scarred, brown, little middle-aged woman—here on the edge of the world, watching her son perform those things which once she herself could have done.

Green light pouring from the wizard's eyes, fire from his mouth.

Seven jewels in a silver bottle.

A goblin-headed staff, with a moonstone set in the goblin's mouth.

Squidslayer drifted nearer to the wall. Jenny saw in the thick dark hide the bright eye, like a little star. The whalemage opened his mouth and let something float out into the choppy waters: a broken stick, gnawed by sea worms until almost no wood remained. It had on it a goblin's face, eaten away like a leper's, with a white jewel still in its grinning mouth.

Many times during her term in the green prison of a jewel, Jenny had wondered about Caradoc. She remembered Gareth—or was it the old King?—saying that Caradoc had been a merchant prince of Somanthus Isle. He'd been a haughty man who'd once courted Rocklys of Galyon, warrior-maiden and cousin of the Regent. It might be she'd loved him, in her way. At least she'd trusted him—or trusted the one she thought had been him—when he came to her saying, *I can get you the regency of the South, in place of your incompetent cousin.*

I can make you ruler, so you can rule everything right.

You poor fool, she thought wearily. *You poor vain fool.*

She saw again the vision she'd had then: a man walking along the seashore, exhausted and frustrated after a night of trying to conjure power. Like hers, she understood, his powers had been slight. And he had been unable to find a teacher. Over many decades, laws against wizardry in the South had kept those born with its power from getting the teaching they needed. Foolish laws, she thought, for they simply prevented the mageborn from learning the things that would keep them out of trouble, for those born with power always knew ways to get into it.

So it had been with Caradoc. She wasn't certain that at one time she wouldn't have made a foolish, dangerous bargain in order to have power.

She wasn't entirely sure what she'd do now, if offered the chance to have her power again.

Most mages were warned by their masters—she had certainly been warned by hers—to beware such dreams.

She knelt on the stones, reached out, and took the drifting staff in her hand. He at least had the sense, she thought, to remain silent while Folcalor sang love songs to him, calling to him to lift his own voice in answering music. His body was gone, devoured by fish; it only remained for his soul to join it in death.

Great ocean of darkness, Squidslayer's voice hooned in her mind. *Music warm singing. Leaping happy forever.* Jenny knew that this was what the whales saw when they thought of death. She understood also that the whales were not capable of smashing so small an object as a jewel. She felt sorry, holding the staff, knowing that Caradoc had never stood a chance. But as long as the stone existed, there existed also the possibility that Folcalor would find it and put it to use. That there was a power in it she did not doubt; nor that what Folcalor sought involved mages imprisoned in this fashion.

Ian held his hands out over the water to sing his thanks to the whalemages as Jenny turned toward the shore.

And in that moment, the wet wood of the goblin-headed staff burst into flame in her hand.

Jenny dropped the burning staff with a cry, sprang back and slipped on the wet stone, fell—and lunged forward on bleeding palms, bleeding knees, trying to grab the brand as it bounced once on the rock and fell into the sea. Behind her Ian said a word she didn't think he knew and flung himself down by the place, grabbing in the water. "Where is it? Can you see?"

A wave smashed on the rocks, soaking them both. Jenny said the same word Ian had and stripped off her plaids, her coat—

"Don't be an idiot, Mother! You'll never find it!"

"If I don't find it, I'm sure we'll learn what became of it in short order." Jenny pulled off her heavy skirt, shuddering in the icy wind, and started to yank off her boots. "Folcalor is a Sea-wight. He has power through water, and he's been searching for this jewel for weeks, maybe months." Squidslayer swept so close to the breakwater that Jenny could have put out her hand and touched his side, then he upended and dove down close to the massive stones of the wall. Jenny had a confused mental image of huge square blocks of granite, weed-grown and dark, of broken pillars and tumbled masonry all tangled together with the cold red kelps of the northern seas, the broken skeletons of ships, and the brown skulls of long-drowned mariners. It lasted only a moment in her mind, then vanished, and the waves crashed again, soaking her.

"Along there," Ian said, wrapping her in her plaid. Another whale showed close to the wall some thirty feet back, then dove. Jenny and Ian hastened along the uneven stones, catching their balance, Jenny shuddering in the flaying wind. She'd have to dive in eventually, she knew. The whales weren't capable of reaching into a crevice as small as some of those among the broken pillars. She only hoped Folcalor hadn't summoned some of the strange creatures she'd seen hovering around the demon gate below the ruin of Somanthus Isle.

Ian cried out.

Turning, Jenny saw a man climb out of the sea.

He had been a young man, fair haired and handsome, with a gold ring in one ear. One eye was intact and the other nearly so.

The eyes had been blue.

She didn't think he was one of the fishermen who'd drowned last night, but he hadn't been dead long. The rocks at Eldsbouch were ship eaters, and His Majesty had spoken of a Southern vessel that had been driven against them a week ago.

"Jenny." The seawater—or maybe worms—had done something to

the vocal cords. "And Ian." He coughed and spit seawater tinged with rotted black blood. "So this is your idea of rescue? Smash the final refuge of my soul and 'release' me to a 'better world'? I'd have thought better of you, Jenny, after all that was between us."

The swollen eyelid winked. A few brown teeth showed in a grin. "Not to mention you, my dear boy."

Ian's cold-reddened face flushed with rage. He started to speak, but Jenny raised a hand to touch his shoulder. "It was the demons," she said softly. "The demon in him, and the demons in us."

But she understood now that even as the physical bond between her imprisoned soul and her demon-ridden body had let her feel every sensation of those endless, savage ruttings during the days of her possession, so had Caradoc been aware of what his body—with Folcalor in possession—had done to and with hers. And she understood, too, that the Southern wizard had come to an accommodation with his imprisonment and had enjoyed at least some of what it brought him.

Something moved in the young sailor's soaked clothing. Drawing his shirt aside, Caradoc pulled a long pinkish worm from his flesh and dropped it into the water off the rocks. "I knew if I waited long enough I'd outsmart them," he said. "Old Folcalor—and fate. But I need your help, my dear."

"*Outsmart* them?" Jenny asked, shocked. "Folcalor will be on you like a hawk on a . . ."

"On a piece of carrion?" The dead face grinned. "*He* thinks. He thought he had me when he sent his little silver devils poking around the rocks for me. He even tried to seduce old Squidslayer, though what you could offer those things except bales of oysters I can't imagine . . ." He waved a flaccid and crab-nibbled hand at the blue-black shapes lying a few yards off, washed by the waves. The jewel must, Jenny thought, have settled on the mouth of the corpse, lodged deep in some niche in the rock wall; she remembered how Caradoc had forced the Icerider children to put jewels in their mouths so their souls would be imprisoned in the crystals' hearts.

"I will say they kept the demons from finding me until your boy told the whales what to look for. I don't suppose it even occurred to you to save *me,* while you were saving all the rest of that gullible rabble."

"You should be the last one," Jenny said thinly, "to scorn the gullible."

"I was *not* gullible," Caradoc snapped. "Had I not been exhausted—and had my concentration not been broken at a critical moment—I would have been able to keep my wards of protection strong the first time I summoned Folcalor. I'll certainly be better prepared next time. But as I said, I'll need your help. This thing certainly isn't going to last me." He slapped his chest, which gave squishily beneath the sodden shirt. "I haven't the demons' ability to keep a corpse going for weeks, but I learned a few things, living side by side with Folcalor six years. This poor sod didn't have much magic in him, that's for certain. You and your boy can help me get a nice bandit, or some stupid brute of a fisherman whom nobody will miss . . ."

He broke off when he saw Jenny's look of horrified shock. "Oh, don't stand there with your mouth open, my dear, as if I'd asked you to tup sailors at a penny a time. Though considering all that Amayon had you do . . ."

"I was Amayon's prisoner and his puppet."

"And you didn't enjoy it? All those tears and screams were genuine?" He must have read the truth in Jenny's disgusted eyes, for he shrugged, and said, "Well, some people don't know how to make the most of their opportunities, I must say." He looked from woman to boy in silence for a time, studying them as he must have studied buyers in the corn markets of Bel, gauging them. He seemed to be seeking some clue in their faces, in what he knew of them, for a way to gain their complicity and assent.

"So what can I offer you, then?" he asked at last. He put his hand to his chin in a gesture Jenny had seen him make when he spoke with Rocklys of Galyon, so the commander wouldn't realize that the man who had courted her, the man she knew and trusted, was no longer looking at her from those pale brown eyes. "What coin will buy the help I need? This corpse stinks even to me, and I can feel the worms creeping around in my guts this minute, and the crabs burrowing along my backbone. Would you help me for the sake of the memories I have, that Folcalor left in my mind? Images, recollections, spells? The instructions that were given him by Adromelech, his master, the Lord of the Hell of the Sea-wights? The name of the wizard whose body he's taken on now?"

"Do you know it?" When Caradoc spoke the archdemon's name the ghostly form of him rose in Jenny's memories, the being Amayon knew as lord. A figure loved and hated, feared and obsessively adored. Intelligent, like Folcalor, but without Folcalor's sly grossness, without Folcalor's greed for pleasure. Cold, wise, hungry beyond human conception for those things that would feed him or satisfy his pride.

"I might," the wizard said.

"Why is it Folcalor who is seeking you—seeking all the wizards—and not Adromelech?" Jenny asked. "Is he in rebellion? Seeking to rule this world in Adromelech's stead?"

"Jenny, Jenny," Caradoc sighed. "After running in tandem with Amayon, you still don't understand? It's all swallowing and being swallowed to them, you know, torturing and being tortured." Some of the angry pride went out of his voice, and condescension tinged it—the condescension of a man who has always considered himself smarter than others and seeks to instruct, not for the sake of the pupil but to hear himself called wise. "They want power, want to absorb and control. They need that dominance, even as they're being eaten themselves."

Jenny shivered, remembering what Amayon remembered: feeling, for a moment, what the demon felt. The unslakable, inflammable hunger to prove himself stronger than others. To have dissolving souls weep in his belly, to play the game of bargaining with them. It was a desire that satisfaction never slaked, only irritated to a craving still more urgent.

"Adromelech tortured Folcalor in ways we cannot even conceive. Tortured him and fed off his pain. He does that with all the demons, of course, but Folcalor more than the others because Folcalor was his lover and his deputy. They all love one another, and hate one another, and feed on one another to some degree. They cannot die, and do not forgive. If he could do it, Folcalor would devour the lady of the burning mirror, to use the power he would gain from her against his lord. It's all revenge."

He shrugged again. Clouds were moving in to cover the sun, and waves broke heavily on the rocks, stinging Jenny's face with icy spray. Jenny had brought her halberd with her but didn't think she could cover the dozen feet between herself and Caradoc quickly enough to surprise him, for the rocks were uneven and slippery.

"Is that what Folcalor wants, then?" she asked. "Revenge? How would conquering the South have given him that? Why did he take the souls of wizards and prison them in crystals? Why make us his slaves?"

"Ah, Jenny." The living dead man smiled patronizingly. "There is slavery and slavery. Did you think you were his slave?"

And she heard in his voice the voice of a merchant who always had some other plan up his sleeve, some information with which to negotiate. She raised her head, alarmed. "You don't plan still to bargain with him?"

"Me?" He made his face look indignant. "After all he did to me? How could you think so? Look over there." His gesture was so natural, his voice so convincing, that she did in fact turn her head, following the direction of his hand, and so was unprepared when he bounded across the distance to her and struck her full-strength on the side of the head with the hammer of his fist, hurling her into the choppy sea. Weighted down with plaids, Jenny was pulled under, coughing and fighting. She heard Ian cry out, and beyond that only the thud and roar of the ocean on the rocks. Desperate, she slithered free of the heavy cloth and scrambled onto the rocks in time to see the big man pinning Ian facedown on the other side of the seawall, holding his head underwater.

With a shrill scream of rage Jenny was on him with the knife she wore always at her belt, but Caradoc twisted out of the way, shoving her back. Ian crawled to his hands and knees, gasping, and Caradoc flung himself off the seawall and into the harbor's calmer waters, vanishing into the bay like a chunk of iron.

Jenny and Ian knelt for a long time on the breakwater's uneven stones, dripping and shivering and clinging together, but they saw no sign of the blond head breaking the waves. Squidslayer and two other whalemages glided through the channel into the harbor, to the awe and horror of the folk onshore, and searched there. King Mick broke one of old man Gorge's teeth keeping the fisherman from putting out at once with his son and a boat full of harpoons. Later Mick and his own sons went out, with their boat and nets, dragging for the body until darkness and rising wind drove them in.

"I doubt it had the strength to get ashore, you know," the innkeeper said comfortingly that night as he brought hot wine to Jenny and Ian by the Great House fire. "It could stand, and talk, as you say, but if it was one of those Southern sailors . . . Well, it'd been in the sea for over a week. My boys and I will search the country round about and destroy the thing, however much of it we find. How long could it last?"

Caradoc might have been lying about the recollections he'd gleaned from close contact with Folcalor's mind; about the memories that had been left in him, as the memories of how to fashion a demon gate had been left in Ian's and Jenny's. Jenny tried to hope so, for the sake of the Winterlands—and for the sake of the world.

A man was waiting for John Aversin at the foot of the shallow steps. "Lord Aversin, no!" he called, rising as John's hand went to his sword hilt. John felt the stab of cramp in his right arm and stepped back to get the broken pillar of the crypt door at his back.

Right, he thought a moment later. *Let 'em take you in the passageway that leads to the burning mirror. That'll make a good impression on the inquisitors.*

Or was this man someone Amayon had spoken to in a dream?

A second cramp bit his thigh, pain stealing his breath. On one knee he forced his numb fingers to close on the sword hilt, swinging to his right to meet an attack.

But there was none. Only the diminutive gray-haired mage hurrying toward him through the tangle of brown vines and snow, fur-lined coat skirts flapping, gloved hands fumbling with his scrying crystal. "That is Lord John Aversin, is it not? Of all the people in the world . . ."

John swung back from a fast check of the landscape—frost-white morning, what remained of last night's powder snow broken only by the tracks of the two horses now tied in the ruined garden above them, no advancing guards of the Regent's council in sight—and held his sword at the ready. Master Bliaud, who like Jenny and Ian had been possessed by Caradoc's demons, halted uncertainly, and John felt the shimmer of further magics in the air like the threat of rain.

"If it's all the same to you, I'd rather you didn't go shoutin' it to the landscape."

"Eh? Oh." Bliaud looked worriedly over his shoulder. "Oh, you needn't worry. I wasn't followed. Or accompanied." He dropped his scrying stone, bent awkwardly to pick it up, and dusted snow from the back of his fur-trimmed robes where he'd sat on the steps. "I was particularly careful about that. The voices warned me . . ." He hesitated, hand at mouth as if he'd said too much.

Gingerly, John sheathed his blade and climbed to his feet. He flinched back a pace when the Southern mage would have come closer, and Bliaud, finally getting the hint, retreated, leaving a distance of about twenty feet between them.

Not, John reflected, that twenty feet or a hundred and twenty feet would do a bloody bit of good if the wizard wanted to lay him out with wringing pain or stop his breathing, for that matter. He'd fought the man—and others of the short-lived Dragonmage Corps—and had come to understand why men feared and hated mages and had passed a thousand years of laws to limit their power and influence.

Still, he felt better with twenty feet between them.

"And what voices are these?"

Bliaud let out a nervous bleat and looked around him again. "In . . . in dreams. They told me my house was being watched, which is absurd. Completely absurd. Prince Gareth promised me—promised us all—that no one on the council blamed us—well, hardly anyone—for being overpowered and possessed . . ."

"But you still hear 'em whisperin'," John said quietly, and saw Bliaud's eyes shift.

Like Ian, the elderly sorcerer looked as if he hadn't slept since the last full moon of summer.

Jen and Ian have one another, he thought. *Neither of 'em can speak of it—all Jen can do is sit in pain so deep she can't even help her own son—but each knows the other went through it, too.*

Bliaud, despite his two well-meaning sons—*And the Old God knows what they thought of their dad's behavior*—was alone.

"I don't . . ." Bliaud wet his lips. "I don't ever listen." He drew a deep breath, and John knew he lied.

Every night, he thought. And every night remembering, as Jenny remembered, the evil he had done in those days when the world was one vast joyous holocaust of colored fire. Knowing he'd done those things and knowing the pain the demon had put him through and knowing, too, the penalties—fire and the wheel and the executioner's knife—and wanting it anyway. Wanting the demon back.

Bliaud's eyes met John's squarely for one moment, naked and begging.

He was not begging to hear him say *I understand*–he could see, John guessed, that he understood. He was begging to hear, *It's all right. No one will blame you. Go back.*

The old man turned his eyes aside. In a quiet voice he said, "They told me to bring things here: clothing, and food, and silver, and gold as well. They said I should lay wyrds of disguise about myself and my horse, that none might see where I went." His glance shifted past John's shoulder to the archway of what had been the crypt door, visible now in winter with the dying of the vines. Something altered in his eyes: curiosity, realization, hunger.

To break that longing gaze, John said briskly, "Well, let's have 'em, then. I'm clemmed."

Bliaud looked back twice over his shoulder as they climbed the steps to the old garden. *If I was on Gar's council,* John thought, *I'd have this one's head, no error.* He felt the heat of the ink bottle against his flesh, under his doublet, and wondered if Bliaud knew it was there.

And he wondered what he could do about it if the mage decided to take it from him.

But Bliaud offered him no threat, merely sat on a fallen pillar, keeping wards of concealment and misdirection–probably utterly unnecessary in the emptiness of the Bel Marches–in place while John shaved, even weaving spells of heat to warm the air around them and the water in the old marble pool, so John could bathe before he changed his clothes. "You have no horse?" Bliaud remarked at one point. "Did you journey far?"

His eyes were on the cuts John had taken from the shining things–and, John was aware, on the pile of his clothes.

"Farther than you'll know." John dried himself roughly and fast and collected the ink bottle first thing. It had been a toss-up whether to keep it thonged about his neck or to leave it concealed in his clothes while he washed.

"Did you ... I mean, were you working for ... That is ..." Bliaud waved his hands uncertainly, the gold stampwork on his blue leather gloves glinting in the rising sun, and his glance shifted to the vine-draped hillside below them, to the dark eye of the crypt. "I understand from my sons that you were in debt to the demons—that you owed them a teind and were doing their bidding."

"Gaw." John pulled on his breeches, then his boots, shivering where the cold winds breathed through the heat spells. "If that's what's bein' noised about me, I'm lucky the Regent's never sent troops back north, ain't it?"

"Is it true?"

He stamped his boots into place and got into the clean shirt and his doublet, tucking the ink bottle and the bag of flax seeds out of sight. He looked back up to meet the old man's desperate eyes.

"Master Bliaud," he said, more gently than he'd thought he would speak to one of Aohila's servants. "A month ago me son Ian tried to kill himself because of a demon whisperin' to him in his dreams. The demon that was in my Jen won't let her rest—not that it's truly there, or able to speak out of the Hell to which I sent him when they left you, no more than that's really me dad shoutin' at me in me dreams."

Bliaud looked quickly away.

"If you called 'em back," John went on, buckling the straps of his doublet, flexing his arm in a jangle of chain and spikes, "it wouldn't heal the pain you're feelin' now. It'd only let 'em drink that pain and laugh at you when the Regent had you killed for the Realm's sake. You know that."

The little man nodded. A wealthy gentleman of good family in Greenhythe, he'd lived most of his life, John recalled, in genteel retirement, keeping his talents discreetly concealed so as not to bring upon his family the stigma of being mageborn in the South.

He'd only ridden north the previous summer at the behest of the Regent, who'd said the Realm needed mages to survive. And the very tutor to whom he'd entrusted himself had raped him of mind and will, imprisoned his self in a sapphire's heart, and put a demon into his body.

He had asked for none of this: pain, shame, memories more foul than the worst of nightmares, and emptiness—that awful sense that without the demon, there could be no more joy in life.

He'd only wanted to help.

It was all in his eyes.

Then he wet his lips with a hesitant pale tongue and asked, "Did you . . . Do you have a demon helper, a demon guide? May I see it?"

Were I king, John thought as he later saw Bliaud ride away with his unloaded packhorse, his shimmer of snowy mist and illusion, *I'd have him killed tonight.*

For the good of the Realm.

And maybe meself as well.

Chapter 9

The gates of paradise lay beyond the Hell of Winds.

Aversin was never sure whether the Hell of Winds was actually as he saw it or merely an illusion of some demon intent on trapping him and Amayon in howling lightless mazes forever. Or intent on *something*, anyway.

It was hard to tell about Hells.

The place didn't even make the marginal sense of the Realm behind the Mirror of Isychros or the wastelands roved by the Shining Things. Bridges spanned gaping, endless abysses, and broken railless stairways climbed the wet black cliffs, but they seemed built for no purpose. "Are they just for decoration, like?" he inquired when, hammered by exhaustion, he insisted they stop in a circular stone pit like a dry well that offered some shelter from the winds. "Or is this a regular route from Ernine to that place I saw in the pool?"

The pit was floored in thin flat slabs of crystal that cut his leather sleeves like razors. Holding a piece of it up to the weak greenish light Amayon had called into being, he saw that one edge was beveled; it was the same kind of dark-hued glass that the hunter woman in the Hell of the Shining Things had carried about her neck to identify demons with.

"You don't understand." Amayon looked annoyed, as at a child's questions regarding the color of the sky. He was trim and clean, not even wet from the spray flying down out of the darkness. With two days' growth of beard, and mud and rain slicking his clothes and hair and spectacles, John wanted to slap him.

"Well, it'd be a waste of both our time to ask if I *did* understand, now, wouldn't it?"

"Every Hell has a secret." Amayon gave him a sly red-lipped smile. "And every Hell has a lord. Mostly you never see the lord, but guessing the secret can be the difference between . . ."

"Life and death?"

The demon laughed; a thin bright tinkling sound. "Silly. What are those? Guessing the secret can be the difference between getting out and not getting out."

Even had the demon guide not been with him, John would have known enough not to follow the lights he sometimes half glimpsed—cold and green, or warm doorways of inviting amber—at the ends of mysterious stairs and causeways. In a gully filled with fire he saw a chained man who looked like his father, weeping and dragging at the bonds that held him to the rocks. There were other people there as well, half glimpsed through the smoke. "It's illusion," John said, "isn't it? Like the whisperers in the Mire?"

And the demon smiled sidelong at him and said, "Human souls have to go someplace when they die. Go down and speak to him."

The man looked up with heat-demolished eyes and shouted something to them, where they stood on the bridge above. John couldn't hear above the roaring and crackle of the blaze. He could have been crying, *Help.* He could have shouted, *John.*

"It's like the whisperers." John held up the dark fragment of glass he'd found, catching the reflection in it as the hunter woman had done. The fire was gone—illusion—but there was something in the pit, something cloaked in shadow and impossible to see clearly. It might still have been his father.

"Whatever it comforts you to believe," Amayon said. And the demon purred almost audibly at the taste of doubt and guilt and pain as John walked across the bridge and away. Nevertheless, though John saw no other evidence of other demons—if in fact the illusion was that of a demon—he noticed that Amayon kept close to his side and didn't attempt any little tricks.

Unless of course opening the gates of paradise was a trick.

If it was, it worked.

That first day in the green warm sweetness of meadow and woodland, all John did was sleep. He stoppered Amayon in the ink bottle and set snares and warning traps all around the thicket of laurel and wild roses where he lay down, though he'd seen no sign of any creature larger or fiercer than a roe deer. His sleep was like drowning in tepid water. He dreamed of Jenny, healed, brushing her long hair again—it had grown in gray, like fog in moonlight—and of Ian and Adric as young men, talking in the sunset of a rich autumn with promise of a plentiful harvest to come. The light was waning as he woke, but it seemed to be summer here, the woods fragrant with briar and honeysuckle. He spent an hour in the fading light scribbling on his scraps of parchment: the apparent route through the stone mazes, the fiery sigils that had marked the gate to paradise, the broken glass in the pit.

How had the glass come to the hunter woman, who looked as if she had been born and raised in the Hell where she was trapped?

All Hells have a secret, Amayon had said.

If he wasn't lying, of course.

Then he ate some of the bread and fruit Bliaud had brought him—for he wasn't sure whether tasting the fruits of paradise would have the same consequences as those of Hell, and he wasn't ready to risk delay—and lay down and slept again.

Fairy lights wakened him, and fairy music.

They circled him like butterflies, bobbing spots of luminosity in the cobalt velvet of the night. All the meadow before him was starred and frosted with the light of similar rings, and in the trees where the ground was lower he saw a young stag browsing, fey lights wreathed and sparkling on its horns. Only when he reached out his hand to those gently glittering powder puffs of light did their true nature become obvious.

Pain lanced his palm where they bit. Shoots of cold pierced his arm, taking his breath. He tried to shake them off and couldn't. He whipped his knife from its sheath and sliced them away, but their stings remained in his flesh, he felt them bore deeper, each twisting and hooking with a separate, greedy life. He dug at them, the blood trickling down, and the pink and blue lights settled on the dripped gore. They reflected sickly greenish in the fragment of beveled glass, he noticed before dizziness swamped him and he dropped to his knees.

The more lights drew near. They fastened on his wrists and face and dug through the sleeves of his shirt, staining the linen with blood. The stag walked nearer, tilting its head, and squirrels, chipmunks, and rabbits soft as baby's breath emerged from the thicket's shadow, fairy light glowing green from their greedy eyes.

John managed to yank the stopper from the ink bottle as his

fingers got cold and numb. Amayon cursed, kicked the nearest demon bunny aside, and snatched up another one, biting through the soft fur of its neck. Blood squirted horribly; the demon sucked up blood and life while the rabbit bit, screamed, and manifested claws and mouths and tentacles to rip at him. The other creatures retreated, and grinning like a mad dog Amayon pursued them, catching the little pink stinger feys and popping them into his mouth.

He came back, smiling, to where John lay among the ferns with sweat streaming from his face as the pain went deeper and deeper still. "I think it's been five hundred years since a human got into this Hell," the demon boy said conversationally, seating himself among the ferns beside John's shoulder. He plucked a violet, savoring its scent, and tucked the blossom behind his ear. "I gather he didn't last long. Well, longer than he wanted to, anyway."

John tried to speak and couldn't, jaws aching from the effort not to scream. He knew that would come, too, and soon. He managed to say, "Aohila."

Men don't leave me, she had said. It was a good bet demons didn't, either, and he saw the change in Amayon's face at the mention of her name.

The anger at being reminded that he, too, was a servant vanished at once. "Wonderful how a little sting will make anyone hide behind a woman's skirts," the demon mocked. "But don't worry." He leaned over John and stroked his face with a grass blade, the mere touch engendering a wave of nauseating agony where the things the stingers had turned into wriggled and dug through muscle and nerve and flesh. "I won't let you die."

Then, with the air of a connoisseur settling himself to sweetmeats and wine, the demon lay back on the ferns to enjoy an extended feast of pain.

There is slavery and slavery, Caradoc had said.

And, *Did you think you were his slave?*

Jenny pondered those words as they passed under the gatehouse of Eldsbouch and took once more the overgrown trail south.

"Obviously, our bodies were slaves," Ian said, pulling his plaids more closely around his face as ice-laden winds ripped through the sparse trees. Returning to the inn after his near drowning, he had slept almost twelve hours. Waking, he'd wrought weather spells against the coming storm but Jenny wouldn't have laid money on how long they'd hold.

At least until we reach Alyn Hold, she prayed to Ankithis, father of storms. Once again, she felt naked, unable to protect herself with anything other than hope and trust in the gods. She had no idea whether this would be enough.

"Somehow," Ian went on, "I don't think that's what he meant."

"Nor do I." Jenny glanced back over her shoulder for a glimpse of King Mick and his sons dragging their net one last time through the violent waters of Migginit Bay. There was still no sign of the animate corpse. She tried to hope that the worms and the fish had completed their interrupted repast, but her dreams would not permit her this comfort. "I was Folcalor's prisoner in the crystal. I—the real part of me—was never his slave."

"Would we have been later?"

Jenny shivered in the plaids the whales had retrieved for her from the sea. "I thought that being his prisoner was the worst that could happen," she said at last. "Seeing what Amayon did—feeling what he did—to and with my body. Not being able to do anything about it."

Ian looked away.

She leaned from Moon Horse's saddle to touch Ian's wrist, letting him know that she understood. "Now I wonder if your father didn't get us out before the worst."

"It will be all right with him, won't it?" Ian glanced back at her, eyes dark and shy under the shadows of his curiously jutting brows. "You going away—going back to Frost Fell . . . ?"

Jenny sighed. Even on the road, dreams of Amayon still came to her: dreams of his passion for her, of the passion for life, of the brilliance of magic and power that she had felt when he had inhabited her flesh. Possession by a demon was not a simple matter, not merely alienation from one's own body while another personality ruled it. Since true death had not severed soul from flesh, the bonds of feeling were strong—strong enough, in most cases, that if exorcism was performed within the first few days, the displaced soul would return. The soul retained the shape of the flesh, as Jenny had found out in the crystal. Hold the hand of her body toward fire, and Jenny, in her crystal, would feel the warmth.

That had been one of the horrors of her imprisonment. It was one of the worst parts of the dreams.

And, it seemed, it had been one of Caradoc's consolations.

"We come together and we move apart," she said in time. "It happens all through life. I was hurt—I was badly hurt—in that final battle, and I'm still hurting and angry. And I was taking my anger out on your father for things that probably aren't his fault." *Like lying with the Demon Queen?* the anger in her soul whispered. *Like going to her instead of coming to me, in the plague?* "I will always be a part of his life. A part of yours."

He looked down at his hands for a moment, clumsy in their worn gloves on his mare's reins. "Does that mean yes or no?"

"It does," Jenny agreed gravely, and he glanced up quickly and laughed.

They camped that night in the ruins of what had been first a fortified manor house, then an inn. The walls had been rebuilt a little, and it was a favorite camping place for the few merchant pack trains that wound their way between Alyn Hold and the sea. The old kitchen still had most of a roof on it, and it was here that they bedded down, kindling a small fire in the brick hearth and tying their horses near. Ian's drained powers had recovered enough to let him set a ring of ward signs around the outbuilding walls, but Jenny and he both agreed that sitting awake in shifts that night wouldn't be a waste of their time.

She dreamed of Amayon again that night, and of Folcalor, crouched somewhere in darkness. Somewhere close, she thought. Caradoc had spoken of a wizard whose body the demon now rode—if he'd been telling the truth. But her magic was gone, and she could not search her dreams as she used to. She dreamed, too, of John, lying asleep in a hollow place of bare red-black rock, his drawn sword under one bandaged hand and his spectacles clutched protectively in the other. She thought he looked exhausted—thin and haggard and filthy—and where his sleeves were pushed up over his forearms and his torn shirt hung open to show his chest, she could see the marks drawn on his flesh by the Demon Queen.

When she woke, consumed with the heat of her changing body,

she knew she would sleep no more that night and told Ian to rest. The boy sorely needed it; he was unconscious in moments and muttered in his sleep words she could not understand. Whether he spoke of his own demon Gothpys or of Folcalor she could not tell, nor did she ask him in the morning. Again and again she tried to conjure recollection of her dreams of Folcalor: where he had been and what things had surrounded him that might lead her to his hiding place or give her a clue as to the body he now wore.

But beyond the fact that he was in a place of darkness, she could see nothing. There were jewels there, she thought: enormous jewels on his many rings, but jewels also like the sapphire and peridot and smoky quartz in which she and the other mages had been imprisoned. But there were so many of them in the hammered silver dish at his side—handfuls—that they could not be prisons for the souls of mages. There were not that many mages in the world.

In the morning Ian was able to scry the territory for signs of bandits or Iceriders and to see in his crystal that all was well at the Hold.

Why cripples? Jenny wondered as she saddled Moon Horse again and helped Ian strap up the packs. *Why the old as well as the young?*

They planned to lie that night at the Dancing Cow in Far West Riding, from which spot—weather permitting—they should be able to reach the Hold by the following night. But when they stopped at sunset, still an hour or two from the small isolated settlement, for Ian to scout the country ahead of them in the scrying stone that had been Jenny's, the boy's eyes widened sharply. "There's trouble," he said.

"Where?" Jenny leaned forward instinctively then sat back, furious and hurt, remembering that she could call nothing in the crystal's heart. "What?"

Ian looked up. "Far West Riding," he said. "Bandits. They're attacking the main gate. I guess Grynne hadn't gotten it shut for the night yet; it looks like the gate's still open. And they're trying to get over the wall in that place where the mortar's no good."

"John told them to fix it last spring," Jenny moaned.

"But why would bandits attack Far West Riding?" He stared down at the crystal again, angling it to the sliver of witchlight he'd called in the fading dusk. They'd stopped just below the crest of Whitelady Hill, in the bare miles of what had been farmland, and the snow that stretched behind them was broken here and there by blue-brown ridges of half-ruined stone walls and lines of long-dead trees. "There's nothing there except the inn and Father Drob's temple and a couple of farms."

"Look at the Hold." Jenny glanced beyond him to the thick yellow-gray sky above the hill. No smoke yet.

"I can't see it." The blue feather of light brightened, shining coldly in the eyes of their horses. Moon Horse turned her long ears inquiringly, sensing the trouble in Ian's voice. Ian's horse was the one John called "the Stupider Roan," to distinguish it from its marginally less blockheaded brother, and would not have sensed trouble had a regiment of goblins danced around it in a circle. "Nothing." Ian looked apologetic. "I'm tired, Mother. It could be only that. I didn't do well yesterday, either. I kept losing the images . . ."

"Or something's happening there," Jenny said, her voice hard. "Something someone doesn't want you to see. Can you see anything?"

Ian shook his head. Scry wards frequently worked by deception—for instance, showing any mage who sought to view a place what that place had looked like at some other time than the present. But just as often they simply blocked any perception at all. And scrying was a skill new to Ian since he'd been possessed, and one that he could not utilize consistently.

It had taken Jenny years of practice before she was able to see where and what she willed every time.

But coupled with the attack on Far West Riding, this failure was far too pat to be chance. "They'll be watching the road," she said. "Check the countryside around the town."

"Marcon's farm," Ian said after a moment—and he didn't, Jenny noticed, have any trouble seeing that. "They're burning the thatch on the house and the barn. I can't see . . . There. Marcon and Lylle and the children are all right, hidden in the cave. The fields south of the town look clear."

"We'll go in that way, then." Every fiber of Jenny's nerves prickled and screamed with the knowledge that something was happening at the Hold. Siege, probably, by bandits who'd gotten hold of scry wards at the very least. Her mind raced to the certainty that Muffle and the greater force of the Hold's strength would make for Far West Riding the minute they knew. *Yes,* she thought, *there,* as smoke plumed up into the sky. That would bring Muffle.

And the Hold would be attacked.

In the dead of winter? Madness.

Or some very, very good reason to do so now.

A chill of foreboding in her heart, she swung onto Moon Horse's back and urged the tired mare around the side of the hill and down toward the burning farm.

They swung wide to avoid the bandits attacking Far West Riding's outlying farms and came upon the town itself through the freezing, black, and windy night. Ian called the weather, howling gale and driving sleet, and the defenders, who were still mostly indoors and could keep their bowstrings dry, gained an advantage. Ian laid, too, spells of panic on men and horses: illusions of armed warriors and attacking wolves that distracted the robbers until they were felled by arrows or stones. Exhausted from the summoning of the whalemages and the steady, grinding effort of working the weather for days, Ian was by this time barely able to summon power at all. But there was no single body of attackers, no overall commander or coordinated thrust, so it was easy enough for one band or another to retreat, cursing and floundering in snow.

Whipped and frozen by the storm winds, Ian and Jenny entered the inn of the Dancing Cow, the largest building of the town, in which most of the inhabitants had taken refuge. Dolly, its proprietor, pressed food and hot cider on them, but Jenny would take little. "We'll be moving on tonight," she said shortly. "We need horses, if you can spare them." She glanced sidelong, worried, at her son, who slumped on a bench before the fire, face ghastly white.

He looked up, however, and made John's thumbs-up sign of readiness to go on, and gave her the flicker of a smile.

"Whatever you need," the innkeeper said. She was a big woman and at times like these wore a man's mail shirt, looted from some long-ago robber, that she had adapted to her full-breasted form—she was the town blacksmith as well as the innkeeper. "My Jeb tells me we've rounded up five of the robbers' horses already, and they're main fresh. One of 'em's my stallion Sun King that Balgodorus Black-Knife stole year before last."

"Black-Knife," Jenny said softly. "I thought so."

The storm was growing less. Ian could possibly have brought it back in force, but to do so would have slowed their own journey as well as inconvenienced the bandits, and in any case Jenny was fairly sure Muffle and the Alyn Hold militia were still advancing toward Far West Riding's relief. Moreover, calling storms was a dangerous exercise for novices. Often, once summoned, storms would not be dismissed, and their force would build and cause great destruction. An hour after midnight she and Ian set off once again on the rutted and broken military road, riding as swiftly as they dared on borrowed horses, starflashes of blue light running along the ruts and potholes before them and turning the steadily falling spits of snow to diamonds.

In the dead dark before morning they met Sergeant Muffle on the road with a dozen of the men of Alyn Hold, heavily armed with spears and bows.

"Jenny!" Muffle spurred his thick-limbed mount through the muck to her and leaned from the saddle to clasp her hands. "And Ian! We saw smoke at sunset. Far West Riding, Bo here says." He gestured to the young brother of the priest of the green god at the West Riding temple.

"Bandits attacked the gates." Jenny pushed back her hood and drew down the plaids that protected her face. The white-and-brown wool cracked with ice from her breath.

"Bandits? At this time of year? Are they insane?"

"No," Jenny said. "What they are at the moment is probably attacking the Hold."

Her brother-in-law cursed and swung his horse around as if he would ride back immediately, then wheeled again. "Ian?" he said. "You're a wizard, you'll be able to see . . ."

And the boy shook his head. "I can't," he said, his breath a blue-white glitter in the witchlight. "I've tried four times since we set out from the Dancing Cow, and I can't. Mother says it sounds like a scry ward."

"Cragget blast 'em! They can't get past the walls, though." His heavy face creased with anger.

"They can," Jenny said, "if they've magic enough to sound and look like you in the dark and the storm."

Ian scried back behind them to Far West Riding and the countryside round about. Though he saw a dozen or more bandits hiding from the cold, there were no signs of organized regrouping. Therefore Muffle and his riders turned their horses and made in a body for the Hold again, slowed by the swollen drifts, the trees that had blown down on the road. Jenny's hands and feet ached from the cold, and her eyes smarted with the slash of the wind. Beside her Ian clung to his saddlebow, and she wondered where John was tonight.

At the hour when in summertime the sun would have stood high above the trees already, a kind of gray glimmer began to water the darkness, and Jenny made out the rolling shapes of the fells. This bleak country was her home ground, and she identified each ridge and humped shoulder of stone by its name, familiar even under the blanket of snow: Cair Gannet, Cair Dag, Skep Tor, the Sleeper. Standing stones crowned their crests, a reminiscence of those who had dwelled there before the kings, and broken bridges guarded the way over ice-locked becks.

Smoke poured in a column over the Sleeper's backbone, the white smoke of burning roofs and burning walls. The smell of it charred the morning air.

As before, they swung wide of the road, which would be watched, and came through the cranberry bog on the far side of Toadback Hill. Jenny, Muffle, and Ian left the horses and most of the men in the ruins just past the hillcrest and made their way up on foot until they could look down on the Hold: white smoke, gray smoke, the pale silky flicker of orange flame.

"They've broke the gate!" Muffle made as if to run back to the horses, and Jenny caught his arm.

"Look again," she said, though the panic that had seized him was reflected in her own heart: Maggie, Adric ... maybe John, if he'd returned. Sparrow and her children. Muffle's wife, Blossom. Gilly, Peasey, Moonbeam ...

"The gate's still closed," she said.

The big man looked again. "That's the kitchen burning, though," he said. "And the blockhouses, the gatehouse roof ..." Along the walls forms could be seen running, the flash of steel in the pallid morning light and the flash, too, of water thrown on flames. As they watched, two men with poles managed to heave the whole gatehouse roof down over the wall, scattering bandits away from the ram that had been set up before the gates themselves.

"Magic," Jenny said softly. "Magic of some kind. Fire spells are the easiest of wyrds to set."

"And the easiest to quench." Ian's face was set, thin and old as a skull's, and his eyes burned a feverish blue. He was gathering himself, focusing all his magic, all his power.

He knew what Muffle knew: that even if the gate still held, if the attackers had some way of sending fire spells within the Hold, the defenders couldn't last long. Jenny saw a man on the walls leap back, striking at the flames that burst spontaneously on his sleeves and back. He was still slapping at them when an arrow from below the wall took him through the chest. A spot of flame appeared on the stable roof, growing rapidly to a flower and then a blaze.

"I can't work the counterspells at this distance," Ian said softly. "Muffle, will you ride down with me?"

"No." Jenny's hand closed over his wrist. "Look down there: the man with Balgodorus, the man in green with the scraggy beard."

Ian frowned, not understanding. "That's just Dogface the bandit," Muffle said. "He rode with Crake and that blond fellow . . . What was his name? A small-time thief and a slaver. Nothing to worry about."

"Except that he's dead," Jenny said. "I know. I killed him—poisoned him—at Brighthelm Tower, eight or nine days ago when I rescued those people from Rushmeath Farm. The bandits were led by a dead man then, too."

There was silence. A sortie of bandits threw themselves from the burning ruins of Alyn Village against the Hold walls, raising siege ladders, scrambling up ropes. They were squat forms, smaller than the other bandits and armored heavily in glittering spikes. Jenny could hear their shouting: the hoarse, growling polysyllables of the gnomes.

"Dogface is dead," Jenny said. "As poor Pellanor was. A demon inhabits his flesh, as demons can. Setting fires is probably all he can do, from the limitations of being in the flesh of a nonmage. And there may be other demons among Balgodorus' men as well. If you use magic against them, Ian, they will take you through your spells, as they took me."

The boy looked at her blankly. It was almost as if, having readied his mind for battle, he was shaken at being drawn back from it. Jenny was familiar with the sensation. She held his gaze with hers and in a moment or two saw his eyes change. He looked past her at the flames, and the distant shouting of men was borne to them with the smoke on the wind.

His lips parted and closed again, as if he could not even frame the words, *What then?*

Jenny closed her eyes, understanding what had to be done.

She, who had no magic but who understood magic, could do it. Her flesh understood an alien flesh and an alien power.

There was a power circle that could be made to draw in the greatest of power: the harmonies of the turning stars. Long study had given Jenny an exact awareness of each planet, each star beyond the daylight sky; she knew also where the veins of gold and silver ran deep beneath the Winterlands rock and where underground rivers could be used to build trines and quarts to amplify and reflect the powers of sky and earth. Thus it was, to be a mage.

Exhausted, shaken, battered from six days' journeying, and from summons of the whalemages, Ian had little power left of his own. But through the soul of a wizard, power could be drawn and focused, as crystal focuses light.

And Jenny's flesh remembered. Jenny's bones remembered. There was a part of her mind, her essence, that had never returned from the brief days when the form of a dragon had been given to her as a gift, and with it a dragon's magic.

Morkeleb the Black had asked her, after battle with Folcalor had burned out her own power, if she wanted to return to being a dragon again, to return with him to the Skerries of Light. What she would not do for relief, for escape from a grief she could not bear, she would do, she understood, for her children, for her sister, for her friends.

It was as if her heart remembered how to do it. Only the power was lacking.

The circle was made in what had been the temple of that nameless town on the hill; standing in its midst, Ian looked very small. Jenny mounted what had been the campanile, a ring of hollowed stones, all its floors long since burned away but still nearly sixty feet tall. The stair wound dizzily up the inner curve of the wall. From the top she could see the Hold, and the flames rising higher.

Adric was there. Maggie like a silent kitten just learning to hunt. The bandits . . .

She closed her mind to them, seeking the cold diamond perfection of a dragon's mind. Below her Ian made the passes, called the white plasma of energy from earth and stars and air, and Jenny remembered what it had felt like to draw that power through her own hands. She had thought she would have felt it, but she didn't. She only saw her son performing the gestures that focused the mind, heard now and then a snatch of the words he cried out—the names of the stars from which he sourced his power.

Will the demons feel it? she wondered. *Feel it and come swirling down on him before he finishes, to catch him through the spells he weaves?*

She couldn't tell, couldn't see.

She could only follow what he did, as if counting in her mind what should be going on.

Power flowing. Power surrounding her. Power filling the empty column of the tower and shining in the air.

She felt nothing. And her son looked very tiny on the hillside far below. The sky around her was cold blue patched with the scattered white of breaking cloud, wide and windy and empty as her bones. There was nothing in her heart to tell her that she was anything but a simple woman standing on the brink of emptiness, waiting to hear a sound that would never come.

But her mind rebuilt the memory of what it had been to be a dragon. Rebuilt the glitter of that alter-self: milk-white scales and diamond spines, wings like cloud and smoke.

A mind that desired but did not love. A heart like the one she had seen in her dream: a casket of jewels locked with a crystal tear.

The soul of a star-drake that had once been a woman.

If the sky spoke her name, she could no longer hear it. Nevertheless she spread her arms, took two running strides, and leaped from the top of the tower, calling out to the sky, to the power, *Now.*

The heat of transformation took her in its hand. Not piecemeal as a flower blooms, but whole and burning at once: wings and horns and maned bird-bill head, claws and tail and magic like a cascade of opals. The music of a name that was hers.

Desires that were not human desires. Awareness of things that no human would even consider.

Her wings sheared air, her will bearing her, as the wills of dragons did. Below her everything changed—not the burning wild beauty of demon perceptions, but clear, cold, crystal and small. A little figure in a little circle on the stone pavement of a little temple, staring up in wonder and terror and delight. She knew his name was Ian, and she knew she'd borne him nine months in her belly, and she knew she loved him—if she could remember what love was.

Not a thing of dragons.

Still there were those in the burning fortress who would die if she did not save them, and though she felt detached from them—they were after all humans, lives like short tangled ribbons that would end soon anyway—she remembered at least that she had promised someone she would keep them from being killed today.

And so she struck.

Men were running, screaming. She remembered there were demons about and so she did not use magic beyond the magic that she was, which enabled her to fly and indeed to live. But she did not need it. Wheeling in the smoky air, she plunged down over the walls, spitting the acrid burning slime that was the weapon of dragons and seeing men fall and clutch their smoking flesh, howling in pain. She recalled that as a demon she had imbibed pain, but it meant nothing to her now.

She veered close, dipped her wings, struck again. Horses flung their riders and ran away; she marked their courses with her opal eyes, remembering her hunger and thinking, *Later.* Her mind triangulated all things in the landscape: burning towers, the course of every man through the flaming shells of the village, the little cluster of men on Toadback Hill pointing and shouting. Arrows flew up from the bandits, and she sailed effortlessly over them then stooped when the shafts fell back and caught up one man in her claws, carrying him aloft and dropping him. She snatched and seized another and sent him spinning away, razored to bits.

Then there were no more men. They had fled into the woods, into the gullies, into the snowy hills beyond the village fields. She spread her wings and circled the Hold, slow and soaring on the thermals of the fire. Someone was down there that she cared about, she thought, but she could not remember who it was. Exultation filled her, a healing glory of magic in her flesh.

Magic was in her heart, which had been starved of it since summer's end.

Dragon music inundated her soul.

She lifted clear of the smoke and the shouting of men, away from a single shrill voice calling a name that had once been hers. Wind in her face, cutting the cold clouds, she flew away to the North.

Chapter 10

It was evening when John came to. He didn't know how many evenings later it was. One at least, and an endless night of sliding in and out of agony worse than the rack, worse than breaking, worse than anything he'd read about in the more appalling books that had survived the centuries.

Amayon was sitting on the fern bank beside him. A pair of long silver tweezers and what looked like a hooked needle lay blood-tipped on his knee. He was just eating the last of a clutch of wriggling, gore-clotted, finger-long things of hooks and teeth, crunching them happily, like a gourmet devouring crayfish. He was smiling.

"They're better," he informed John, "the bigger they get. I didn't know that. They absorb pain, too."

John rolled over and groped with fingers that would barely move for the ink bottle, still on its ribbon around his neck. The Demon Queen must have placed a wyrd on it, he thought, that kept Amayon from simply throwing it away.

"Oh, don't be an ass," the demon said as he caught a bore worm that was attempting to crawl away through the grass. He crunched it in his small white teeth. "It was only luck that you were able to get the bottle open when these things got you. Do you think you're going to be any nimbler the next time you blunder into something you think looks pretty and harmless? If you do think that, I wonder that you've lasted this long. Lady Jenny's help, I expect."

"That's it," John said, trying to breathe. "She's been rescuin' me every day of me life and barely has time to make bread or braid her hair, and fair fratched she's been about it, too." He felt nauseated, and there were small deep cuts on his arms, on his chest where his shirt had been torn open, on his belly and on the calves of his legs. He felt dried blood on his temple and assumed there were cuts on his neck and face as well. They were starting to bruise up, too. He'd look, he thought, like he'd fallen down a flight of stairs. Everything hurt.

He dumped eight flax seeds into the ink bottle and heard Amayon spit curses at him as he dropped off to exhausted sleep again.

He woke feeling a little better. Possibly the Queen had laid some magic on his flesh that would let him recover from injuries sustained in Hells; perhaps it was one of Miss Mab's spells, written on him before he passed for the first time behind the burning mirror. He half expected to find evidence of some other devilment Amayon had performed while he was incapacitated with pain—pouring out or befouling his food or water, for instance, or smashing his spectacles—but found nothing. He wondered what inducement Aohila had extended for Amayon's good behavior.

It would help to know, he thought, painfully tying his shirt together and rebuckling his doublet. If magic differed from one Hell to another, there was going to be some point at which the spells she'd placed on the demon would fail, and then, John thought, he'd better watch out.

And if Amayon broke free, then what? What was freedom, to the children of Hell? Would he return to Adromelech? How much did the Lord of the Sea-wights know about Folcalor's activities in the realm of mortal men? Perhaps he'd return to Folcalor? Whose side was Amayon on, the little weasel?

Or would he just stay on in whatever Hell he found himself, a nasty little swamp gyre who tormented humans and demons alike for the pleasure it gave him, until the lord of that particular Hell sucked him up?

He supposed Amayon was right about his needing the demon's help to get through paradise to the place where—according to the dim dreams rising into the back of his mind—the gateway to the next Hell would lie. It was enormous labor even to walk, and when he cut a sapling in a thicket the stump of it spat smoking black ichor at him that he barely dodged. Aversin generally carried a couple of silk scarves in his pockets for use as anything from tourniquets to strainers, and one of these he wrapped around the wood to protect his hand as he limped along.

Fat lot of use I'll be, he thought, *when I find this chap I'm supposed to bring back to her.*

The chap who killed the girl with lavender hair in the Hell of Walls.

The thought was not enough to get him to release Amayon from the bottle.

Memories rose disturbingly to Aversin's mind as he passed through the scented beauty of groves and streamlets, as if he had walked this way already and taken careful note of the route. He sensed there were other things in his mind as well, things he'd dreamed in the mirror chamber and wouldn't recall until he required the knowledge. *And you couldn't have given me a bit of a word about butterflies?* he thought bitterly.

There were things in his satchel now, along with the bits and pieces he'd taken from Jenny's workbox, that he'd never seen before and had no idea how to use, or why: an earthenware pot of what appeared to be ointment, a small heavy cylinder of black metal and glass.

Master Bliaud had given him things as well: thick-linked chains of silver, gold coins minted by various kings of Bel. The weight of it cut a channel of pain in his shoulder and sapped his breath, and he would rather have had the equivalent weight of water and food. Birdsong rippled from the trees as he waded through summer flowers; once he heard voices, like young maidens laughing, and he went to ground in a cave and didn't move until that gay music faded with the fading of the afternoon.

The light departed, and the light returned; but there was neither sun nor moon, and the velvety lapis sky was without stars.

Such, he was coming to understand, was the nature of Hell.

The marks on his flesh—the traced spells of the Demon Queen—shone with a kind of pale silvery shimmer among the bruises. They were visible at all times here, not just now and then as they were in the world of humankind. He wondered again if Amayon bore such marks beneath that quilted velvet doublet and what the Demon Queen had done to him.

Perhaps it wasn't surprising that the demon would take vengeance where he could on the man who'd sent him behind the mirror into the Hell of his enemies.

He still didn't open the bottle.

He reached at last a place among the trees where a waterfall tumbled sparkling from high rocks to a moss-cushioned pool—the place where his memories ended, as if he had reached a mountain's top and saw no further road beyond. From his pocket he took the dark fragment of beveled glass he'd found in the Hell of Winds, and using this as a mirror he searched the glen, one tiny portion at a time. It took him nearly two hours of aching concentration, but at last he found it: the sigil of the gate. He'd made a note of its shape and position on their entry into paradise, and into the Hell of Winds before that.

It was written on the waterfall itself, as if flickering light shone there from behind. Something underwater tried to take a bite out of his calf as he waded through the bright laughing pool to trace the sigil with his fingers, as he'd seen Amayon do. Later he found tooth marks on his boot from something with a mouth as large as a small wolf's.

The waterfall turned to smoke where the sigil had been. He stepped through it into what lay beyond.

It took John almost three days to guess the secret of the Hell of Walls.

He might, he thought later, have understood it sooner had he let Amayon out of the bottle and asked his advice. But he doubted it. Amayon would have taken too much delight in confusing him, and he would not have believed anything the demon said.

It was a Hell of noise, of walls, of crowds of creatures that looked human. It was certainly the place he had seen in the puddle in the mirror chamber: the place where, somewhere, he would encounter the Demon Queen's absconding lover in his hall of golden lamps. *Another reason to keep Amayon prisoner,* he thought, huddling into a blind and bricked-up doorway while the featureless black sky rivered down stinging rain. The demon would almost certainly have been able to locate Aversin's quarry more quickly; he would have captured him, bound him, taken him to Aohila in return for his own freedom and left John a prisoner in the Hell of Walls forever.

That first night, he thought death would have been preferable.

A man—or what appeared to be a man—detached itself from the endless, jostling crowd that joggled and yammered in the canyon of colored light among endless walls and crept toward the niche where Aversin sheltered from the rain. All the seeming people wore glistening caps and cloaks as they scurried on unimaginable errands in and out of buildings that lost themselves far overhead in darkness and cloud; this creature was no different. But it—he—smelled of filth, and his stubbled face was eroded with sores. He smiled a vacant smile, visible in the light that reflected down the alley from rectangular blocks of white light, like the hothwais of the gnomes, suspended above the streets.

John half drew his sword and let the blade catch the light. The shabby man halted, ankle-deep in the water that flooded every street and alley hereabouts, and for a moment his hands wavered uncertainly before his face, as if he was confused by what he saw. Then he shambled away and crawled into one of the great dark metal refuse containers that lined the alley, creeping with roaches and mold.

John did not sleep that night. At one point he wondered if in fact this place had day or night. The jostling crowds in the colored glow of the streets never seemed to lessen. Mosquitoes—actual mosquitoes, he realized shortly—swarmed in whining clouds. Later, a small band of young men and women dodged along the alley, shabbily clothed, their skin brightly painted, smelling of dirt and bearing things they handled like weapons. He heard them speak, and the voices in his mind formed words, as had the voices of the hunters in the Hell of the Shining Things.

Demons? he wondered. Servants of the lord of this unimaginable Hell? Or prisoners as the hunters had been—as he himself was, and would be forever if he could not find the man he sought.

Day came. The rain ceased for a time, but the gray blank overhead smelled of more. The crowds increased, unbelievably. Warily, John moved out among them, and though they gave him wide berth, he wasn't the only one he saw heavily armed. The noise was dizzying, the sides of the buildings plastered and patched with garish lights and flashing panels of color. Panels of pictures, too, that moved as if living: tiny as a thumbnail or towering a dozen stories up the side of a building whose uppermost floors were wreathed in low-hanging cloud.

These pictures spoke, and music—if it was music—rivered from them, but because the speech was artificially produced he could not understand what was being said. These moving images seemed to be a series of short plays or demonstrations. Watching them, he knew to put the ointment from the Queen's terra-cotta pot on his face, for his skin, which had itched within hours of coming through the waterfall, was reddened as if burned, and he was nearly bitten to death by mosquitoes.

He had no time to waste, he knew. He had food and water for a week of short rations, three days of which would be needed to get him back through paradise and the Hell of Winds. So he hunted through alleys that were only slots between the buildings.

There was no end, apparently, to the city. Certainly in all the time that he spent there he never saw anything that was not walls and pavement and pictures mouthing senseless words and noise. Sometimes he would enter the buildings–heart hammering, for he wasn't entirely certain that they were truly buildings–but many of them seemed to have no doors. He was for a long while unwilling to descend into the tunnels from which people, if they were people, poured constantly, for he could hear roaring and clattering from below, like the passage of great beasts or machines.

On the third night he found the place where the girl had been killed. The night had turned cold and the wind came up, unfelt if one traveled the avenues but howling strong enough to knock a sick man down at the crossing of every street. Tiny waves raced across the murky water that stood in the streets, the water itself pushed by the storm far beyond its usual limitations, lapping the dark buildings, the metal bases of the grillwork walkways and duckboards built up from the older pavements, the scarified feet of the elevated trackways where dark trains roared by. Aversin was aware of the gangs that prowled the storm-blasted alleys, creeping into areas where the glaring lights failed.

He had his lantern with him, however, and by its wavering light was able to recognize the place he'd seen in his dreaming. The pattern and shapes that scribbled every foot of the walls were the same–obscene drawings, gigantic writing, simplified pictograms of things he did not understand.

It was easy to see the bloodstains.

The wind's screaming grew louder. The water splashed softly around John's boots, and rats–the only animals he had seen here so far–plopped and scuttered as he neared the huge dark shapes that had flanked the woman in his vision. Rubbish bins, he knew now, the size of the poorer houses in Alyn Village. Kneeling, he fished gingerly under one of them and found the heel of the dead woman's shoe: vivid pink with chevrons of black, unmistakable. The lantern's light gleamed on something else under the scummy water. Taking off his iron-backed gloves he held the light down close and with his fingernails picked up a broken, flat link of an ornamental chain.

Gold. Next to it, nearly buried in nameless muck, were broken fragments of what appeared to be glass, thin and infinitely fine. It was the first glass he'd seen, for most things—furniture, dishes, clothing found in the refuse bins—all seemed to be made of the same stuff: *plex,* he had heard it called, the same word used to describe either hard stuff or soft. He probed farther and brought up the curled remains of what looked like a glass shell.

For a long time he stood with the thing cupped in his hand beneath the lantern's shuddering light.

Sea-wights.

Maybe he should have expected it, he thought, looking around at the inky shadows, the wavery golden ghosts of the lantern's light. God knew there was water enough. If the archwight Adromelech had sent Folcalor to enslave the mages in the world of humankind—if he'd long ago given humankind his help in sealing Aohila and her demons behind the mirror—why wouldn't he have sent some other wight to make trouble for the inhabitants of some other Hell?

Small odds for his own survival either way. As he carefully stowed the remains of the shell in his doublet, his fingers brushed the ink bottle, and he wondered, *Can Amayon call his brethren?*

Can he touch the dreams of the humans here, as he touched the dreams of that poor lad Browson in the Darrow Bottoms?

One more thing to worry about. He had only a day's food if he wanted any hope of making it through the Hell of Winds, and no clue as to where to go from here. Would Amayon know of a way to contact Aohila? Was that what she was counting on him to do? To eat or drink in Hell was to put yourself in the power of its lord, and he couldn't imagine what the lord of this place would be like.

Wind yowled around the corner, whipped his long wet hair, and put out the candle in the lantern's horn frame.

Blackness swallowed him. Sea-wights would be watching him, he thought—plus the demons native to this Hell, servants of its lord.

Someone in a room many stories above the alley lit a candle—the shaky light was unmistakable. John wondered where they'd gotten it, for he'd seen neither sheep nor bees in Hell. The light drew his eyes, then guided them past the window itself to the black cutout of the skyline hundreds of feet overhead.

The gale had shredded the cloud cover that he had for three days mistaken for sky. Now the rags of gypsy clouds fled across the slot between building and building, harried by the remains of the storm.

And between them, beyond them, stars.

The Watcher, with his shining belt and his red-eyed dog. The Hay-wain perpetually circling the North Star.

True stars and true sky, not the strange colorless nowhere of Hell. The waning moon was just rising, as it should have been three days after he'd seen it over the midnight ruins of Ernine.

The understanding burst upon him that the human beings who thronged this place were not akin to the lost hunters who roved the Hell of the Shining Things. The disappearance of the Demon Queen's marks from his skin did not mean the presence of a magic greater in this place than hers.

He was not, he realized, in Hell at all, but in a mortal world like his own.

An old man named Docket who ran a bookstore helped him find a room. "The very same thing happened to my brother's son," he said, shaking his snowy head as he tidied the bright-colored plex squares called chips, the finger-long 'zines—whatever 'zines were—and the ancient, fusty volumes of bound paper and plex that heaped the shelves of the farthest of his little third-floor rooms. "The big drug companies just don't keep good enough track of their formulas. Now, my brother's son ate candy that was mostly phrenzoicaine—which is pretty harmless as long as you go on taking it and don't switch brands—but that reacted with some Powder Blue a friend gave him at a party, and for weeks he hadn't the slightest idea about where he lived or who he was. He's lucky his wife was there to get him home. He still has short-term memory problems, though I think he'd be better off if he didn't keep eating Buddle Pies. Those things have CPN in them and that just plays hob with everything else you take. Absolute hob."

He patted John's arm comfortingly. "You'll remember in time."

"Thanks," John said, and made a mental note to avoid candy, Powder Blue, and Buddle Pies—whatever Powder Blue and Buddle Pies were.

"Fourteen hundred creds a month," the landlady of the run-down building old Docket took him to said. "Thirty, if you want the screen covered." She gestured to the enormous moving picture that dominated one of the room's windowless walls. "That's high, I know," she added, as if expecting argument, "but that's what the agencies charge for subsidy, and they won't take a day-to-day prorate. Here's the volume. Rent goes up fifty credits for every day the volume goes below five."

She touched a button at the bottom right of the screen. The voices and the brain-numbing music could be lowered but never completely eliminated. It helped that John hadn't the least idea of what those people on the screen were saying, because if he had, he was certain he'd have been driven genuinely insane in hours. He wondered how many murders were committed or apartments were sacked simply because that endless yammering covered any hope of hearing an invader.

John paid her with a piece of the Demon Queen's silver, and the way her eyes lit up—and Docket's bulged with shock—he guessed that precious metals were as uncommon in the city as wood, leather, wool, or anything else that came from nature.

When she skittered away, clutching the coin as if it were a jewel, he was aware of the old man regarding him with uncertain wariness in the white glare of the single square of illuminated tile—ether lights, Docket called them—that filled the room. "You want to be careful, my friend," the old man said gently. "Best not to let people know you have things like that, if you have any more of them. The deep-zone gangs have informants everywhere here, and they're not to be trifled with."

John had already encountered the gangs that came in by scutter boat from the flooded streets and empty ruins drowned fathoms deep. He understood, from things Docket had told him, that in addition to buying the more potent and unpredictable drugs like Blood Red and Lovehammer, they made stimulants of their own and as a result behaved with unpredictable violence if crossed.

"I'll be careful," he said.

There had to be someone, he thought as the old man left. He braced the only chair against the door. Someone knew the girl who'd been killed, or someone had seen something or knew something. Had the killing been entirely random the Demon Queen would not have shown it to him. He needed a place from which to watch and listen, to learn the signals that were a hunter's livelihood and life.

That narrow strip where she'd been killed, the streets and alleys where the water lay ankle-deep and sometimes not even that, was the place to begin.

The girl had been well dressed. That pink shoe he'd found was new, and if silver was treasured, gold must be valued here like life itself. The girl had been driven into the alley, but she'd come from higher and drier ground beyond.

And somewhere in those wealthier zones, a man in dark spectacles sat in a green leather chair, fingering gold.

Amayon could probably find him in a night.

John leaned one shoulder against the wall and contemplated the frolicking images on the ad screen—the bouncing and looming pictures of boots or bottles or faces—and touched, beneath his shirt, the hot angry heart of the ink bottle. Dimly, as if from the end of an infinite corridor, he thought he could hear the demon cursing him.

An incomprehensible place, he thought, but at least a place that was neither evil nor good—only dangerous and interesting and a hell of a tale to tell Jenny if he managed to get out of it alive. He prowled into the tiny plex cubicle and twisted and poked at the levers there and was rewarded—to his delighted astonishment—with a miniature waterfall of hot clean water such as he'd seen on the ad screens.

I'll definitely have to figure out how this works before I go back, he thought, stripping out of his sodden and filthy clothes and stepping in. *I wonder if we can rig one up at the Hold.*

Chapter 11

"Demons walk the streets of this city, my friends." Bort TenEighty leaned impressively across the table littered with cups—plex table and plex cups, since the House of Two Fragrances wavered somewhere in that deadly neverland between a coffee house and a mere café—and stabbed a thick finger at the other members of the League of the White Black Bird. "I've seen them. Mark my words, it's they who took poor old Docket."

Measuring coffee beans into one machine that would grind them, dumping the resulting grit into another machine that would actually do the brewing, engulfed in an aromatic miasma of steam and heat and thumping music that almost but not quite drowned the ad screens that took up most of two walls, Aversin listened. Not a lot of people in the city—which he still sometimes thought of as the Hell of Walls—were able to filter through conflicting sounds to pick out those in a single timbre, like a voice, and in any case the Demon Queen's spell of comprehension definitely helped. Nearly everyone drinking coffee in the brightly lit green-and-yellow room either had a personal sound environment system—PSE, for short—or had chipped their favorite recordings into the table players. Sometimes, John was amused and irritated to observe, both.

"You really think so?" SeventyeightFourFive asked. John had heard his name variously as *Poot* or *Garrypoot* or *Gargies* from the other members of the league, but SeventyeightFourFive came up on his cred when it was his turn to pay for the coffee. He was a thin young man with a long nose who always affected black clothing. The corneas of his eyes had a yellow tinge that Tisa Three—short for ThreeThirtyfive—who worked with John behind the counter, said was typical of cut-rate Priority Four plex eye jobs, whatever that meant.

"He's a wizard," Bort said. "Who else would have done such a thing?" His voice dropped, but he was so accustomed to dominating conversation—as he did every morning and evening with various members of the league at their regular corner table—that he could be clearly heard. "He said he'd seen them, too. Late in the night they creep along the verges of the wall or glow where they slip into the water: things like silvery lizards, shining in the dark. Double vanilla latte tall no-fat mocha cinnamon burned," he added into the table mike.

"Get that, would you, Moondog?" Tisa asked. It was the League of the White Black Bird that had started calling John *Moondog,* after a character in a book: a professor of literature who went mad and believed himself to be a dragon slayer. The staff of the House of Two Fragrances had very quickly picked up the nickname.

John didn't mind. He'd found employment mostly as a means of learning: Had he been in a strange city in his own world, he would have worked as potboy in a tavern, just to listen to what people said. *Not up to Jen's trick of spreadin' her awareness over the countryside and hearin' voices on the wind, but we do what we can.*

"The wet zone's shifted in the past two years," Clea Seventy-sevenNine said. "Docket's store is definitely inside it now."

John's attention sharpened. He knew now that the area where the girl had been killed was called the wet zone. The House of Two Fragrances, being in an older building, had actual windows, which looked out onto Economy Square, and the glare of the reflected neon outlined Clea's long nose, her awkward chin, and the unkempt tail of gray hair that hung wet down her back. "There's weird folks in there." She was the oldest of the league, a tall rawboned woman who carried her weight in her belly like a man. Her dark eyes were kind and her voice soft. Among the excruciatingly fashionable women who patronized the H2F during this, the evening shift, she stood out in her homeliness, her dumpiness, and the mismatched brightness of her garb.

It was the same with all the members of the league, a loose congeries of friends and acquaintances who seemed to have taken the big corner table as their headquarters and meeting place at any hour of the day or night. The computers they often brought and plugged into the table outlet were good quality, according to Tisa Three. But they dressed like the poor, or like clerks and shop walkers and inputters, in loose baggy pants or anonymous tights, sloppy tunics or sweaters, plex ponchos bought from streetcorner bins and cracking already with a month's use. They were among the very few who didn't dye their hair either gaudy taffy-bright hues or jet black, and as far as John could ascertain, most of them eschewed the drugs that were nearly universal in the city. Tisa and the rest of the staff at the H2F complained about this, because most of the preblended coffees came mixed with White Light or Lovehammer or whatever the bliss of the day might be.

"And a lot of weird drugs," Clea went on. "This might just be a case of some poor goon getting his dust cut with drain cleaner and taking it out on whoever crossed his path."

"Nothing was missing." Bort shook his head and stroked the savage auburn bush of his beard. "And nothing was disturbed, except for one book—SeventyfiveTwoOne's *A Companion Beyond the Limits.* It had fallen on the floor behind the counter."

"Woo, spooky." Tisa squinnied to the machine beside John and mimed a sarcastic gesture of panic shock. "You listening to those guys?" She was a delicately pretty girl, thin with the manicured thinness fashionable among the rich and among those who wanted to look enough like the rich to be accepted by them. Her hair was dyed hyperfashionable snowy white—like the girls in the ad screens—and was dressed in tiny braids and lacquered loops held in place by gold clips with enameled blue butterflies. Under the transparent finish of one of the more expensive "masks"—as the skin ointments were called—her face was painted to enhance its natural pallor. She was, John guessed, seventeen or eighteen. He also guessed she prostituted herself part-time, as many girls—and boys, too—did along the wet zone's fringes: not for money, but for clothes and jewelry, for gym or cinema subscriptions, for occasional rent or com-co bills, or for hits of high-priced drugs. She certainly hadn't paid for that gold-and-blue hair clip herself, or the bracelets of real gold that circled her knobby wrists.

"Shouldn't I?"

Tisa rolled her eyes. "Moondog, *honestly,* what manhole did you come out of?" She handed a gray-suited salaryman a triple-strength espresso and a muffin with a brilliant smile—and a copy of a card printed with her com number—and turned back to John a moment later.

"Those guys are weird," she explained patiently. She reached up and straightened the collar of the shabby, cinder-colored shirt he wore. "They're crazy. You've got to be careful. They all think they're *wizards* or something. I've *heard* them."

"And that's worse than doin' your job and not thinkin' anythin' at all?" He nodded toward the clientele in the main body of the little bistro, most of whom were snatching a quick break after their regular work hours before returning to spend an extra two or three hours doing whatever they could to impress their superiors with their diligence, whether there was actual work to be performed or not. A couple of laborers lingered over coffee, heads adorned with holo-hats that played over and over fragments of advertisements—one of the more annoying ether-based miracles. There were students, too, from the art, 'ware, and tech schools, jacking their notebooks and PSE systems into the table relays, surrounding themselves in the noise of their choice to drown the clamor of those whose backs bent studiously twelve inches from their own.

"No," Tisa protested with the indignant promptness of one trained by years of advertising to believe that she was freer, different from, and better than others and therefore deserved to buy a more expensive mask or some Pixilon treatments to make her hair longer and shinier. "But I've been in that old guy's crazy store."

SixtysevenThree, the evening fetch-and-carry man, came through the door behind the counter, and Tisa and John slipped back through to take their break, climbing a narrow stair of high-impact plex to the storeroom above. The storeroom was situated just below the relay chamber where crystals refracted, channeled, and focused the ether that powered the air circulation, lighting, water pumps, and computers for the entire building, and the concentrated vibration there gave John a headache if he stayed more than a few minutes. He suspected this was one reason why NinetysixThou, the manager of the H2F, had made it the employees' break room.

There was a relay crystal in the room itself to power the coffee machines and table jacks. It was about three inches long and the thickness of Aversin's little finger, unobtrusive in its gold-wired cage in the middle of the low ceiling. The gold cage was, of course, surrounded by a far more substantial lockbox of perforated metaplast, and there were two more metaplast ceiling boxes installed behind the stores of coffee and filters and drugs, ceiling boxes that John was pretty sure housed illegal relay crystals to pull energy for which NinetysixThou wasn't paying Consolidated Power. On his first day of work, a week and a half ago, he'd climbed up on the table and examined the crystals as well as he could. They seemed to be identical and, he'd later learned, were manufactured as casually as potters in Alyn Village manufactured cups. His headache had increased when he'd come within a few feet of the lockbox.

With crystals by the dozen in every building and more relays of them glittering on their thin masts above every street, no wonder everyone in the city used Pink Sunshine and Let's Get Happy and a dozen other substances to remain calm enough to function.

"That old guy, Docket ThreeFiftyfiveTen?" Her voice tilted inquiringly at the end of the sentence as if to ask if he was familiar with the shabby bibliophile, but in the next breath she went on as if assuming he was not. "I mean, if he's a wizard and all that–if they're *all* supposed to be wizards–how come he's running this crummy bookstore and living in one room in the back? How come TenEighty is like forty-five or something and all he does is input and teach a city rec class? That SeventysevenNine woman still lives with her mother! If they can do magic, how come they're not rich?"

She perched on the corner of the table and dotted Sero-Yum on her tongue to kill her hunger, followed by a couple of dabs of Pink Sunshine–a gift from an admirer–to make it through the rest of the shift. "I know you don't read, but that store he runs is full of *books* and stuff–really old paper books, I mean–about how to make magic and call elemental spirits. And those guys *believe* it! You see them sitting around comparing recipes for how to make gold out of breakfast flakes or how to talk to houseplants. They're losers, Moondog."

"Maybe magic's not about money?"

"Oh, come *on*!" She leaned back a little, crossed her long legs, and considered him as if trying to add up the shabby clothing and old-fashioned spectacles, the scars on his arms and the gray in his long hair. She'd been the one who, at their mutual landlady's request, had gotten him the job at the House of Two Fragrances, and it was her artless evaluations of the various drugs, behavior stimulators, and addictive foods and candies that had alerted him that paradise wasn't the only place where nothing was as it seemed. "What's cooler than money? And let me tell you, the boyfriend who's picking me up tonight has *really* got money. What are you, some kind of philosopher?"

"Some kind," John assented with a grin.

Old Docket had accepted without comment or surprise Aversin's disappointment that the volumes in his shop, and even vocal recordings, were incomprehensible to him and had spent hours telling him how the world worked, something even the people born in the city mostly didn't know. John suspected the old man's advice about gangs and scams had already saved his life, if for no other reason than that it had permitted him to keep Amayon bottled up and out of mischief.

And now the old man was gone.

Demons.

With the conclusion of his shift John walked Tisa to her rendezvous with Lots of Zeroes, as she referred to her latest inamorato, through the slanting rain across Economy Square. Vendors, salarypersons, and students jostled him on their way into, or out of, the subway and el-train stations situated amid a tangle of 'zine racks and steaming snack carts, flickering holo-hats, chattering PSEs. On every building enormous ad screens trumpeted the virtues of Embody shoes ("The circles on the soles make the magic!") or Ravage clothing or Devour'Em candy or any number of drugs–not that it was always easy to tell what was being advertised–and, lower down, twisting ropes of neon spelled out incomprehensible letters over the windows and doors of bistros and shops, a constant battery of color, shape, and sound.

Parting from the girl at the far side of the square, he turned down Old 21st Boulevard, the thin puddles of the square's pavement deepening gradually underfoot as the crowds diminished. By the time the boulevard crossed 187th Avenue, there were no more ten-story ad screens, and the buildings shortened and narrowed. Past 186th, water stood in the street to the level of the curb. The air reeked of sewage, chemicals, and salt, and it droned with mosquitoes.

Three or four years ago, according to Tisa, 184th Avenue had been the official boundary of the wet zone, the street her mother had told her never to cross, though of course she had. The buildings along it were mostly tall and mostly "secure," as they said–meaning they lacked windows–and such windows as there were glowed with the white even light of ether spots and tiles. Duckboards had been set up on bricks. Cofferdams raised the doorsills of the biggest shops, permitting them to continue on the first floor.

Metal shutters or grills covered the few street-level windows. Distantly, in the pitch-black alleyways, John could hear the whistling of the gangs.

Old Docket's bookstore occupied four rooms of what had been long ago a luxury flat on the third floor of a building on the Avenue of Galaxies. Aversin had a thirty-gram crystal flashlight that had cost him most of his first week's paycheck, and he flicked it to high to examine the prefab plex stairway that ran from the drowned sidewalk grills up to Docket's door. John played the light along the edges of the steps and particularly on the railings and the jambs of the door but found no sign of struggle. The door itself was unlocked, but the shop's front room hadn't been entered. If gangs had been responsible for Docket's disappearance, the computer would be gone, obsolete as it was. Used chips sold for a half-cred a pound. Moreover, according to Old Docket, most gang members favored a mix of Brain Candy and Lovehammer, a combination that inclined its users to vandalism.

The small room was lined, floor to ceiling, with scuffed racks of red plex filled with book chips. Each thin, smooth chip was about the length of John's forefinger and half as wide, inscribed with the title in meaningless symbols. *Popular hooey,* Old Docket had scoffed, gesturing about him that first evening. *Three-quarters of them are assists. Maybe you could read an assist? They got a vocal track to them so you can follow along with reading. Though most of the gangboys, they can't even follow those unless they're rewritten to be simple. The assists are the purple chips,* the old man had added as John fingered a chip wonderingly. *The yellow are rewrites.*

Four readers, their screens white, crowded together at the front of the shop before mangled green plex chairs. With Old Docket's help John had tried to make sense out of a purple assist, a novel called *Thunderhump.* The recorded language on book chips would not speak to his mind any more than the transmissions of the ad screens did.

What, if anything, he wondered, playing the flashlight's hard white beam around the three-sided polyplex counter, had the old man told the League of the White Black Bird about him?

A book lay on the floor in the fenced-in square between the counters, shoved nearly under the computer. John swung himself over the counter and pulled it out. It was thin and small but a real book, similar to what he knew and treasured at home. It had a hundred or so sof-plast pages covered in a hard shell of blue plex.

Had it been dropped there in the scuffle? In spite of Tisa's disparaging scorn, Old Docket kept the place scrupulously neat. Books of all formats–actuals with pages, three different sizes of disks, old-fashioned thick chips and the newer thin chips–heaped the shelves and edges of the readers in every room, but nothing was ever suffered to lie on the floor or pile up on chairs.

Not being able to read was a hindrance, of course. John left the book on the corner of the counter and walked down the narrow hall to the room where the actuals were kept. Its window had been bricked up as a security measure at some time, and an ad screen partly covered the spot. The amount the advertisers paid of any apartment's rent was calculated by the number of hours the screen was left at half volume or higher. This one was turned down to a volume exquisitely calibrated to balance with the rent.

All things considered, it was a miracle he heard anyone else enter the shop.

"How could they have gotten in?" a voice in the front room asked, and John hit the dimmer on his flashlight and stepped back fast into the shadows between the bookshelves. With the ad screen displaying seminude girls playing doink to a bouncily brain-numbing tune–*what are they advertising? sand? doink? pink shoes? the girls?*–it was impossible to hear sounds in the front room, and of course now he could not turn down the sound without giving his presence away. But he felt the vibration of feet on the flooring and edged into the room where Docket kept outmoded disks and chips, staying behind the archway that led into the front room again.

It was Bort TenEighty, Garrypoot, Clea, and another of the league–a leathery, bearded man called Shamble who wore a laborer's cheap bright poly-knit and a holo-hat that enacted and reenacted the image of a very fat man exclaiming, bug-eyed, the once-comical punchline of some incomprehensible commercial play.

It was Garrypoot who had spoken. "Wouldn't there be some sign if it were demons?" the boy went on. "Smashed furniture?"

"You think demons are the way they look in the vids, dear boy," Bort reproved. He turned over the chips stacked along the edge of the nearest reader. "As if any creature would traipse around the city seven feet tall with special effects zapping out of its horns and eyes and tail. They wear the bodies of men—men with eyes like broken glass. How do you think they've been able to do the alley murders?"

"That's demons?" Shamble came over from turning down the front-room ad screen. The jingly doink tune behind John sounded all the louder. "The freelancers in the deep zone make crazy drugs."

"If it was drugs," Garrypoot added. "It might have been some kind of initiation rite."

"It was demons," Bort said somberly. Like John, Bort was near-sighted and one of the few people in the city to wear spectacles. Old Docket had told John, when he'd pointed out the various members of the league one day, that for some reason Bort was unable to undergo the procedure to correct the poor eyesight with which at least three-quarters of humanity was born. His spectacles consisted of a single strip of crystalline plex that fit his heavy, dark-browed face from temple to temple, modeled over the bridge of his lumpy nose. Its curved lens was subtly faceted, so the pale blue eyes behind it always appeared to be shifting their size and placement. "They eat pain. Live on it, as we live on food."

"Well, not really." John stepped around the archway behind the fat man's shoulder; Bort and the others nearly jumped out of their shoes. "They don't eat pain anymore than we eat music. But they live on it and for it, the way opera geeks and rock fans live on and for what comes out of their systems." He scratched the side of his nose. "Only of course music doesn't destroy those who make it. Not right away, anyhow."

Garrypoot's eyes bulged. "You know!" he whispered reverently, and Bort tilted his head, regarding the lithe unprepossessing form from behind his faceted band.

"What know you of demons, Moondog?"

"A bit." John held out the blue-covered book. "What's this one called?"

"It's Bransle's–" Garrypoot began, and Bort laid a hand on his young friend's shoulder to silence him.

"Why do you want to know?"

"'Cause me guess is the demons pretended they were customers." John crossed behind him to the counter and pointed to where he'd found the book. "There were others on the counter?"

Bort nodded toward one of the reader tables. "Just that. SeventyfiveTwoOne's."

"Any way of findin' out who bought 'em?"

"I could tap into the cred numbers," Garrypoot offered. "They'd be filed in the computer, and I could trace the buyers."

"If the demons were fool enough to let Docket put their cred into the reader," Bort said. "I wouldn't, were it me." Garrypoot, who'd come around the counter already and flipped the power toggle, looked at John inquiringly, asking what to do next.

"I notice there are no empty spaces on the shelves," John said. "It looks like Docket had 'em out and ready for a customer who'd queried beforehand. It's what I'd do, if I wanted to meet him here after closing hours."

For a moment Bort and Garrypoot looked at one another. Then Bort said, "Check."

While the younger man called file name after file name to the softly glowing screen in search of recent correspondence from the Op-Link, Bort asked again, more quietly, "What do you know of demons? Don't tell me you're one of us?"

"And who," John asked, even more softly, "is this *us* you're talkin' of? Wizards?"

"In a manner of speaking." Bort folded his arms and settled his chin in its deep scraggy beard; he was heavy and pudgy, but oddly powerful despite cheap, ill-fitting clothing and the sour air of failure. "Surely you've seen how now and then a black bird will be hatched that isn't black but white? And how the other black birds peck it and drive it from the flock because they cannot endure its whiteness?"

"Well, it ain't so much an aesthetic choice as a defense," John remarked, realizing as he spoke that the language used in the city had no word that distinguished raven from crow from blackbird. They were all *black birds*. The only other birds he'd seen were the carnivorous pigeons that infested the city as rats did, and what were called *wild birds*, meaning any of a dozen varieties of sparrow. "Black birds *do* flock, you know, and a white one's goin' to get 'em seen in the trees by somethin' big and nasty and hungry, which I hope isn't the case with you and your friends and me."

"Oh." The heavy man looked momentarily nonplused. "Oh, that's why they do it? Not the only reason, of course," he went on, swiftly resuming his ponderous dignity. "And in any case the metaphor remains valid. We are those born misfits in this world–born with an understanding, a sensitivity to, forces and emanations beyond the comprehension of the average run of humankind. We understand that there are things–powers–beyond what human eyes can see."

"Magic?" John shoved his hands behind his belt buckle and leaned his back against the counter. "Or stuff like what keeps the lights goin' and how come we can see whacko games and hockey that're taking place a couple thousand miles from here?"

Bort waved impatiently at the ad screen. "Plasmic ether was the refuge, the fallback, of those who craved cheap and easy solutions," he said. "It's a natural force, like steam or gravity or electricity. But I believe that its very pervasiveness has contributed to the downfall, the death, of true magic."

"Magic did exist," Shamble added, his weak blue eyes catching a fragment of neon from outside and seeming to burn in the gloom. On his head the fat man did a thousandth bug-eyed double take and mouthed the catch phrase that had made the image famous. "We know it did. It has to have. And we who were born with it still in us, in a world where it no longer functions, are condemned to a lifetime of being misunderstood."

"The great mages have all been persecuted," Bort agreed. He sounded as if persecution were at least recognition of specialness. "The knowledge has been passed down in secret, corrupted by those who do not understand. But the wise, like Old Docket, kept it safe." He gestured toward the back room, to the stair that ascended to a further floor, where the old bookseller had had his cluttered sleeping chamber.

"And in the past thirty years, with the Op-Link, we've been able to contact others like ourselves, in all parts of the world," Clea added. "There are areas and nodes on the Link where the children of magic come to trade experience and advice with one another. The Link may be able to help us find Docket, or learn about demons–"

"Or let the demons learn about you." John had heard about the Op-Link from Old Docket, though it made as little sense to him as personal enhancement institutes or embodiment training.

Bort drew back, startled. "I– What? Why?" He had clearly not realized that Docket's disappearance might have anything to do with him.

John sighed. After a lifetime in the Winterlands it was difficult to remember sometimes that there were people who didn't look through doors before stepping out. "Listen. Last summer I was twilkin' near killed because a demon lord set about collectin' mages. He combed the Realm for 'em, tricked 'em out of hiding. His demons took over their bodies, and he kept their souls. Now you tell me the likes of you are spreadin' word about how you're wizards all over the public computer lines, and you don't think . . ."

"I've found the book titles." Garrypoot's voice broke across John's words. The youth looked back over his shoulder, the pale glow of the screen playing across his ratlike face. "Moondog was right, Bort. Both the Bransle and the *Companion* were mentioned in the same correspondence, two days ago, asking Docket to wait after closing. The message was signed Wan ThirtyoneFourFour."

"ThirtyoneFourFour?" Bort's heavy shoulders dropped, and for an instant he resembled the fat comic actor hovering faintly above Shamble's yellow cap. "*ThirtyoneFourFour?* Are you sure?"

"I traced the log-on code," Garrypoot said. He looked scared. "It was a genuine transmission."

Bort and Garrypoot looked at one another disbelievingly, then at Clea, at Shamble, at John.

"All right," John said after a moment. "So who's this Wan when he's at home? D'you know him?"

Clea laughed, as at an absurdity. Bort only shook his head. "Not being millionaires, of course we've never met. But we've heard of him on the news. Everyone has."

"Wan ThirtyoneFourFour is the first man to come back from the dead," Clea said.

Chapter 12

"Mother."

She heard their voices, far-off and clear. The dragon dreams in which she slept were like sleeping in a world wrought all of brown topaz that refracted every separate sound and scent and vibration to crystal distinctness. She could hear snow falling in the Gray Mountains, moles whispering as they turned in their sleep.

But the voices caught at her mind. She didn't know why.

"You're stupid," the younger boy said. "Of course she'll know who we are. Dragons know everything."

Indeed we do, she thought. *Indeed we do.*

She knew they were two boys moving on foot northeast through the thick woods five miles to the south of her. She knew that though the younger bore a little sword they were no threat.

They had lost their mother, by the sound of it, though the elder—she turned her mind upon them, seeing within as dragons can—was old enough to take care of both himself and the younger.

The older boy was a wizard, as humans reckoned wizardry. The nimbus of power shone dim around his head and shoulders. Adolescent humans were seldom strong in their powers until the flesh from which they sourced their magic ceased its changes from child to adult. She didn't know why she knew this, or why the children looked familiar to her.

Heretofore her dreams had been dragon dreams: sailing on the wind above ice fields and rocks; absorbing the magics of sun and air as if she'd long been starved; dreaming of the other star-drakes, wherever they were, in the mountains or the ocean's heart, or among the Skerries of Light.

Why did she dream of lost children?

"Dragons may know everything," the older boy, the wizard-boy, said, "but she may not remember who she is. She may not remember she's our mother. She may not be able to turn back."

"That's stupid," the younger declared. He was stocky and red haired. "*You're* stupid."

The young of any species generally smite those younger still who treat them with disrespect–it is a way of making oneself safe–but this older boy only sighed and said, "Yes. Yes, I am."

The white dragon considered the boys for a time in her sleep.

She had laired in the crypt of an old temple that had been built to some human god and was now overgrown with dead briars under an eiderdown of last night's snow. There was some gold there, though robbers had been at the place, long ago. Still, there was gold enough for her to sing to, gold into which to pour the music of her mind and heart and have it reflect back a thousandfold the heart-shaking beauties of the everlasting world.

She felt the goodheartedness of the old temple's priests, who'd stayed to keep their god's honor fresh in the minds of the local people; felt the grief and terror and tragedy of their death at the hands of bandits; the peace and wonder of each slow-passing season, each nesting bird, each fox kit raised and taught to hunt and to go forth to meet the winter moon.

All these things, and a thousand sad shining sweetnesses more, resonated from the gold, soothing and healing her heart.

The children were seeking their mother.

In her dream the white dragon blew on the gold again. It seemed so long since she'd basked in the glory that dragon magic calls from gold. Every joy, every hour of content she had ever felt, every beauty she had ever been aware of, came back to her from it, easing a hurt deep in her heart for which she had neither memory nor words. The children presented no threat to her, no more than the hungry deer that scraped the snow in quest of brown ferns. There were bandits in the woods, a small group of them, following the boys' tracks. *Slave traders,* she thought, and recognized two or three as being among the men she'd driven from the walls of the citadel.

Now why, she wondered, had she done that?

She remembered doing it, but could not remember why.

The wizard-boy should be aware of them, but watching through her dreams she did not think he was.

It was often so, with adolescent mages.

"Maybe she's gone off to be a dragon forever," the younger boy said. "I think that's great. Papa says the dragons live on islands way out in the ocean, and hunt and fish and sing songs. That's what I'd do if I could."

She saw the boy's grief like blood drops shed in silence in the snow.

"If she wants to do that, yes," the black-haired elder boy said. "But we have to ask her at least to come back till Father returns. Because of the demons."

Demons.

The white dragon dreamed of demons.

Those memories, too, the gold refracted: a kaleidoscope of rage and pain and horror, of slavery and rape. Because she was a dragon she saw all these visions dispassionately, understanding them for experiences, for things that she now knew.

She had demon memories as well, clarified and magnified through the gold.

She was in Hell, watching Adromelech the archdemon torture Folcalor. She saw them clearly—Amayon saw them clearly, Amayon whose memory this was. Amayon sat on the steps of Adromelech's dais and clung to the blaze of the archdemon's power. He absorbed and warmed himself in the howling, obscene agonies of Folcalor's humiliation and pain. He absorbed, too, like the crumbs and leavings of a feast, some of the archdemon's sensual delight.

This was what it was to be a demon, the dragon understood. This was what it was. When Adromelech withdrew Folcalor from the fire, on the point of dissolution, he took the victim in his arms and breathed into him all the pleasure he'd taken from Folcalor's pain and made Folcalor love him.

Ah, my little wight. Ah, my little treasure.

And Folcalor said, *I will serve you as you served me.* For Folcalor was the most intelligent of the Sea-wights, coldness and patience added to their will and their greed and their vast malicious anger. *I will devour you, piece by piece, as you daily devour me.*

Of course you will, my child, Adromelech chuckled indulgently, *of course you will.* And with his clawed forefinger he put out Folcalor's eyes and let him creep around the room blind, burning him as he crept, with Amayon giggling, lapping up the pain, behind.

They all love one another, and hate one another, and feed on one another to some degree, a man had said to her once on some sea rocks, waves smashing high over their heads. *They cannot die, and do not forgive.*

What does he want? she had asked the worm-riddled dead man, with his blue decomposing eyes. She was aware of him, too, shambling and stumbling through the freezing wastes of the fells, lying down in the snowdrifts to keep the rot from overtaking his corpse, hearing the Demon Lord's sweet singing in his crumbling dreams. *What does he want?*

In the gold's shimmering reflections she saw Folcalor clothed in the body of a gnome. White hair tinged faintly with pink flowed down over his brocaded shoulders. His hands she knew already, thick and heavy and ringed with the faceted gems of the gnomes. And she knew his greenish, watchful eyes.

The chamber where he was had a pool in its center, six or seven feet broad and brimming with water through which leafy beryl light flickered up. Folcalor's jeweled hand passed over the water, and in it the dragon saw the image of an old man weeping. *Bliaud,* she thought. *His name is Bliaud ...* And he wept as if he had lost the last and dearest thing that had made his life worth living. In some part of her heart the white dragon knew what that thing was.

Folcalor leaned over the pool and whispered, *"Blood in the bowl, peace in your soul. All will be whole."*

The dragon's opal eyes opened, and she knew there was something she had forgotten—something about the demon.

And the lost boys knew what it was.

Waking, she heard their voices crying out. The bandits had reached them, had fired a poison arrow that struck the wizard-boy's leg. Even at this distance she smelled the blood and smelled in it the poisons that would tangle his magic and keep him from using it against those who attacked. She smelled, too, the flesh of the man who'd shot the arrow, smelled decay and death.

The white dragon whipped among the pillars of the hidden crypt like a snake. She crashed forth in an explosion of dazzle and circled once above the snow-covered woods to get her bearings, silken wings spread. Gray clouds lay low over the white-choked vales, the wind-scoured fells. There had been snow last night, and more was coming. She rose into those silent vapors, blending with them, white as the mists and snow. She knew the land's shape, and the way the hills wore their garment of heather, knew their stilled streams and ponds. Ears and heart and the memory of older dreams took her to the bare black trees where the bandits had laid hands on the boys.

The younger boy had cut a man with his child's sword, and the blood lay glaring on the snow. The man he'd hurt was holding his bleeding thigh and cursing while the others held the boy and beat him. His brother, disarmed and weak from the poison, struggled against a dark-bearded bandit who bound his wrists with a thong. This bandit was saying to their leader, a stocky dead man with demon eyes, "Better be worth it is all I got to say." Then as the white dragon dropped down out of the mists overhead, the dark-bearded man looked up and screamed.

The white dragon ripped with her claws at the bare treetops that prevented her from tearing straight down on them. One of the bandits grabbed the smaller boy and tried to run with him; the boy shoved his boot between the man's legs, tripping him, and the man got up and ran without him. The demon leader, the stocky man once called Dogface, started toward the boy, but the white dragon ripped another tree and flung it between him and his prey. "Mother!" the older boy cried.

The bandits were gone. Their leader, after a moment's hesitation, followed, though slower and looking back. The white dragon spat fire after them but did not pursue. She hung soundless above the trees, her opal gaze that could triangulate on a rabbit from five hundred feet fixing on the boys. Sinuous as a water snake, long tail swaying back and forth for balance, she cleared herself a place to pass through the interwoven branches of bare oak and bare elm, then raised her great wings and settled through the hole.

"Mother!" the older boy said again, and the younger, who'd gone to fetch his small sword where the men had thrown it aside, came limping up, his face mottled crimson from blows, holding his side. He looked up at the dragon in silence. Neither, it appeared, had ever heard that one should not look into a dragon's eyes.

"Mother?" the boy said a third time.

"Are you really our mother?" the younger boy asked.

Absurd. Human infants.

Yet she knew them.

Ian, the wizard-boy was called. The warrior-child was Adric.

A third child. Surely there was a third?

Gently she extended her long neck toward the wizard-boy, who shrank back from her in fear a little. But because the bandits had bound his wrists and ankles, even had he not been weak from the poison, he could not run. He shivered, staring at her in wonderment and shock: staring at her narrow birdlike head framed in its mane of fur and ribbons, horns and whiskers; at the glittering razors that guarded every joint and spike and spine.

These boys seemed so fragile to her, and suddenly, curiously precious. She saw this boy not only as he was—weedy and thin with a nose too big for his face—but as a red-faced infant sleeping after the exhaustion of birth, as a toddler staggering across a flagstoned floor—*where?*—as a child huddled with his brother in the quilts and furs they shared in a tower room at night, telling stories about the exploits of a hero called Lord John.

As an old man, healing those who came to seek his help, blue eyes undimmed, with a mane of milk-white hair.

She reached her mind into his mind and body and wrapped his self in her power. With a touch, a whisper of her mind, she blew away the poisons from his organs and brain and blood, as she would have healed another of her own kind.

As she *had* healed another, she remembered, once upon a time.

She drew back her head and considered the boys again.

Human children. Not a thing of dragons.

I will trust the Lord of Time, she had once said, *as humans must, who cannot will pain away by magic.*

As humans must, she had said. *As humans must.*

She had spoken to a dragon then—a dragon as she herself was. It seemed to her that she had been a dragon as she said those words, but as the image became clearer in her mind she saw things differently.

Human. Woman.

Once a wizard. Once a dragon. Then only a woman, trusting in the Lord of Time like everyone else.

Ian? She spoke the word hesitantly into his mind.

"Mother?"

Power-circle path? She called to mind the route by which she had gone into dragon form from her woman's flesh. It had in it an element of skill, like the adeptness that the hands learn in playing the harp, when the mind hears the music and the hands form it without reference to the single consciousness of this finger or that. Like the steady rocking motion of the spindle or the loom.

But she couldn't touch either its beginning or its end.

"Do you want to come back?"

Magic, she thought, remembering. The comfort and wonderment of calling dreams forth from gold. The idea of surrendering again the glitter and glory of dragon flesh, dragon power, was unendurable.

But she knew, too, that if she remained in her dragon form, she would forget. Time is a different matter to dragons. It would be easy to return to the Skerries of Light and let the seasons pass over her like shining wings. When next she returned, Ian would be a man and John would be old.

Old without her.

Show me the path home, my son.

"Of course the regular medical establishment denounces the whole thing as chicanery." Bort paused beneath the red-and-gold awning of a Happy Snack stand and handed the woman there his cred. She slipped the silver end into the reader and poked the square button marked with a single Happy Snack icon four times, then doled out the slightly flattened, greasy, cheesy balls of meat in their wrappers of dough. Clea had a Veggie Snack. John could detect absolutely no difference between the snacks and suspected there wasn't any. "But the doctors at Free Life Institute do seem to have found a way to raise the dead."

They took the Celestial Line subway to 509th Avenue, emerging to jostle well-dressed crowds of salarypersons and students, club-goers and civil servants bound for home or for work as if it weren't an hour and a half short of dawn. Within the terminal below Garrypoot's apartment, neon still flashed and music still blared. Ad screens, holos twice life-size, dazzling sculptures of light all proclaimed the virtues and wonders of Lovehammer and Ravage, Embody and Speedy-Cred. Everything smelled of damp concrete, and the echoes went through John's head like an ax.

"Free Life is a joke," Clea added as they made their way to the escalators. "The process is supposed to cost at least two million, plus a stay at a reorientation clinic out on the Purpleflash Line."

"Is it, now?" Despite John's warning, none of the quasi-wizards seemed to think twice about the fact that one of their number had been kidnapped. At least they seemed to regard themselves as perfectly safe in the crowd. John, maneuvering to stay on the outer edge of the little group, strained his senses trying to keep an eye in all directions at once, logging faces that looked briefly familiar, clothing that caught his eye more than once. Meeting, momentarily, the eyes of those who passed, seeking the demon glitter he'd seen in Ian's, and Jenny's, during last summer's horrors.

Mostly they just smiled, peacefully engrossed in Brain Candy dreams.

"But nobody really knows," Garrypoot said. "The institute has the families sign nondisclosure agreements, and I heard on *Yammer*—that's SevenDoubleohNine's talk show," he added, seeing John's puzzled expression, but the explanation, like many in the Hell of Walls, didn't explain much, "that SixtysevenFiveThirtythreeFourteen's girlfriend was harassed and sued when she leaked to the press that Sixtyseven-FiveThirtythreeFourteen was brought back after that stroke he had last year. SixtysevenFiveThirtythreeFourteen?" he repeated, as if he expected John to have heard of that person, whoever he was. "The head of Op-Link? The guy who revolutionized global communication? There was all that hoopla about him dying and leaving everything to his girlfriend, whatever the hell her number was . . ."

"EleventyFive," Shamble provided. The holo wavering above his cap did its three thousandth bug-eyed double take of the night. John had seen at least fifty identical versions in the subway and its stations, plus several hundred others equally silly. He had no idea how he was going to write *those* up in his notes.

"Eleventyfive. Except he turned out not to have died after all?"

"It was a hell of a scandal," Bort said. "Surely you heard . . ."

"Oh, yeah." John nodded. "That. Sorry." But he saw Clea's eyes cut sidelong to him.

Above the vast shouting cavern of the terminal, the underground lobby of the apartment building itself was nearly as large. Kiosks dispensed Jollybites and Dazzleyummies, plex scarves and ointment masks and little vials of Have A Nice Day; the scents mingled with the sweet yeasty odors from the building's Food Central on a garish mezzanine guarded by blank-eyed building enforcers in blue. The noise was awesome.

"Anyway, only the extremely rich can afford to get it done." Garrypoot slipped his key into the slot of the elevator that led to the apartments themselves. The teeth-gritting vibration of ambient ether transmission was trebled in the enclosed metal box, made worse by the tiny relays in Shamble's hat and the elevator's ad screen, which perpetually received from the purveyors of candles, satin sheets, crimson underwear, or young boys and girls. "And they're the ones who can afford to keep the wraps on whether they get it done or not."

"And what's the medical establishment got against raisin' the dead?" John contemplated the commercial in fascination. The others took no notice of the on-screen proceedings at all.

"Their contention is there has to be some kind of large-scale organ piracy going on," Clea said. "Cloned subs are pretty good–my mother's had her colon replaced twice–but with systemic failure or a Type Three syndrome you can't replace more than one. Free Life won't say where it gets its organs from, or release any information. In fact they pooh-pooh the whole idea of raising the dead, at least in their public statements."

"Wan ThirtyoneFourFour is the son of the head of Speedy-Cred." Garrypoot led the way into his apartment, two rooms with a kitchenette and a small ad screen in the bedroom, turned down to low. Most of one wall of the living room was occupied by an enormous window that looked out over the white curve of a beach, pine trees rustling in the whisper of a breeze along green-fringed cliffs. Stars shone in the clear dark sky, winter's constellations, a comet burning small and clear and low above the sea.

John wondered where that actually was, or if it existed at all. The colors had the overemphatic hue he'd learned to associate with animated vids.

Still, they had to have learned about beaches and cliffs and pine trees somewhere.

As always–as a thousand times in the days of riding, of climbing, of picking his way through this clamorous carnival–he caught himself making a mental note to tell Jenny of this, and thought, *If I see her again.*

The pain in his heart was so sharp he had to push the thought instantly away.

Jenny.

Ian.

Dear God, I hope Muffle's looking after him . . .

But who'd look after Muffle and the folk of the Hold, if demons were truly on the march?

"Nobody wanted to say where ThirtyoneFourFour picked up AOAD syndrome," Bort went on, "but it was in all the vids when he was brought into the Econo-Health Emergency Clinic and died there of it. Of course his mother denied it. Then about a month later they were saying, *No, no, no, it was all a rumor and here he is, alive and well.*"

Bort, John knew from nearly two weeks of observing him and the others of the league, was addicted to the sleazier newsvid shows. *Pure gossip,* Tisa had declared scornfully. *Makes me sick.* Yet she could quote rumors about the personal lives of celebrities for hours.

"ThirtyoneFourFour and his wife divorced a few months after his resurrection or procedure or whatever it was, and he left the place they had out on the Blueflash Line and got an apartment closer to the heart of the city. He's been making the circuit of the clubs ever since, picking up the fancy girls. One of that little Tisa Three's girlfriends dated him for a while."

"You know where his apartment is?" Fascinated, John tapped a discreet button under the window's sill. The shower in his apartment had cured his fear of touching anything, but he still half expected carnivorous butterflies. The image there melted into that of the subway station downstairs. *It has to be a direct link,* John thought. He'd noted the fry-bread vendor with a holo-hat of the Ravage logo, and she was still on duty, dipping crimson syrup—which, Docket had warned him, was highly addictive—onto a platter of dough. *This must be what it's like for Jenny with a ward spell.*

"The Universe Towers." Garrypoot didn't even look up from the enormous computer setup that dominated the other side of the parlor. "Seventieth through seventy-second floors. Give me another five minutes and I'll have the entry codes."

He touched through a series of blue, red, and green screens filled with symbols. John tapped another button under the windowsill and was rewarded with what had to be a view of the outside of the building: He could think of no other reason for reproducing a scene of gray monstrous monoliths and jammed streets lit by ad screens under a slow, steady rain.

How would you even make notes about this? he wondered, bemused and at the same time deeply sad. *How could you make it make sense to whoever might have to come here again?* He felt he'd wandered endless miles from the Winterlands, so far that nothing was left to refer to: no trees, no earth, no animals save roaches and rats . . .

How would he tell Jenny and the children about this? Always supposing he got the chance.

Be there when I get back, he willed silently, desperately. *Just be there.*

"Who are you?" Clea cleared a double handful of book chips off a small hassock near him and sat. "And where are you from?"

"I was just beginnin' to wonder that meself," John countered, finger-combing his long hair back to twist it into a warrior's topknot. "Where's anyone from?"

Clea shook her head. "You've dealt with demons before," she said. "You know what you're looking for and what it should look like. And you think magic is more natural than its absence."

"What?" John grinned at her maliciously. "And the lot of you wizards?"

The older woman smiled. "You know as well as I do what I mean." She glanced back at Bort and Shamble, bent over Garrypoot's shoulders, kibitzing as the boy marked and transferred symbols to a handbox jacked into the main terminal. "We . . ." Her voice stumbled a little, stuck a little, on the words. "We were born knowing, born different. When I was a little girl, I felt like those children in the old stories, the stories they never make into vids: the ones where the sprites switch one of their babies for a human child. Well, I've always felt like I'd been switched."

She looked down at her hands, big and soft and clumsy, hands that had never done work. Her voice grew wistful. "I always felt that one day I'd find my real people. But in the meantime I had to make the best of living with people who weren't concerned with . . ." She shook her head.

"I can't even say what it was that I was looking for, and that they had no notion existed. I can't say 'music' because my mother listens to music and says she likes it. I can't say 'friendship' because everyone I know has friends and wants friends, though . . . though not quite the kind of friends and friendships I've looked for all my life. Maybe it's just hunger for affection I never really got, because my mother isn't an affectionate woman, though she'll claim she is. Magic is an answer. I've studied it all my life and it . . . it makes sense to me. The idea of it helps me. These others . . ."

She gestured back to them with a sigh: Bort, dark and clumsy with his bristling beard and glittering spectacles; Shamble reaching down past Garrypoot's bent, greasy head to stab a callused finger at the screen.

"They are my family. Sometimes they drive me crazy, but they understand. We are all seeking what we pray one day we will find. More than anything in the world, we just want it to be real. But you . . ." She touched his arm, turned back the edge of his sleeve where the sword scar he'd gotten at age nineteen from Balgodorus Black-Knife bisected his forearm, close beside a small red mark left by dragon acid. "You've found it. You know it's real because you've seen it. And I'd like to know where."

John smiled. "So would I," he said. "Where, I mean, for I haven't a clue what *where* is about these days." He twisted an elastic band around his hair, which worked far better than a leather thong—*there has to be some way,* he thought, *to manufacture it in the Winterlands.* "If I said, it wouldn't mean a thing to you because the place I come from, and the places I've been, don't exist."

"Are you a . . . a kind of demon hunter?" She laughed self-consciously and said, "There was a vid called *Demon Hunter* out a couple of years ago. Awful special effects—buckets of slime and fake eyeballs."

John plucked at one of his spare elastics, stretched between thumb and forefinger like a crude bowstring, and thought about the Hell behind the Mirror of Isychros. "Is that me regular job, you mean?" He shook his head. "Not usually." He linked his arms around his knees and leaned back against the vid screen, remembering the Winterlands: the gray moors rising and rising, one behind the other, with the rain sweeping their tops; the way the air smelled when he stood at his study window at night and saw nothing–no light, no buildings, no trees–just shapeless lands lost in darkness; the way his fingers hurt from cold.

Jenny, curled among the furs of their bed, dark hair like a sea among the pillows, all the cares she carried day to day smoothed from her face by sleep. Little Maggie, red haired and dark eyed, making spiderwebs of his aunts' spinning wool.

Clea's hand on his wrist made him startle. He hadn't realized he'd shut his eyes.

Her eyes met his, troubled. "Homesick," he said to reassure her. He took off his glasses, rubbed the bridge of his nose.

"Has it been long?"

Over by the terminal Shamble was saying, "The key code for building maintenance workers at Universe is pretty easy to duplicate, and I know a guy who rents out the uniforms."

"Even if ThirtyoneFourFour has all three floors and keeps a single entry, there'll be vents into the other levels . . ."

"That's another thing I haven't the faintest idea about," John said quietly. "I've been away for weeks. But the demon gates don't take account of time. The snow that was fallin' when I rode from the Hold won't have melted yet from the ground."

"The Hold," said Clea softly. "Is that your home?"

He nodded. The smell of the wind when it set from the heath, of wood smoke on the air, the bark of a dog unseen across the moor on a misty night. Jenny playing the harp.

"What is it you're looking for? And why?"

Bort's com signal beeped, a swift flutter of sound. He unclipped it from his belt, glanced at the source code, then toggled the line open. "TenEighty," he said. John had watched old Docket and Bort and his landlady TwelveNinetyseven when they took coms, and generally if it was someone they knew they'd say either their nickname–like Bort–or a casual greeting like, "Yo," or, "What's up?"

"Yes," Bort said. "I know him."

A silence. *Now why couldn't I have had a com last summer,* John wondered, putting on his specs again, *when I was that desperate to get hold of Jenny to tell her Ian had been kidnapped? Everything would have been dead easy.*

It seemed very far away, and his desperation then to save his son seemed simple compared to the darkness in Ian's soul now, to Jenny's silent pain and his own cautious, weary loneliness.

Would ether crystals work in his own world? And how could he use them to power a com?

"Thank you," Bort said. "We'll be there in an hour."

He fingernailed the toggle to close the line.

"That was the District Two Hundred enforcers," he said. "They found Docket."

"Alive?" Clea's whole face brightened, then faltered at Bort's expression.

"Not . . . exactly," said Bort. "They found my number stored in his com. They say we'd better get over there."

Chapter 13

"He was like this when we picked him up," the enforcer said. He snapped his fingers in front of Docket's eyes; they did not even blink in response, though the old man was breathing through a slack, half-open mouth.

"And where was that?" Even Bort's usual pompous bluster seemed quelled by the cold lights and hard echoes of the District Building, and John felt his hackles lift for no reason he could readily comprehend. The District Building was dirtier and more crowded than anyplace he'd encountered outside the wet zone and had a smell to it that he hated without being able to identify. Ad screens plastered the walls nearly edge-to-edge, some of them displaying the usual playlets about fashionable restaurants or apartments, some showing scenes of violence and horror: young women being beaten up, children being tormented by men in the leathers and makeup of the gang, an old man sodomized by a hulking youth in blue face paint and spikes. At the front counter a clerk in gray expressionlessly keyed in a complaint by a woman at the head of a very long line. Another clerk doled out plex cards bearing what John understood to be numbers.

After being given such a number on their arrival at District Two Hundred, he, Bort, Clea, and Garrypoot had waited nearly two hours to be ushered into a filthy cubicle smaller than a cow stall at the Hold, where they'd waited a further hour before the enforcer arrived with Docket.

Or what had been Docket.

"We found him over on Two-oh-ninth Avenue." The enforcer consulted the information felt-penned on the old man's chemical burned and mosquito ravaged forehead. The bookseller made no response, simply stared ahead. By the smell of his clothes he'd wet himself during the night. A thin drip of saliva dampened the white stubble on his chin.

"He was disoriented and unable to speak or help himself. He doesn't appear to know his name or where he is." The enforcer spoke as if from a memorized script. His voice was soft and rather light, at grotesque odds with his shaven head and overmuscled bulk. His small fair beard was neatly clipped. "Please enter information about yourself and signal when you're ready to sign him out."

He swiveled the keyboard of the desk terminal around so Bort could use it, and left.

Bort sighed and began to input.

After the fifth screen John jerked his head at the doors. "Can't we just take him and leave?" People were coming and going from the waiting area as their numbers were called. Nobody seemed to be keeping track.

"We need to sign ourselves as responsible," Clea explained when Bort raised his head with an exasperated growl. "We'd never get him past security if we didn't."

"He hasn't committed any crime, has he?" John pointed out, perched on the corner of the desk beside the old man, his boots dangling above the trash-littered floor. Old Docket was barefoot, and when John gently searched the pockets of his trousers and shirt—he wore no jacket—they were empty. "I thought he had a com."

"He probably did when they found him," Shamble said. "Shoes, too." He glanced nervously around him. The subliminal hum of ether relays was nearly audible here. Inadequate shielding, John guessed. Everyone in the huge waiting room was shouting, quarreling, or making repeated trips to the three vending machines dispensing Peace—which the Human Resources Bureau handed out free—that occupied the only wall space not filled with ad screens. "He's been in a holding cell for a couple of hours. That means we'll have to renumber his credit."

"Curse," Clea said without heat. "Like we didn't have enough to do finding out what's wrong with him. I'm just glad someone called. Unclaimed indigents often disappear when the enforcers pick them up," she added, glancing over at John. "The government denies it, of course, but if you match up numbers on the Op-Link, there's a certain amount of evidence that Metro-Sec—the firm that contracts security for about half the districts in the city—is owned by the same megacorp that owns Renewal."

"Renewal?"

"The chief supplier of transplant organs," Shamble said dryly. "Poot, do you want to get in line for a number for a doctor? This might just be some kind of a drug reaction, but I've never seen anything like this."

"I have," John said. "And getting him to see a healer probably won't help. Where's Two-oh-ninth Avenue? Anywhere near the Universe Towers where this ThirtyoneFourFour lives?"

Shamble and Bort traded a glance. "Universe is on Two-oh-ninth Avenue," Bort said. "About three-quarters of a mile from here."

The white dragon bore the boys to Frost Fell, one in each claw, Adric gazing down in hungry wonderment at the ground. Seeing the house made her remember still more clearly how it had felt to be a woman, and to love. It made her remember, too, with a distant dispassion, the pain and the grief of dreaming of John in the arms of the Demon Queen.

As a dragon she was free of Amayon's calling, free of the dreams of dizzying pleasure that came from drinking others' pain. She shivered at the thought of going back. That would, she knew, be bad.

But how bad, she had no guessing.

Ian had to rest a day, for echoes of the poison's hurt lingered in his veins, keeping him from concentrating. The following morning he was better, and under the white dragon's guidance he drew out a great circle of power on the hilltop behind the house, open to the silvery sky.

In this the dragon lay and opened her heart to those cold roads that led magic back to human dreams and human flesh.

The power of transformation took her: heat, cold, a hammering as if she lay naked to the buffeting of a thousand years of storms.

Distantly she heard Ian calling to her. She tried to reach out to him in reply but could not; she could only lie on the bitter ground twisting in an agony that was worse than childbearing, worse than losing her powers of magic, worse than anything she had yet endured. A hundred times she tried to reverse what she had begun and return to dragon flesh, but she had given up the dragon power and could find no way back. Yet it seemed that she could not go forward into human form. What form her flesh and bones retained she knew not, only that her flesh burned and her bones hurt as if racked and broken and twisted to shards; her whole body was drowned in pain and heat.

She cried Ian's name. Weeping, she cried John's, feeling her strength ebb, like a woman who cannot bring forth her child yet whose body will not cease the pangs of birth. Again and again she thought of Amayon, but the part of her that remained a dragon and felt no love told her that Amayon, being a demon, would only laugh at her pain. She slipped back into the darkness of dreaming and sought desperately for John, but John was gone.

Dead? she wondered. *Would I have known it if he died or went to be a servant of the Demon Queen?* Images flooded to her mind, and she could not remember whether they were things she had seen with her own eyes or merely figments Amayon had sent her in dreams to torture her: John and the Queen lying together, John letting her drink the blood from his arms and wrists.

John standing above Ian's dead body, in the snow of Frost Fell, saying, *This was your doing. This was your doing.*

That was true, she thought. She had wanted neither of the boys, had wanted no child to interrupt her meditations, her striving for power. It was hard to breathe, and it came to her how easily she could die, like a dragon releasing its hold on the earth and lifting into the sky. The thought appealed to her: a simple solution, and beautiful.

John will get along without me, she thought. He always had. It was what she had demanded that he do, and her sons as well.

Jenny.

Like a cuckoo, she thought, *I bore them and flew away.*

Jenny, this is not true.

A voice of gentleness, speaking through the darkness of those terrible human dreams.

You left them with one who loved them. You did as you must, to become what you became.

As if she lay at the bottom of a storm-ravaged ocean, she looked up and saw another layer of dreaming, the still clarity of dragon dreams, miles above her head in the light.

Stone, sea, and sky; deep silence unbroken even by birds. Consciousness that spread and listened to the waves, to the winds, to the age-long lattices of what the rock had been and would be. A heart like a core of invisible flame.

What is truth, Jenny?

She saw truth laid out in a very simple pattern, a line leading from dragon to woman, and back.

It took all of Ian's strength, and all of her own, to call her back from the meshes of silvery darkness where her mind had wandered. To her horror she saw how near to the dark country of no return she lay; with more horror still, she realized how much she wanted only the relief that is found in its bornes.

Cold enveloped her just before she fell asleep. She opened her eyes and saw Ian and Adric running toward her with blankets in their arms and fear on their faces. "I'm all right," she said, and she fell a thousand miles into sleep without dreams.

Waking, she lay for a long time in her bed in the house on Frost Fell. She knew she ought to speak to the people who came and went around her—Sergeant Muffle and his mother, the stout white-haired Aunt Hol, and sturdy Cousin Dilly—but could not bring herself to do so. She felt very cold, numb and weak as if only water remained in place of her bones.

The magic of dragonhood was gone. Dreams of the demon seethed below the level of her consciousness, whispering to her from the dark. It was hard for her to remember why she ought to live.

"Mother, we have to warn the King somehow."

Ian's voice, miles away. She didn't know whether she actually opened her eyes or not. The scene in her mind was dreamlike, a boy in grimy leather and plaids sitting on the edge of a bed in which a woman lay. The woman was tiny, shriveled and brown like a mummy, with a scarred face and bald head and twisted hands.

"We have to get word to them in the South. The bandits that seized me and Adric—they said to the man with the bow, *He's the witch boy.* It isn't just Folcalor hunting us, Mother. He has allies, more than we knew. And he's growing stronger."

Not us, *my child,* Jenny thought with weary resentment. The memory of her lost power was for a moment a handful of ashes, and she wondered again if John was dead. That would be the bitterest jest of all. As a dragon in her dreaming she had sought him all through the world and had seen nothing of him.

How could he be dead, and I not know?

"I've been trying to contact Master Bliaud, Mother, and I can't. Can you hear me? Please, please answer me if you can!"

He put his hands on either side of her face, and she opened her eyes, sleepily looking up into his. She saw his features alter with consternation and grief.

Then the door behind him opened, and the dragon Morkeleb came into the room.

Dreaming? Jenny wondered absently. Or was this merely how one saw when one was dead?

She could not precisely tell whether Morkeleb walked in his human form or as a dragon: She had seen him as a dragon reduce his size to barely larger than a cat's, perfect as those statues of coal they made in the far outer villages. In human form he had appeared to her to be a man with long gray hair, a thin pale man neither old nor young, a man with the sort of face a dragon might wear if he went masking as human. She thought this was probably how he appeared now because neither Muffle nor Aunt Hol nor the boys seemed particularly frightened, though they would not, she noticed, come too near him.

Thus she saw him sometimes, in the timeless vagueness that followed, sitting beside her bed and holding her hands. At other times he appeared to be a dragon, his narrow birdlike head maned in ribbons, but the hand she held, save for its claws, was a human hand. His eyes were always the same, and sometimes it was only the eyes that she saw, and all the rest invisible as smoke.

She saw the eyes and heard the voice speaking in her mind.

You said that you would remain among the living, and be my friend.

I did not know then how bad it would be, she said.

She felt as if something had been cut out of her bones when she had given up dragon flesh and dragon power a third time. The strength to finish the transformation had had to come from somewhere, and there had been nowhere for it to take root. She closed her eyes.

For a long while she was aware of him silent and unmoving beside her, only breathing and at rest. For herself, Jenny felt as if she looked out over the gray peaceful silvery nothingness of death as if overlooking the ocean from a high cliff. It was restful to know only that the choice was there. Then she heard Adric say softly, "Are you really a dragon, sir?" She opened her eyes to see the boy standing next to Morkeleb, hands clasped behind his back, studying him intently.

He wasn't, Jenny noticed, wearing his sword. He'd left it wrapped in its belt on the hearth, beside which Ian slumbered in fitful dreams.

"I am," Morkeleb replied gravely. "Are you really a human being?"

The boy drew himself up. "I am Adric Aversin, son of the Thane." He hadn't combed his hair, and both his eyes were blacked from the bandits' blows. He looked at Jenny and said more quietly, "Will Mama be all right? Can you save her with magic? Mama says dragons are magic."

"I know not whether your mother will live." Morkeleb tilted his head a little to one side, a gesture wholly reminiscent of his dragon form; the white crystal gaze rested on the boy, as if, Jenny thought, for the first time he was trying to understand without anger or envy these things that had drawn her from him. It seemed he wanted to understand what it was about them that had made her forsake immortality and dragonhood only to be with them, to see them every day. "And I have surrendered my magic, lest the use of it blind me to an understanding of what the universe truly is."

Ian, who had waked at the sound of their voices, raised his head and regarded the dragon with sudden thoughtfulness in his eyes.

"Can't you take it back," Adric asked, "long enough to help Mother, and then quit again?"

"Adric," Ian said, shocked, "stop being a toad." He got to his feet and crossed the small room, his face haggard, old beyond his years in the firelight. Standing before the dragon, he asked quietly, "Are you saying that even death—even the death of someone you love—will teach you something about the nature of the universe?" He did not meet the dragon's eyes as he spoke, looking down instead at the long white hands with their black claws, still holding Jenny's; but he did not flinch.

"That's stupid," Adric said. Ian shoved him to silence him.

"It is what I am saying," Morkeleb replied. "Yet I think, too, that she is beyond my healing. I have done what I can. But dragons heal one another, and she is not of dragonkind anymore. It is up to her." Turning back to her, he touched her face and said, "Do not leave me, my friend."

Through his fingers she felt the heat of the dragon fire, like the core of the sun.

It is not a thing of dragons, Jenny said, *to pick out quarrels with death and time.*

Nor is it, Morkeleb replied.

She understood then that it was no longer of concern to him what was a thing of dragons and what was not. He had become what he was, dragonshadow or something else. The pride in him was gone, even the pride that would have held him aloof from these two children of humankind. The power that she felt within him was no longer magic as she had known it, but something else.

As she—she understood now and suddenly—was something other than what she had been or thought herself to be.

My friend, she said, and opened her heart and her life. She let him breathe his warmth into her, accepting life back within her flesh—accepting all that life might bring.

With life came grief: for John's anger over their son, for his absence, for her lost magic.

And then, cold and terrible, came the recollection of the dreams of Folcalor. The hand with its gold rings passing across the well, calling image after image. A gnome in the North. A mage in the South.

Demons under the sea, clustered, green and shining, around the gate that the whalemages had closed. Waiting to enter this world, to make it their battleground in their wars against one another, for vengeance and pain. Their hunting ground. Their orchestra for the arts of terror and pain, and their gateway to every world and Hell beyond.

There is slavery and slavery, the dead sailor had grinned. *Did you think you were his slave?*

"Morkeleb," she said, "can you take me to the South, to the court of the King?"

"It is what I came here to do," he replied.

Since all of them had been awake for close to twenty-four hours, Bort voted for dinner and a night's sleep before undertaking an invasion of the Universe Towers.

"If they took him sometime after he closed up last night," John pointed out, "he's been like this for the best part of a day, and in my world at least, it gets harder to bring 'em back the longer they're out of their bodies." So they rode the subway back to Garrypoot's apartment, which was not only the closest to District Two Hundred but also the most secure and the best equipped. The young tech looked decidedly squeamish at the suggestion that a mindless and incontinent old man be confined there but, after one glare from Clea, didn't say so. "If a victim of possession can be exorcised within two or three days, he'll usually recover. After that it's pretty chancy."

"You mean Docket's–" Garrypoot looked hastily around him at the other occupants of the subway car, who were in any case staying as far away from Docket as possible, and lowered his voice. "–possessed?" He seemed caught between horror at the implications of the situation and awe that at last he was given an opportunity to deal with true magic. "You mean there's a demon inside him?" He dropped to a whisper, and he leaned around Shamble to look into the old man's blank, staring eyes.

"Not exactly. His mind and his soul–his self–were stripped out of him, but no demon went in in its place." John edged aside as a couple of neatly dressed inputters got on, bound no doubt for a late shift at one of the city bureaus, and gave them a friendly smile. They took one look at Docket and shoehorned themselves into the already-packed rear half of the car. It was fortunately not rush hour. "Didn't think it worth the trouble, probably, there bein' no magic here. I wish I could talk to Jen about this one–Jen's me wife–but I think it'd stump her as well. I've got a guess at what's goin' on," he added, as the train slowed and there was a hissing crackle, the lights dimming. There must be water in the tunnels–the stench was a giveaway. Now and again the trains had to turn back, crackling and hissing, for miles. "But there's no way of tellin' till we get into ThirtyoneFourFour's flat."

Back at his apartment, Garrypoot hooked his com through the terminal and put in a call to ThirtyoneFourFour, making note of the system relays it passed through: "He's in the wet zone," he said. "Clear out where it's deep, it looks like: Ninety-fourth and Old Thirtieth Boulevard."

"ThirtyoneFourFour?" Clea said disbelievingly, looking from the bathroom door where she was gently sponging Docket in the shower stall. "The deep gangs will kill him out there!"

"That's where the relays feed." The boy cut the signal before ThirtyoneFourFour could respond. "He's been back from the dead once. Maybe it makes him immortal?" He glanced inquiringly, hungrily, at John.

"He *is* immortal," John said shortly. Dobbin the carry beast came to his mind, bleeding legs rotting beneath him as he staggered up the black rocks of the Hell of the Shining Things. "He doesn't care whether ThirtyoneFourFour dies or not." And, seeing Garrypoot's puzzlement, he explained patiently, "He's a demon, Poot. He quit being ThirtyoneFourFour back at Econo Health Emergency. The demon's just riding the body like a horse. The main question is, how long will it take him to get back?"

"Oh, I have the security codes," Garrypoot said reassuringly. "We should have all the time we need."

Aversin said nothing. But he wondered how much Amayon could hear in his onyx bottle. Could he see, as Jenny had spoken of seeing in dreams? And how long would it take him to contact his fellow wights with the news, *Get back at once, they're raiding your flat?*

Shamble came in with black maintenance coveralls labeled UNIVERSE TOWERS in white. Nobody in the city ever asked why you wanted to rent whatever you wanted to rent, be it plex earrings or assault weapons. It was enough trouble just to keep a roof over your head—literally, for those who slept outdoors in the chemical rain started to deteriorate very quickly after a night or two—and your meds paid up. John had never particularly liked the grinding cold and hunger of living in the Winterlands, to say nothing of the possibility of being killed or enslaved by bandits, but he was beginning to understand that there were worse places.

The Celestial, Infinity, and Presidential lines all had stops under the Universe Towers. Shamble, a welder and a worker in metals, had done repairs at Universe Station, and he led them unerringly through the half dozen levels of walkways and overpasses and branching tunnels all clogged with 'zine kiosks and vendors of drugs and sausages. John glanced over his shoulder and around him at the crowds and shadow all the way. The door to the maintenance stair opened readily to one of Garrypoot's bootlegged key cards. After a long climb up sagging plex steps through darkness that hummed with mosquitoes and reeked of rats and sewage, another key card admitted them to the ether feed-control room. The shielding there was a thousand times better than at District, but nevertheless the vibrations were blinding.

Garrypoot jacked his hand-terminal into one of the dozen black boxes ranged along the wall and quickly fed in a series of commands. "Done," he said. "Auto-security on floors seventy through seventy-three is going to think everything is just fine for the rest of the cycle, which should be the next"—he checked his watch—"hour and forty minutes. By that time we should be out of there and gone."

And none of Garrypoot's machinations would gain them a damn thing, John thought—fighting the chill of panic—if Amayon had already summoned reinforcements.

They took a maintenance elevator to the sixty-ninth floor. John half expected it to be incomprehensibly dizzying, but it was no different from being in a room built on the side of a high mountain. It was only a room, in what was clearly a servants' area. From there another stair led up, starting and ending in small maintenance chambers hidden behind discreet doors.

"If the Towers are for the rich," he whispered as they mounted the stairs, "why do they have ad screens in the servants' section? They can't need the rent knock-off, surely?" Those they'd passed on the floor below had been huge, numerous, and prominently placed.

"Are you kidding?" Garrypoot replied. "The servants would quit if they didn't have screens."

Baffled, John shook his head. In many ways the Hell of Winds was easier to understand.

He had thought—had hoped—that Wan ThirtyoneFourFour might be the man he sought, the face he'd seen in the water before the Mirror of Isychros: that his quest might end here and soon. But the photographs that dotted the walls of the nearly bare study, the huge gray living room, were of a younger man, fair and blue eyed and so perfect of feature John wondered aloud if the pictures were some sort of idealized animation.

"Well, in a way they are," Bort said. He kept his voice low as they prowled to the uppermost level of the three, testing doors as they went. "He's had a lot of work done. You can tell by the cheekbones." He chuckled a little at John's naïveté. "You don't think any of the rich are born that beautiful, do you?"

Even so, as they passed swiftly through the ample halls, through rooms sparsely scattered with comfortable furniture and tastefully shuttered screens, John looked for the chamber he'd seen in the water: the heavy curtains stamped with gold, the candlesticks and statues and bowls of bright-gleaming metal.

But there was none of that here. The walls were plastered and painted light cool hues. Wide electronic windows displayed mountains and sunset clouds, so exquisitely coordinated with one another that had he not known better John would have thought the flat truly was a house set on a mountaintop in some beautiful fastness. Even in these rooms, the roaches endemic to the city flicked away under baseboards and behind expensive curtains as they approached, and something about their presence made John's hackles prick. When they ascended the stair to the upper levels of the apartment, the insects grew more numerous still. The air-conditioning was powerful, but every now and then he caught, as they passed shut doors, the fugitive reek of blood.

In a double-locked chamber on the third level of the apartment they found what Aversin expected. The room was set up as a sort of workroom, with terminal, multiple screens, and a small table brightly bathed in light. A stream of ants crept from a ceiling vent, across wall and floor, to disappear beneath a second shut door leading to an inner room. On the lighted table lay the things John sought, in foamplex boxes such as takeout food came in.

One box contained five jewels: three sapphires, an amethyst, and a ruby, all good quality and all cut in facets after the fashion of the gnomes, a method apparently common in this world. "Naturals!" Bort held the ruby up to the light, awe in his voice. "Not synthetics, I mean. Ether crystals are technically diamonds, in that they're crystallized carbon charged to align polarities, but they don't bring the price a natural diamond would. These were probably bought at estate auctions. You don't get naturals of any kind on the market, seldom even see them at gem and metals nodes on the Link."

John nodded, barely hearing. Gold rings and gold chains and neat bundles of gold wire evidently unraveled from some kind of ethertonic equipment were heaped in another of those little boxes. A little scale sat nearby, for weighing the gold.

"I always wondered if that was one reason magic quit working."

Shamble extended a reverent finger to touch the gems. "All the books talk of using jewels, but of course most jewels now are synthetics. I don't think I've ever seen one that truly came out of the ground."

John picked up the thing that lay next to the scale—a gold hair clip decorated with a blue enameled butterfly. Stuck in the dried blood on it was a single long snow-white hair.

"What's this one?" Garrypoot took an extremely dark amethyst from the box where it had been set apart alone.

I should have guessed. I should have seen it coming. A lifetime of protecting those who could not protect themselves coalesced into a terrible regret.

Oh, Tisa.

He set the hair clip down and gently removed the gem from Poot's hand.

"This one," he said, "is what we've come to get." His hand shook a little as he wrapped the gem in his handkerchief and tucked it in his pocket.

Tisa leaning against the corner of a building, waiting for her mysterious Lots of Zeroes to come take her to dinner. *The one who's picking me up tonight has* really *got money . . .*

Her elfin grin as she'd waved good-bye.

Against his chest, he felt the onyx ink bottle warm and knew that Amayon fed on his horror and his guilt.

His fear, too, maybe. The rising uneasiness, the sense of time running out. Wan ThirtyoneFourFour was rich. He'd have a fast boat and a crew of private-sector enforcers capable of dealing with any deep-zone gang that got in his way—if the gangs weren't already in his pay or thrall.

"Okay," he said quietly. "Now let's get out. First we've got to find . . ."

"Moondog—"

John crossed the room, though he guessed by Bort's tone what was behind the door that Bort had opened, the doorway into the inner chamber. He guessed it would be bad. No attempt at cleanup had been made, neither after the latest splashes and stains and puddles had been laid down last night, nor on numerous occasions before. Roaches swarmed, fled as the ether panel on the ceiling lit up. The ants just went about their business, as ants will.

"What in the name of Hell . . . ?" Shamble and Garrypoot trailed at his heels, stared in shock through the door.

"Aye," John said softly. "In the name of Hell." Some of the hair stuck in the blood here, too, was white. "Hasn't anyone ever told you lot what demons do?"

They gazed at him, sickened, would-be mages who had talked casually of demons and magic and spells. *Children,* John thought, switching off the light. Shamble was probably his own age and Bort a good seven years his senior, but children nevertheless. Like young Prince Gareth, who'd sought him in the Winterlands thinking heroes and dragons resembled those in the ballads.

"Pain is what they do." He walked back to the table and pocketed the five natural jewels. Not, he thought, that a rich man like Wan ThirtyoneFourFour would have a lot of trouble finding others, but at least this would buy the next-targeted victims some time. "Chaos is what they do. I don't know how he keeps it from the servants, but maybe in this world, too, it's possible to find people who don't care what their masters do, so long as the pay's good—and anyway I'm sure there's a drug for that. There seems to be for everythin' else."

He picked up also the golden hair clip, the rage in him rising with the smell of the blood from the other room, the stink of roasted flesh. The hair clip, he realized, had the only depiction he'd seen of insect, animal, or bird since he'd come to the city.

His hand was shaking.

"I came to this world to find someone," he said softly. "Someone who collects gold. Poot, why don't you download everythin' off that terminal, and then we get the hell out of here."

Chapter 14

They passed Wan ThirtyoneFourFour in Universe Station. The private Redstreak line had a terminal there, on the level above the public lines. John glimpsed him through the triple-thick glass that enclosed the exclusive precinct, recognized the fair hair and impossible cheekbones as he and the White Black Birds descended the crowded stairway to the jumble of home-going salarypersons below. ThirtyoneFourFour, clothed in neat and very expensive black, was—as John had known he would be—accompanied by two very large shaven-headed men who looked like enforcers, men with the bleak, glazed look of strong drugs in their eyes.

Heat flared in the onyx bottle against John's chest. ThirtyoneFourFour turned his head as if at a cry.

"Not that way! What are you doing, Moondog?" Bort pounded after John as he slipped and dodged through the crowd. The barriers designed to protect the private lines' customers from the common horde was all that saved them, slowing the thugs, but Aversin heard the whining report of a handgun as he plunged down the escalator, ducked around a corner. He wasn't sure, but he thought he heard another soft, snarling shot and a struck man's cry.

Of course. They're all drugged. They won't dodge. He flung himself onto the nearest train. "It's the wrong line, you fool! You'll end up on Nine-seventy-fifth Avenue!" Bort wailed from halfway down the platform. The doors hissed.

Aversin didn't stop trembling until he reached Garrypoot's apartment, where Clea was trying to get Docket to drink a little milk. "I gave him the widest-spectrum antibodies I could get." She looked up despairingly; milk was dribbled everywhere. "He isn't running a fever, but he won't eat or drink. He could have caught anything—he wasn't wearing mask, and the mosquitoes carry IADS and AOAD . . ."

"Lay him on the floor." The old man had been good to him, chatting for hours about gangs and computers and how to survive in the city: all those things that Amayon would have lied to him about. He fished in his pocket for the amethyst. Master Bliaud had worked spells, he recalled, to return the imprisoned mages to their proper bodies, but such spells had no meaning in this world.

Gently John opened Old Docket's mouth and placed the gem inside. He watched the bookseller's eyes, but they remained blank. Mageborn, the old man still had no idea how to come out of the jewel in which he'd been imprisoned, and there was no wizardry, no adeptness, in his flesh itself.

"Bugger all." He removed the jewel and wiped the spittle off it on the hem of his shirt. "We'll have to do this the hard way. Poot wouldn't have such a thing as a hammer about, would he, love?" He could only hope that if he released it, the old man's soul would find its way back to its body. Did they *have* hammers here?

It turned out they did, a little to John's surprise. He hunted around the apartment until he found a small tray of high-impact plex, which he set on the floor as close as he dared beside the old man's head, then wrapped Clea's scarf over Docket's eyes for protection. "Hold his nose and mouth," he instructed. "When I say *now*, let him breathe. On the count of three. One, two—" He set the jewel on the tray, raised the hammer high. "Now."

The door opened. "What—?" Bort cried as the hammer smashed down, shattering the amethyst inches from Docket's lips. Clea snatched her hand clear as the old man gasped, coughed, flailed with one hand.

"Where—?" Docket choked as John whipped the handkerchief from his eyes. "What—?"

"You all right?" John looked into the terrified gray eyes.

"What happened to me?" The old man caught at his hands and stared in shock at Bort, Garrypoot, and Shamble as they entered the apartment, shaking rain from their ponchos and caps.

"Really, Moondog," Garrypoot fussed, "we've been on the subways for hours trying to find you and now you just . . ."

"The demon," Docket gasped, and the others fell silent. "The demon . . . spoke to me . . ."

"What demon?" John asked softly. "What was his name?"

"Folcalor," the old man whispered, then burst into tears.

* * *

"Should we call enforcement?" Clea paused in the corridor as the digitalized numbers above the elevator doors phased into one another. She'd wrapped herself in her plex poncho again and coiled up her long gray hair under a cap. The bright lights of Poot's building were disorienting; if it weren't for the afternoon sunlight that bathed the illusory landscape outside—inside?—Poot's window, John would have had no idea whether it was day or night. All he knew was that he was exhausted and not likely to have pleasant dreams.

"You mean the chaps with the little cubicles, and they hand you a number and you wait in a line?"

She looked confused. Long used to being the law in the stead of an absent King, John was already sorting through various plans for dealing with the problem himself. Expecting help from that lot in the cubicles was akin to expecting help from Ector of Sindestray.

"Besides," he added gently, "I'll not send men against demons, and them not believing in 'em. Would you?"

Clea shook her head. Bort and Shamble, who'd clearly thought that their part in any rough-and-tumble had been fulfilled, traded uneasy glances.

"It's one of the problems in havin' power, see," John explained. "It's yours for a reason. And that reason involves helpin' those who don't have it, whatever the cost. That's what makes us different from the demons."

He kept a sharp eye on the crowds as he walked the White Black Birds across to their platforms. "You call Poot the minute you're home," he said. "Don't get out of sight of help, and lock yourselves in, and for God's sake watch your backs." And he remained on the platform until the subway whisked them away to sleep among the families that did not understand them and to work at jobs to which they could never accustom themselves.

Then he returned to Poot's apartment and called in his resignation to the House of Two Fragrances, knowing that, fascinating as it had been, its purpose was fulfilled. He slept a little after that but didn't rest easy until the league reassembled slightly more than twenty-four hours later for coffee—which Garrypoot sent down to Food Central for and which was dreadful—and pizza, a food John had every intention of attempting to make when he got home.

If, he reminded himself, he got home.

"Why gold?" Bort asked. "Most of ThirtyoneFourFour's correspondence concerns acquisition of gold from estate sales and attempts to sell it on the Op-Link nodes. He uses about ten different avatars and a whole flak-field of financial screens, but I think we've traced most of them." His lumpy, saturnine face was haggard, and he couldn't have had more than five hours' sleep before going to work in the anonymous bureau that paid his rent, minimum food, and Priority Three meds. He had a class to teach, too, at one of the local rec schools: Literature of Mysticism. According to Tisa, he had exactly two students.

"Now, I know all sorcery requires gold and silver, in pure quantities," Bort continued. "Synthetics don't seem to do, any more than synthetic jewels do. The black nodes—the Link nodes devoted to occult studies—routinely advertise it to buy and sell, in far greater quantities than have ever been on the market. But why? What is it about gold?"

John shook his head. "You're askin' the wrong person," he said. "I'm just a demon hunter. I know it has properties other metals don't, but what those might be you might as well ask the bugs in Poot's kitchen."

Poot swung indignantly around from his keyboard, mouth open to protest, and the others laughed.

"Accordin' to Jenny—me wife . . ." *If she is still me wife,* he thought, with a stab of the old pain, the old love, the old rage in his heart.

As his voice faltered he felt Clea's questioning, gentle gaze touch him.

"Accordin' to Jenny, gold holds certain kinds of magic, or can be made to transmit certain kinds. She says it sends wizards daft when somebody pays 'em off and cheats with an alloy, 'cause then they've got to work around it for as long as they've got that metal, or go through the nuisance of assayin' it clear."

"It says that in ThirtynineThreeSeven's *Occult Encyclopedia.*" Old Docket fumbled eagerly in his pockets for the book chips he routinely carried with him and sighed with frustration. The other prisoners in the holding cell had relieved him even of those. After a night's sleep, the bookseller had only vague recollections of what had happened to him after Wan ThirtyoneFourFour and his two private enforcers entered his store, though he remembered ThirtyoneFourFour holding a gun to his head—grinning and laughing—and putting a purple jewel into his mouth. He had been, he said, imprisoned in a place made of purple crystal. There a demon had spoken to him, though he could not now remember what the demon said.

"Well, anyway, it says in the encyclopedia," the old man went on, fluffing his white hair with a thin hand, "that powers sourced from the sun, the earth, or fire can be stored indefinitely in gold, and that those sourced from the moon, the stars, or water can be stored in silver."

"That's in the *Elucidus Lapidaris,* too," John agreed. "Gantering Pellus says you can source what he calls cold magic from the silver . . ."

"NineSeventy talks of warm and cold magic!" Docket cried excitedly. "Do you have this Gantering Pellus on you?" John's eyes widened in astonishment until he realized that book chips of all twelve volumes probably *would* fit in a pocket. "Or would you be willing to record what you remember . . . Oh, all right," he added as Clea yanked the sleeve of his borrowed pajamas. "Gold is superior because magic contained in gold can be retrieved more strongly and more completely, whereas sourcing magic through silver is more complicated and less sure. The noble metals store and transmit powers, and crystalline formations store information and patterns of energy. And, in fact, crystalline energy alignment is critical to the sourcing and transmission of common plasmic ether."

"So what do the demons want with it?"

"Don't know." John chewed his pizza thoughtfully and nudged his spectacles back onto the bridge of his nose with the back of his wrist. "Could be near anythin', and the Demon Queen sent me here with a great bloody stack of the stuff, bad cess to it. And given that Wan's collectin' it, too, my guess is she planned I should use it as bait to catch me man, same as Wan is. Because any bets the man I'm lookin' for's a mage."

Their eyes devoured him. They were scared and fascinated, all their dreamings coming true in forms that horrified them—as frequently happens, John reflected, with dreams.

"Then why would ThirtyoneFourFour be trying to sell?" Garrypoot asked. He had deeply grudged putting up Old Docket for the night and had been even more upset by the amount of water Clea had used to clean the old man up—"I ration that water *very carefully!*" he'd said. But the prospect of using his skills on the Op-Link to track actual demons seemed to have mollified him.

"Most of these transmissions are about trying to sell over the Link or to find information about other buyers, who of course are hiding their real identities behind avatars as well."

"Is that usual?" John had a momentary, appalling vision of networks of demons all tapping away on terminals. *Let's not tell Aohila about the Op-Link . . .*

"On the occult nodes it is," Bort said. "You can't imagine some of the crazies out there. People who want . . . who want some kind of power. Any kind."

He fell silent, as if hearing in his own words an echo of self. For a time he gazed at the window, which had been switched to show the entrance to the elevator in the subway station below. Behind the faceted band of his spectacles his blue eyes looked weary, battered by the fight against the realization that he was exactly what Tisa had called him: a loser. Crowded and cramped in a world of tiny apartments, endless noise, employments that had no meaning; unfit for the tasks that made one rich, unfit as well for the simple solutions demanded by the frustrated and the drugged. Never married, never destined to be anything but what he was: a dreamer of dreams that could never come true.

"Why won't magic work here?" John asked quietly. "Did it used to?"

Bort opened his mouth to give the usual swift replies about modern civilization and ancient truths, then closed it again. He tugged on his unkempt beard, considering the seethe of humankind in the window for another few moments, then shook his head. "I don't know." He looked at John with tired eyes. "It's so difficult to tell, from the books. Because of course all those books were written by people who . . . who wanted very badly that it should. I think magic did work at one time here, yes, thousands and thousands of years ago. But that's very difficult to prove. So many records have been lost, and those that remain aren't easy to interpret, particularly now. Funds are shorter and shorter for anything that doesn't immediately pertain to energy management and public health. At least three of the major document repositories were in what is now the deep zone. The buildings were abandoned after the 'ninety-seven quake, and what with so much other damage, document retrieval was classified Priority Five. Which means they were simply left there to rot. The fact is, simply, that nobody really cares."

He folded his hands and looked down at them for a time while beyond the window, only a few yards down it seemed, salarypersons on their way back from dinner to voluntary overtime jostled among the kiosks and snack carts, the ad screens and holos and whores, each surrounded in a tight little cloud of private music and prefab dreams. A couple of gang boys crossed the platform and climbed onto a subway car, the more respectable citizens giving them wide berth; they openly wore assault weapons holstered at their belts and slung around their crimson-jacketed backs on bandoliers. The building enforcers watched them warily but didn't challenge them.

Not a thing of building enforcers. John recalled the voice of the dragon Morkeleb in his mind and grinned.

There were demons out there, he thought. He saw Shamble step from a subway car and make his way toward the elevator, shabby jacket pulled close around him and a new holo-hat—this one displaying a clip from a popular holovid play—glowing and posturing above his head.

Demons, and a fugitive mage.

Aohila's lover? Or had that, like the purpose of the water from the enchanted spring, been a lie? The man knew something, or had something, that the Demon Queen could use—of that John was certain.

A gate into his own world?

Abilities she needed to obtain some further goal?

Did he dare turn the man over to her before he learned the truth?

He wished he could ask Jenny what she thought was going on.

He wondered where Jenny was, and if the pain lodged in her like a poisoned arrowhead was growing less. He wondered if Ian was recovering from the grief that had been eating him alive, and if Adric was looking after his brother and his mother. What a hell of a thing for a child of nine to have to do.

I'm only doing the best I can, Son.

He wanted suddenly, desperately and with all his heart, to go home.

The door chime sounded. Old Docket got up to get it and admitted Shamble. In spite of the jewels safely in his pocket John felt a stab of uneasiness whenever any of the league went out of his sight.

In this world Folcalor's demons could have no use for mages' bodies, which could not be utilized to do or channel magic. Yet he wanted their souls.

Souls imprisoned in jewels.

As Ian's had been imprisoned, and Jenny's.

As the unknown mage's would be, if the demons learned where he hid. Was that what Aohila wanted?

"Any of you seen the news?" The welder leaned to the screen, touched in a corner menu. The teeming confusion below flicked away, replaced by a scene of gray rain, afternoon light, and chaos.

Smoke half-obscured the vision, but John realized he had to be looking at a picture of the deep zone. Monstrous buildings; blocks of darkness; the rain-flecked glint of foully iridescent water; square, collapsed shells or monolithic islands defining street upon half-drowned street. Like islands, the roofs of some of those blocks bore trees, the first Aversin had seen in the city. Sickly vines trailed from windows, from holes blown in the walls. In the distance more buildings yet, more walls; iron-hued streets disappearing into infinity with the glare of neon and ad screens and ether light illuminating ash-colored clouds. Mists floated above some parts of the screen. The view drew in, as if descending over one huge block.

It took him a moment to realize those were bodies lined up on the roof, or parts of bodies. Smoke still rose from the piled debris that had been used for a pyre, but it didn't obscure the ropes and manacles that bound the bodies together nor that the postures were not those of people who had been dead when the fire began.

"The enforcers say it's a gang war," Shamble said. He folded his skinny arms, eyes somber with shock. "This footage was shot by an independent. Far as I've heard the enforcers aren't going to investigate."

"Gang war?" Clea came out of the kitchen alcove, coffee filter in hand. "Those are women and children. The gangs don't kill each others' families." She dried her hands on her tunic, sat on the back of the couch. "The enforcers know that. Where is that? If that block there—"

She pointed at the pyramidal mass of pillared ruins. "–is the old central records office, then that must be . . ."

"Ninety-fourth Street and Thirtieth Avenue," John said softly. "Just at a guess."

The others looked at him in surprise. "I didn't know you knew the city," Clea said.

"I don't. But that's where ThirtyoneFourFour was yesterday. And what happened there," John went on quietly, aware that his breath was coming shallow and fast, remembering the bloody walls and straps, the gold hair clip with the blue butterfly, "is exactly what's in Gantering Pellus' *Encyclopedia,* and in the fragments of the *Liever Abominator,* and in every other old tome that ever speaks of what happens when demons start wars in our worlds."

Jenny and Morkeleb left Adric and Ian at Alyn Hold and flew south the following night.

"What about Balgodorus?" Ian had asked during the council they held in the kitchen of the Hold: she and her sons, with Muffle and Morkeleb. In his dark rough robe the dragon appeared human enough unless looked at closely. But the bones in his face were odd, the suggestion of bird remaining in the jut of the nose and the narrow lines of the forehead framed in silky gray. His eyes were a dragon's eyes, and he smelled like a dragon and not a man.

"After the fright Jen put into him," Muffle said, "he's likely running yet. It's winter, lad," he added, seeing his elder nephew's doubtful expression. "Yes, they attacked the Hold. But they can't mount a winter siege. They'll freeze."

"If they were still bandits, they would," Jenny remarked. "But I suspect Balgodorus is a mercenary now, working for Folcalor. In whatever guise the demon now wears; a gnome, I think. I dreamed . . ." She frowned, struggling to catch back the elusive dragon memories.

"If it's a gnome, it has to be the one who's behind their buying of human slaves," she said at last. "Whether Black-Knife knows his master is a demon or not, his resources are greater than they were when he had to live off the land."

"Remember, too," Morkeleb said in his soft human voice, "that demons can bend human thought and human will through dreams, whether or not they have human magic at their beck."

Muffle had nothing to reply to that and only scratched at his unshaved chin.

Jenny had been a little surprised, upon their return to Alyn Hold, that Morkeleb had remained visible to all. She had half expected him to retreat into the defenses of illusion, as she had seen him do at other times when he walked in human form among humankind. But he had spoken even to Aunt Jane, listening with a kind of hesitant interest to her diatribe upon the shortcomings of her sisters, her nephews, and the castle maids. He made few comments and showed little expression, but in the tilt of his head and the wordless watchfulness of his diamond eyes, Jenny saw an unfolding curiosity, a striving to understand from within that which he had previously only observed.

It is not enough, she thought, a little wonderingly, *that he surrender the easy comfort of gold's music and lay aside the magic that makes events bend to the will rather than the currents of chance and time. He has taken a step beyond his pride and treads new territory, perhaps for the first time in his life.*

"I can't take on a demon," Ian said. He would rather not have raised his eyes to meet those around the table, so he forced himself to look first at his uncle, then at his mother. "When I . . . when first I met Caradoc–Folcalor–he played a trick on me, getting me to touch the demon. When I tried to use magic against it, it burned my hand. It . . . it came up the magic, as if I'd thrown it a rope. It came into me through the magic. Even when I tried to defend against it, it used the spells of defense. I don't know how it did that."

"For me it was the same." Jenny pulled the white wool robe she wore more closely around her shoulders, feeling a chill even in the warmth of the kitchen.

On the other side of the big room Aunt Jane said to Sally the cook, her voice loud in the silence, "You add a little honey to those apples and they'll be fine. My mother used to mix in cardamom, but I say those new-fashioned spices only spoil what the Green God gave . . ."

"What do we do if they come back?"

"What you can," Jenny replied. "The important thing to remember is that what they want is *you,* Ian. Not in a thousand years have demons shown such strength. We don't know if there's some other method by which they could enter your flesh against your will and drive you out yet again. You should never have come looking for me as you did."

Ian colored and looked away.

"You should never have come alone." Jenny reached across the table and took his hand.

"Oh, and what am I?" Adric demanded indignantly. "A little brown dog?"

"Yes," Jenny said, ruffling his hair, at which he pulled away, striving for a man's dignity.

"You're a little brown dog who could be used as a hostage," Muffle put in grimly. "I told the pair of you your mother'd be back."

"I'm not sure that I would have, though." Jenny looked around at the smith. "I might have—I'm not sure. But I had forgotten who and what I was. I think in another few days I would even have forgotten why I was lairing up near Frost Fell and would simply have taken wing for the Skerries of Light. And you wouldn't have inquired why I was there," she added, turning to Morkeleb, "would you?"

I would not have wished to, the dragon replied in her mind. But he said, for the benefit of those around the table, "Perhaps not. Or not soon enough. We perceive not time as you do. It is true that the murmur of the demon has troubled my dreams, but it is true also that it is one rumor among many, and I had no reason to pursue it with my thoughts or seek for it in my dreaming. Having known the demon's mind, Jenny, you perceive his calling as others do not."

"You did well," Jenny said, touching again her son's hand, "to seek me. And you, Muffle, did well to try to keep him from doing so."

"We were afraid you'd fly off," Adric said. "It's like when a falcon breaks her jesses and gets away. You've got to have Mim go after her alone—the falcon, I mean—because she knows and trusts him. Mim's Papa's falconer," he added for Morkeleb's benefit. "If everybody in the hunt goes chasing a falcon, she'll be gone. We thought—I thought—you might be scared or something."

"As I was," Jenny said. "In any case we won't be gone long. But Prince Gareth must be warned that there is danger of demons still in the land. Almost certainly Folcalor will make another attempt to gain control of the Realm, to further his rebellion against his lord Adromelech. There's a connection there, too, I think, with the slaves they're buying. In spite of all Ector of Sindestray's efforts, there is no law against being possessed by a demon, only against trafficking with them; but I suspect Master Bliaud has gone into hiding nevertheless. Gareth will surely know where he is. The old man has to be warned not only to look out for himself but to guard his sons, who might be used as hostages for his compliance."

"Demons," Aunt Jane sniffed, fishing salt pork from the brine barrel in a great greasy whiff of salt. "As if we haven't troubles enough. I told that nephew of mine . . ."

Following the conference in the kitchen, Sergeant Muffle clanged the meeting bell above the Hold gate, summoning the folk of the Hold and of Alyn Village to assemble in the hall. Farmers and brew wives and laborers for hire, the baker and the priest–men and women she'd known all her life–greeted Jenny as they came in, as did their children. "Dearest, you've got to put some flesh on your bones," Sparrow said, hugging her–Sparrow, who was even shorter than Jenny and weighed barely more than a good-sized dog–and Peg the gatekeeper kissed her on her bald head and said, "Things'll look better come spring, you'll see."

All of these Morkeleb greeted with quiet courtesy, introducing himself as a friend of Jenny's from the North. When the conference started he settled himself among the grandmothers and the children, in the shadows behind the pillars where the hall's stonework ran into the living rock of the hill on which it was built.

"We ran off the bandits," Muffle told everyone when they'd made themselves more or less comfortable on trestle benches, on the hearth bricks, or on the bases of the pillars that ran down the center of the big chamber in a double line. "But from what Jen tells me they'll be back. And from what Jen tells me, there's magic afoot and a-brewing, and foul things abroad. Some of you may get dreams about how you should kill this person or that person–maybe me, maybe somebody else . . ."

"I get dreams like that all the time, Sergeant," his wife, Blossom, joked and got a general laugh. "I thought everybody did."

"Well, don't pay 'em any heed, woman," he retorted with a grin. "These folk that're using magic of one kind or another will be trying to get hold of Master Ian." He nodded toward the boy sitting uncomfortably on a stool at Jenny's side. In the crowd Jenny picked out the boys Ian had played with less than a year ago: Muffle's son Rok and her own cousins from the Darrow Bottoms, boys growing into the farmers and hunters of the Winterlands, having no other choice of what they would be. No more than John had had, she thought, when he'd wanted to be a scholar and was told he was the lord's son and therefore must become a warrior whether he liked it or not.

"So you may get dreams about doing something with Master Ian," Muffle went on, his voice grave. "Killing him, maybe. Maybe taking him out into the woods with you, or giving someone a way into the Hold, or luring out Master Adric into a trap. These people who'll bait their traps through dreams," the blacksmith said, looking around him now at the quiet faces, still bruised or scabbed from the attack three days ago, "they'll seem to you more powerful than they are. Well, maybe they are powerful. And they may promise you all sorts of things, good or maybe bad. But I think you'll know if your dreams aren't what they ought to be, for such dreams don't usually have the taste of real dreams," he said. "And if that happens, come and tell me.

"Because those who'll send you the dreams will lie. Whatever they tell you they'll reward or punish, it's a lie. And all that will happen is doom for us all. Do you understand?"

There was silence. Looking out over the faces—the scared, uncertain eyes—Jenny wondered suddenly which of those people—Muggy Dim the baker or Mol Bucket the cow maid—might already have dreamed a poisoned dream and heard Folcalor whispering seductive little rhymes to them in their sleep.

"Any questions?" Muffle asked.

Adric, of course, piped up with, "Why is the sky blue?"

"Any questions about this?"

There was a hush in which the wind that had begun to blow from the north whined and sang around the walls of the Hold and drove smoke down the chimney to make Granny Ivers cough. Then Granny Brown—an old stringy woman who had been midwife for many years on the outlying farms, who was eccentric and weather-beaten and now sinking into an unaccustomed sweetness in her old age—spoke up.

"When will Lord John be back?" she asked.

And Muffle looked aside without replying while Jenny thought of that question, which she herself would have asked of the God of Women had she believed in any power or justice in the world.

Would he believe her, she wondered, when she told him she was sorry for what she had said? For her rage at his dreaming of the Demon Queen? She wanted at least to have that chance.

She glanced at Morkeleb, seated next to the old midwife, but he was listening to something four-year-old Ammi Dim was telling him about her kitten.

At length Muffle said, "I don't know, Granny. I don't know."

The day was failing when the meeting broke up, and as usual half the village stayed for dinner. Jenny extricated Mag from the weaving room—"Magic," the child explained, holding up a horrifying knot of Aunt Umetty's wool—and then found a thick skirt and sheepskin boots for herself, and a leather bodice with silver clasps. Over this she put on her heaviest plaids and the sheepskin coat she'd worn to Eldsbouch.

"Now I know why you lived all those years at the Fell," Ian said, coming out into the cold blue snowlight of the court. Jenny laughed. It was the first laughter to pass her lips in months, and it surprised her, almost hurting her throat. It came to her that it was not a thing of dragons to laugh. "I guess Father has his own Frost Fell up in his study. I never thought of it before."

Ian tucked his hands under his plaids, his breath golden smoke in the lantern light from the doors. The warmth of that glow colored his cheekbones and caught threads of carnelian in his hair. Through the door they watched Adric speaking to this crofter or that yeoman, small square hands shoved behind the buckle of his sword belt, Mag listening, silent, at his heels. The bruises on the boy's face were swollen and black; Jenny saw Peg the gatekeeper reach out, concerned, to look, and saw how her son pulled back. Another child might have made a show of the wounds, seeking praise or pity. Adric's gesture was impatient: *Good grief, that was* yesterday.

He will be a lord, she thought. Thane of the Winterlands, body and bones, with none of the doubts and division of soul that tormented John.

Lord Aver, she thought, remembering that big red angry man, *rest easy in your grave. You have your heir.*

As, she supposed looking at Ian, *Kahiera Nightraven has hers.*

And whose heir, she wondered, would silent Maggie turn out to be?

"You'll be back soon?" Ian asked.

Jenny nodded. She picked up the bundle Cousin Dilly had brought for her: food and a little money, medicinal herbs and a blanket, a bottle of water and a couple of clean shifts. Morkeleb stood in the kitchen doorway, shaking his head and softly thanking Aunt Jane and Cousin Dilly for their offer of hospitality for supper. Not human, Jenny thought—wearing his human form like a colorless garment. Darkness within dark, with a diamond glimmer of eyes.

Morkeleb the Black, dragon of Nast Wall.

Star-drake and dragonshadow, treader of the farther dark.

Seeking the knowledge of new things as the ancient king of legend was supposed to have learned them: by being transformed by a wizardly tutor into beasts or fish or birds, to walk among the humble of the earth.

It was time to go. The last of those leaving had taken their departure, and through the hall's open door she heard those who were staying to supper setting up tables and moving benches about amid banter and laughter. There'd be dancing later, she thought. Her stiff hands flexed at the recollection of the music of her harp.

It had been months since those songs had even flickered in her mind.

"Take care," she said, and Ian hugged her close. "If your father returns . . ."

What?

"Tell him I love him," she said. "And that I'm sorry for the darkness that fell between us. That I'll do whatever I can to make amends, if amends are possible."

Ian glanced at the beetling shadow of the wall, where last they'd seen Morkeleb standing—Jenny felt rather than saw the stir of wings and spikes and snow-flecked mane—and then at his mother again, asking if she truly meant what she said. Then he smiled and said, "I'll tell him."

Peg had closed the gates of the Hold and run the portcullis down nearly to the ground. She waited in the dark of the gatehouse now, sitting on the drawbridge's wheel. She gave Jenny a quick grin—

they'd played together as girls–and opened the postern; Jenny kissed Ian again and ducked under the portcullis' spikes.

Morkeleb had risen like a bat from the courtyard shadows and circled now in the moonlight above the wall, small enough that Jenny could have taken him like a falcon on her wrist.

But instead it was he who took her up. Growing in size as he descended, the full moon's light blazed through him as if he were smoke and dreams. His shadow where it passed over Ian's face was a mottle of silver and ash; his wings did not obscure the stars. Jenny lifted her arms to the descending claws. Ian raised a hand in farewell.

The world fell away, amber flowers shrinking in cobalt dark and snow. Wind smote Jenny's face like frozen razors. Together they passed over the village and into the bitter lapis night.

Chapter 15

It is the whole art and pleasure of wights to cause suffering.

John Aversin stared for a long time at the slow pull of waves on the silent beach.

Gantering Pellus, he automatically identified the words that rose to his mind. *The Encyclopedia of Everything in the Material World, Volume III.* He could call to mind the merchant he'd bought the decaying volume from and smell again the snow that had fallen on the winter night he'd copied out that passage.

An ordinary drunkard demons seldom possess, unless they beguile him into welcoming them. Yet those under the influence of certain drugs, which render the mind as if dead, demons may enter, either thrusting forth the souls of their victims or prisoning them in their own bodies. In villages near the places where demons dwell, the inhabitants are known to bind the bodies of the dead before burning them, that demons not enter into the corpses.

That was from Cerduces Scrinus, though the volume he had was fragmentary. Every time he shut his eyes he could see the news-vid and the smoking, twisted bodies on the roof, the red-dripping walls and the ants creeping over the straps on the chair.

He could hear Tisa's laughter as she waved good-bye to him at the corner of Economy Square.

Once entered into the world of men, demons have two goals: to cause pain and death for sport, and to open gates to others of their kind.

Open his eyes, and he saw the peace and beauty of that artificial world, wherever it was. Close them, and he saw the charred dead or a gold-and-blue hairclip lying on a table. Or else Jenny, with the demon fire in her eyes, raising her head from the wine-soaked and bloodied pillows of her bed in Rocklys' camp, smiling at him.

Take care of yourself, love. Take care of our son, if you're able.

Behind him the voices of Bort and Garrypoot yammered on over the noise of Garrypoot's PSE, which favored discords, screams, and random thumps without rhythm: *Rhythm is so* obvious*, man.*

"Names of people who inquired about gold . . ." Garrypoot was saying now. "Cross-referenced . . . files in the black nodes . . ."

"What about people who wrote to Old Docket about books?"

Please enter information . . . Signal when you're ready . . .

God of the Earth, no wonder these people all take drugs.

The smell of coffee. The rustle of clumsy skirts. Clea settled cross-legged beside him and held out a cup. "Unless working for H2F has made you so sick of it you'd rather have something else."

He shook his head but didn't touch the inky brew. "I take it the enforcers didn't look for the killer of any of the murdered girls."

"They say they did. On the news, I mean. I don't think anyone has been detained for it. I've been watching–we all have–since Bort came up with this theory that these killings were caused by a demon. To tell you the truth I don't think anyone really cares."

"And that?" He tapped the button that cut in the news footage again. *Why footage?* he thought. *Feet of what?* Around the edges of the main image one or two small boats flicked through the rank dark waters of the streets. Toward the mist-thick horizon the suggestion of movement stirred beneath the fouled surface of the water. The buildings marched on, deeper and deeper submerged, until only the cornices of some showed above the flood. *How far?*

"Our stuff, is how the gangs speak of what goes on in the deep zone." The woman's lank gray hair brushed John's shoulder as she leaned to touch the buttons below the screen again. It was a wider vista of the city than any he yet had seen, and still it had no end. Black monoliths marched to a sour blurred horizon, a lunatic blaze of neon and ad screens, as if the streets were all in candy-colored flame. The ubiquitous glitter of ether masts shawled the whole. The deep zone snaked through the left-hand half of the screen, vast patches dark where the power had failed, the water orange in places with

chemical ruptures or haphazard attempts at mosquito abatement. In the deep zone, spots of light burned here and there among the ruins, red, like the campfires of shepherds on the hills.

Over all, black clouds reflected the city's rancid glare.

"If a gangboy rapes your sister or your wife or your daughter, you speak to the gang council about it, not to the enforcers," Clea went on. She sounded shocked, as if unaware that this was how bandit gangs operated. As if she thought the city wasn't the Winterlands in other guise. "If it was one of the council that did it, you bite your tongue and hope the council doesn't start thinking that your loyalty may be at question because of it."

She touched another button. Evidently there was no more "footage" of the old portion of the city, the portion built before the waters began to rise. The angle of the image shifted a trifle, but against the grimy sky the broken buildings still loomed, poisonous water deep around their walls.

"Bet TwentyTwelve—she's one of us, one of the league—lives in the zone. She says in the deep zone it's worse. People live there, die there, nobody knows how many or how they do it. They creep out to the dole stations for food and drugs, then slide back in their paddleboats and turn half of it over to the presidents and leaders and champs and generals and whatever the heads of their gangs call themselves. Sometimes whole families just die of disease—cholera or the fever or IDS—overnight. Sometimes the deep-zone boys hire themselves out as enforcers. But even Bet doesn't really know what goes on out there. It could be anything."

Silver salamanders crawling along those mold-eaten buildings, wise with the wisdom of Hell in their eyes. Or maybe, John thought, some poor lost soul of a champion's son sells his wit and his sword to buy the books he was never allowed to read as a child: to buy, maybe, a deal with the King to return law to the abandoned lands?

Give it over, Son, he reflected with a sigh. *It'll never work. They'll do for you every time.*

Demon war.

"Now, here we have something."

John opened his eyes at the glee in Bort's voice. The image on the window had returned to the starlit beach, the slow-rolling breakers. The constellation of the Watcher had risen a little to show the passage of time.

"We matched ThirtyoneFourFour's lists with those who visited Old Docket's node and cross-referenced through the commercial sites of gold purchase on the Link," Bort explained as Clea rose and went to look over their shoulders at the terminal screen. "I expect this Corvin NinetyfiveFifty person, whoever he is, bought magic documents from Docket under other avatars, but this was the first contact. It must be twenty-five years ago."

"He has," crowed Garrypoot. "Look. See? The same number comes up when I run a trace . . ."

"Can you find out who he is?" John asked. "And where?"

"Who he is," Clea said, folding her arms beneath her shawl, "is the foremost researcher into etheric transfer theory in the world."

Bort and Poot turned from the terminal to regard her in surprise.

"If he's the same Corvin NinetyfiveFifty my mother worked with in the nineties. He may not be. Mother says he was elderly then."

"It's 9550-73421-93." Garrypoot read the sequence off the screen.

"I don't remember the whole designation, but Mom'll have it." She walked to a corner of the tiny living room and flipped open her com, blocking her other ear with a finger while Bort paged through half a dozen screens.

"Whoever he is, he shows up a lot on the nodes specializing in precious metals and gems," the fat man reported. "He uses a dozen avatars . . ."

While Bort reeled off incomprehensible details, John settled back to gaze at the velvet night, the too-large, too-beautiful stars.

Odd, to see them all like this, almost exactly as he saw them through his telescope on the tower roof at Alyn Hold. Old friends. He picked out Belida's Mice and the Hay-Wain and Old Master Greenstaff with his lantern. The full moon, ripe and huge as yellow fruit—even the dark plains, the pale rings, were the same, preternaturally clear. Three weeks, he saw, since he'd emerged from the crypt of Ernine to find Master Bliaud waiting for him. When he returned, would it be to find the moon thus? Or would it be that dwindling half circle, or somewhere in-between?

"Is that accurate?" he asked Bort, pointing, when the inputter came over to the couch beside him.

"If it isn't, Garrypoot's paying an obscene percentage of his salary for a counterfeit." The not-quite-wizard studied the sky critically, and John recalled that even when it was cloudy, Jenny could tell him where any star lay in the heavens. Thus it was to be a mage, to source one's power from the light and the true name of each of those distant fires. "But a counterfeit would have to be awfully good to get by him. Astronomy's a special hobby of his. And that looks right. Look, there's even old Doomsday Two."

He pointed a chubby finger where the fringe of trees blurred the dark line of the cliff. A spot of brightness trailed a thin, pronged ravel of light. "Nice animation," he added. "They run in satellite projections."

The last statement meant absolutely nothing to John, who only said, "And about bloody time."

Bort raised his brows.

"Well, it's months late." John folded his arms around his drawn-up knees. "I mean, if that's the mate of the one that showed up last summer. Accordin' to Juronal the thing was a double, with the mate turnin' up seventy-five days after its elder sister. Cerduces Scrinus says they were in the sky at the same time, but he was writin' a hundred and ninety years after. It's been damn near seven months."

"The news mentioned that." Bort slid to the carpet beside John and toggled buttons with a practiced finger. Small cut-outs appeared over the larger window, like bright colored squares of paper pasted on the false window: diagrams of spheres and rings and balls of fire. "At the comet's first appearance during the Dua Dynasty the interval between the two heads was thirty days." He fed in a command, and the explanatory diagrams—whatever it was they explained—wiped themselves neatly away, taking with them cliffs, ocean, and trees. Only a stylized black waviness remained at the bottom to indicate hills. The stars stood untwinkling in the cobalt sky. Even after three weeks of marvels, John was stunned by the simplicity and beauty of the construct.

"This is what the sky looked like back then," Bort said. "You see the first head of the comet was still in the sky at the time of the second head's appearance. The second appearance, during the Interregnum, was, as you say—" Another block of graphics flashed into being

in a corner. "—seventy-five days after the first. One point for your Master Scrinus. As you see—" Nothing if not pedantic, Bort tapped the quasi-window, leaving a faint greasy smudge. "—there's a gravitational lag building up with the widening of the comet's ellipse. They can tell it's the same comet by the iron content, which is very high for cometary spectra, and by the multiple tails. The Astronomical Institute predicted this appearance to the day."

He tapped in another string of instructions, leaving John with a window full of stars—and what was presumably the animated image of the comet's slowpoke mate as it had looked a thousand years ago—as he turned to Clea. "Is it the same NinetyfiveFifty?"

"Apparently." She gestured with her com. "But according to Mother, Corvin NinetyfiveFifty, toward the end of his employment with AcuPro, was altering his appearance like an actor, trying to look older."

"Older?" Garrypoot swiveled on his chair. "Every executive at my job spends thousands getting gray erased from their hair and wrinkles lifted so they can look 'contemporary,' as I think they say. You're dead if your boss thinks you're going to pull experience on him."

"Older," Clea affirmed. She picked up her coffee cup—John was still trying to figure out why the stuff never got cold—and carried it back to the couch. "She caught him at it one afternoon at lunch. Said once or twice she saw where his white hair was growing in black."

Bort looked baffled. John only said, "Was he, now?" The face in the water had been curiously ageless, like a statue's. Soft immobile lips just barely beginning to wrinkle above the delicate chin, the white cheeks free of spots of age. He wondered what the flesh around the eyes looked like, behind the mask of black glass. Or was that why the man wore the dark spectacles? "How old did he look to be, and how long did he work with your mum?"

"Well, Mother worked as a tech for about twelve years with AcuPro. NinetyfiveFifty was senior systems analyst. When Mother came to the company, NinetyfiveFifty had been there about seven years, but most of the people who'd been there when he started were fired on one pretext or another—and some of them pretty obviously pretexts, Mother says—within five years."

Clea settled on the couch where Bort had been, turning the iridescent plex of the mug in her big, clumsy hands. "Mother says he'd start with complaints and disciplinary actions, some of them for things that didn't happen: relays being left open or foci left on when she *knew* they'd been turned off. Files were altered. In one case—an old man only a few years from retirement—a vid loop was altered to show him copying secured data. So she said she knew when she got her first d.a., she'd better start looking, because there was no fighting Ninety-fiveFifty when he made up his mind that someone had been there too long."

"What a son of a bitch," Bort remarked, annoyed. "I've heard of that kind of thing being done by bureaucrats who don't want to pay an advanced salary, but—"

"According to Mother, the teams at AcuPro were allotted extra for experienced personnel. She said the pattern was clear after a few years, but she had no idea what was behind it." Clea sipped her coffee, made a face, and set the cup on the floor. "But, as she said, the handwriting was on the wall. And it's better to get out with a good report than a file full of d.a.'s and complaints. And, she said, she wasn't getting any younger."

"No," John said softly. "And that's the awkward bit when your boss has been around as long as you and isn't gettin' any older. Starts to look bad. How long was he with the company altogether?"

Clea shook her head. "That'd be easy enough to find out through the Link," Bort said.

"Just as a guess," John said, "I'd say he was there long enough that he couldn't cover up the fact anymore that he wasn't an old man—and long enough to find another job where he could darken up his hair a little and start claimin' forty again. Which I'll bet," he added, "is round about the age he gave for the next place he worked. If he's the feller I'm lookin' for, that is."

Bort and Clea regarded him very oddly. Magic of some kind, John thought, in a world where human magic didn't exist . . . Yet if he has magic, why use makeup and dye to look older? Why not an illusion of age, as other mages he'd known had used illusions of youth? It was something else . . . Something stolen from the Demon Queen?

Was that why she sought him?

Bort retreated to Garrypoot's computer again, and Clea leaned back against the round, black, too-hard cushions, staring at the artificial night with its artificial stars.

"What're they called?" John asked in time. "The stars? What're their names?" There were things about this world he had no idea how he'd ever explain, when he finally had time to write of what he'd seen—slugmuffling parlors, for instance, or the Doop—but the stars were a comfort to him, old and faithful friends. Besides, Jenny would thank him for telling her whatever he could about their nature and behavior: The more a mage knew of any source of power, the clearer and stronger that power would be.

"Now?" Clea made a soft sad whisper of laughter. "Three-nine-fifty. Three-eleven-thirty-five." She put a twist of romantic mockery into her voice. "Oh, now that's a mellifluous one: two-three-eighty-five. Doesn't it just have a song to it like the chiming of bells?"

"And what were they called," John asked, "by all those people who should have been wizards?"

A ghost of a smile brushed her lips. Like Jenny, a woman of no great beauty and, like Jenny, growing old. She had the prim mouth and awkward body of the perpetual virgin, too odd to have been wanted or wed by those raised to regard only the stunning beauties portrayed by advertising. Maybe it was simply because she had been caring for her mother all these years.

"What about you?" she asked. "Are you a mage, in the world from which you come?"

"Gaw, no." John shivered at the memory of how the demons had trapped Jenny through her magic, of half-recollected tales concerning his mother and the things she had done. Pain went through him, and a longing to be with the people he knew, away from these stunted children, this wretched flooded city where nothing had room to flower but mildew and despair.

"But he is," she said. "NinetyfiveFifty. The one you seek."

Was he? John wondered. *A mage who had conquered death and time?*

"Your mum didn't happen to say," John said, "where this Corvin's workin' these days? If he went to the trouble of dyein' his hair and gettin' a lot of innocent people fired, it's got to have been so he could get another job."

"True, your lordship."

John grinned, conscious of his coffee-stained shirt and holed boots.

"And if we can find where he works all day, we can sure as check see where he goes to take his shoes off at night."

South of Cair Corflyn, where the King's governor tried to protect too much territory with the attenuated tatters of a garrison, the Snake River lost its way in the woods of Wyr, sinking into marshes and bogs amid the ruins of farms. The lands had been the breadbasket of the Realm before plague had followed hard on the heels of years of floods.

They are like tales, each inscribed upon a grass blade, your people, Morkeleb said as Jenny scanned the coarse sable woods below in search of the firefly clusters of village lights. And the image rather than the words entered her mind. For the first time there was no anger at her or at them, that this was so. *Is it truly what you wish?*

Each blade is a world. She gave words for the first time to what was in her heart concerning even such people as Aunt Jane—or Balgodorus Black-Knife, for that matter. *You see the spot of sunlight on the ocean's surface, and yet the ocean beneath it is miles deep. This is what I am, Star-Treader.*

You are more.

No, she corrected him. *Being human is more than you think it to be.*

To that he had no reply, but she could feel the music of his thoughts, like the silence between stars.

As they flew over the Snakewater country Jenny strained her eyes for the villages she knew: tiny knots of houses set on stilts above the marshes, ruled by their little wild kings. There was one above a pond called Cantle Weck where she knew she would be welcome, but when they drew near it she could find no points of brightness there. Ice flashed in the glimmer of the setting moon as the dragon circled down upon the place, and Jenny smelled old ash long cold and the stench of decay.

"Bandits as a rule don't come into the Snakewaters," she said worriedly, peering through the skeletal blue light. "There don't seem to be any houses burned, either."

There is the smell of sickness in the town, the dragon replied. *A smell of death.* And he put the smell in her mind as he smelled it: the stench of wrongness, a swift series of images of fever, delirium, purging, running sores. And beneath this miasmatic awareness, other images still: images of those who survived the sickness lying in their little round huts, too weak to seek food or to build up fires in the hearth, watching the snow fall outside with despairing eyes.

Each blade of grass dying, and dying with it all the stories, all the recollections, all the invisible treasures of the heart.

Would you descend, Dragonfriend? I sense no one alive.

She forced her lips tight shut and covered her eyes with her arm, trying not to think of the children she had helped birth in that village, who'd run to her giggling when she walked down the shore. Morkeleb circled her with his thoughts, saying nothing, and when they went to ground on an islet in the marsh near Cantle Weck he did not immediately leave to hunt but remained beside her while she wept. At the tail end of the night, she dreamed for a time of the infants of dragons swooping through weightless blackness, playing with weightless balls of opal fire.

Chapter 16

She was sleeping when Morkeleb left her, in dawn mist thick and hued like iron, to hunt for a cow he heard wandering thin and starving among the bare black reeds and snowy stillness. *It was uncared for,* he told her later, returning, *and none searched for it; I hear nothing and no one living in all these marshes.* Jenny thought again of Sparrow's account of the sickness in Alyn Village and cursed that she had not the ability, as dragons had, to stretch out her senses over the lands. She huddled her plaids around her, then kicked them irritably away as a raging wave of heat surged from her protesting flesh and migraine stabbed her vision with momentary, swirling fire. *You'll only go mad with grief and rage,* she thought, *if you start wishing for all the things you once had.*

Sleeping again, she dreamed of John, saw him inconspicuous amid more people than she had ever seen packed tight into a vast dirty dreary room. Dreamed of him sitting at a table gazing into a strange-shaped glass box, bluish lights and strange patterns of colors reflected back from his spectacles.

Folcalor's voice whispered soft and childlike in the deep hollows of her mind. *"Blood in the bowl, make sick men whole."* And a man's thin, age-spotted hand dipped into a gold basin filled with blood and came forth clasping a fragile glass shell.

"Blood in the bowl, peace in the soul."

Her eyes opened to the fading of the chilly winter daylight. Morkeleb lay near her, and in his proximity she felt none of the cold that transformed the waters of the marsh to hard greenish ice; the dragon was little more than a ghost, his shadow barely to be seen in the increasing shadows of night. He listened, and the pale lamps of his antennae glimmered with a queer foxfire light as they moved.

Under white jeweled stars they crossed the sleepy provincial fields and meadows of the Farhythe and the Nearhythe, and the bony back of the Collywilds between them. They saw the lights of little villages whose bells carried to them through the deepening night. The moon's brilliance let Jenny make out every wall and fence and hayrick, but no one below sounded alarms. Even in full daylight it was difficult to see Morkeleb, and he extended his aura of shadow to cloak her as well. As they passed over the town of Queen's Graythe—the principal trading center of Greenhythe—and later over Yamstrand, where the white phosphorus turned the ocean's brim to luminous ruffles, Jenny smelled pyres again. In her mind she had the image of a chain of such conflagrations, like watchfires relaying warning of danger, stretched from the Snakewaters south.

Smoke rises from the walls of Bel, the star-drake said as the white teeth of Nast Wall clove the sky. In the silver-spangled sea the Seven Isles shouldered, dark patches trimmed and dotted with lights: Somanthus and the Silver Isle, Zoalfa and Ebsoon, the wide pastures and rich farmlands of Sarmaynde and the bright falling springs of Glaye. Of Urrate only a black small spike remained, the highest peak, where the temple of the Green God had stood before the island's destruction by the demons under the sea.

Jenny shivered as Morkeleb circled along the arc of the island chain.

Between Somanthus and Urrate the abyss lay where she had fought Folcalor while the whalemages held the other demons at bay. Among those rocks Caradoc's staff had lain hidden. She seemed to hear the crooning songs of the Sea-wights as they waited for the gate to be opened. As they waited to pour into the world again.

Pyres burned in the fields outside Bel. Coming in over the water with moonset, Jenny saw slanted columns of smoke and heard the tolling of the bells.

I like this not. Morkeleb crouched, no more than elf light and bones, among the trees just above the great landward road that ran from Bel to the little town of Deeping, which nestled around the gates of the gnomes' Deep at Ylferdun. The dragon had destroyed Deeping five years ago. Jenny could feel his recognition, his memory of the place in flames. *There is the smell of plague upon the land, and voices crying out in the city. But in the Snakewaters I dreamed of demons, and I hear them whispering still.*

He settled on his narrow haunches and then lay cat-wise again, all his spikes and scales glittering and the bobs of light that tipped his whiskers sparkling like unseasonal fireflies in the dark.

When the star-drakes journeyed from world to world, we would hide ourselves and listen, some of us sleeping and dreaming, others mounting watch over those who slept. These images Jenny saw in her mind, wordless marvels: Centhwevir blue and golden, Hagginarshildim pink and green, others of the dragon-kin she had met and known all sleeping in the strange light of alien moons. *Dreams would pass back and forth among our minds and those of the shadow drakes, the dragonshadows, who partake both of waking and sleeping; the dreams, also, of those who walked in those unknown realms. There is an ice floe on the backbone of Nast Wall, where the waters divide. From there I can listen to the city lands of Bel, and deep into the caverns of the gnomes, and even across the marches eastward to Prokeps and the lands of Too Many Gods.*

To your voice also will I listen in my sleep, Jenny, while you walk among men and speak to your little King.

She straightened her plaids and her sheepskin coat and felt a flash of gladness that she didn't have to worry about rebraiding her hair. It was far less cold here in the South than it had been in the Winterlands–she sometimes thought it would be less cold in Hell than there–and snow only sprinkled the high foothills of Nast Wall, where the black watchtowers of the gnomes loomed above the Ylferdun gate. Looking up into the white endless crystalline eyes, she asked, *How far can you hear, in the deeps of your dreams?*

Through her mind flashed the images of her children: Ian wrapped in his plaids by the reflected glow of torches in the hall, smiling a little at his aunts' bustling hospitality; Adric chatting with grown men about cattle and fortifications and horse doctoring as if he were already the Winterlands' lord; and little Maggie, silent, watching, with who knew what intricate knots of awareness behind her mouse-black eyes.

I know not, Jenny. His voice was gentle, a touch of peace. *As the pool deepens, it widens. Did I sleep a thousand years, I could perhaps hear the voices of every child born to women on this earth, and the names they called their cats.* He blinked at her; she seemed to see points of fire glimmer as he settled himself and tucked his wings, and all the spikes and spines and ridges of his armor for an instant caught the starlight, then vanished, as he was more and more apt to do.

It is hard, she said, *not to know. Not to be able to see.*

There is always something, he said, *that one cannot see, or do, or have.*

But she had seen him speaking with the old women at the Hold who had lived a lifetime of happiness and grief without ever going farther than Great Toby; had seen him with the children there. For the first time she felt that he understood.

From the air she had seen that Bel's landward gate stood open so the dead-carts could come out. Pyre light glared ahead of her in the mists as she walked toward the walls, using her halberd as a staff. Once when she turned back, she thought she saw a shimmer of ghostly light rise on silk wings from the hill above the road and circle toward the mountains with the first dawn staining the cloud-bolstered winter sky. She walked on.

Around the gates all was madness. Torchlight fluttered on either side of the great triple archway, and in the fields carters threw down the bodies of the dead from their wagons. Wood was heaped everywhere, and grimy men stumbled with weariness as they built pyres. Jenny saw that some of the bodies, laid out waiting to be burned, were wrapped in cheap rags and old sheets, and others in costly white wool embroidered in bright colors. She did not have to be told that the contagion was claiming rich and poor alike.

She passed among them like a ghost and entered the city with the late winter dawn.

Once she was within the walls, it was clear to her that the healers had no more notion of where to look for the plague's source than she had. Smudges of herbs and sulfur burned before some mansions, and through the gates of others, even at this hour, Jenny saw women swabbing down the house fronts and dooryards with vinegar the smell of which cut the air like a knife. Incense and the halitus of burning meat breathed upon her from the gates of every temple and chapel she passed.

Bel stood upon five hills, the tallest being given to the gods. But its companion hill, broader and fairer, bore the gilded turrets and many-hued roof tiles of the House of Uwanë among a lacing of bare-branched trees. Around the King's house the wealthy, as the wealthy do, had built their pillared dwellings, and as she made her way through the streets, Jenny saw how many gateways bore the yellow sigils of contagion, how many glass windows flickered with lamplight where physicians sat with the sick.

In one flower-carved arch a man in robes of cut velvet pleaded with a little band of the King's guards. "It's too soon to say he's dead. Far too soon. The sickness debilitated him, of course it did, but his fever's abating." He beckoned, his hand laid on the forehead of the child on the bier, a boy of about fifteen years old.

"The sickness has taken turns like this before," the father went on, in the faltering voice of one who chatters to save himself from doom. "He'll be . . . still . . . like this. You'd be ready to swear he's gone, and then his eyes will open."

The chief of the guards did not come near, nor extend his hand to feel the child's face. Rather he signaled his men to take up the bier and carry it away.

"At least give me an hour!" the father pleaded, his voice breaking. "The healers will be back then and—"

"The King's law is clear," the chief of the guards said. His face was like stone, but Jenny heard in his voice a note that made her wonder whether he, too, had lost a child. "The dead must be taken out of the city and burned lest the contagion spread."

"But it wasn't the contagion that killed him." The man spoke too quickly, his eyes darting from face to face. "That . . . that he's sick with, I mean. You can see there's no sores . . ."

"I'm sorry, Lord Walfrith," the chief said more gently. "The healers say that your son had all the marks of the sickness. They bade us fetch his body away. We can't risk the disease spreading further."

"At least let him lie in the family vaults!" The father clung to his son's hand.

"I'm sorry, my lord." A priest, clothed in the gray of the God of Healing, gently disengaged Lord Walfrith's grip. "It cannot be."

The father began to weep, and Jenny moved on through the half-light of the cold streets. She remembered Ian and Sparrow and others, speaking of the strange sickness that had seized Druff Werehove and Genny Hopper's child. Nothing in the old books Caerdinn had preserved of ancient times, nothing in John's vast collection of learning and nonsense at the Hold, had spoken of this kind of power in demons—at least not for the past thousand years.

The gates of the palace stood open. But the outer court, where vendors and petitioners and sightseers usually milled, was empty. Generally petitioners got no farther than this—certainly not those who made their appearance dressed in a peasant's leather bodice and sheepskin boots—but Jenny had been made welcome in the palace before and knew to go to the guardhouse and ask the man there if he would send a page to Lord Badegamus, the Regent's chamberlain, telling him of her arrival.

"Tell him it's the Lady Jenny Waynest," she said, making her voice as impressive as she could and wishing absurdly that she were half a foot taller. "It is a matter of importance touching Lord Gareth."

"I don't doubt as he'll see you, m'lady," the captain of the men at the gate said as one of their number crossed the deserted flagstones, his boot heels clacking, toward the palace hall. "Even after all that's passed I've heard him speak well of you." He offered the words to her like a gift, as if in comfort, but Jenny was aware of the way other guards jostled discreetly to get a look at her from the shadows of the watchroom. "Bedded *how* many of the rebel cavalry in one night?" she heard one man whisper in awe. She was glad she stood in shadow that hid the dull blaze of color she felt rise through her neck and face.

She could not even turn to these men and say, *It was the demon that took over my body, that did those things!* If John did not believe her, why should they?

Instead she asked the captain, who seemed to be a kind man, about the plague. "As I came through the Snakewaters, I saw whole villages stricken with it and pyres burning in the Hythe," she said. "What have the healers made of it, or the scholars at the university in Halnath?"

"They've made nothing, m'lady." The captain's lean dark face hardened. "Nor can they cure it, four cases in five—and that fifth case I think is mostly chance. It's a fever that won't be brought down by all their herbs and purges. Five days now it's been in the city, and less time than that, from the first outbreak in the Hythe till it reached us."

Another man, a thin discontented-looking lancer, added, "For once the rich, who leave the city when the summer fevers come, have to suffer with the poor."

"Shut up, fool!" the captain snapped. Jenny saw real and immediate rage in his eyes and remembered the dead boy in the gateway and the father's weeping as the guards and the priest tried to take the youth's body away. Turning back to Jenny, the captain said, "My lord Regent's nearly distracted, my lady. People are saying—if you'll excuse me saying it—that it was the wizards that joined with Lady Rocklys, when she rebelled in the summer, that planted the seeds of this in vengeance for her defeat. Though myself, I served under Rocklys, five years ago, and she wasn't a woman to—"

He turned quickly and saluted. Jenny saw the guardsman who'd gone to deliver a message to Gareth's chamberlain. To her surprise the chamberlain himself bustled at the man's mailed heels. Badegamus, gray and stout and resembling nothing so much as a rosebush in bloom in his fluttering array of archaic mantlings, executed a proper and lengthy salaam, just as if, thought Jenny, she wasn't a skinny, scarred, hairless woman about whom guardsmen sniggered in corners. "Please come with me, my lady," he said.

A lone petitioner sprinted from the gate to catch the chamberlain on the way across the court. Badegamus deftly fended him into the arms of the guard. "It's imperative that I speak with Lord Gareth soon," Jenny said, her voice echoing a little in the damp arched passageway that ran beneath the hall. "Please ask him . . ."

"My lord requested that I take you straight to him," the chamberlain said. "It is I who must beg forgiveness of *you,* madam, for not allowing you time to bathe and change your raiment. But my lord Regent was most insistent." His voice was trained and melodious, like a deep-toned woodwind skillfully played, but Jenny heard the flaw within it and looked up quickly. Under the heavy cosmetics, his face had creases of exhaustion and grief and the pallor of a man who has not slept.

She was taken up a back stair and down a dreary servants' hall illumined by a single window high in a gable. With one gold-painted fingernail the chamberlain scratched at a small door, the other side of which Jenny guessed would be hidden by paneling and paintwork. "Come," a muffled voice said.

A smell of sickness and lamp oil, of clothing days unwashed.

Prince Gareth stood up from beside a carved bed, its curtains looped back to show the wasted, fragile shape of the girl within.

"A god sent you." He'd been weeping. He fumbled to put on his thick spectacles, then gave it up and simply crossed the room to take Jenny in his arms. His stubbled face was so haggard with grief, so changed by weariness and by eyes swollen with tears, that for an instant Jenny did not recognize the boy who had come to Frost Fell five years ago begging for help against the Dragon of Nast Wall. She felt him tremble as he clung to her, a six-foot child begging for a mother's comfort. Badegamus tactfully disappeared through the door in the paneling and pulled it silently closed behind him.

"The doctors say she's dying." Desperation cracked Gareth's voice as he led Jenny across to the bed. Skeletal, blue lipped, and blotched with red blisters, Gareth's wife, Trey, lay on the bed.

Chapter 17

GeoCorp Offices had an entire district named for them, an endless subway ride on the Eternity line and virtually identical to every other portion of the city John had seen. A major subway station serviced the complex's lowest levels, larger even than that below the Universe Towers. Every niche and wall and angle of its ceiling blazed with crystalvision ad screens and shrieking neon: Gorgeous women applied Cover-Blaze and godlike men sipped or sniffed or shunted Brain Candy or Blue Heaven. Spiked and shaven-headed gangboys jostled along the platforms in groups, glaring warily to the right and the left with drug-burned cinder eyes; enforcers glanced at them and looked the other way. A dole office occupied one level of the station, and beggars shuffled restlessly in the line, thin and hungry-looking but smiling contentedly as they received their handouts of proto-chow and Peace. They smiled at the enforcers who chased them onto the trains or up the stairs to the rainstorm above, smiled at the rich who pushed them aside.

Music hammered the walls, the ceiling, the floor. Mosquitoes whined above the puddles. Everything stank of piss, chemicals, and smoke.

"There's supposed to be a truly excellent theatrical bar on Six-oh-seventh Street just off the square," SevenNinetynine, Clea's tiny crimson-haired mother, remarked. She minced along at John's side in her high-soled red shoes and bright red-and-white dress with the air of a dowager promenading her gigolo, her lacquered coiffure dancing with gold clips. More gold—thin chains such as Tisa's lovers had given her—flickered on the schoolgirl-smooth flesh of her throat. No wrinkles marred her plump lips, no crow's-feet desecrated the corners of her sapphire eyes. Only the eyes themselves were old: hardened, cynical, and weary to death of struggling. They, and the oddly silky texture of her skin, were the only things that spoke of true age: two bitter truths in the gorgeous lie of her face.

This must be what Clea meant, John thought, *when she said, "My mother's had a lot of work done."* He was coming to know the look of "a lot of work." He only wondered what that "work" consisted of: something to think about, next time he heard a ballad hymning eternal youth.

"I almost never come here," she added, pausing beside a vendor's barrow to look at more hair clips. "All the good dance clubs are down in the Seventieth District. Isn't this darling?" It contained a holo chip—which John only knew as the thing that made the annoying animated images dance and posture on holo-hats—that created a very tiny animated couple who appeared to be making love in the wearer's hair.

"Has eight color settings," the vendor pointed out eagerly. "And a sound chip. You can pipe in an audie from your own system as well, so they can say any names you like."

John thought about the eyeless creatures that lived in Aohila's hair and wondered if she'd like one of these for her birthday, if demon queens had birthdays.

"Shouldn't we watch the platforms down here as well?" Bort glanced nervously at the slow-churning sea of humanity clustered around the incoming trains. He had to shout over the vendor's thundering PSE, and SevenNinetynine's, which she'd raised in volume to compete.

"Oh, NinetyfiveFifty would *never* take a subway, I don't care who's after him." SevenNinetynine paid for the hair toy, produced a key card from her handbag, and minced toward the bank of elevators that ascended to the building above. "I know there are analysts and engineers who live downtown and take the regular trains, but NinetyfiveFifty was an absolute recluse. Even in those days he had his own pod and hired an enforcer to follow him to work. Well, with those spectacles he isn't exactly unobtrusive, now, is he?" She almost had to shout over her own music but didn't particularly seem to notice.

"Specs?" John said curiously. "Dark ones, that hid his eyes?"

"Yes, darling. Do you know him?" She smiled up at John and melted a little against his side, like colorful ice cream. "But of course you're right, dearest," she added, turning her head to study Bort and Clea. "Why don't the two of you keep an eye on the corporation elevators over there? He should be out soon. He never cared about impressing management with extra shifts. Goodness knows he didn't have to.

"She does stand out so," she added to John, in as much of an undervoice as was possible with a PSE blaring earsplitting harp adagios all around her, as her daughter and Bort obediently headed toward the other bank of elevators and she insinuated her arm into the crook of John's elbow and led him into a softly lighted glass bubble for the ascent to the building above.

"And of course those friends of hers are *completely* hopeless. I trust you're not a magus of exalted lineage cast by some sad twist of fate into a world unworthy of your talents? Bort's a perfectly sweet boy—" Bort was forty-five. "—but one *can* have enough of the cruelty of fate." She withdrew a tiny enameled vaporator from her handbag and took a revivifying sniff. "Now, look as if you wrestle wealthy old hags for a living, darling." She offered him the vaporator with a flirtatious wink; John grinned and shook his head.

"They goin' to give us a problem if we just hang about in the executive lobby and all?"

"Oh, my *dear* boy." She smiled languishingly up at him. "You obviously haven't had enough experience with the way executives conduct their lives."

Obsidian mirrors dominated the walls of the executive lobby, gilt pillars and statues breaking up the lush expanses of gloom. What seemed to be acres of empty space was dotted with sma' tables at which men and women in sharply tailored, quiet-hued clothing sat while beautiful girls and handsome boys ran and fetched chilled drinks, tiny trays of rice crackers and fish roe, and exquisitely wrought porcelain thimble cups of pink, blue, and yellow powders and pills. "They never mix them strong enough in places like this," SevenNinetynine commented, flagging down the handsomest boy, tapping her credit into the tray holder, and taking a sniff of Golden Glimmer. "I've had stronger at a church luncheon. Why are you looking for NinetyfiveFifty? What's he done?"

Her eyes glinted, suddenly avid behind her screen of sweet vivacity, and John remembered Clea saying her mother regularly searched her room, though she was nearly fifty and her mother seventy-five. "Whatever it was, it must have been just *decades* ago. So far as I've ever been able to ascertain, he's done nothing for the past fifty years but invent more and more efficient relays and processors."

Would a mage know how to do that? John wondered. *If he's got spells on him to keep age and death at bay, he'd have time to learn.*

"He was working on a replicating splitter when he was at Acu with me. It made them a fortune, of which he kept a solid percentage. A replicating splitter divides the etheric stream without weakening the energy, something you can't do with electricity. It made for a staggering increase in power output from a single generator, you understand. How it operates I'm still not entirely certain—I'm a dead loss below submeson level. Will you have a drink?"

John shook his head. He severely missed Aunt Hol's barley beer and the sweet, musky southern wine, but he'd seen too many of his erstwhile neighbors at TwelveNinetyseven's lodging house indulging in the local alcohol to have the slightest inclination to trust the stuff. Most everything here—alcohol, some coffees, most foods, all drugs, and even certain vid shows—as far as he could tell, was designed by its makers to be addictive in a fashion he did not understand. Docket had warned him of this. He wondered if Amayon would have, or would simply have laughed in delight at John's belly cramps, seizures, and depression of withdrawal as he'd laughed at his agonies in paradise.

John sipped his tea, eyes following the people who emerged from the lifts, wondering who they were when they went home and what they did. Men and women both seemed to follow the pattern of every salaryperson he'd seen in dyeing their hair quiet shades of dark brown or black. They all looked young and they all looked like they'd "had work done." Most of them crossed at once to the smoked-glass doors at the far side of the lobby, where they slipped cards into a slot then went to join friends at one or another table. In time the small green lights in the tables' centers would brighten when their private pods were ready at the doors. Each table also had a com, a terminal, and a pop-up screen, and even during conversation, everyone continued to make calls or tap keys until the moment the light went on, in case their supervisors chanced by. As he and SevenNinetynine passed between the tables he caught whiffs of personal music, but there was none in this corner but that of his companion, who toggled it down a little to permit speech.

"They have the same set-ups in their pods, too, you know." SevenNinetynine tasted half a rice pat and set it back down on its fragile ceramic plate. Like most wealthy women she was thin—only the poor, evidently, were fat here. Clea had explained that most of the toppings on rice pats were made with half-and-half molyose and scrunnin, substances that were at once addictive and repellent, so those who did not wish to put on flesh continued to buy food that they then had no desire to eat. "Half the executives at this level are still in their offices, you know, and will remain there until nearly midnight so their security codes will register the fact on the mainframe. Which is something, I'll grant him, NinetyfiveFifty never did."

She tilted her head inquiringly, regarding John with brilliant and rather dilated blue eyes. "You never did say what you want him for. He must be *ancient* these days, you know."

"A woman he once loved sent me to find him," John said, reflecting that this was more or less the truth, all but the *woman* part. "That's all." He touched the dragonbone box in his pocket; felt, too, the heat of Amayon's prison glowing against his skin beneath his shirt. He'd feared to bring the demon along but feared still more letting the bottle from his sight. "I mean him no harm."

"Just as well." SevenNinetynine clicked her tongue a little in disapproval of a passing executive with dark purple hair and a suit to match. "Because even when he worked for Acu—and goodness knows *that* was when dinosaurs walked the earth!—he had the most astonishing security systems around his office, his private lab, everyplace he was likely to be. He came up with good reasons for it, of course, reasons that the corporation believed anyway—every sort of tale about industrial spying and concept theft—and he was such a genius at subatomics they'd do anything to keep him, including putting in electrofused silicate door frames and taser emplacements. He was certainly worried about something. I can't believe it was just the likes of you."

"It isn't," John murmured. "Though meself, I'd not want to get on the bad side of the lady he loved and left."

"Good heavens!" SevenNinetynine turned her face quickly aside and moved a little so that a gilt nude concealed her from the main expanse of the lobby. "If he's had work done, it's the best I've ever seen! He doesn't look a day past thirty-two!"

Turning in his chair with the air of a man watching a pretty waitress cross the room, John observed the man who had just stepped from the elevator. SevenNinetynine's estimate was generous. In fact Corvin NinetyfiveFifty looked about Jenny's age—forty-five—with dark hair just beginning to streak silver at the temples and lines just beginning to settle into his pale, somewhat mottled skin. Under the silver-gray perfection of expensive suiting his thin, stoop-shouldered body was beginning to acquire a little paunch, but he did not move like a man who was elderly fifty years ago. Even those executives who had had their jowls tightened and crepy necks smoothed, their wrinkles excised and their bodies carefully massaged and exercised and electrotoned to the illusion of youth—even these moved, in time, like the old men and women they were.

It wasn't just the illusion of healthy middle age. It was reality.

No magic I have heard of, John thought, *will do that.*

He glanced back at SevenNinetynine and saw fury at her mortality in her despairing eyes.

It lasted only a moment. NinetyfiveFifty slipped his card into the slot by the door, then went to a nearby table to order a drink. John was interested in the placement of the table: close to the bank of doors that led into the pod trains, tucked into a corner so anyone who came near him would come from one direction only.

It was the table John would have chosen had he been expecting trouble.

He slipped his hand into his doublet, palmed the dragonbone box, and caught the tiny neck of the bronze flask with a finger. *Now?* he wondered. Did his prey have to see him plunk the seeds or whatever they were into the trap for the magic to work? A lunatic vision drifted through his mind of himself performing this rite before a thoroughly unimpressed and unaltered NinetyfiveFifty: *I beg your pardon, young man, but aren't you aware that magic doesn't work in the city?*

How would he explain *that* to the Demon Queen?

Well, let's give it a try anyway.

He was starting to get to his feet when NinetyfiveFifty raised his head, the dim lamps flashing on the dark glass that hid his eyes. John froze in his tracks, knowing suddenly and without question that behind that darkness lay something inhuman, something that could not be concealed as age could be. For a heartstopping instant he thought the scientist was looking at him. Then he heard the elevator doors open behind him.

Wan ThirtyoneFourFour stepped into the lobby, two handsomely suited and extremely large men in tow.

Bugger. With great presence of mind John sat at the nearest vacant table and pretended to look through his pockets for a key.

The onyx bottle burned against his skin.

His eyes the lunatic eyes of a demon, ThirtyoneFourFour strode across the lobby. His grin was a demon's grin. His hand went into the front of his jacket, and John remembered the dead girl in the alley, blood splashing in the scummy water. Remembered the gold in white foamplex cartons in the dim-lit chamber in the Universe Towers. NinetyfiveFifty was rising from his seat.

Don't give yourself away till you have to, John thought.

The next instant four men seemed to melt out of the crowd in the lobby, men who, John realized later, had all entered within the five minutes preceding NinetyfiveFifty's arrival.

Like those with ThirtyoneFourFour, they were neatly dressed in standard business attire, though in dark blue instead of black, and they were all very large.

Wan ThirtyoneFourFour palmed a gun. John was already ducking when one of ThirtyoneFourFour's enforcers yelled, "What the . . ." in anger.

And all hell broke loose. Each of the scientist's men produced a weapon, and techs and executives of both sexes looked up startled and a little puzzled, then belatedly flung themselves out of their chairs as thin cold fire flashed. Bullets or lines of ruby light tore smoking holes in tables, walls, human flesh. Wan staggered, and two of NinetyfiveFifty's men tackled him. John saw blood pour down the side of Wan's head, but the demon kept lunging against the grip of the enforcers, kept firing at NinetyfiveFifty with wild, raking shots, regardless of where they went.

NinetyfiveFifty darted like a lizard for the pod doors the moment the shooting began. Alarms shrilled, lights exploded, men scattered like scared bugs; John looked around for SevenNinetynine and saw her duck a line of laser light and reach a gilded statue in two quick steps. *Cover?* There seemed to be better cover available, but she was pretty drugged up.

The pod door flipped open. Two more enforcers emerged from it to open fire on Wan and his surviving henchman the moment their own employer was inside. Building enforcers slammed into the room, assault weapons ablaze. The pod door snipped shut, and an instant later the light above it turned from red to green, indicating the pod was gone. Beside John a waitress had fallen, clutching her belly, weeping over the blood welling between her fingers; the handsome young man who'd brought SevenNinetynine her Golden Glimmer five minutes before lay dead just beyond, a green plex barb buried in his eye.

Enforcers were rounding up everyone in sight. John made a dash for the statue, caught SevenNinetynine by the wrist; she already had her key in her hand and managed to summon the elevator and slip in before anyone got to them.

"You all right?" he panted as the glass floor sank away under them, plunging to the subway station below. He was trembling, the waitress' spattered blood sticky on his hand. He saw Amayon's face in his mind, dreamily sighing in the azure twilight of paradise.

"Just fine." SevenNinetynine took another sniff from her vaporator and smiled as if nothing had happened. A tiny logo on the cylinder identified it as Midnight Dewdrops: *No matter how trying your day has been,* Old Docket had translated the ad screens for him. She held out the drug to John; he shook his head. "Are you sure, dear? You look pale."

A dozen people had just died in the room above them. A score or more injured, some of them desperately. He'd seen worse after bandit raids, but in those cases it had made a kind of sense. John understood bandits. He looked down into SevenNinetynine's eyes and saw only the drug.

She smiled. "Optiflash Yellow," she said. "Special house line Twelve-twelve."

"What?"

An impatient little frown creased the flawless brow, "Optiflash Yellow," she repeated. "Twelve-twelve. The pod line he took. It goes straight to the Yellow Circles." Her manicured fingers fumbled with the vaporator, and she took another whiff of it, and another, before shoving it back into her handbag with a curse.

"They never make those things strong enough anymore," she said. "The Yellow Circles are one of the elite complexes, guaranteed trouble-free—which means everyone and everything going in is screened. They put in a separate food-shipments line after one of the gangs staged a raid on the Red Circles through a food train. You'll have your work cut out for you, it looks like."

She stepped out of the elevator and made a beeline for the nearest kiosk, which bore a holo of a dancing vial scattering glittering lines of pale blue powder that dissolved into stars. John followed more slowly, still seeing Wan ThirtyoneFourFour, who'd only wanted to live a little longer, handsome as a god, a hole through his head and a grin on his very expensive face. Still fighting.

Like poor old Dobbin, he thought. *Ridden to death and beyond.*

Coincidence, that the demon attacked Corvin NinetyfiveFifty just ahead of my finding him?

Amayon, me pretty lad, remind me to dump something gie unpleasant into your little bottle with you.

It meant he had to act fast, for by the sound of it Corvin NinetyfiveFifty was rich enough to change his hiding place easily.

And it meant as well, of course, that now Corvin NinetyfiveFifty would be expecting company.

"I can't do it." Jenny looked down at the blistered, pain-taut face of the woman on the bed. Her voice trembled, seeing in Trey Clerlock's face the horrible mirror of her own: aged, hair shorn with the fever, scarred from the malady's sores. Seeing, too, the young woman's belly swollen with child, the child whose life sapped the strength of its mother, robbed her of the strength to resist.

Her eyes blurred with tears as she looked up at Gareth, towering awkwardly beside her. "I can't do it anymore." She stammered, the full horror of her impotence coming to her: that she could not save the life of this sweet young woman, her friend's wife; could not save her friend's child. Her hand pressed quickly to her mouth for a moment, then she took it away. "I'm not a healer anymore, Gareth. My magic . . ."

"Try," he whispered.

She tried.

Through the forenoon she sat by Trey's bed, bathing the girl's forehead and cleansing her sores with tinctures she'd wrought last year, before her magic had failed. The fever herbs—willow bark and slippery elm that the healers had already administered—she boiled and cooled and gave her again. As she worked, she drew the signs and sigils of healing on the girl's lips and eyelids and belly; made the passes and whispered the words of power, of healing, of balance. But she felt them sterile, no more than the mumbled hocus-pocus of her days of impotence as a young girl, after Nightraven had left her and before Caerdinn had begun to teach her the true words of power. In those days she'd pretended, making up spells from remembered fragments and omens seen in dreams and had wept when nothing came of them. Sitting beside Trey's bed, she wept now.

She cried for the dying girl, and for the man who sat beside her, watching with despairing intensity. For the child that would never be born. Wept for herself as well, watching herself as if she saw that little northlands girl again, like a child at a mud-pie party, pretending stones are cakes and miming the presence of cloaks and tablecloths and feathered hats when there is only air in her hands.

The baby was dead in Trey's womb. She did not need to be a magewife to know this. Pressing her hands to the thin milky skin she felt only stillness and knew that the young woman would survive neither a purging of the fetus nor the sepsis of its decay. The fever had killed it, as it was killing the mother long before the child's death would have its inevitable effect.

Rain swept the terrace outside, and the great dark curtains that cloaked the windows stirred and bellied with restless, gusty life. Once Jenny sat back, blind with exhaustion, and said, "Everything that healers could do has been done."

"Please," Gareth said. Just, "Please." Behind the glass of his spectacles his eyes begged her to make things other than as they were.

At about the hour of noon, Trey of Belmarie died.

For a long time Jenny sat, holding the girl's thin hand and remembering the shy sixteen-year-old who'd risked the mockery of her brother and her friends and lent Jenny a dress so the older woman wouldn't be embarrassed before the malice of the Southern court. She remembered Trey's love for Gareth and her gentle dignity as the

Regent's wife when Jenny had seen her two years ago; her instinctive kindness in dealing with the mind-broken old King.

Where was Trey's daughter Millença, she wondered, to whose naming day she and John had come? Taken sick also?

But she could not ask. Gareth lay stretched across his wife's body, silent and shuddering with shock and pain. She could only stroke the trembling shoulders, touch the wisps of barley-colored, dye-streaked hair. She said nothing, for there was nothing to say. After his sobbing ceased, Gareth lay for a long time, face turned away from her and toward the face of his wife. He did not speak, though twice or three times he drew a long deep breath and let it out in a sigh.

At last he stood up and raised Jenny to her feet. "You did what you could." His words came out small, like a message from a stranger written and memorized years ago. "You have to be weary. I'll have Badegamus get you a room."

Gray light leaked through the half-open curtains. Rain still struck the tiny windowpanes with a noise like the beat of waves. Last night's lamp smoke clogged the air in the chamber, and Gareth's face wore a shuttered look, beyond anything but exhaustion.

"I'll stay here with you, if you don't object."

The Regent shook his head. "You need sleep." To the scratching at the door he added, "Come." It opened to admit a servant with a pot of coffee and another of tea, and a plate of honey and rolls. The chamberlain followed, face still the careful mask of one trained not to burden others with his griefs. He glanced toward the bed, eyes asking what it would not be good manners to speak, and Gareth said, still in that small careful voice, "She lives."

Jenny glanced quickly up at Gareth, but he averted his face.

"Lady Jenny has done all she can and advises that ... that my wife be left utterly undisturbed. There is ... there is an herbalist in town I've sent for, who may be able to refresh her." Gareth had resumed his spectacles to speak to Badegamus, and behind them his eyes were a stranger's. His hand, when he took Jenny's arm, was alien, stiff, and halting as he propelled her across to where chamberlain and servant stood. "Please take Lady Jenny to her room, and send Captain Torneval and twenty men here to me."

He has lost his wife, Jenny thought, *and his child. It is not for me to speak up and say to another person, "He's lying; his wife is dead."* So she let herself be led away through the bedroom's small airy antechamber and the suite beyond, then along a terrace shuttered against the hammering rain and toward the wing and the room where she and John had stayed two years ago as the Regent's guests. Looking back through the long corridor of rooms she glimpsed Gareth still standing at Trey's bedside looking down at her, and though she could not read his face, his whole body seemed braced as if for a whipping.

In her room she ate and bathed and put on the sleeping robe the servants had left for her. The gold-stamped crimson curtain was caught back, and through the window's small round panes she made out the distorted shape of the terrace outside the royal chamber. Two guards flanked the door that led into Trey's room, indistinct blobs of red.

Gareth himself had ruled that the bodies of the dead must be burned, not laid in the tombs of their families.

Even Trey, she thought. *Even Trey.*

As she watched, the terrace doors opened. A tall figure emerged, wrapped in a hooded cloak—Gareth, by his height, though the uneven panes made it impossible to be certain. He neither spoke to the guards nor paused, only drew the hood more closely over his head and hurried down the terrace and across the garden, the cloak nearly tripping him as he went.

When he had passed from sight, Jenny opened the window and slept with the charnel smell of the city drifting above the rain smell and the earth smell from the garden. She rose with the tolling of the evening bells, dressed, and returned to Trey's rooms, knowing that if he'd returned Gareth should not be alone. Passing along the terrace she heard no outcry of mourning. Gardeners and guards alike still wore the red and gold of the House of Uwanë, not mourning black. When she reached the door into the vestibule of the royal rooms, Jenny found the guardsmen still at their posts.

"I'm sorry, my lord," Captain Torneval was saying to the tall red-haired man who stood before him in a scholar's black robe as Jenny entered. "My lord Gareth said none were to be admitted until his return. My lady Trey needs her sleep."

Jenny opened her mouth and closed it again. It was not for her to announce—to guardsmen, to the servants lighting the lamps, and to whomever else cared to carry the gossip abroad—the death of the Regent's wife before the Regent himself was ready to bear the public display of sorrow.

"Did he say where he's gone?" the man asked. Jenny recognized the scholar as Polycarp of Halnath, Gareth's cousin and the master of the Citadel University. "Or when he'll return?" At summer's end Polycarp had sided with Ector of Sindestray in voting to imprison John for bargaining with the Demon Queen. Jenny had hated him then for it. Knowing what she now knew of demons, she understood. She knew, too, how difficult that decision had been.

"My lord," she said now, stepping up to him, and he turned his head, startled.

"Thank you," he said to the captain of the guards. "I'm glad to hear she's feeling better. I shall speak to my cousin on his return." Taking Jenny's arm, he led her out of the lamplit vestibule down a flight of black marble and malachite steps into the garden.

The rain had lightened, though by the smell it would return. A pillared belvedere stood on the edge of a sedge-fringed pond, and in its shadows they sat.

"Trey is dead," Jenny said quietly. She drew her cloak tighter about her, for the winter evening was cold. "Gareth posted guards around the room and left about an hour after that. This was about noon. If it's true that all the bodies of the plague's victims must be burned at once, I can understand that he'd want a little time. The guards—and the priests of healing—seem adamant about it."

"And well they should be." The master glanced across the garden at the crimson-cloaked warriors on the terrace. He was a fox-faced man and, like Gareth, tall and thin and nervy. Now he looked worn down. He was a scholar, like John, and as John would do, she thought, he must have sought long in the libraries of the university for some answer to this new scourge.

"He said something about an herbalist in the town—" She broke off as the master's white hand bunched in a sudden, angry fist.

"This was all he said?"

Looking into his face, she nodded. By his voice there was something more.

The master was silent a long time, like a man debating how much he could reveal. He seemed to be seeking some omen among the scars of her face, the thin small wrinkles of age, the blue knowledge-haunted eyes.

Then he sighed. "There is a man in the city who is said to raise the dead."

Pellanor in the firelight. Dogface in the snow. She felt a thousand years old.

"Is it true?"

"I don't know." Rain made gold rings in the beryl water where the light from the terrace windows crossed it. It damped the charnel smoke from beyond the city's walls, but still a whiff of decay smudged the air. Somewhere close a woman was crying, jagged and weary and beyond hope.

"The priests don't like it," Polycarp said at last. "*I* don't like it."

"No." She thought of a dead sailor on the sea-hammered rocks, pulling a long red worm from his guts; a man's hand dipping into a basin of blood and coming out with a glass shell.

"It's as if . . . as if my dog died suddenly and in his prime, and a man appeared next day offering to sell me another, saying, 'I hear your dog has died.' "

"Yes." She felt bleak inside, and furious. For Gareth, and for Trey; for the weeping lord in the gate of his big house, begging men not to take his son's body away.

Where was John, she wondered, and how might she get word to him that she and Gareth and the Realm all needed help?

"I've read, and studied, and searched far into the nights." Polycarp rubbed wearily at the inner corners of his eyes. "First it was just for some mention of this sickness. But there is none, no ailment that sounds like this. Afterward it was for word of any, even in the remotest antiquity, that could raise the dead."

They were silent, and in the silence the patter of droplets on the water sounded loud. Looking across the pool and into the gray mist, Jenny saw the hard wrinkled face and jeweled hands of the gnome mage in her dream. She visioned herself trying to piece together a mosaic of bits of stone and tile, knowing all the while that the picture she would produce would be terrible to behold.

John asleep in a dry well, sheltering from howling wind. John staring into a glass box, with the strange bluish radiance of it playing across his beaky face and turning his spectacle lenses to rounds of blank light.

"What can I do?" she asked.

"Will you go to Ylferdun Deep?" Their eyes met for a time, and she saw that he recalled her hatred. But he, too, had felt the grip of the demon, had heard it whisper in his dreams, and this made an understanding between them. "The only mage whose learning I can trust," he went on, "the only mage untainted by the demons last summer–is Miss Mab, the witchwife of the gnomes. I've tried to see her, but King Balgub of the Deep put her under house arrest, which still has half a year to run."

"You know that my powers are gone," Jenny said softly.

"I know," he said. "But I know, too, that you're a lady of the Winterlands. And you know the Deep. If any can reach her undetected, it is you."

Chapter 18

It wasn't until she reached the First Hall of Ylferdun Deep that Jenny knew for certain she was being followed.

From the gates of Bel to the village of Deeping, which lay outside the gnomes' great doors, was the walk of most of a day. Leaving before the market women even began to cry their milk and nuts in the streets, Jenny avoided the paved road and made her way along the hedgerows that marked the fallow fields, her plaids blending with the winter landscape. Rain fell, obliterating her tracks. Wind bit through her damp garments, and she longed for the days when she could have wrapped herself in a scrim of magic and walked unseen down the high road.

Still, her lifetime in the Winterlands served her well.

She skirted Deeping. The town was smaller now than it had been, and the tanneries, where so many of the original populace had taken refuge and been killed, had never been rebuilt. In five years the woods behind them had encroached to smother the broken walls, and brown ferns stood around the well that the leather workers had used. But the clock tower above the market square had been repaired, globes and vanes and numerals glinting gold in the evening light. The clothing of the men and women coming down from the Deep's iron doors glowed like poppies against the mud and old snow. Above everything the vast rusty darkness of Nast Wall gouged the clouds.

Morkeleb. Jenny reached toward him with her mind in the mists and glaciers where he laired but didn't know if he heard.

Morkeleb. It had been winter, like this, when she and John and Gareth had ridden to Deeping to seek him. The smell of the woods and the wet chill in her bones had been the same. The fear had been cold behind her breastbone. In her heart she saw John then, standing in the stirrups of his warhorse Osprey—a big dapple slain by the dragon the next day. She saw his eyes narrow behind the cold glint of his spectacles as he listened to the silence of the Vale; saw the flex of his mouth, the bent shape of his nose.

In the days of her magic, she thought, she would have known were he dead. But now she did not know, and her vulnerability terrified her. Had she been unable to sense him in her dragon dreams because it was not a thing of dragons to love? She had sensed her sons.

She put the thoughts aside, climbing over them as a dragon rises over obstacles in flight. *What will come is what will come.* She had other things to occupy her than gnawing fantasies about John eloping like a schoolboy with the Demon Queen. Pellanor had been raised from the dead for a purpose. The gnome wizards were buying slaves who could not work for a purpose. Folcalor, for a purpose, was invading the dreams of every mage his mind could touch.

Whatever was happening, Miss Mab, whose spells had sustained John in his quest behind the mirror, would have at least some idea of what to do.

If she could reach her.

Jenny stole as far as she could along Tanner's Rise, then descended to the square before the market hall and crossed it through the gathering evening to the gates of the Deep. She waited patiently until a large group of merchants emerged with baskets on their backs, drawing the notice of the gnome wardens. The day was ending, and torches were being kindled in fantastic iron holders beside the gate. Soon the market's doors would shut. She passed through without being seen.

As at the opposite limit of the delvings of the gnomes, where an eastern gate looked out into the town of Halnath, this western boundary of the underground domain consisted of a market hall where the gnomes brought metalwork, jewels, and their renowned weapons to trade for the produce of humankind's farms. John had been wounded about here, she thought, as the straw mats that covered the vast floor crunched a little under her feet. Did his blood still mark the stone beneath? Did Morkeleb's? Where the glittering bulk of the dragon had stretched, a brightly draped stall sold painted pottery; a barrow heaped with apples occupied the place where his head had lain. Jenny smiled, thinking of what the dragon would have to say, not on those facts but on her bemusement at them. *Time is time,* she heard his soft voice echo in the dark of her mind. *And all things pass and are renewed.*

The plague did not appear to have reached Deeping Town, but the market was thinly populated, even for this time of evening. Jenny idled over a selection of silk kerchiefs until one of the gnome guards at the inner doorway went to speak to a market woman. Even so she thought the other guard saw her, and she had to walk quickly through the hall beyond. "Madam, wait," he called out to her, and she pretended not to hear.

She was in the Deep.

For quite some time she thought that it was one of the gate guards who pursued her, intent on asking her business or telling her to leave. The way the gnomes looked at her as she passed through the public spaces of the upper levels fed this impression; she heard one of the gnomewives in the arched Hall of Sarmendes say to another, "Spreading the plague . . ." and guessed that the Lord of the Deep had told the guards to keep humankind out. So she quickened her step and sought the downward-leading passageways as soon as possible, ways that led to the warrens of this or that powerful clan: storerooms, well chambers, private chapels to the Ancestors where a thousand candles burned. In her wake she caught the echo of boots with a gnome's quick, soft tread and hurried still faster, ducking into shortcuts and passing through rooms filled with wheat sacks or oil or wool.

When first she'd entered the Deep, to heal the dragon Morkeleb and to find the medicines that would save John's life, the thought of getting lost had terrified her. The Deep had been empty then, the gnomes all fled before the dragon. Morkeleb's mind had guided her through the narrow passageways, the endless stairs in darkness. Had she lost her way she would have starved.

Since that time, however, she had entered the Realm of the gnomes on several occasions, twice under the dragon's guidance. Survival in the Winterlands depended on knowing where you were and what was around you, and in the days when she had had to make do with slight powers, she had made it a point to know always where she stood in relationship to the things of the earth, from which even tiny amounts of power could be sourced. At summer's end she and

Morkeleb had sought out Miss Mab after the Council of the Gnomes had placed her under arrest for helping John; so she had a good idea of how to find her way to the ninth level, where lay the caverns of the clan of Hawteth-Arawan.

Now she patiently dug through her trained memory for the stairs and alleyways through which slaves tugged burdens, the walkways along the pipes that pumped water from wells deep below. The lamps here were dim, and they smoked with cheap oils and fats that stained the rock of the walls with their soot. The walls were clean, though, for the gnomes were a fastidious folk. Twice on her circuitous way Jenny saw slaves—human slaves—scrubbing the limestone around such cressets or washing the reflectors behind them.

More than one pair of soft boots pattered behind her now, and there was a muttered whisper too distorted by echoes to understand. She realized that she risked not simply the failure of her errand, but enslavement herself.

Fear needled through her, and she slipped down the first stair she saw with the dim intention of backtracking and losing her pursuit in the storerooms around some ancestral sanctuary. Through a narrow doorway she passed into a kind of servants' hall where two women—humans—labored over a smoking stove; she fled silent as a bird through a thickly curtained door, which let into a chamber where a fountain poured water endlessly into a basin of stone.

A small archway let her into a narrow stair, stretching into darkness beside a stepped waterfall illuminated only by the fewest and feeblest of lamps. She descended the stair at a run, the shallow steps favored by the gnomes making her knees ache, though she was little taller than a tall gnome herself. Far above her in the dark she heard a soft alto voice say, "There she goes."

Jenny caught up her plaids and fled. She thought there would be a door soon through which she could evade her pursuers but there wasn't, not for many hundreds of steps. Her thighs and calves throbbed and she panted in the cold, but the footfalls drew closer. She heard the clatter of weaponry on metal buckles, the dry hollow rattle of arrows. When at last she found a door, it was on the other side of the watercourse and led into a long tunnel she did not know, the stone of its walls and floors undressed and unfinished. A great draft blew hot and steady all around her. *A ventilation corridor,* she thought, *leading into the mines.* That meant traps and pitfalls, but nevertheless she ran, her hand on the wall to guide her as they left the realm of the lights, the boots behind her running also.

One turning, two—darkness ever deeper and the clatter of feet coming closer. They could see her, she thought—gnomes' sight in darkness being clearer than that of humankind. *They haven't called out to me to stop,* she thought. *That must be because they know—*

The floor vanished from beneath her feet. She cried out and just had time to roll herself together, protecting her head, as a jagged floor smote her and pain lanced up through her left hip and thigh, taking her breath away. She tried to rise and couldn't; above her, the clack of boots came slower. They'd heard her fall.

They'd known the trap was there.

Dim light reflected on the tunnel ceiling. It was a hothwais—a stone or crystal charged to hold light—steady and cold. It showed her the lip of the drop over which she'd fallen, a dozen feet above her head. Not a pit as such, she saw now in the wan glow, but a small rough cavern, perhaps seventy feet at its widest. There were other tunnels, higher up the other walls; some had bones beneath them. A ladder dangled from one, but when she tried to stand and limp toward it the pain in her leg made her nearly faint.

"There she is."

She got a glimpse of them—three squat armored shapes—just as one loosed an arrow that took her in the shoulder with such force as to throw her down.

The other two were nocking arrows to their bows. Pain like a burning knife went through her shoulder as she rolled, then crawled into the shelter of the drop-off itself, where they would have to shoot straight down at her; the cavern even curved a little in, below the lip of the tunnel floor above. One gnome cursed, and another said, "One should do it." He sounded like a tradesman talking about logs on a fire.

The light dimmed as they walked away. She heard the tap of arrows replaced in quivers, a voice commenting, "We'll need to make a report to Rogmadoscibar . . ."

One should do it.

Sickness washed her in a terrifying wave, and she felt her breath start to slow.

They had not been trying to turn her back, she thought. Had not wanted to enslave her.

Their orders had been to kill her.

The arrow was poisoned.

"You understand," Shamble TenSevenTwentysix said, squinting behind smoked magnifiers at the white-hot tip of his soldering iron, "that nobody really knows what magic is, or why it worked. Or why it stopped working."

"Come to that," John replied cheerfully, "I don't know what plasmic ether is either, or why it stops workin' three or four nights a week in my apartment just when I'm on me way to the bathroom, bad cess to it."

"Oh, that's just the crystals going out," Bort explained. "They don't maintain the relays into the wet zone." He came through the apartment door and maneuvered carefully between the plex table that took up two-thirds of the room between Shamble's kitchen niche and the narrow bed, and looked around the cluttered surface of the table for somewhere to put down his burden: the giant bundle of pale green flimsiplast he and Garrypoot had spent most of the evening running out on Garrypoot's printer.

Shamble's apartment was hot, and it stank. It was the size of Garrypoot's bedroom and was situated in the very center of an enormous megablock in the Seventy-ninth District; the heat came partly from the portable forge that took up whatever floor space wasn't already occupied by the table and the bed. John couldn't imagine what the neighbors said about it, if they noticed; evidently the heating and cooling systems in the megablocks never worked very well. Neither did the shielding on the ether relays: His skull felt as if it were filled with rattling steel balls. An enormous ad screen was turned up full volume, and another dominated the little toilet cubicle; floor-to-ceiling industrial shelves jammed the remaining wall space, overflowing with books, both paper and chip; readers; half-disassembled terminals and at least three working ones; bales of wire; boxes of coal and wood for the forge; packets of herbs and powders; crystals; and dust. The place reminded John rather of Jenny's house at Frost Fell, though it smelled like Sergeant Muffle's forge in spite of the triple-strength air-suck installed over the usual kitchen vent and powered by an eight-way etheric splitter rigged in the power outlet.

Other splitters dangled from the wiring all over the room. The kitchen niche was written over with what John guessed were anti-roach wards, though they looked nothing like the wards Jenny wrote against mice and insects; in any case they worked not at all.

"Ether is a natural force," Bort went on, "a little like electricity or gravity. It exists everywhere and is the result of interaction between molecules. Magic is the operation of the will, without physical instrumentality. There's no reason—" He touched the dragonbone box John had laid on the corner of the table. "—for this to be anything other than its component elements. Certainly no reason for a man's spirit, his soul, to . . . to be absorbed into it and trapped, while his body . . . What? Dies? Dissolves? What will happen to him when you put whatever it is . . .

"What *is* it that you're going to put into the box to activate the spell?"

John scratched the side of his long nose. "I dunno. She said, 'Bring him,' and then, 'Here's this box, Son.' I assume if I open it in his presence and drop these little oojahs in—" He shook the bronze bottle, which tinkled musically. "—there'll be a connection, but I'm buggered if I know what." Yet as he spoke the words he felt a shiver in the dark of his mind, where dreams begin, and he knew perfectly well what would happen.

"What worries me, after what Clea's mum said and that ballyhoo at GeoCorp this afternoon, is gettin' to this Circle place and gettin' in."

"I think this should take care of that little problem." Bort smugly tapped the plast. "Garrypoot cut into the Optiflash and Circle records for the security codes on both the passenger line and the supply train. We have maps, plans, schematics . . . The house registered to Corvin was a private dwelling that was turned over to its present owner by deed of gift in the year Sixty-four of the current administration—that is, close to eighty years ago. The Circle was built around it."

"Was it, now?" John said softly. "He looked gie spry for his age."

"He's a mage." Passion and grief and devouring envy echoed in Bort's distorted blue gaze.

"Finished." Shamble put down his soldering iron and pushed up the guards from his eyes, revealing the slightly yellowish corneas of a cheap government transplant. He was a thin man, tall and stooped and unclean, who spent every spare credit he had on the materials required for the working of magic as described in his ancient texts. He eked an existence by cooking for himself, rather than buying at the building's Food Central, and by spending water-ration credits on high-quality fuels rather than baths. His obsession, John gathered, had cost him a wife and a child at some point.

Perched on the back of the room's single chair with his feet on the book-cluttered seat, John thought of Jenny in her house on Frost Fell, pursuing her solitary dreams of power. And now with no more to show for it than this poor man had.

No wonder she had turned inward, to despair and hate of all things.

"This should do what you've described," the metalworker went on. He held up the small cube of dark brown bone that John had given him, one of the few fragments of claw and tail left when the flesh of the golden dragon of Wyr had dissolved into dust. He'd carried it in his satchel, with flax seed and silver and whatever else magical he could find, through paradise and Hell. "I've laid spells of the unity of essence on both this and the box you asked me to make."

With the smallest of his graving tools he touched the box, a careful copy of the one Aohila had given John before the Mirror of Isychros: dragonbone, silver, and opal, though the opal was far smaller. "Thaumaturgically they should be the same thing, both as one another and as the original box."

John picked up the two boxes, turned them in his hands. The workmanship of the one Aohila had given him was infinitely finer, of course. Demons presumably had centuries to perfect their arts. Inside it was finished smooth: He flipped the lid open, and shut, and open again, knowing he might have very little time, when he finally came face-to-face with Corvin NinetyfiveFifty, to make up his mind about what he should do.

The thought of rescuing from her clutches the man who'd bought the dead girls' gold bracelets from the demons wasn't one he relished. His every instinct told him there was something uncanny and deadly about the mage he'd come so close to in the lobby of GeoCorp, something that Aohila might turn to terrible use if she had it in her power.

Or something that might continue to do evil in this world—or another—if permitted to walk free.

On the original box's inner surface Shamble had etched one of the gate sigils copied from John's notes, a sigil that was reproduced on the small square of dragonbone and silver now lying in the metal-worker's callused hand.

"Of course," Shamble said with sudden shyness, "there's no way of telling whether the wards I've worked are as strong as those of the demon. In fact, I'm sure mine aren't—wouldn't be, that is, if magic worked at all here." He handed John the little graven bone square and the bronze bottle, then took a sip of his coffee, now bitter from sitting too long.

"It might be it does, you know." John closed both boxes and bestowed them, the bottle, and the dragonbone sigil in separate pockets of his doublet. "It may be things have changed so much you're not sourcin' the magic properly anymore—at least that's what Jen says is usually the problem when magic that used to work quits workin'. Though you'd know more about it than I do."

"No," the smith said simply. "And that's the . . . the sorrow of it. We don't."

There was a deep sadness in his discolored eyes, and John remembered Jenny standing in the winter moonlight, scarred hands folded and slick scarred pate bowed, tears like diamonds on the shiny burned patches of her cheeks, mourning what had been hers, the only thing in the world that she had truly loved.

Loved more than him, for all his hopes that it would be different. Loved more than her children. Maybe more than her life. He felt no anger at her, nor pity—only a deep sadness and a wanting to speak to her again.

"We've tried everything, over the years," Shamble went on softly. He scratched absently with his dirty nails at the small round scars left by the removal of cancers from his chin. "We've gotten in touch with everyone we think is like us, everyone who has an interest in these matters. Everyone who has had these . . . these dreams of power, these dreams that cannot be explained. From all we can tell, people used to be able to draw power from their own bodies, and from the stars, the earth, the sea. Used to be able to do the things we dream of doing.

"They could heal others of malaria and tuberculosis and cancer just by laying their hands on them and drawing circles in the dirt with silver and blood. They could see what was taking place miles away, or across centuries—see it accurately, and every time they tried. But something's changed, and we don't know what. Maybe some combination of stars and planets has shifted, but if so we can't find it in all Garrypoot's astrological projections. But we just don't know. My old master . . ."

He paused and grinned a little self-consciously. "You'd like this," he said.

"Oh, Shamble," Bort sighed, "now really isn't the time to play show-and-tell."

But Shamble had turned away.

"There was this book, you see," the smith said. "I got it from the man who taught me to work in metal—another welder, but one of us: one who would have been a mage. He taught me to make knives and blades."

From beneath his bed he brought a box and took out a sword. "How about this, hunh?"

Bort sighed heavily and rolled his eyes. But John hefted the weapon, gauging its weight and balance. It was two or three inches shorter than his own blade and handled differently, but it balanced well. The steel was fine grained and beautifully wrought, the grip wrapped in silver wire braided with red cording. Runes were etched over hilt, guards, pommel, and spine.

"It was the sixth or seventh sword I made," Shamble said. "I wove into it all the demon-killing spells I could find in Docket's books. I made one or two after this one, but they just didn't turn out as well."

"It's good," John said, and the smith flushed with pleasure. "It's gie good. I don't know if it'll slay demons, but it's a fine blade." He stepped clear of the other men as much as was possible in the confines of the tiny apartment and swung the weapon carefully, cross-cut and then down.

"You can have it," Shamble said shyly, "if you want."

"I'll take it." John stepped back to grip the smith's hand. "Thank you." From the small bundle he'd fetched from his own room he brought his own sword and laid it on the table. "You can take this if you'd care to. It's not magic or anythin', but I've slain a dragon with it—well, cut him up a bit and finished him with an ax—and chopped up cave grues and weird critters in Hell and any number of bandits."

"You don't have to do that." Shamble touched the worn hilt, the stained grip, his fingers reverent and awe in his face. "I mean, it's yours. It was your father's."

John shrugged. "It's just a sword."

Sheathing the new weapon, he turned in time to catch Bort's eye. Bort had been thumbing through his pile of looted files, and his face now wore, for an unguarded second, the expression of weariness, of defeat, he'd had a day or two ago in Garrypoot's flat.

He's a mage, Bort had said of the man they hunted, and John saw those words reflected now in the discontented pain in Bort's eyes.

He's a mage.

John went to stand before him. It was a moment before the in-putter looked up. "If he'd the slightest intent to help you," John said quietly, "the smallest interest in other mages in this world, you don't think he could have found you? He's been all over Docket's node on the Op-Link. He's known how to get hold of you for twenty years and more. He's hidin', Bort. He wouldn't thank you for comin' to him, and he's gie for certain not going to help you."

Bort looked away. "No," he said, in a low voice. "No, of course not. Of course not."

Lying on Garrypoot's couch that night—if Amayon was the one giving away his position, his own room in the wet zone too easy a target—John dreamed of Bort.

It was Bort's dream, actually, he thought. Bort's dream because what he saw was Bort's apartment, cramped and even tinier than Shamble's but filled, like Shamble's, with books and readers and terminals, with bottles and pots and baskets of the things by which wizards of old had worked magic, or had thought they worked magic. There were crystals and crystal spheres, mirrors of obsidian and quicksilver, phials of amber floating in brandy. There were skulls and teeth of small animals and birds, carefully preserved and written over with runes. A circle had been drawn on the floor, and the charred pottery bowl in its center still smoked. Heat-cracked fragments of bone dotted the circle's marked-out quadrants, and John guessed Bort had spent the evening, after they'd parted at Shamble's, engaged in divination, trying to make up his mind.

As he watched, the smoke in the bowl slowly formed up a shape, like a ghost drifting in darkness. He recognized Amayon's face. When the eyes opened, they were Amayon's blue brilliant eyes.

"Of course he'd tell you Corvin will refuse to help," the demon said in a voice, John thought, that Bort half remembered—a familiar quiet alto like someone Bort had once known. "He won't be able to trap this mage, deliver him up to the whore of Hell, if Corvin has warning that someone other than a demon is on his trail."

Bort turned on his narrow bed and emitted a fat man's glottal snore. The weak green glow of the smoke illumined the dirty dishes and finger-smudged books. The ad screen's cold reflection flickered and danced, damped down quiet and further buried by muted music. In the artificial deeps of the small quasi-window, stars that hadn't been visible for decades burned too brightly, and the comet combed her shining hair.

It was like his own study in Alyn Hold, John thought: books and implements and trappings of the person he had all his life wanted to be, the person forever denied. *At least,* John thought, *I could hate me dad—poor, driven sod—for burnin' the books and demandin' I be what he was: killer and warrior and protector of me people.*

Who can Bort hate for takin' his dream from him?

"All these years Corvin has hidden," Amayon whispered, and the scene began to blend and shift into the images of another dream. "All these years he's thought himself safe."

And John saw what Bort saw: ancient stone walls and smoke-discolored rafters. A frail, genial-looking old man sat at his desk among scrolls and cats and dappled sunlight. The exile mage of legend rose with a sigh of longing, going to the window.

"All these years," Amayon murmured, "looking for—waiting for—someone he can trust."

"Fools." The old man sighed and stroked his silver beard. "Fools, who say there is no such thing as magic." John thought his face vaguely familiar from dozens of ad-screen playlets. "Everywhere around them it lies, and yet they cannot see." He stretched his hand toward the leaves that grew thick around the window, and as his fingers touched them, light flickered between the fingers and the tender young growth.

"There must be someone out there," the old man said. "Someone able to learn, someone strong hearted enough to bear the knowledge, wise enough to see beyond demon lies and demon pawns. Ah! I cannot bear it, that I might take the knowledge of where to find magic with me to my grave! The answer is so simple."

Within the dream the images faded, collapsing on themselves. The last thing John saw before he woke—the thing he thought about for a long time, lying in the pale light of the artificial stars, the artificial moon—was Bort TenEighty, last mage in the Hell of Walls, sitting in his undershorts on crumb-imbued carpet, staring at the diagram of divination and the burnt bones scattered across it like errant constellations of unreadable stars.

In time John got quietly to his feet and touched the activation key of Garrypoot's computer. Poot was working a late shift; he wouldn't be home for an hour or more. John flipped to the opening screen with its simple, bright-colored icons. After a moment's thought, calling back what Bort and Garrypoot had earlier done to obtain a second copy of the Optiflash specs, he opened the list of marked files, counted back in his mind, and flagged three files to print.

He hoped he'd counted right. Folding the flimsiplast small, he stashed it in his doublet with the Demon Queen's dragonbone box and the ink bottle containing the whispering soul of a demon. As he was pulling on his boots, belting his new sword around his hips, the orange light flashed once more on the printer, and one more sheet spooled out.

AVERSIN
DON'T BE A FOOL. YOU'LL NEVER MAKE IT
INTO CORVIN'S STRONGHOLD WITHOUT ME.
AMAYON

John dropped the sheet as if it had turned to a live spider in his hand. He watched it as it crumpled, then melted itself into a ball, a puddle, a smudge of fireless ash.

* * *

"Someone's watching Bort?" Clea stepped aside from the doorway of the flat and signed him to silence with a glance at the door behind which her mother still slept. "Who is? How do you know?" She wore a faded caftan, and her wet gray hair was dressed in a shabby knot. She smelled of soap, incense, and coffee: the scents of early waking, early meditation in the stillness. The apartment was in an older building and had a wall of windows that opened onto a narrow terrace, but ten feet beyond, another building loomed, cutting off the light. The terrace was littered with trash, stacked with boxes of old clothes and packaged foods, draped in plastic sheets against the weather. On the ad screen a pair of grotesquely elderly people copulated to soft rhythms barely heard, huge smiles on their toothless mouths.

"Demons." John held out to her the handful of flimsiplast. "We can't have him help us for fear of them knowin' now, see? We've got to move, and we've got to move now."

Chapter 19

They took the Universe Rail: coal-sack darkness, flickering lights, men and women jostling for seats or clinging to handles from the car's low ceiling. There were children onboard, too, though they were children with the faces of tired adults, slack eyes dim with Let's-Be-Good and Happy Time. A mother handed her five-year-old daughter a little sniffer of Peace to keep her from fidgeting. They carried their drugs in big gaudy plastic bottles shaped like weapons or the semihuman characters of cartoons, clipped to their belts or knapsack straps in imitation of gangboy bandoliers. John couldn't look at them. He kept seeing Adric's face.

"We get off here," Clea said. "Bet said she'd meet us at the Free Market in the Ninety-seventh Avenue station. Bet Phenomenal," she added, as they stepped onto the broken concrete platform of the old 211th Avenue station. "The gangfolk don't like to come up top."

The 211th had been constructed before it became customary to route the subway directly into the megablocks. It had been looted even of its benches, and old bones mixed with the garbage heaped along the tiled and gang-scribbled walls. After the train pulled out, Clea led the way, rather gingerly, to the end of the platform and jumped down into the track bed itself; she flicked on her flashlight and walked with her shoulder to the wall, hurrying because there was no catwalk here and the next train might catch them before they reached it. Water stood in puddles in the track bed, and mosquitoes roared in frustration around their faces and hands, nearly blinding them. John guessed it wouldn't be long before this part of the line was abandoned.

Their footfalls whispered in the dark. Enormous rats scurried a little distance from the light, then turned and regarded the intruders speculatively. John unlimbered his sword from the foamplex tube in which he carried it and held it ready. The vermin weren't any larger than the rats in the lower levels of gnome delvings, but he hadn't particularly liked fighting those, either.

But the rats kept their distance. Now and then the darkness throbbed with the passage of distant trains in other tunnels, or the floor vibrated where another rail ran above or below. Gradually the headache that had become part of his life faded a little as they got farther from the ether relays, and looking up, he saw that the crystals along the tunnel ceiling had been looted as well.

"We're below the Crenfields," Clea whispered. Echoes carried her voice away into the dark. She said the name as if John should know it, and when he looked blankly at her, she added, "This part of the city's dead above our heads."

"Why? What happened?"

"Long story," she said and did not tell it. When she turned her head he saw a glint of tears in her eyes.

They came to an empty station, boarded up, its platforms littered with bones knee-deep: human, rodent, the withered carcasses of roaches as big as John's hand. Clea scrambled awkwardly onto the platform and guided John to a stairway descending four levels that John could see, though they only went down one. The bottom of the stairwell was drowned in dark foul liquid. Roaches swarmed the walls, and the mosquitoes were like carnivorous dust motes in the glints of Clea's flashlight. There were bones on the landings, on the steps. Something moved in the water, and John thought he saw a flash of quicksilver two levels below. The cold air brought him the smell of sulfur and blood.

They followed another line, this one flooded to the edge of its catwalk. John strained his senses for the stealthy spatter of droplets from some wet silvery back, for the smell of demons, but the stench of rats and human waste and chemicals was overwhelming—the flashlight gleamed on huge slicks of them, orange and green and black. Could demons inhabit the bodies of rats? Of mosquitoes? Now there was an unpleasant thought.

There was light ahead—not the white glare of ether but the dirty yellow warmth of torchlight. He heard the scrape and jangle of music—actual music, not the product of PSEs. The reek of garbage and excrement grew overwhelming, and smoke blurred the light. "Ninety-seventh Avenue?" he asked, and Clea nodded.

"Bet says it's bad manners to walk around with a weapon in your hand," she warned him. "And some of the folks there are pretty paranoid from too much Brainhammer. But keep it ready."

John wasn't sure what to expect, but the Free Market wasn't so very different from the market at Great Toby: Coarse vegetables, packages of food ranging from the cheapest Soyovite to the most delicate pinkfish and sauce merveil, pots, clothing new and old, PSEs, and weapons were offered for sale, mostly on blankets spread on the concrete but sometimes arranged on planks and trestles. Two metal garbage cans had been converted to barbecues, burning wood that looked like chopped-up furniture, and women cooked sausages and chunks of what could have been either pigeons or rats. A young girl with astonishingly checkered hair danced on a blanket to the music of a long-necked three-stringed psaltery and a hand drum, the first instruments John had seen in the city.

Everyone was stoned. Everything from Peace on up to Flying Dreams was being sold, cut-rate: "Fell off the back of the train, man; I found it on the tracks." John turned from purchasing a large slingshot from amid an assortment of submachine guns—he'd been searching for days to find a tree to provide a forked branch for one, and this one was metal—and nearly tripped over a lanky gangboy with white and purple stripes on his face, sitting on the edge of the platform staring blankly into the tunnel's flooded darkness.

"Probably Lovehammer cut with Purple Delight and Rust-Be-gone," Bet Phenomenal remarked; she was short and swarthy and had most of her hair shaved, after the fashion of the gangs. Under a layer of red-and-yellow mask she was pretty, though the colored ointment covered a scar on her chin and another beside her left eye. "That's the big kick these days. I found somebody who can take you into the Circles." She nodded toward a stout gray woman by the nearest drug emporium, haggling over a coffee mug full of Pink Sunshine with Peace-induced calm persistence. "EleventySeven's got deals with most of the gangs to let her through, and there's darn few who're willing to go near the Yellow Circle or Red since they've started contracting enforcement there to World Peace."

"World Peace?" Clea's eyes widened. "Yipe. They're heavy-duty enforcement," she explained to John. "Mostly they don't even report intruders to District," she said. "The intruders just disappear."

She spoke in an awed voice and looked disconcerted when John just nodded. But it was only the Winterlands all over again.

"A couple of our friends tried to get in on the goods train last year," Bet corroborated. *Our friends,* John had been told by Old Docket, was the way the gangfolk referred to themselves. "Nothing was heard from them again. Not even bodies. These are not folks you want to mess around with." She glanced up at Clea. "The thing is, the old Celestial line runs clear under the deep area between here and there—it's flooded, I mean, but there's clearance for EleventySeven's boat."

"No," John said. He looked around him at the shadowy market, the figures with their shaved heads and gaudy masks. Evidently the Free Market was a place where gangfolk could mingle without violence erupting—he saw at least six different color combinations. "Can she take us over the surface?" The ink bottle was hot against his flesh, and he knew, as surely as he knew his name, that Sea-wights lurked and whispered in the waters over which they would pass.

At least on the surface there was somewhere to run.

"It'll cost you more," Bet warned as EleventySeven shuffled toward them, a harpoon over one shoulder and a flamethrower holstered on her back.

John produced one of the Demon Queen's gold coins from his doublet and palmed it carefully to show the gondolier what it was. "Not a problem," he said.

EleventySeven blinked. "Not a problem here, either," she replied. "This way."

Aboveground the buildings were empty. The ghastly eye pits of blown-out windows stared, and sometimes whole sections of wall gaped, to expose broken-off segments of floor, shattered stairways, and elevator shafts like bone and entrail within. From ankle-deep—as elsewhere in the wet zone—the flooding in the streets rapidly deepened, an arm of the deep zone thrusting far into the city where low ground had been, and EleventySeven kept her harpoon in hand as she guided her ether-powered scutter boat close to the mold-slimed walls.

"What are they?" John whispered as the brown water broke momentarily across the rounded back of something beneath that sank away again with a flurry of fins.

The gondolier spat. "They don't bother me; I don't bother them."

Peering down, John thought he saw the flicker of something silver, or perhaps he imagined it. He might, too, he thought, only be imagining the whining hum of other engines, other boats, skimming through the hellish wet twilight behind them.

Clea had replayed yesterday's news footage of the deep zone for him in her apartment, manipulating the images to show the Yellow Circle, which had been visible at the edge of the screen. They had been built, she said, to protect those wealthy enough to afford dwellings within their rings of protection and enforcers, but at least half the buffer zone that surrounded them now lay anywhere from six inches to four feet deep underwater, and many of the culverts leading out of the Yellow Circle were stagnant channels filled with mud and weeds.

Given a week, John thought—studying the open space of flooded concrete, the towering wall and guardhouses beyond—he might have been able to figure out some safer way of doing this. But he didn't have a week. He'd be lucky if Corvin hadn't already changed identities and fled.

And the gods help me if he picks someplace worse than this to hide out in.

You can't do this without me, Amayon had written. John wasn't sure that he could, but he dreaded the thought of what the demon would do once their quarry was captured, a prisoner in his little bone-and-silver box. Only one of them could bargain with Aohila.

There was movement in the water behind them again, barely seen in the gloom among the buildings.

"Those things come out into the open zone?"

EleventySeven shrugged and took a sniff from the black government-issue vaporator that hung around her neck. "Not the big ones."

"That makes me feel *so* much better." Clea barely glanced up from the nylon fanny pack through which she was digging for the various key cards she'd reprogrammed from Poot's columns of numbers. She looked like a dumpy shopper digging for her cred.

"This should do it." She extracted one of the several slips of plastic. "I hope Mother doesn't miss her private pass to the Marvelous department stores–store keys are the easiest to reprogram because the stores do it month to month. Goodness knows how Garrypoot got the Circle codes."

"What if he didn't get the right ones?"

"If he didn't get the right ones," Clea said, with a wry glance up at the guardhouses that thrust out from the wall over the wide apron of flooded concrete, "we're both in real trouble."

She was trying to sound nonchalant–presumably like the tough and beautiful heroines of the cinema films Tisa Three had been so addicted to–but John could see her hand shake a little as she strapped the black nylon bag around her waist again. "Not both, love," he said gently. He tucked his spectacles inside his doublet, took a felt marker from his boot, and held out a hand for the key. "Just show me which end goes into the lock and give me the rest. I think our friend here'll get you back to the station."

"Don't be silly." Clea shoved her cap into her pocket, pulled on a pair of latex gloves that, she had said back at her mother's apartment, would in some fashion keep the Circle enforcers from tracing her presence in the house should they be so lucky as to get away undetected. "If anything goes wrong, you'll need someone who can read and use a computer."

"If anything goes wrong, those enforcers will make pâté out of the both of us without askin' our names."

Before them, the water lay brown and cold and rain pocked. Sheets and patches of what looked like orange mold dotted the surface, on which bobbed unspeakable debris. In places the concrete showed dimly through.

"Here." Clea produced a small spray can from her belt and shot a dose into each eye, then sprayed her face and neck and handed him the can. "If there are demons following us–if they were watching Bort's apartment–do you think I'd make it back to the station without meeting them? The tide's been coming in for about three hours now. The water's not going to get much deeper."

"Just as well." John sprayed his face and his eyes, unshipped his sword from his side, and lowered himself over the gunwale. The water was warmish and oily, deeper than his head in the alley but only chest-high where the concrete apron had been put in when the Circle was built. Could Amayon communicate better with his brothers through the medium of water? he wondered. Or were things past the point where it mattered?

As Clea slipped into the murk beside him he heard it again: the whine of a small etheric engine somewhere in the alleys. Wan Thirty-oneFourFour and his merry men? Or gangboys whose drug-addled minds the Sea-wights would presumably have little trouble ousting from their overmuscled bodies? No magic in them, of course, but command of a small army with lots of automatic firepower wouldn't come amiss if you were after someone.

"Let's go." Submerging his head, he glided fast for the nearest drainage culvert in the wall.

Even had his eyesight been normal he doubted he could have seen much under the cloudy water. It stung his eyes even through the protective spray, but his sense of direction had been honed by two decades of automatic attentiveness to small cues, and his outstretched fingers touched the submerged foot of the wall only a yard from the culvert. The concrete shelved toward the wall until it was only a foot or so deep, but he sensed something brush his leg, loathsome and sleek and the size of a dog. It made no move against him, and when his head broke the surface in the concealment of the culvert, he saw nothing. Clea came up beside him, shivering a little; John sprayed his eyes again, put on his spectacles, and peered through the grill.

There was open ground there, the first he'd seen in weeks. The rough rolling terrain had once been planted with trees and dotted with what appeared to be ornamental buildings. The dead trees still stood, mummified by the chemical-imbued rain. Huddles of ruins clung to the sides of some hills, wherever they hadn't been in the way of newer houses or the pylons that supported the three train lines that brought in servants and enforcers, supplies, and—the uppermost of the three—the inhabitants of the Circle.

The houses were the size of most apartment blocks in the older part of the wet zone, rooflines showing over stained, ugly walls that only enforcers ever saw from the outside. Many walls bore bullet scars or the long streaks of ether probes and laser fire. Thieves before them had come to the same conclusion about accessibility through the servant or supply trains.

Clea, John thought desperately, *forgive me.*

Then he unslung the ink bottle from around his neck, took his slingshot from his pocket, and fired Amayon's prison through the grill and into the roughest and highest ground he could see.

"Come on."

He pulled off his spectacles and led the way along the wall toward the next culvert, a hundred feet away underwater. By the time he and Clea came up in its shelter there were enforcers already at the first grill, and John knew he'd guessed right.

Corvin NinetyfiveFifty had some device that detected the passage of demons and had told his bodyguards to investigate any alarm.

Clea slipped the card into the lock of the culvert grill. The metal groaned as John pushed it inward, but the steady drumming of the rain would keep the enforcers from hearing. He closed it after them and, donning his cap and spectacles once more, snaked through a snaggle of ruins to a wall that would hide them, Clea following close behind. Across the hundred feet or so of open ground he could see the other culvert and hear the voices of the enforcers echoing through it, broken snatches under the sound of the rain. He heard them rattle the grill and find it firm.

With the rain coming down, they wouldn't remain there long.

When he saw a light come on in one of the guardhouse windows, John moved. Creeping close to the earth, he retrieved the ink bottle and slung it again around his neck. "Is the demon in there?" Clea whispered, and John nodded. The tall woman looked far less ambling and clownish with her hair in a knot and mud streaking her face. She would never, John thought, survive in the Winterlands, but she was doing better than most of the rest of the league would.

Bort?

He didn't like to think of what might happen if Amayon or one of the other Sea-wights truly got hold of Bort.

"Why don't you leave it?" Clea ducked low, following John's example as best she could as they zigzagged toward the first of the houses. There were random motion detectors on the grounds, but these could be shut down for ten minutes at a time from the various transmitters; Clea studied the incomprehensible figures Bort had pulled from Garrypoot's computer and inserted one of her cards into the appropriate slot. "According to this, NinetyfiveFifty's put these . . . these demon wards all over the grounds. They're not like the regular security."

"Aye, but if they work on an alarm system to the guardhouse, is it possible to shut down the alarms?" John touched the ink bottle. "And I'd be tickled pink to bury this and forget about it forever. Only there are at least a couple of other demons abroad in the city. Amayon would be able to bring 'em to him and get out. Completely leavin' aside that I need him to get back to me own world—and deliver Corvin to the queen—I can't let him go rovin' about loose here after I'm gone."

He blinked myopically at her through wet-beaded glass. "You saw the vids of what Wan and his boys did in the deep zone. Thank the gods you didn't see that room in Wan's apartment. When demons come into a world, to fight one another or to make use of humankind, they start killin' like that for the sport of it. We have to do whatever we can to bring their defeat. It'll be one of the gladder days of me life when I can deliver Amayon back to the Demon Queen and have done with the whole bloody business."

"And will you then be able to live happily ever after?" Clea's lips formed the ghost of a smile as she turned back from the disabled alarms, but there was genuine concern in her eyes.

John thought about Ian, and about Jenny. About his son drinking poison and his wife standing in the frost-hard moonlight with desolation in her face.

"I'll give it a try," he said.

Jenny felt the touch of Morkeleb's mind on hers. She saw him on the fanged black promontory that stood above the glacier, wreathed in cloud and ice, heard him speak her name. He called out to her, spread wings like a galaxy of glittering lights, and rose into the mists.

All around her in the rocks was the whisper of demons.

They were waiting for him.

They knew I'd try to find Miss Mab, she thought, despair a cold needle in her heart. *They were waiting for me. No wonder I was able to get into the Deep so easily. And now they wait for him.*

Morkeleb, no! She tried to fling her thoughts into the dragon's mind, as once she had been able to do. But dragged down by exhaustion, by the chill grip of the poison that numbed her lungs and heart, she didn't know whether he heard her. She thought not.

Whether it was in truth a vision, as she used to get in dreams, or only the delirium of the poison, she did not know. She seemed to see the Sea-wights, little shining quicksilver things that rose to the surface of a well—the shallow-curbed well she'd seen in her dragon dream—in their glass shells. Shedding the shells, they whipped like glistening vermin through the darkness and the rocks. Opening her eyes—or dreaming that she opened them—she could see them clustered on the rocks, amorphous and vile, watching her with bright black beady eyes as they drank her pain and despair.

Get away from me! She wanted to scream, and could not. *Get away!*

Jenny, Jenny, they whispered, *surely you don't mean it. You welcomed Amayon once upon a time. You loved him.* And they screamed with laughter at her fury and her shame.

He's coming. She saw him in her mind—maybe truth, maybe only the visions they sent her, as once they'd sent her the vision of Ian killing John. She saw the black glitter of wings, the dark shape descending on a little-known watch window high in the mountain above. The gnome guards fled in terror, and the dragon contracted in size to whip through the narrow tunnels, down the twisting stairs.

If he uses magic, he is theirs. She remembered how in last summer's battle she had tried to wrench Ian from them with magic, how the demon Amayon had caught her by the magic itself, drawing her in like a fish on the line, tangling in her flesh, flooding her with that glorious, disorienting fire.

Surrender your magic, Morkeleb had cried. *Let go.*

And she had not let go, hoping against hope that her strength would be enough.

She fumbled at her belt for the knife she carried, with some dim notion of opening the veins in her wrists, to be dead before he came so that he would not put forth his power to save her and not be trapped by his love for her, as John had been trapped by the Demon Queen. Then she thought, *I am the only one who knows about Trey. About these resurrectors, these healers of the dead—these things that promise whatever they think you'll believe, call to you in whatever voice your heart will heed, like the Blood-wights in the Wraithmire.*

And Morkeleb had said, *Do not leave me, my friend.*

There has to be a way out. A way to intercept him. Pain seared her as she tried to draw herself forward into the lightless cavern, pain in her injured hip and a great endless weariness that encompassed her whole self. There had been other entrances, one of them with a ladder, she recalled.

She dropped over a rift in the floor and fell again, not far, eighteen inches or so, but she landed hard on broken rock. She felt cold, as if she lay in water, but it was only the poison drinking away the last of her strength.

A gnome in the Deep, she thought, *using a well to bring the Sea-wights through. Folcalor must have seduced one of the Wise Ones of the gnomes. Was he powerful enough to get past Miss Mab's family? To take the gnomewitch now and imprison her in a crystal?*

Why imprison?

Why crystal?

Did you think you were his slave?

She sank down on the stone and thought, *I can't.*

A questing mind touched hers from out of the darkness, the peace and stillness like the flow of wind on rock and sea. *Jenny . . .*

MORKELEB, GO BACK!

Then the roaring crash of an explosion, somewhere very close. Echoes snatched the sound and flung it, crashing from rock to rock; the stones beneath Jenny's body heaved and trembled, vibrated with the impact, and through it she heard the demons laughing like the crazed chittering of birds before a storm. A huge roiling cloud of dust and grit poured down on her like water.

And after it, silence.

Chapter 20

Nearly five hundred houses stood in the Yellow Circle, walled fortresses in a world no longer concerned with the way things looked out-of-doors. By this time it was raining hard enough that Clea had to wipe off Garrypoot's map two or three times before she could read it, orienting them as they slipped among the ragged hummocks, the tumbledown kiosks, the pits where—Clea said—swimming pools had once been. Twice trains went by overhead, windowless cars rattling and shaking: old, scarred with bullet pocks, and filthy with corrosion and smog.

"That's the *Houseboy Special*," Clea whispered. She and Aversin crouched in a smelly grotto large enough to hold a ball in. There were drains in the floor—that was the most John could figure out about its original purpose. "Security on it is unbelievable, but two or three times a year I'm told there are still attempts to get into some house or other. Bet tells me the Phenomenals don't even try anymore."

I'll bet they don't, John thought, remembering what Shamble had told him about the enforcers' connections with organ-supply houses. But, of course, demons wouldn't care how many of their mounts—or their drug-addled pawns—ended up being carved into collops and parceled out to those in need of new livers.

Whatever Corvin had—or was—Folcalor wanted him badly. Adromelech wanted him.

And Aohila wanted him.

And where does that leave me?

He touched the dragonbone boxes in their separate pockets, the bronze bottle, the bone square that bore the enchanted sigil of the gate. It was worse than having magic himself, worse than being Thane of the Winterlands: this hideous sense of responsibility, of holding catastrophe in his hands.

And no clue—not one—as to what he should do.

From her belt com Clea put in a call to Circle Central Security, gave a code from one of the flimsiplast schematics, and reported a repair on the pylons that supported the supply train. The supply train ran on the lowest pylons, but crossing the rail from the pylon to house 1212 was still a cautious exercise in balance, forty feet above the torn and flooded ground. Aversin had already marked out a place to cling near the sliding doorway, to wait for the doors to open with the arrival of the next train; but when they reached the place he saw that the sliding doors stood a foot or so ajar.

Something had been scribbled on each leaf of the door, sigils that he half recognized with a cold touch of dread.

Demon magic. Demon signs.

"Bugger," he whispered.

He looked back at the woman who clung gamely to the metal struts just below him: Jenny's age or a half decade older, graying and homely with lines of laughter and concern in her face and the pear-shaped figure of a woman who spent her days in comfortable chairs reading. Not a fighter. Not a wizard, possibly not even had there been magic in this world.

But she was willing to help, to put her life at risk—her soul at risk, if Folcalor and his minions were collecting them in jewels—to thwart evil, in whatever form it appeared.

All the more reason, he thought, not to be party to evil himself, unknowing.

"Listen, love," he breathed. "We're behind the fair. Demons are ahead of us." He hesitated a moment, then added, "Bort may be with 'em."

She put her hand to her lips quickly to hide the flinch of her mouth, as she had always hidden what was going on inside her. Bort had been her friend for twenty years and was maybe the only person who understood the needs of her mind and heart.

Then she took her hand away. "You'll tell me what I can do to help him?" she asked.

"I'll tell you if I find it out," he said grimly. "But right at the moment, just don't help him against me. Please. No matter what he says or does." All it would need, he thought, was to have Clea stab him in the back.

She nodded, her teeth clenched hard. "All right."

He sighed, feeling as he had felt seven months ago, when he'd ridden against the blue-and-golden dragon at Cair Dhû: when everything had been simple, and his life was the only thing he had to risk. "In we go, then." And he swung up and slipped through the broken doors.

The alarm system had been torn out at the wall box. That was the first thing he saw in the neat small chamber filled with shelves of packets, boxes, bottles, cans. The second thing he saw was Bort.

Demons had killed him.

That was very, very obvious.

Clea gasped, turned convulsively to vomit out the open doors. John strode after her and caught her, knowing that like most people she'd miscalculated the violence of the physical reaction and would probably fall. "Oh, horror—oh, horror—" she whispered, and her whole body trembled as he gripped her arms. "What . . . ? How . . . ?" Under protective ointment and spray her face was nearly green.

"Love, I'd send you back but I don't think I can," John said grimly. "Stay with me and stay close because it's the only way I can protect you. They got at him through dreams." He settled Clea against the doorjamb, hurried to the nearest portions of Bort and found, under the spattered blood and scattered entrails, half a dozen keys and a crumpled sheet of flimsiplast: Garrypoot's codes and schematics. No indication of how long ago he'd betrayed them, or what he'd told.

They'd let him lead them in, thinking to the last he would come face-to-face with that kindly silver-haired mage of his dream. They'd deceived him by his dearest wish, as demons were wont to do.

He wondered if they'd taken his soul from his torn body and imprisoned it in a jewel just before he died.

"Curse it," he whispered and checked again the dragonbone boxes. This wasn't just a matter of tucking something away in case of need, like that second silver flask of water from the Hell of the Shining Things. His choice might unleash destruction on his own world—or Aohila's vengeance. He wiped Bort's blood off his hand as best he could before taking Clea by the wrist. "Don't look," he whispered and led the way to the stairs.

The door at the top stood open, propped by the body of a man. A gangboy, by his half-shaved head and gaudy green-and-orange ointment mask. His body had been half torn to pieces by bullets and laser fire, his painted face distorted by shock, horror, and pain. There was tumult in the room beyond; John pushed Clea back and peered around the doorjamb, keeping low, which was all that saved him, for a second gangboy fired at where his head would have been, had he entered standing. The young man strode forward. John drew his sword and lunged in a single movement, catching the man in the groin and ripping upward. The gangboy grinned, twisted away from the blade with his intestines dangling, brought the gun around . . .

And lurched away, torn apart by the heavy-caliber bullets that spattered from within the room, allowing John to duck aside. The big man in the black clothes of one of Wan ThirtyoneFourFour's enforcers, who had fired the rescuing shots, shoved a second clip into the weapon and let off a burst of shots at John, but John was already moving, ducking, rolling behind the gilded ruin of an upholstered couch. A beefy man in the dark blue suit of one of NinetyfiveFifty's enforcers was already there, gasping as the last of his blood pumped from a shattered chest cavity. John's mind registered details: three gangboys, four enforcers in black. Another dead man in blue. Wan ThirtyoneFourFour himself, armed with a short sickle-shaped sword and a submachine gun, firing into the locks of a door at the room's far side.

And the room itself, lush with gold and tapestries–golden candlesticks, golden vases, curtains flashing with the precious metal woven into them. John caught up the dead bluecoat's semiauto and plunged, panting, into the shelter of a bookcase. On the blood-soaked carpet near him lay one of the twisted gold bracelets of the lavender-haired girl who'd died in the pool in the mirror chamber. Bait, for Folcalor to locate his quarry, the former owner's death itself merely a passing game. Then a line of red laser fire ripped toward him, and he flung himself behind another couch, then sliced off the head of the enforcer who sprang over its top and down upon him.

For a wonder the man died. Not all were demons, then, only enforcers who'd die for pay.

One of the gangboys came around the side of the couch at him, and John opened fire with the dead enforcer's gun. The kick nearly knocked him off his feet, but at that distance he couldn't miss. When he scrambled up, he found the room empty, the door at the end open. The gangboys were gone, too, leaving a trail of blood down the hallway.

There was shouting from somewhere, and the stink of burned polyester and roasted flesh.

"You got the house plan?" John demanded as Clea darted into the room and started to help herself to fallen weapons. She pulled out the schematics. "He'll be in the lab—it's on the third floor. How do we get to the crawlspace under the roof?"

It was entered through the library on the third floor. John flung the onyx ink bottle up the back stair ahead of him and set off the demon trap there: a blast of fire that belched out of nozzles set in the concrete wall, the heat suffocating. At the top and the bottom of the stair sprinklers drenched the walls—and John and Clea, waiting at the foot. When the whole show ceased, John retrieved the bottle, slinging it around his neck again as they climbed.

Smoke filled the upper floor of the house. The sound of shots and the roar of flames told of other demon traps. *You can't kill demons,* John thought. *All you can do is destroy their horses—and their pawns.* One of NinetyfiveFifty's bluecoats lay in the library, dead in a ghastly pool of blood-tinged vomit.

Of course, John thought. *All it'd take is one enforcer gettin' a little more swacked than usual on Brain Candy, one demon dream about pourin' Roach-B-Gone into the guardroom coffee.* It could all be over before Wan and his henchmen—or the green-and-orange gang, which seemed to be a separate operation—even got there.

Demon war—Folcalor and Adromelech taking sides, though who was on what side wasn't clear and probably didn't matter.

In the crawlspace the smoke was worse. John found the only way he could proceed was on his belly, where a little air remained underneath the roil of smoke. Still he was coughing, nauseated, and dizzy when he passed close over the main fight and then the area above what he guessed—from the forest of pipes rising up from floor to roof—was Corvin's laboratory.

That's where his real defenses will be, John thought.

He listened, gauging the sounds. Bullets tore through the ceiling between the century-old rafters, smoke and flamelets spitting up through the holes. He edged past the fight, leading Clea by the hand. The woman followed gamely, though her face was blanched with shock. She carried a couple of guns, but by the way she held them it was clear she probably wouldn't be able to fire. A little way on, among the vents, the ceiling was cooler, and John could hear below the single quick scuffle of feet.

The poison had gotten all the bluecoats, then. A mutter, stifled by the room's insulation; a single voice's sobbing whisper. Then he heard the sudden, terrible crash of a weight against the door. Feet fled to the farthest limit of the wall. A voice panted, a hopeless little, "Unh . . ." and John thought, *They're coming up the outside wall to the lab window.*

It's what he himself would have done.

He's surrounded.

Jen used magic against them, he thought, *and they seized her through it.* It might not work that way here, but it was clear Corvin didn't see it as an option.

If the demons get him, he thought, *either Wan or the gangboys, I'll have to get him away from them.*

He thought about those cold, guarded floors in the Universe Towers, and the room with the blood on the walls. About the deep zone, and the dark waters there teeming with the gods knew what.

I would really, really rather not have to do that.

"Clea?" John whispered. "You think you can find your way back to the pod stage and get out of here?"

"I don't know." Her hand tightened unconsciously on his arm, a reflex of terror at the thought of having to go back through this horror by herself. "I'll try if I have to."

"Right. Stay up here till I yell. And if I don't yell . . ."

Clea looked at him, scared—desperately scared.

And no matter who won the fight below, John thought, she was right to be scared. If he had any sense, he'd be scared, too.

Demons on both sides. And the gods only knew what defenses Corvin had. Bort dead.

He guessed that sight was in Clea's mind as well.

"If I don't yell," he said quietly, "forgive me, if you can."

She said, just as softly, "I've got a gun. I'll use it."

"Gaw," John said. "I'm gie sorry."

He heard the crash of the door breaking in below him. Turning, he aimed one of the submachine guns at the floor just above those sounds and opened fire.

There were howls, shouts, the wild pinging rattle of bullets bouncing everywhere, and without stopping to think or give the defenders time to think, John kicked his way down through the weakened boards and dropped into the lab itself.

He had only the dimmest vision of a long chamber, gray with sicklied light through a broken window whose sill was spattered with blood. There was an impression of machinery such as he'd seen in the cinema show Tisa had taken him to: oscilloscopes, etheric relays, splitters, readers, screens—all veiled in smoke that burned his eyes and seared his throat. Dead bluecoats on the floor, bodies knotted with their last agonies. And clearer than all else, the slender little man he'd glimpsed in the GeoCorp lobby, pressed against a wall staring about him in horror and despair.

Corvin NinetyfiveFifty. Mage and scientist and lover of the Demon Queen. And the gods knew what besides.

The window at the room's far end smashed open, and one of the gangboys leaped through, gutted and shattered by bullets and still grinning, ready to fight. John emptied a clip at him, the impact of the bullets knocking him back through the window, then swung around to fire another weapon at two of Wan's enforcers coming through the broken door.

"Storeroom?" John yelled. "You got one?" There were literally hundreds of ether crystals in the room—big masthead-size jewels, not just the little relay gems—and the searing howl of them went through his skull like a revelation of the gods.

"I . . . through there."

John grabbed the thin arm under its expensive dark suiting, thrust Corvin ahead of him through the door he'd indicated. A narrow chamber and a narrower door, lined with metal. Perfect.

He whipped his sword from its sheath, braced himself back in a corner near the door, weapon in hand.

"Who are you?" Corvin gasped. "Who . . . ?"

"Friend of yours sent me." John stepped in fast, cut the hand and arm from the first gangboy through the door, then kicked the gun in one direction and the limb in the other as the gangboy plunged through, spitting blood and grinning, dragging out a knife with his other hand . . .

Which John promptly severed, followed by the head. Eyeless, the torso flopped and kicked. John took a moment from dealing with the next gangboy through the door to cut the hamstrings on the first. No sense taking chances. The second gangboy was only massively high, not possessed of a demon that would keep dead flesh alive; he died and John caught up the weapons of both, emptied them into the dark-clothed enforcers who followed them through the door.

Silence outside. The stink of burning plex, blood, cordite. Corvin leaned against the wall, gasping with shock. His dark spectacles had jolted loose, and he tremblingly shoved them back into place, face half turned aside. "I . . . thank you," he whispered. "I owe you my life. They . . . These . . ."

"Demons," John said softly. He was panting, covered with gore and slime and dust, but he felt curiously calm now, as if he had all the seconds he needed for what he had to do. "Why're they after you? Who are you and what are you, that they want you as they do?"

Corvin stared at him, eyes invisible again behind the dark of the glass. But Aversin sensed those eyes darting, seeking some other way to reply than the truth. "I'm a . . . a scientist," he stammered. "For years I've worked with etheric energy, chaneling in power from other dimensions, other worlds than our own . . ."

"Hells, you mean?"

Corvin only looked at him.

"Is that why they're after you? Folcalor's demons?"

"Folcalor?" Corvin asked. "It's Adromelech, the Lord of the Sea-wights, who sent demons here to . . ."

Above their heads, above the ceiling, John heard Clea scream.

The next second bullets roared, rained through the shattering ceiling as he dragged Corvin out of the way, sheltering behind the metal cabinets, plunging for the door.

With a tearing crash Wan ThirtyoneFourFour leapt down through the ceiling, gun and sword gleaming in his hands.

John shoved the table at him, knocking him off balance; sprang across it to slash at the wrist that held the gun. Wan cut at him with his own blade and tried to bring the submachine gun around on him, but the severed tendons would not respond. The next second the crippled gangboy, still rolling and flopping about the floor, lurched against the table's legs, knocking John sprawling. Wan leaped in, cutting and slashing, and John twisted, hacked, cutting half through the possessed creature's neck and then slashing at the backs of the knees.

Wan went down, lurching, leaping up, and John grabbed Corvin's arm and dragged the scientist through the door and into the lab, slamming the door behind him. "Does it lock?" he yelled as the door lurched and started under his grip. Corvin, in shock, made no reply, so John jammed the nearest submachine gun under the latch as a temporary bar, grabbed Corvin's arm again, and shoved him toward the door.

As they passed beneath the hole in the ceiling Clea dropped through, dust covered and bruised but unhurt. "He came up through the crawlspace—" she started.

"Taken care of. Run!"

The house below them was an inferno of smoke, heat, spreading fire. Two possessed gangboys met them on the stairs, blazing away with semiautomatic fire; Clea fired back, the weapon's kick slamming her against the wall. The bullets went everywhere, but the attackers retreated for a moment. "Window!" John yelled, and plunged through the smoke into the nearest room.

Like the chambers downstairs it was filled with gold: vases, candlesticks, hangings that were embroidered and woven with the precious metal. Ether crystals formed a circle, mounted on small masts, in the midst of which stood a green leather chair. The vibration of the unshielded gems was blinding. John ripped aside the gold-woven curtains that covered the window. The rope by which the gangboy demons had ascended to the lab a story directly above was still attached by its throwing hook to the sill overhead. Smoke poured from every window of the house, mingling with the rain; distantly, John heard the whine of sirens, the steady terrible *whacka-whacka-whacka* of aircars nearing. The building looked odd from the outside, dirty and grim after the opulence within.

"Thank you," Corvin gasped again when they reached the ground. A dead gangboy lay on the pavement. A dead enforcer—one of Corvin's, and this one had been shot to death—huddled beside the wall.

You never knew, in a demon war.

"I can't tell you how much I owe you."

"And what d'you owe those others?" John asked. He wiped the sweat from his face, the cold rain flicking his hair. "All those the demons killed so they could take whatever gold they had, to track you, lure you out of hiding? The demons must've killed a dozen of 'em, not to mention your enforcers, poor saps."

A stray bullet cracked on the pavement near them. Evidently

there were gangboys still in the house, still possessed of demons and still intent on getting their quarry.

Aohila's quarry.

The being she wanted so badly—or wanted so badly to keep from Folcalor—that she'd destroy the Winterlands.

"For the last time," John asked again. "Who are you?"

Corvin looked at him for one long moment, then turned and tried to flee.

John took the Demon Queen's box from his pocket, opened the bronze bottle, and removed what she had given him: six tiny beads of gold. He dropped them into the box.

Corvin screamed once—desperate and inhuman—and dissolved into smoke.

Chapter 21

John walked Clea from the subway platform to the door of her mother's apartment. "Will you be all right?" he asked.

Corvin's pod, which they took using one of Clea's keys, had been not only private but deluxe. It had included washing facilities—so they had removed all obvious signs of violence—and a spare shirt whose sleeves were two inches too short for John's arms. But John and Clea were both still disheveled and shaken. They left the heavier armament onboard when they deserted the private line at the 65th Boulevard station and switched to the Interstice. Clea dumped in a public washroom the latex gloves she'd worn.

"I'll be all right," she said.

Nightmares, John thought, looking at her eyes. What she'd seen in the lab, and the pod's entry platform, seemed to be burned there. Bort's face.

Nobody should have to know those things.

"I'm sorry," he said.

She shook her head. They passed in silence through the terminal below her mother's apartment building, through the swarm and clamor of the mobs, the noise, the stinks, and the etheric, whining hum that never ceased. Ad screens and holo-hats. Pink Angel and Lovehammer. A doomed swarming world unaware of all they had lost, all they were losing every day. "You're done here, aren't you?" she said. "You'll be going home?"

"Aye. I hope." He stood a step below her as she carded the elevator door. "I owed the Demon Queen two, and by God I've gotten them for her."

"And what will she do now," Clea asked, "with what you'll give her? Or will you give her the box?"

"Oh, I'll give her the box, all right." John fished the second box—Shamble's box—from his pocket, and with it the dragonbone cube that bore the sigil of the gate. "Whether I'll use this—whether it'll work, once I get to me own world again . . ."

He shook his head. "I wanted to see him—to see who he is, and what he is. To ask why the Queen's so ettled to have him, and never mind that abandoned-lover guff. To guess if I could what she'll do with him, once she's got him in her power.

"She and her people came out from behind the mirror once, a thousand years ago, and brought down a peaceful Realm into blood and chaos. The Hellspawn don't die, and they've got gie long memories. They've waited a long time to get loose again."

He took the round bone box, the demon's box, from another pocket, and flipped it in the air. "This poor sod was only hidin' out, after all, and that scared of her. No tellin' what I'd do if I could, to keep from bein' taken back to her. And yet he lied to me."

"So what will you do?"

"Find Jen," John said. "If she'll still have anything to do with me. Or maybe old Master Bliaud, if he hasn't gone so deep into hidin' he can't be found. Someone who'll be able to use the water I fetched from another Hell to speak to Corvin in his box here. Before I do anythin' I've got to know who Corvin is, and what he is—what power he holds. And I'll have to be fast about it, once I get back, for the Queen'll send plague again to my people if she thinks I've cheated her. It's hard to know . . ."

He broke off and pushed up his spectacles to rub his tired eyes. "When you start playin' about with demons, it's hard to know where anybody stands."

"Including yourself?"

"Aye," John said, with a faint grin. "Includin' meself." He took Clea's hands and drew her down to him to kiss her gently. A gray-suited salarytech passing in the hall viewed John's battered leathers and bruised, scabbed face, then hurried on her pharmacologically unconcerned way.

"Warn the others." John stepped back from Clea, his hands still holding hers. "Docket and Shamble especially—I'm willin' to bet Shamble's a true mage, whatever might be said of the others. And take the warnin' yourself. There are demons yet about. They're strong—how strong I don't know—and they want the mageborn for ends of their own. Keep a watch on one another, and stay away from all them things—Pink Sunshine and Peace and Put Your Brain in Your Pocket . . . Demons trapped me wife through the use of her magic. I think they'll trap you through those artificial dreams."

Clea nodded. Her voice was wistful. "Will your wife be all right?"

In her eyes was something he hadn't seen before. Her fingers held his as if reluctant to release the contact. "That I don't know," he said softly. "And what's *all right*, anyway? You mind how you go."

"I will."

For another moment their hands held. Then she turned away and went inside. He heard the lock clack behind her.

Hands deep in his pockets, sword hidden in a ratty bundle of raincoat and tubing, he ambled down the hall and took the elevator to the subway station once more.

He took the Interstice line as far as it went toward the wet zone and got out at the last station, where the water stood in dark streams between the tracks and the mosquitoes hummed louder than the failing crystals in the ceiling. A catwalk extended into the darkness. It was a half mile to the next station, with the water getting deeper over the rails. His flashlight gleamed on its solid obsidian sheet, on the swirling insects' wings.

Somewhere far ahead of him firelight cast ruddy smears on the glistening walls, and he heard music, the blare of a PSE. A free fair somewhere. People he wanted to talk to, to ask about what had happened here and what was happening still, if they knew.

Maybe they didn't, any more than the solitary hunters had in the Hell of the Shining Things. Maybe they just got on as best they could.

In his satchel, along with the two boxes of silver and dragonbone, he carried a wad of paper and parchment and flimsiplast, written and crossed and overwritten in a grubby palimpsest—notes to occupy a decade of winter nights, if he lived longer than the next twenty minutes. Was there any more to the world than the city? Why did it always rain? Who made the drugs, and what was ether and how did it work?

And other things as well, he thought, thinking of Clea's hands holding his outside her mother's door. *Other things as well.*

But you couldn't be two people.

The same way Jenny could not be both a dragon and his wife.

The passageway broadened around him. The white ether glow glistened on wet tiles and filth, on the concrete arches of ceiling, on the red eyes of rats. Out of habit—for he wasn't sure if it would work in this world—John drew a circle around himself in felt-tip pen on the concrete and opened the onyx ink bottle.

"How *dare* you?" Amayon's voice shook, his mulberry-blue eyes blazing with rage. "How *dare* you treat me like a . . . a common servant? A broom to be put in the cupboard until the floor wants sweeping? You could have gotten yourself killed—"

"And let you fall into the hands of Corvin's enforcers?" John tilted his head a little, the ether light making flashing circles of his spectacles. He was aware of how tired he was, and that he ached all over—bruised, weary, thin with the thinness of one who dares not eat or sleep. And aching in soul worse than in body. "Or maybe of whichever bunch of demons isn't on the side you've chosen?"

Amayon spat, and the spittle smoked where it struck the pavement.

"I didn't do so ill." John touched the pocket where the dragonbone box lay hidden. "I found our boy. The Queen'll be pleased."

"She is never pleased." Amayon's rosebud mouth twisted with emotions impossible to describe. "Don't you realize that yet, you puling twit? She is *never* pleased, and nothing that you do is *ever* enough. Do you think your service to her is done?"

John was silent.

"Do you think she hasn't been playing you like a puppet? Do you think she's telling you the truth about who and what this Corvin is, and why she wants him in her power? Are you as crassly stupid as that? Cast the box away! Throw it into the water. You have no concept of the ill that you do, Aversin . . ."

"No," he said softly. "No, I haven't. But nor am I like to learn it from you, or from any demon—particularly not those who'd be in that water waitin' to nip up that box and pass it along to Folcalor if I did as you say. So maybe it's best I just give her what she wants, and see where we are from there."

Amayon studied him for a moment, blue eyes icy with rage. By the demon light that played around them John could see the Demon

Queen's marks on the boyish face, as if a finger dipped in silvery fire had traced whorls and signs on his flesh.

"Yes," the demon said at last. "It is best to give her what she wants." He turned and led the way down the platform, to where a metal door had been let into a niche in the wall. When the demon's hand touched the latch John saw—though he couldn't tell whether it had flickered into life then or had always been there—the sigil of the gate.

John drew his sword.

It was as well that he did, for the men who seized him from both sides as he stepped through did it so quickly that he probably couldn't have defended himself at all had he not been ready. The place into which the door opened was dark—a cellar or crypt, by the low vaulting overhead—but John's eyes were adjusted already to the dark of the subway tunnel. He slashed one man across the face and turned to kick his attackers on the other side, opening a gap in the group. Boxes, barrels, the smell of coals—his mind registered them, and the more familiar stinks of mildew and potatoes. A voice shouted, "Get the bottle!" As a hand ripped the ink bottle free of the cord around his neck, he knew the voice.

Ector of Sindestray. Treasurer of the Council to the Regent Gareth of Bel.

He was in Bel.

Probably, he thought as he dodged behind a pillar, shoved a pile of boxes over onto his pursuers, *in the vaults under Ector's own town house.* That would be the logical place for Amayon to betray him.

All this went through his mind in instants as he ran, not toward the stairs, which would be guarded, but toward the chute he knew all town houses had, to let barrels and provisions and coal slide straight into the cellars—the equivalent, he reflected wryly, of the Circle's goods trains. He thrust the trapdoor aside and scrambled up and through, blinking in the bright cool light of the cobbled street, disoriented and shaken.

Bel, he thought. His own world. His own home.

Gareth.

The Regent was his friend. In the summer, when the old King had condemned him as a demon trafficker, it was Gareth who'd secretly engineered his escape. At a guess, Ector of Sindestray wouldn't even mention to Gareth, *Oh, yes, he did happen to come into my cellar one day and my men finished him off . . .*

Ector's town house stood in the fashionable quarter of town, eastward toward the hills and not far from the palace. John dodged down the first narrow street he saw before the councilor's men could emerge from the house, then ducked around a cart carrying boxes—coffins?—and dodged into an alleyway between the tall houses. Voices shouted in the street behind him. It wouldn't be long, he thought, before they got on his track.

At a corner near a market square a niche in a moldering wall housed a statue—old and disgraced by a million pigeons—of the forgotten Lord of Time. John worked his boot toe into a crack in the brickwork and thrust himself up to the level of the niche—it was some five feet from the ground—and wedged the silver bottle of water from the spring and the Demon Queen's box of silver and dragonbone among the dirty rummage of guttered votive candles and rats' mess around the old god's feet.

He hesitated, Shamble's duplicate box in one hand and the little bone gate sigil in the other, hearing the shouting come nearer and remembering . . .

The plague spots on Ian's face.

The winds and illusions of Hell.

The dead on the roof of a deep-zone ruin, slaughtered for no better reason than because demons were at large in their world.

I can't, he thought.

He raised the cover of Shamble's box and dropped the sigil inside.

He shoved the box into hiding, dropped to the pavement, and ducked into the marketplace, sword sheathed and walking fast. He felt glaringly conspicuous in jeans and Corvin's too-small shirt. The day was cold but bright, clouds scudding over the houses of stone and timber and plastered brick that looked so small after the terrifying megablocks of the city. He hadn't realized how badly he'd missed the air and sky and the mere absence of rain. As he jogged down an alleyway, frozen and half choked with dirty snow, his mind identified the smell of smoke, of pyres, a charnel stink.

Plague? In winter?

A small and twisting street. That congeries of red and blue roofs ahead should be the palace. *Let's hope our boy Gar is at home and not on some country estate or off at Halnath lookin' up ballads about Dragonsbanes. If worse comes to worst, the Lady Trey'll stand up for me till he gets . . .*

"There he is!"

John yanked on the trap of a cellar cover and found it locked. An arrow struck the trapdoor; he sprang back, ducked, turned . . . And saw that the alley dead-ended in an eight-foot wall. Trees on the other side—a garden—

"Don't try it."

John stood still.

"Turn around," the same voice said. It was a man's, and deep, not like the Earl of Sindestray's light tenor yap. John turned and faced the men. They wore the red livery of the royal House of Uwanë. It was their commander who had spoken.

"Shoot him." Lord Ector came panting around the corner a moment later, Amayon jogging unruffled at his side. "He has trafficked with demons."

"Take me to see Lord Gareth," John said quietly. Enough of them had bows that at this short range it was a choice between surrender and a brief career as a pincushion. "I'm his servant and the Thane of the Winterlands still."

"Not since you sold yourself to the Hellspawn!"

"That doesn't give us the right to kill a man," the red-clad commander said. John recognized him as Torneval, a senior captain of the King's guard, a thin dark warrior from the marshes beyond Halnath. The guards all looked exhausted and grim, with the unshaven appearance of men pulling too many shifts. The smell of burning, the emptiness of the marketplace as he'd passed through, the cart bearing coffins . . .

"Put down your sword, Lord John."

They searched him, roughly, for weapons. "What did you do with the box?" Amayon demanded.

Torneval frowned at him, and Ector said, "My nephew." His brow puckered a little as he said it, as if some anomaly crossed his mind, but he quickly put it aside with a little shake of his head. "It was he who warned me Aversin would be using the vaults beneath my house to meet with demons."

A dream, John thought, looking into those puzzled eyes. Bort and the gangboys evidently weren't the only ones who had had strange dreams.

Amayon even wore the blue-and-white livery of Ector's house, his dark curls hanging to his shoulders. Goodness knew what he looked like to the Earl of Sindestray, or to the men of the guard. He held the ink bottle, stoppered tight, in his blue-gloved hands.

"He had a box wrought of brownish bone, about so large, strapped with silver and lidded with a single opal," he said. "This was a . . . treasure . . . he stole from our house."

Torneval glanced back at one of his men and said, "Follow where he ran and fetch it."

"He's lying to you." John lunged despairingly against the men who bound his wrists. "He's a demon, he's trying to trick you—"

Ector struck him hard across the face. "Be silent or I'll kill you where you stand."

"That's the peril of demons, Lord Torneval," Amayon sighed sententiously. "Once a man sells his heart to them, no one is ever sure of him, or of anyone who comes near him. I'm told that in times past such mistrust brought kingdoms to ruin."

"I want to see Lord Gareth," John repeated grimly as they led him from the alley and toward the palace. "I've that right."

"Oh, my dear Captain, you'd be a fool to let him! His influence over the boy is such . . ."

"Give our lord Regent credit for knowing a dangerous man when he sees one." Torneval's voice was dry. By the sound of it he had as little use for the treasurer as John did. To John, he said, "It may be a little time before he can speak with you, Lord John. His lady is sick unto death; he has watched by her side now for three days. Yes, Marc?"

The young guardsman returned with the dragonbone box in his hand. "I found this, Lord."

Aohila's, John thought, recognizing the finer workmanship and the solid opal lid. He gritted his teeth. *So much for a month's quest through the marches of Hell.*

"That's it." Amayon held out his hand for it. Torneval shot him a wary glance and gave it to Ector, but as the men started off again the treasurer passed it to the demon—almost, John thought, without being aware of what he was doing.

"I'll tell Aohila that you were delayed, shall I?" Amayon fell gaily into step at John's side. "Or shall I ask her to visit you in your cell and preserve your soul alive even if she can't do anything about keeping your body from being broken and burned?" His voice was too soft to be heard even by those men who walked on either side, but he laughed at John's stony face. "Or would you like to send her a message, begging her help? I'll even promise to deliver it. It will give me great pleasure, in fact."

"Fuck yourself," John said quietly. "I assume that's what you spent your time in the bottle doing anyway."

Amayon laughed again and halted in the thin winter sunlight of the market. None of the guards, nor Lord Ector himself, seemed to notice that he'd stopped. John pulled against the grip on his arms, twisting to look back, and saw the demon standing, arms upraised in triumph and delight. Then Amayon laughed again and waved farewell, and skipped away, twirling his ink-bottle prison around and around on its scarlet ribbon over his head like a child playing with a toy.

For three days they starved him. This was customary in the South for those condemned to burning alive.

Thus it is that the prisoner's spirit may be rendered docile—Polyborus again—*and he give those in authority little trouble in leading him to the ground of execution.* John could read the words in his mind every time he shut his eyes.

Gareth came on the second night, a beaten and exhausted Gareth who seemed to have aged ten years. "Forgive me." The Regent glanced up as the guards in the corridor above the cells pulled away the ladder and closed the grilled trapdoor that was the tiny pit's only source of light. "Lord John, I . . ."

John shook his head. "You've grief enough by the sound of it," he said. "I'm gie sorry about Trey. The guards say there's a plague." He'd overheard them speak of it through the long day just past. *The Demon Queen?* he wondered. *Folcalor?* He saw Ian again, tossing in fever, tongue swollen, face flushed. The descriptions of the current plague were much the same. How after a thousand years had they gained this power? And what could be done about it?

He didn't even have Corvin to bargain with now. And Amayon

was gone, the Old God only knew where, to make his own treaty with the Demon Queen.

With unsteady hands the young man took off his spectacles, rubbed eyes red-rimmed with fatigue. When John had seen him at the burned-out camp on the banks of the Wildspae, after the battle at Cor's Bridge against Rocklys, Gareth had been exhausted, sickened by the violence of combat and the shock of his cousin's betrayal, but he'd had the look of a man who would recover, given rest and food and time.

Though the cell was ill lit–torchlight fell through the grillwork from the corridor overhead–and the guards had taken John's spectacles, still he could see that Gareth was thin now, not with a boy's weediness such as he'd had when first John had met him, but with the unhealthy thinness of a man whose body has given way under too great a sorrow. His face was haggard and lined. His hair hung lank, unkempt, and the mousy brown was streaked with gray. There were bruises under his eyes.

"Trey–" He stopped himself. Then, "Trey died." And seeing John open his mouth to speak comfort he added quickly, "She's all right now, though. There's a man in the city, a healer. A very great healer. She died the day before yesterday, and he . . . he brought her back." He raised his eyes, and John tried not to look as if he'd been struck in the heart with an arrow of ice. Gareth's voice shook with emotion, gratitude, awe. "He brought her back."

He's the first man to come back from the dead.

Go ahead, John thought. *Tell him.*

Tell him the woman he adores is a demon.

Tell him to kill her, to burn up her body alive, so she won't end up like Wan ThirtyoneFourFour. So your people won't end up like Tisa Three, or those poor deep-zone families on the news.

In the silence the creak of a guard's boot leather in the corridor sounded loud.

"This . . . this was last night. I think last night." Gareth swallowed again, fighting to keep his voice steady. "Trey, I mean. I don't really remember. I've been so tired, I slept the clock around, they tell me. When I woke, Captain Torneval told me you were here. But Trey . . . last night she sat up, weak, but . . . but well. She smiled at me, so . . ."

He shook his head furiously, thrusting away memory, thought, pain, joy. Tears of thankfulness crept again from his eyes. "I'm sorry, John, so sorry. Ector claims he told me the day you were taken, I just . . . I just don't remember." His hand clenched convulsively. "Please, please, forgive . . ."

"Gar, no," John said quickly. "Gaw, you did what you could . . ."

The young man shook his head. When he touched John's arm, John saw how the rings had turned on his fingers, so thin the fingers had grown. "Ector announced your arrest to the council this afternoon, while I was sleeping," he said. "He saw to it Father was there, though Father barely knows who he's with these days. And with the plague, and the rumors that have been going around . . ."

"About what?"

Gareth ducked his head a little, looked aside in embarrassment. "About demons," he said, after a long time. "About . . . about you trafficking with demons, to bring about the plague."

John was silent, cold, furious, shaking inside. *Amayon,* he thought. *That filthy little bugger was thinking about this, all that time in the bottle. Sending dreams to Ector, who of course was willing to believe anything. Setting this up. Setting* me *up.*

"I'll get you out." Gareth's voice was unsteady. "I swear I'll get you out. Midnight, tonight . . ."

"Well, if it's midnight tomorrow," John remarked, rubbing the side of his nose, "I'll be a good deal slower on me feet. What about Jenny?"

The young Regent startled, as if at something forgotten and suddenly recalled. "Jenny . . ."

"Have you heard aught of her?" Without John's spectacles Gareth's face was little more than a blur, but the way he said her name told John that he had heard something.

"She was . . . she came here. To the palace. Yesterday . . . the day before . . ." He shook his head, brow folding, struggling to think past the haze of exhaustion and grief. "It was three days ago. She was with Trey when Trey . . . She was with Trey." He couldn't even speak the words again. "I didn't . . . I don't remember . . ." He passed a hand across his face, panic in his tone at so hideous a mental lapse.

Trust a demon to blur that recollection from your mind, John thought.

"Find her," he said. "Tell her I'm here. Tell her . . ."

Tell her what? That now I'm in trouble I'm sorry about all I said?

His heart pounded at the thought of her. Had Amayon betrayed her, too? Was she locked up here somewhere as well?

"Polycarp," Gareth said, struggling to recall. "Polycarp said he saw her. He said something . . ."

"Just find her. Promise me. And tell none others of this, not even Trey." Seeing Gareth stiffen indignantly, he added quickly, "For her own good, not that I don't trust her. After you find Jen, one of you needs to go to the marketplace at the foot of the hill, near Ector's house. There's a statue of the Lord of Time in a wall niche down one of the streets near there. There's a silver bottle, and a box made of bone and silver, shoved in behind the statue and the candles and all. I need 'em, but it must be only you or she who gets 'em."

Gareth nodded. "I'll get them myself. And I'll find her, I swear it. I haven't been myself. I know she's somewhere in the palace; Badegamus would have told me if anything had happened to her."

If Badegamus knew.

"And send me down some food," he added, trying to calm the hammering of his heart as Gareth signed the guards to lower the ladder again. A prosaic enough request, when Jenny could be locked in some hole in greater danger than he, but when he stood to bid his liege lord good-bye—he'd had to sit down halfway through the interview from sheer lightheadedness—the floor seemed to rock under his feet. Even with the Regent assisting him, an escape from Bel wasn't going to be easy, and he might end up having to run or swim or climb. "Anythin' at all—potato skins, bread crusts, whole roast oxen . . ."

"Torneval will bring it." Gareth had to whisper the words; the guards stood above them, framed against the torchlight at the ladder's top. He visibly restrained himself from clasping John's hands and said in a firm voice for their benefit, "I will see you ere the sentence is carried out."

Equally for the benefit of the guards—who would undoubtedly be quizzed by Ector, worms rot him—John sank to one knee and bowed his head and stayed that way as Gareth climbed the ladder and the grill was replaced.

Midnight. And by the best of his calculations, it was an hour or so after sunset now.

He sank back, leaned his head against the damp stone. *So much,* he reflected bitterly, *for preventing demon war.* Within weeks, if not days, Trey would have a little room in the palace like Wan Thirtyone-FourFour's, with blood-soaked chair straps and swarming insects. Would that be enough to convince Gareth of her possession? Or would he not learn of it until too late?

And Jenny ... His flesh went cold at the thought of her here. Three days! Had she had the sense to get out? To go into hiding? Had she figured out that Trey was no longer the girl she'd known?

He closed his eyes and saw Tisa Three leaning gaily against the corner of the alley, waving a jaunty good-bye. Saw Old Docket brought out mindless and stumbling from the District cells; saw what was left of Bort on the blood-pooled floor. It would only be carnage from here, and he could think of no way to stop it, no way to turn the rising scarlet tide.

Would Corvin NinetyfiveFifty know? He'd been Aohila's lover—or something. What had he learned from her, aside from the secret of immortality, that could possibly defeat the demons now that they had human rulers and human mages in their thrall? Now that they had reattained powers that had not been theirs in a thousand years?

If we can speak to him, within the dragonbone box. If human magic—or, the Old God help us, the abilities of a human who had once had magic—could use the scrying water as a demon could. If Corvin would speak at all to the man who'd captured him ...

It's got to work. John watched the blurry squares of torchlight on the floor move, brighten, fade with the passage of the guards' feet and shadows and torches. Folcalor and Adromelech turning this world into a battlefield and a playground ...

He felt sick at the thought.

Get me out of here. Torneval, wherever you are, lad ...

Is it midnight yet?

More guards passing. Different voices, asking news of this prisoner and that. He heard his own name, and caught the words, "No trouble."

You want to see trouble, lad, you just come down here and I'll show you trouble.

In another cell a man coughed, desperate and hacking. John

huddled grimly in his corner, trying not to think about how hungry he was, or how cold.

Surely midnight had to be near?

After a long time, the guards changed again.

It was close to dawn before he realized the truth.

Torneval wasn't coming.

Trey. Fear—and absolute certainty—settled in him with the finality of a stone sinking into a quicksand bog.

Lie down with me, love. He could almost hear her voice speaking to her husband, a man desperately weary, torn to pieces by what he'd passed through. *Lie down with me and have a glass of wine.*

Gar, no, he thought, with what little energy was left in him to think anything. *Gar, no.*

And then she'd say to the guards, *Oh, my lord is resting . . .*

Of course, my lady. We'll see to it, my lady.

A shudder went through him at the thought of the fire.

They came for him just before noon.

About the Author

At various times in her life, BARBARA HAMBLY has been a high-school teacher, a model, a waitress, a technical editor, a professional graduate student, an all-night clerk at a liquor store, and a karate instructor. Born in San Diego, she grew up in Southern California, with the exception of one high-school semester spent in New South Wales, Australia. Her interest in fantasy began with reading *The Wizard of Oz* at an early age and has continued ever since.

She attended the University of California, Riverside, specializing in medieval history. In connection with this, she spent a year at the University of Bordeaux in the south of France and worked as a teaching and research assistant at UC Riverside, eventually earning a master's degree in the subject. She now lives in Los Angeles.